Richard Usborne was born in India in 1910. After Oxford, he began a career in advertising, and was a writer and journalist – including a three-year spell as assistant editor to the *Strand Magazine*, the publication in which most of P.G. Wodehouse's stories first appeared. Long regarded as the leading authority on Wodehouse, he is also the author of the classic *Clubland Heroes*, a look at the fiction of Dornford Yates, Sapper and John Buchan. In addition to his several previous volumes on Wodehouse, he edited and annotated the unfinished final Wodehouse novel *Sunset at Blandings*. He lives in London.

Plum Sauce

A P G Wodehouse Companion

Richard Usborne

THE OVERLOOK PRESS
Woodstock & New York

This edition first published in the United States in 2003 by
The Overlook Press, Peter Mayer Publishers, Inc.
Woodstock & New York

WOODSTOCK:
One Overlook Drive
Woodstock, NY 12498
www.overlookpress.com
[for individual orders, bulk and special sales, contact our Woodstock office]

NEW YORK:
141 Wooster Street
New York, NY 10012

∞ The paper used in this book meets the requirements for paper
permanence as described in the ANSI Z39.48-1992 standard.

Library of Congress Cataloging-in-Publication Data

Usborne, Richard.
Plum sauce : a P.G. Wodehouse companion / Richard Usborne.
p. cm.
Includes index.
1. Wodehouse, P. G. (Pelham Grenville), 1881-1975—Stories, plots, etc.—Handbooks, manuals, etc.
2. Wodehouse, P. G. (Pelham Grenville), 1881-1975—Characters—Handbooks, manuals, etc.
3. Wodehouse, P. G. (Pelham Grenville), 1881-1975—Handbooks, manuals, etc.
4. Humorous stories, English—Handbooks, manuals, etc. I. Title
PR6045.O53Z8895 2003   823'.912—dc21   2003054931

Manufactured in the United States of America
ISBN 1-58567-441-9
1 3 5 7 9 8 6 4 2

CONTENTS

Note *viii*

Introduction *1*

Suspension of Disbelief –
Thirty postulates for relaxed reading of P. G. Wodehouse *6*

THE WODEHOUSE GREATS

Psmith *9*

The School Stories *21*

Ukridge *24*

The Light Novels *30*

Lord Emsworth and Blandings *37*

Uncle Fred *48*

Insulting the Wodehouse Way *54*

Bertie Wooster *57*

Jeeves *81*

58 OTHER MEMORABLE PEOPLE AND A MEMORABLE PIG *96*

Gally's Old Friends and Enemies *130*

92 BOOKS *137*

The Other Short Stories *201*

Fictional Authors and Their Books Found in Wodehouse *210*

The French for Wodehouse *215*

How Do I Look (Sound, Etc.)? *220*

NUGGETS
Drink *22*
Church *34*
Children *46*
Menservants *78*
The Female of the Species *94*
Writers *116*
Animals, Mostly Dogs *128*
Aunts *134*
Golf *208*
Smells *218*

Index *223*

ACKNOWLEDGEMENTS

Thanks to Pat Kavanagh and Carol MacArthur at Peters, Fraser and Dunlop, Linda Shaughnessy at A.P. Watt, and the Estate of P.G. Wodehouse for all their help in assembling this present volume.

All the artwork that decorates the book is taken from original Wodehouse sources. The simple black and white line drawings by Kerr were drawn for *Week-End Wodehouse* edited by Hilaire Belloc (1939). The full cover artworks are the original Herbert Jenkins, Barrie and Jenkins and Methuen hardcover jackets. The other cut-out illustrations are taken from the *Strand Magazine* which originally serialised much of P.G. Wodehouse's work.

NOTE

The name Wodehouse is properly pronounced
Woodhouse. The name Ukridge properly rhymes
with Duke-ridge. The name Psmith, its owner
claimed, was properly pronounced Smith.

INTRODUCTION

Sir Pelham Wodehouse, K.B.E., D.Litt. (Oxon), died of a heart attack in hospital on St Valentine's Day 1975 at the age of ninety-three. He and his wife had lived in the village of Remsenburg, on Long Island, New York, for the last twenty years. In tribute, the Remsenburg post office lowered its flag to half mast, just clear of the piled-up snow.

The knighthood had been announced in the New Year's list forty-five days before he died. At that time he was up and about, but only just. Before Christmas he had written to a friend, 'My legs have gone right back on me and I have to walk with a stick to keep me from falling. The other day I came a stinker and bust a rib.' He had to say that he could not manage to go to London and the Palace to receive the accolade, nor even to Washington. The Queen Mother, a great fan of the Wodehouse books, said, 'Why shouldn't I go over and give it to him?' But royal schedules could not easily be changed at short notice. So arrangements were made for a ceremony at the British Consulate in New York, with the Ambassador, Sir Peter Ramsbotham, coming from Washington. But before a date for this could be fixed, Wodehouse died. A fortnight later the Acting Consul General drove out from New York with the insignia and the warrant, and presented them to Lady Wodehouse.

Since 1956 Wodehouse had been American as well as British. He had dual citizenship. He had in fact lived more years of his life in America than in England. His roots were in England and his absorbent youth had been spent there: prep schools, Dulwich College, a spell in a bank in the City and years of freelancing, as journalist, novelist, short-story writer, lyric-writer and playwright. To the end of his life he preferred to write about English people in English settings.

He was the author of nearly a hundred books, ninety-two of them being novels and collections of short stories. None of them was wholly serious: most of them, and the best of them, were farce. He collaborated in more than thirty stage plays, mostly musical. He was in the front rank of writers of lyrics, words fitted to music, especially Jerome Kern's, for the stage. He was an expert writer of light verse, and contributed a great deal to *Punch* from 1902 onwards. For two stretches he was highly paid and (he thought) underworked as a writer in Hollywood. He was happily married for sixty-one years. He had no children of his own, but his wife, a widow when he married her, had a daughter, Leonora, who was a great joy to him and everybody who knew her. He was a very private man, who worked hard and loved working. He made merry, but only at his desk and typewriter. He was a humorist: not a wit, not a satirist. He was a craftsman manufacturer of the ludicrous –

1

words, phrases, characters and situations in intricate and tightly controlled plots. He was not gregarious. He had few close friends. For farce fiction at the rate of about a book a year in a *floruit* period of fifty years he had no rivals.

His books were always young and all his elders, even the stuffed shirts, had been young once. Even the awesome Roderick Spode, Lord Sidcup, had stolen a policeman's helmet on Boat Race Night and was still proud of it. You can be sure, with Wodehouse, that David will defeat Goliath, the schoolboy will outwit the master, the chorus girl will rise to be a star, or, at very least, will marry an earl, the poor will soak the rich, the Pekinese will rout the Alsatian, the curate will get a vicarage, the young man, with a nose broken by boxing or playing rugger for his Varsity, will marry the pretty girl whose kitten he has rescued. Those are the sorts of novels, outside the Blandings and Wooster sagas, Wodehouse wanted to write, and he wrote them exuberantly. Only in his extreme old age did his plots become strained and his flow of verbal felicities, in narrative and dialogue, thin.

He wrote about himself very little, and then in jest. Don't take his autobiographical books all as gospel. For instance, that story of his about being sacked by the bank for defacing a new ledger. He has told that one a number of times in print, and I heard him, at the age of ninety, trying to get it past Robert Robinson's defences in a TV interview. He was never sacked from the bank. As a trainee he had not been any better, or much worse, than the other boys from the public schools who had got nominations to the Hong Kong and Shanghai Bank in the City. But Wodehouse had determined, and known, that he was going to be a writer, and when he was offered a full-time job for five weeks at 5 guineas a week to write the By-The-Way column for the *Globe* newspaper, he said Yes and the bank agreed to let him go. The ledger-defacement/angry-Head-Clerk/banishment-in-disgrace-of-young-Wodehouse made a good story, and young Wodehouse worked it up and sold it in print, more than once. Old Wodehouse knew it by heart and thought Robert Robinson might not.

Do not believe, either, that Wodehouse's attitude to the backlash from his broadcast Talks from Berlin in 1941 was carefree. His selected letters to his old friend Bill Townend, in the *Performing Flea*, may give the impression of 'Silly me! Let's hope it's all blown over now.' But the whole business had wounded him deeply: the knowledge that he had made a fool of himself and the slow realisation that thousands of people, not having heard or read his Talks, thought he had been worse than a fool. He was not prepared to lick his wounds in public, but they never healed.

The Wodehouses had lived in Le Touquet since 1935. They were overrun by the German armies in May 1940. After eleven months of civilian internment Wodehouse had been released from camp and brought to Berlin. It was three months to his sixtieth birthday, and at sixty a civilian internee was released to whatever approved private life he could arrange. In Berlin a German whom the Wodehouses had known in Hollywood and who was now connected with the Foreign Office, suggested he might like to give some talks to America (which had not yet entered the war). Wodehouse was glad of the chance to show that he was alive and well, and to say thank you to American friends who had written to him and sent him parcels. He recorded five thirteen-minute talks. They covered his progression: being rounded up in Le Touquet, Loos prison near Lille in France, Liège barracks in Belgium, Huy Citadel in Belgium and Tost internment camp, once a lunatic asylum, in Upper Silesia.

He knew soon enough that he had made a terrible mistake by going on the air in Berlin. He was a British subject, not then American. He should have said 'No, thank you' to the suggestion of radio talks. But, knowing how utterly non-political his talks had been, he was surprised by the virulence of the attacks on him in England. He could not grasp that, for every one person in England who had heard his voice on the short wave from Berlin to America at English-time 4 am, a hundred had heard the ranting and vulgar philippic that William Connor of the *Daily Mirror*, briefed by the Minister of Information, Duff Cooper, had spat at him in prime time on the BBC National Programme, after the News on a Sunday evening. Connor had called him a hireling of Dr Goebbels, a fool giggling while Rome burned, and a traitor to his country, his class and his old school, Dulwich. The first two of Wodehouse's talks had been broadcast, and monitored by the BBC at their listening-post at Evesham, when Connor prepared his script. The monitorings must have been available to him. It is quite clear that he had not read them.

The memory of, and regret for, those broadcasts from Berlin cast a shadow over Wodehouse's life for the remaining thirty-five years. The knighthood, when it came, showed that he had been officially forgiven. That was some comfort. But he never returned to his native England. Editors of magazines, in England and America, which had, before the war, paid top prices for his short stories and serials, and begged for more, cold-shouldered his agents' post-war Wodehouse offerings. And there are still people today who, as an excuse for not reading him, remember that 'he blotted his copybook in some way during the war'. It is a sad irony that a man who, for a quarter of a century, had backed out of any personal limelight, should have got caught in the wartime searchlights and flak.

In 1961, when Wodehouse was to become eighty, Evelyn Waugh, always a great admirer, prepared a BBC talk as a birthday Tribute and Reparation to 'Dr Wodehouse'. Waugh, in correspondence, had told Wodehouse that he was working on this, and Wodehouse begged him not to attack Connor, with whom, he said, he had now become friends. Waugh complied, I suspect with regret. But, in relating how people had absurdly over-reacted in wartime, Waugh said that, in revenge for the broadcasts, some RAF types had flown to Le Touquet to bomb the Wodehouse villa (Ethel Wodehouse had been moved out a year earlier) and had in fact pranged somebody else's villa. Wodehouse learnt about this escapade when the BBC sent him a tape of Waugh's broadcast. Guy Bolton told me that the thought of this raid, presumably authorised, hung like a cloud in Wodehouse's mind till his death fourteen years later.

There was no truth in Waugh's story. The raid could not have happened unauthorised. It did not happen authorised. The *mairie* of Le Touquet has assured me that, after the German occupation in 1940, no bombs fell on Le Touquet till 1944 when (to suggest that the Allied invasion might land there) the RAF had done some diversionary bombing. Wodehouse never knew that. Evelyn Waugh never knew that; nor, perhaps mercifully, did Waugh know that he had thus saddened, and for so long, the man he so much honoured. Wodehouse came to dislike talking about the whole sad business of his broadcasts from Berlin. He hoped that others would forget it, and he went on working. Work had always been his favourite pastime, and he had a sheaf of typescript and notes for a new Blandings novel in hospital with him when he died. He was also roughing out new stanzas for a song 'Kissing Time'.

His fiction – his world of drones, Drones, fortnight-long house parties, butlers, chefs and valets – was never contemporary, nor had he been part of any such world. He had, in his typewriter, practised, polished and perfected an accent, a world and an outlook which was acceptable on both sides of the Atlantic and ignored Depressions, wars, strikes, ageing and death. Many people have tried, in print or conversation, to place the Wodehouse manner into some exact historical era: to fit Bertie Wooster and his friends, say, into a decade, when they could be taken for real. It never works. The Wodehouse worlds and the three or four Wodehouse languages (Psmith, Jeeves, the burbler, the buzzer) are artefacts.

I had, in 1942, and far from England, what I thought at the time was a revelation on this subject. Syria and Lebanon, Arab countries, had been, as far as living memory went back, ruled by the Turks and the French, and now the British were in control. In Beirut that summer I met an Armenian, a dealer in antiques. Armenians had been third-class citizens, if citizens at all, in the Levant, state-less and detribalised except for massacres and persecutions, for half a century. My friend Dikran's mother had spoken Armenian, Turkish, Arabic, Italian, French and English. She had a stroke at the age of seventy and could then speak only her native Armenian. Dikran spoke most of those languages, too, fluently, though probably badly. I found his English, hesitant at first, extremely odd. It was laced with bits of slang such as 'old bean' and 'pip-pip'. He used the word 'oofy' for rich – a word I myself hadn't used since schooldays. ('Oof' for 'money' had been, in the 1920s, an obligatory jargon word at Charterhouse, part of the strange private language that we had to learn in our first three weeks, and, I am sorry to say, soon came to use without embarrassment.)

I discovered that my friend Dikran had himself been at an English public school, St Peter's, York, just before the First World War. He was, in 1942, for converse with the new master race, groping back to a language he had learnt in an artificial society and had scarcely used at all in the last quarter of a century. Not all of it, but odd bits, came floating, tumbling on to his tongue. The result was nearest to Wodehouse/Wooster prose that I have ever heard, and I am sorry that I did not think to get on to tape our conversations over the arak at the St Georges Hotel. I am also sorry that Dikran so quickly learnt to clean up its anachronisms, and its strange concords of Prayer Book and 'Pink 'Un', military and music hall, cockney and cricket. He hadn't, in fact, read much Wodehouse. If his speech then was a linguistic revelation, it would have needed much more study than I was able to give it before it could be presented as a valid contribution to the identification of the roots of the Wodehouse styles. Certainly one of the fertilisers of the Wodehouse/Wooster language was the Indian babu joke – the florid and idiomatically discordant English spoken or written by 'examination-wallahs' who had learnt from books and who overused and misapplied tags and quotations from the English classics.

In addition to the essays on the Wodehouse greats and the thumbnail résumés of ninety-two books, I have given thumbnail sketches of fifty-eight of Wodehouse's other key characters. I have thought it rash not to collect Wodehouse's fictional authors and the titles of their books. You will notice that two ladies lay claim to *Heather O' the Hills*. But remember that when Wodehouse named his 1929 Blandings novel *Summer Lightning*, he found, too late, that this title had been used twice in England already, and three times in America. He could only hope, modestly, that his story might be 'considered worthy of inclusion in the listing of The Hundred Best Books Called *Summer Lightning*'. I have tried to make a complete roster of the pleasant and raffish acquaintances Galahad Threepwood remembered from his rowdy and unregretted youth.

And, to break up the monotone, I have quoted some nuggets of Wodehouse description, under various subject-heads. I have tried not to repeat any of those in the *Oxford Book of Quotations*. It is open-cast mining to dig them out. Evelyn Waugh said of Wodehouse: 'One has to regard a man as a Master who can produce on average three uniquely brilliant and entirely original similes to each page.' Three to a page, yes, that is about the striking rate of his similes. But similes are not by any means the only nuggets that glow on a Wodehouse page. Mixed metaphors, pulpit sentences deflated by slang, mad logic, clashes of clichés, blissfully botched quotations, absurd images. He worked at these things: they didn't just float together out of his mind. He wrote and rewrote. Evelyn Waugh's son Auberon called Wodehouse 'our greatest literary craftsman'. Yes. His intricate plots may come to have a sameness. His heroes (ugly, athletic) and heroines (pretty, small, with noses tip-tilted, bossy) may change their names and little else. But the language is the thing. The Wodehouse language – pontificating, buzzing, burbling – carries the story, as it has done since it cut loose in the conversation of Psmith.

SUSPENSIONOFDISBELIEF

Thirty postulates for relaxed reading of P.G. Wodehouse

1 It is always hay-harvest weather in England: for 54 holes of golf a day, or for a swim before breakfast in the lake, morning in the hammock under the cedars, tea on the lawn, coffee on the terrace after dinner.

2 Money is something you should inherit, get monthly as an allowance from an uncle, win at the races or borrow from Oofy Prosser.

3 All small dogs bite your ankles.

4 All babies are hideously ugly.

5 All small boys are fiends.

6 All aunts are hell, except Bertie's Aunt Dahlia.

7 All butlers have port in their pantries.

8 Old nannies are a menace. They know too much.

9 Drunk men can be very funny.

10 Almost all middle-aged men, even the most pompous (Lord Tilbury, Sir Gregory Parsloe, Bart., Roderick Spode/Lord Sidcup), were tearaways at some stage of their youth.

11 Country pubs are open all day long and their home-brew ale is very potent.

12 All decent-sized country houses have cellars, coal-sheds and potting sheds for locking people up in.

13 Watch out for girls with two-syllable masculine-sounding shortenings of their Christian names (Bobbie Wickham, Corky Pirbright, Nobby Hopwood, Stiffy Byng). They get the good man of their choice in the end, but they spread havoc on the way.

14 Most handsome men have feet of clay.

15 All young men with wavy, marcelled or corrugated hair have feet of clay and worse.

16 No decent man may cancel, or even refuse, an engagement to a girl.

17 Men and girls in love think only of marriage.

18 Rose gardens turn a girl on.

19 If a young man has a single-syllable Christian name, is poor and ugly and can stop dog-fights, he is sure to be the hero. He may propose to the heroine at their first meeting and try to shower kisses on her upturned face at their second. She will love this, though she may kick his shins at the beginning of such an embrace.

20 A bedroom scene is when you discover someone's made you an apple-pie bed and/or punctured your hot water bottle.

21 Another bedroom scene is when one or more people come and search your room for policemen's helmets, manuscript memoirs, notebooks, jewels or miscreants hiding in cupboards or under the bed.

22 All married couples have separate bedrooms.

23 All bedrooms have on their mantlepieces china figures of the Infant Samuel at Prayer. All these figures are dispensable.

24 Chorus girls are all right and earls (Marshmoreton) and nephews of earls (Ronnie Fish) are very lucky to marry them.

25 Barmaids are all right, and Lords (Yaxley) and Barts (Sir Gregory Parsloe) are lucky to marry them.

26 A country J.P. can call the local policeman and have anybody arrested and held in a cell on suspicion of anything. At his whim a J.P. can send anybody to prison without the option and without trial, legal representation or redress, for up to thirty days.

27 If, for a country house, you need a secretary, a Harley Street loony-doctor, a butler, a cook, a head gardener, a detective or a valet, you go up to London by a morning train and, without having made any appointment by telephone, you find what you want and come back with him or her by train the same afternoon.

28 The night you go to a nightclub is the night it gets raided by the police.

29 If you are arrested, on Boat Race Night or at a nightclub, give a false name and address and they will be accepted by the magistrate.

30 On Boat Race Night in London a young man always gets a bit tight, and it is then his duty to try to part a policeman from his helmet.

Psmith

Enter Psmith (1935) and *Mike and Psmith* (1953), both virtually the same book, made from the second half of *Mike* (1909), *Psmith in the City* (1910), *Psmith Journalist* (1915), *Leave it to Psmith* (1923), *The World of Psmith* omnibus (1974).

Enter Psmith

Psmith is Wodehouse's first adult hero. At Sedleigh he is already the Old Etonian, the grown-up among boys, the sophisticate among the callow. His eyelids are a little weary, and he wears a monocle. In a schoolboy world, where nobody else has done much but play cricket and see the latest Seymour Hicks show at the theatre, Psmith talks and behaves like someone who has swept together ten thousand experiences, and is never going to be surprised at anything again. In his first book he patronises his headmaster, in his last he patronises Lord Emsworth.

Psmith is like a breath of good, stale nightclub air coming through the healthily open, if precautiously barred, windows of common room, study and dormitory. To readers of Wodehouse, he is the link between Awkward Adolescence and the Great After Life. He leads us to the new world of the City, America, gangsters, crooks, clubs, Psocialism and Blandings Castle. Those of us who are unable to dissociate Wodehouse's school books from our own schooldays (a test of their excellence for the market for which they were written) have been, for seven books, moving in the smell of cooked cabbage and old plimsolls, in the sound of bells and whistles and clanging clocks. We have been sitting, if at all, on lockers and benches, with chilblains and spots, red wrists, rude health, huge hungers and bull-calf enthusiasms. Psmith is a lazy man who likes his comforts. He is strongly opposed to missing his sleep, and he quotes a learned German doctor's theory that early rising leads to insanity. Psmith offers us late breakfasts, deep armchairs, the smell of cigar-smoke, the folding of the hands in repose after good lunches in clubland, and a lifetime truce to 'training'. Psmith wafts us painlessly from the School Close to Piccadilly.

Psmith does not despise his schooldays. But he is unsentimental about them. He is finished with them. His father hoped that his one term at Sedleigh might 'get him a Balliol', but Psmith avoids anything so swottish. He looks back to his Eton days without regret and without rancour. At Cambridge he is objective enough to decide that his happiest memory of the school whose Old Boy blazer he wears with his sky-blue pyjamas is of a certain hot bath after 'one of the foulest cross-country runs that ever occurred outside Dante's Inferno'. He would have played for Eton at Lord's in his last half; but in the matter

9

of cricket he is more likely to remember that, in a village match, he had been caught at point by a man wearing braces. 'It would have been madness to risk another such shock to my system.'

The first adult, Psmith is also the first man of means in Wodehouse. There was 'a tolerable supply of simoleons' and doubloons in the Psmith family old oak chest: much more, one feels, than in the Jackson chest. Psmith's father, though eccentric, was County, landed and a man of capital. In the Sedleigh period, Psmith's money is immanent, but unimportant to the story. In *Psmith in the City* the Psmith simoleons are useful in softening the asperities of London clericalism, both for Psmith and for Mike. And in *Psmith Journalist*, Psmith's money is cardinal to the plot. In fact, Psmith returns to Cambridge after that book, the owner of a successful New York weekly paper, *Cosy Moments*. Then his father dies, the money disappears, and Psmith goes into, and out of, his uncle's fish business. Hence the 'Leave it to Psmith! Psmith will help you. Psmith is Ready for Anything,' etc., advertisement on the front page of *The Morning Globe*. A member of four London clubs, and due to be a member of two more, Psmith is without means of support. He needs that secretary's job at Blandings when Baxter is driven forth.

But the job is, in fact, an afterthought. Psmith has been working for Freddie Threepwood at Blandings, not for personal profit, but to get, by a concatenation of events that would follow if he stole the necklace, the £3,000 that Mike Jackson needs to buy the farm in Lincolnshire. When that is accomplished, Psmith takes the job with Lord Emsworth.

Psmith is not afraid of poverty. But he is afraid of being bored. He prefers danger to being bored. And, though this compulsion has produced heroes as innocuous as Water Rat in *The Wind in the Willows* and as nocuous as Bulldog Drummond, it needs a little study in the Psmith and Wodehouse context.

Psmith the buzzer

Psmith might have developed into a Raffles after *Psmith Journalist*, with gun-play and detection providing breezy excitements. His exploits in *Leave it to Psmith* were mildly in the Raffles vein, and there was gun-play in the last chapters. But Wodehouse veered to farce and away from heroics, and the derring-do in his books veered away from revolver-shooting to pig-stealing and policeman's helmet-pinching. The Psmith-type Wodehouse hero does not have to duck the bullets again after the early 1920s. He does, however, seek to avoid boredom still, and (as Psmith did) he uses his tongue as a weapon in that cause. This is the essence of the 'buzzer' in Wodehouse. He buzzes in the hope that his talk will 'start something'. Buzzing cheers him up and makes him feel better himself. But there is always the possibility that it may also cause someone else to do something exciting that will relieve the monotony.

Psmith

Although Wodehouse didn't coin the word till *Money in the Bank* in 1946, Psmith is the first integrated 'buzzer' in the books. He emits radiations of sound. What he says may, or may not, be true. It may have much meaning, or none. But it may be reckoned to lift dull reality a notch or two into the air and, if it starts nothing more than a train of thought to play with, it has done a job. 'Comrade Jackson's name is a byword in our literary salons', 'Comrade Jackson is possibly the best known of our English cat-fanciers.' Both these claims are made by Psmith, in New York, in *Psmith Journalist*, to a prominent New York gangster. Neither is true. But this kind of typical buzzer's remark induces two kinds of danger, plays with two kinds of fire. There is the danger that the gangster will realise that Psmith is engaged in persiflage, and take steps. And there is the danger that Mike, hearing himself thus described, will switch from surprise to giggles. In that case, too, the gangster may take steps. By inducing this kind of danger the buzzer staves off boredom from himself. Buzzing is a conversational excitement-inciter. It is a Wodehouse proprietary patent medicine, and Psmith is its first dispenser.

Wodehouse had been playing with the ingredients of buzzing in his first book, *The Pothunters*. Charteris is 'seldom silent'. Dallas describes his housemaster airily as 'a man of the vilest antecedents' (an echo of Conan Doyle). In later school stories you get Marriott and Jimmy Silver putting their feet up and simply persiflating. These, to change from the chemist's shop to the music-room, are Wodehouse's five-finger exercises which will break into the chords of Psmith, just as soon as that local habitation and name occur. Who is talking now?

> ...there are stories about me which only my brother knows. Did I want them spread about the school? No, laddie, I did not. Hence, we see my brother, two terms ago, packing up his little box, and tooling off to Rugby. And here am I at Wrykyn, with an unstained reputation, loved by all who know me, revered by all who don't; courted by boys, fawned on by masters. People's faces brighten when I throw them a nod. If I frown...

That's Clowes, in the first half of *Mike*, three years, as the fictional calendar goes, before Psmith appears at all: a mere twenty chapters as the pages of *Mike* turn. Psmithery is there, in the keys of Wodehouse's typewriter, waiting to come out. Wodehouse said he got the character of Psmith handed to him on a plate when a Wykehamist cousin told him about a schoolmate, Rupert, son of the Savoy Opera's D'Oyly Carte. He called his fellow Wykehamists 'Comrade', wore a monocle and was orotund of speech. In the orotundity of speech that Wodehouse gave Psmith I think one can hear, also, Sherlock Holmes, Baboo Jabberjee, Beetle imitating King, Stalky, Dick Swiveller, Mr Micawber and, perhaps, Raffles.

But just because Psmith has emerged, and is going to recur, why should the faithless Wodehouse not go on using some of his ingredients for pleasant characters in the books between? In 1915, midway between Psmith's appearance at Sedleigh and his reappearance, in 1923, in *Leave it to Psmith*, Ashe Marson, hero of *Something Fresh*, goes to Blandings, disguised as Mr Peters's valet, to steal a scarab, much as Psmith later, disguised as the Canadian poet, goes to Blandings to steal Connie Keeble's necklace for her husband. And this is Ashe addressing his employer, the testy millionaire:

'I've come to read to you,' said Ashe.
'You fool, do you know that I have just managed to get to sleep?'
'And now you're awake again,' said Ashe soothingly. 'Such is life. A little rest, a little folding of the hands in sleep, and then, bing, off we go again.'

Here is Ashe again, describing to Joan Valentine, who is pretending to be a lady's maid, his success in the servants' hall:

'Let us look on the bright side ... the commissariat department is a revelation to me. I had no idea that servants did themselves so well. As for the social side, I love it.... Did you observe my manner towards the kitchen maid who waited on us at dinner last night? A touch of the old *noblesse* about it, I fancy? Dignified, but not unkind, I think?...'

And who's speaking now?

'The advice I give to every young man starting life is "Never confuse the unusual with the impossible!" Take the present case, for instance. If you had only realised the possibility of somebody some day busting you on the jaw when you tried to get into a cab, you might have thought out a dozen crafty schemes for dealing with the matter. As it is, you are unprepared. The thing comes on you as a surprise. The whisper flies around the clubs: "Poor old What's-his-name has been taken unawares. He cannot cope with the situation."'

No, that's George Bevan, who marries the lady named in *A Damsel in Distress* (1919). Bevan is a playwright, and supposed to be an American, too. Perhaps he met Psmith in New York in the *Psmith Journalist* period, and decided to model his own conversational style on Psmith's.

This business of 'starting something' is recurrent throughout Wodehouse, and in his later years he has made it the mainspring of one of his best girl characters. Bobbie Wickham periodically feels the urge to 'start something' just for the heck of it. Bobbie, a human ticking-bomb, is, in that sense, the female of the species Psmith. In the post-school books the

Wodehouse male ragger, whoever he may be, from Psmith to Lord Ickenham, has to have a good cause, such as helping a friend, as an excuse for anything more than verbal ragging. The female can start something for the purpose of doing down an enemy (Stiffy Byng *v.* the village policeman) or (Bobbie Wickham) merely through boredom. Lord Ickenham insists that all the best girls are apple-pie-bedmakers, preferably of bishops' beds. In fact, prime movers of misrule.

Psmith's buzzing, and the buzzing of all successors to Psmith in Wodehouse, is a one-man verbal rag. Psmith buzzes, not to call attention to himself. That happens, and must be tolerated. He buzzes in order to attract causes for amusement, to make amusement occur, so that he may be amused.

Knuts

Psmith, in appearance and, very broadly, manner, is the Knut. The Knut was not a Wodehouse invention. He was a fashion-eddy of late Edwardianism, though his line goes back to the dandy and the fop of earlier centuries. Captain Good, RN, in Rider Haggard's *King Solomon's Mines*, wore a guttapercha collar, a monocle, matching hat and jacket and impeccable other kit in the African bush, to the amusement of his companions and Rider Haggard's readers, but not to the lessening of his own dignity. *Punch* was making jokes about the Knut at the same time as Wodehouse was using him as part of Psmith.

The Knut was an amiable person. You could laugh at him kindly. He cultivated a 'blah' manner and vocabulary. Some of Psmith's vocabulary was from early Knut sources. 'Oojah-cum-spiff' and 'Rannygazoo', both Knut locutions, were used by Psmith first, and later by Bertie Wooster. When Bertie Wooster used 'Oojah-cum-spiff' and 'Rannygazoo' in the 1920s, they sounded, to the reader too young to have known the Knut language, like personal Wodehouse/Wooster fabrications. In the Wodehouse play *Good Morning, Bill* of which the novel *Dr Sally* is virtually a transcript, Lord Tidmouth, a Knut, says goodbye in six different ways: 'Bung-ho', 'Teuf-teuf', 'Tinkerty-tonk', 'Toodle-oo', 'Poo-boop-a-doop' and 'Honk-honk'.

Knut language, like any other generic slang, substituted for the sake of substitution. It was the manner of the Knut to call a man a 'cove' or a 'stout sportsman'. In *The Lighter Side of School Life* Ian Hay, discussing Dean Farrar's *Eric*, says 'No schoolboy ever called lighted candles "superfluous abundance of nocturnal illumination".' Psmith could have. Psmith, instead of 'tea' says 'a cup of the steaming'. Psmith, first in Wodehouse, plays variations on the already several-times-removed-from-reality imagist phrase 'in the soup'. Psmith refers to '*consomme* splashing about the ankles' and someone being 'knee-deep in the *bouillon*'. He always prefers the orotund to the curt. Instead of 'shoot a goal' he says 'push the bulb into the meshes beyond the uprights'. 'Archaeology will brook no divided allegiance from her devotees', and 'the dream of my youth and aspirations of my riper years' – these are pleasant enough suggestions of pulpit pomp. In the crowded school study they would certainly be given in a parody voice, adding a specific victim to the general parody. The headmaster or the padre would be the local wax figure for the group to stick their verbal pins into.

School talk

Even if Psmith had not first appeared in a school story, one might shrewdly assess that his language and manner had been born and bred in a school society. It is at that impression-able age, and in that sort of confined study-fug, that speech-forms and humour-forms sprout most proliferously and, by applause and fierce criticism, are shaped and tailored for a wider public.

> At English schools in my boyhood, humorists were divided into two classes, both unpopular. If you merely talked amusingly, you were a 'silly ass'. ('You are a silly ass!' was the formula.) If your conversation took a mordant and satirical turn, you were a 'funny swine'. And whichever you were, you were scorned and despised and lucky not to get kicked. It is to this early discouragement that I attribute the fact that no Englishman, grown to man's estate, ever says anything brighter than 'Eh, what?' and 'Most extraordinary'.

This is Wodehouse in *Over Seventy* (1957). 'Silly ass!' and 'funny swine!' may well have been appellations of opprobrium addressed to Psmith at Eton. In that term at Sedleigh covered by *Mike and Psmith*, Jellicoe once says to him. 'You *are* a lad!', and once, 'You *are* a chap!' Perhaps Psmith was too old and formidable for anyone to call him 'silly ass' or 'funny swine' with impunity at that stage; but he was an amusing talker, and he started something in the Wodehouse books. Take a line through Psmith and fifty young heroes and heroines of stories and novels, and you fetch up at the biggest of all the irrepressible buzzers, Lord Ickenham. His talk is like the flail of a tank going through a minefield.

The three buzzer styles

'Don't *talk* so much! I never met a fellow like you for talking!' complained Freddie Threepwood to Psmith in *Leave it to Psmith*. Mike Jackson in *Psmith Journalist* simply fell asleep to Psmith's conversation. It is stated of Psmith that 'conversation always acted on him as a mental stimulus', and he was the more attracted to Eve in the last book because she 'let him talk oftener and longer than any girl he had ever known'. The pleasant Psmith buzz, a rich mixture of glancing parodies, quotations, word-muddles and false concords, contained as ingredients three main, separable styles. Wodehouse soon thriftily and successfully isolated them for the individual use of others. The first he developed for the subsequent buzzers, the conscious maestros of racy conversation, invective and persiflage: Galahad and Uncle Fred, and all those chirpy young heroes of whom testy tycoons say in opening chapters that they are 'a darn sight too fresh'. These are clever men, who talk that way because it amuses them. A second ingredient of Psmith's talk has gone, in later books, to those unconscious humorists at the lower IQ level, of whom Bertie Wooster is the finest flower. Bertie jumbles his words, phrases and concords through innocence and stupidity; he stumbles on his images; he seems only just to be listening to what he himself is saying; and at occasional pinheaded moments he can stop to be intrigued by something he has just heard coming out of his own mouth, like a kitten intrigued by the flicking of its own tail. Such innocents are vulnerable and lovable. But they are burblers, not buzzers.

The third form in which the Psmith manner was bred out is the Jeeves style. In essence that style is the Ciceronian/ Johnsonian. It is the parliamentary or Civil Service style, level, pompous, circumlocutory, didactic. It is the language of leaders, school sermons, toastmasters and treaties. It is funny when used out of place – as by Mr Micawber – and consistently by such as would seem to have no need of it: butlers and gentlemen's gentlemen.

In Psmith this super-fatted style becomes dominant only when he talks to people who would be most dazed by it. In New York, with a six-inch bullet-hole in his hat after a skirmish with gangsters, Psmith addresses three cops with a battery of yard-long sentences, polysyllables and subjunctives:

> 'I am loath to interrupt this very impressive brain-barbecue, but, trivial as it may seem to you, to me there is a certain interest in this other matter of my ruined hat. I know that it may strike you as hypersensitive of us to protest...'

Holmes and babu

Apart from the blah Knut manner, the two strongest influences in the rhythms and locutions of the Psmith language are, first, Conan Doyle's Sherlock Holmes stories, and, second, 'babu'. Wodehouse recalled to Townend (in *Performing Flea*) the excitement of waiting for new issues of *The Strand Magazine* on Dulwich station. Schoolboys and paulo-post-schoolboys of Wodehouse's own vintage, and of Psmith's a decade later, were not only steeped in the Sherlock Holmes stories, but they knew that they could recognisably bandy the language of them with anyone else of their age and class. Stalky and his friends dropped into Brer Rabbit language almost as a code. Wodehouse's first major conversational parodist, Psmith, is constantly echoing Sherlock Homes (indeed, the Holmes *Valley of Fear* influence probably to some extent suggested the plot of *Psmith Journalist*). Psmith has verbal 'lifts' from Sherlock Holmes, with direct quotations of words, and copying of manner. 'You had best put the case in my hands.... I will think over the matter.' 'Do not disturb me. These are deep waters.' '...Omitting no detail, however slight' – these are the parts of the iceberg that appear above the water. In *Psmith Journalist* a snatch of Psmith dialogue is:

> 'It is possible that Comrade Windsor may possess the qualifications necessary for the post. But here he comes. Let us forgather with him, and observe him in private life before arriving at any premature decision.'

There, only 'But here he comes' is a direct lift from Holmes. But we could not be sure of that unless the surrounding rhythms were making us alert for identifications of exact phrases.

The element of Psmith's language that was hived off later for the use of the burblers such as Bertie Wooster is babu-English, and I'd like to take a few minutes here to have a look at F. Anstey's 1897 book, compiled from pieces in *Punch* in 1896, called *Baboo Jabberjee*. (I shall spell it 'babu' from now on.) Wodehouse read all Anstey's stuff as a boy, including, as is obvious from his school stories, *Vice Versa*. But *Baboo Jabberjee* (which is quoted by name in *Love Among the Chickens*) was powerfully seminal to Psmith and the quintessential Wodehouse style of false concords.

Anstey's Hurry Bungsho Jabberjee, BA, is a Bombay law-student in England. He uses the appellation 'Hon'ble' more or less as we say 'Mister' and the *Uncle Remus* characters say 'Brer'. Psmith's appellation 'Comrade' chimes well with Jabberjee. Jabberjee has learnt his English from books. He uses absurdly inflated phrases, and he makes unintentional false concords. He writes, for instance:

> The late respectable Dr Ben Johnson, gifted author of Boswell's Biography, once rather humorously remarked, on witnessing a nautch performed by canine quadrupeds, that, although their choreographical abilities were of but a moderate

nature, the wonderment was that they should be capable at all to execute such a hind-legged feat and *tour de force.*'

Some of Jabberjee's false concords are repeated verbatim by Bertie Wooster. Some of his inflated phraseology goes into Jeeves's vocabulary. Isn't that last quotation, apart from its howlers, rather reminiscent of Jeeves when he muffles the furious Pop Stoker with a chloroform mask of verbiage in *Right Ho, Jeeves*? Jabberjee writes:

'As poet Burns remarks with great truthfulness, "Rank is but a penny stamp, and a Man is a man and all that."'

This is a pleasant skid on the banana skin of education. Bertie and Jeeves, you remember, get tangled up in this same quotation at a moment of great crisis.

Rem acu tetigisti, non possumus, surgit amari aliquid, ultra vires, mens sana in corpore sano, amende honorable – these are gobbets of education that Jabberjee uses and Jeeves takes over. And (this is sad) we find that it was Jabberjee, and not Bertie, who first made that excellent Shakespeare emendation, only conceivable through the ears, only translatable through the eyes. Jabberjee writes: 'Jessamina inherits, in Hamlet's immortal phraseology, "an eye like Ma's to threaten and command".' There are other trace elements of Jabberjee in the wider Wodehouse. Jabberjee, describing an evening of professional boxing matches in a London hall, mentions the NO SMOKING notice, and says that everybody goes on smoking just the same. This point is made by Corky when describing an East End boxing evening in a Ukridge story. Jabberjee's 'I became once more *otto voce* and the silent tomb' is a phrase Bertie evokes once or twice, if perhaps with faint quotation marks in his voice. Jabberjee's mystification at Stratford, on finding that all the portraits of Hon'ble Shakespeare are unalike, and that none bears any resemblance to the bust, is a point which Wodehouse sharpens in an essay. Jabberjee who, like Bertie Wooster *passim*, is plagued by being engaged to a girl he wishes he were not engaged to, speaks of a 'manly, straightforward stratagem' for oiling out of the commitment. Wodehouse gets variations on this happy phrase into the mouths of Ukridge, Bingo Little, Tuppy Glossop and Bertie on separate occasions. Jabberjee, like Dick Swiveller, sucks the knob of his cane. So does Bertie. So does Freddie Threepwood. So does Motty, Lord Pershore, in the early Jeeves story.

Jabberjee introduces himself to 'Hon'ble Punch' as 'one saturated to the skin of his teeth in best English masterpieces of immaculate and moderately good prose extracts and dramatic passages'. Take your line through Ram, an actual babu schoolboy who appeared in *The Luck Stone*, into Psmith the buzzer, Bertie the burbler and Jeeves the orotund, and you may feel inclined, as I do, to pay a passing tribute to F. Anstey for planting a seed in the rich soil of young Wodehouse's burgeoning mind. Or, if you prefer the image, for putting a piece of grit into the Wodehouse oyster shell, so that Wodehouse built it into a pearl, richer than all his tribe of humorous writers.

Psmith is not the first fictional schoolboy whose main characteristic is clever talk, nor is he the last of the schoolboy Knuts. Anthony Pembury at St Dominic's, in Talbot Baines Reed's novel, is the son of the editor of *Great Britain* weekly review, the inheritor of his father's sharp tongue. He is a cripple, so he cannot play games or 'pursue'. But 'he can talk and he can ridicule, as his victims all the school over know.' The Knut with the eyeglass and faultless clothes has become more or less a stock character in Frank Richards and post-Frank Richards schoolboy fiction. Perhaps Psmith is the only example of the Knut with clever talk. The tradition of the Knut in *Magnet* and *Gem* is that he should be a Lord, pronounce his 'r's' as 'w's', and say 'you wotter!!!' with at least that number of exclamation marks. The smallness of his vocabulary fits the smallness of his intelligence, and his vocabulary is further limited by the need to find words for him which have 'r's' to mispwonounce.

Psmith has a large vocabulary and wide range of imagery. Many of his quotations, verbal images and conceits pass into the Wodehouse language, free for all later pleasant characters to use: restoring the tissues; *solvitur ambulando*; making us more spiritual; of all sad words of tongue or pen; Patience on a monument; couldn't find a bass drum in a telephone booth; this tendency ... fight against it; it would be paltering with the truth; not so but far otherwise; I have my spies everywhere; the man who discovered that alcohol was a food long before the doctors did.

Psmith is the first runner in the Wodehouse Non-Stop Quotation Stakes: the recitation, printed as prose, of gobbets from the better-known poets. At one moment he feels like some watcher of the skies, and keeps the feeling going accurately for three and a half lines of Keats. This stands as the record distance, until he beats it himself with four lines of uninterrupted Omar. Wodehouse appropriated this trick, I suspect, consciously or unconsciously, from Dick Swiveller in *The Old Curiosity Shop*:

'An excellent woman, that mother of yours, Christopher,' said Mr Swiveller. 'Who ran to catch me when I fell, and kissed the place to make it well? My mother. A charming woman...'

This is one of Psmith's own quotations, and Jeeves's and Bertie's. And that typographical manner of quoting poetry as prose became a pleasant habit of Wodehouse's. (Mr Cornelius of Valley Fields holds the record with sixteen lines of Scott.)

There are a few rather surprising moments when Psmith positively becomes a conscious wag, almost a buffoon. In *Psmith Journalist*, he has a throwaway line: 'We will now recite that pathetic song, "Baby's Sock is now a Blue-Bag..."' In *Leave it to Psmith* he makes one suspect three or four times that he has been dipping into the works of Dornford Yates and admiring

Berry: when he has to go forth in the night, and puts a white rose into the lapel of his pyjamas and a Homburg hat on his head; and when he describes an aspect of Blandings:

> 'We are now in the southern pleasaunce or the west home-park or something. Note the refined way the deer are cropping the grass. All the ground on which we are now standing is of historic interest. Oliver Cromwell went through here in 1550. The record has since been lowered...'

And when Eve tells him he is terribly conceited, he says: 'No, no, success has not spoiled me.'

Psmith had been 'resting' for eight years after *Psmith Journalist*. In those eight years Wodehouse had written the first of the Blandings saga, the book and the play of *Piccadilly Jim*, *Jill the Reckless*, his first book of golf stories, and two books of Jeeves. For a Wodehouse who had turned so many corners and advanced so far as a writer, it must have been a little difficult to keep the revived Psmith exactly in register with his previous self. Wodehouse said that he had had trouble with the last half of *Leave it to Psmith*, and, indeed, had to rewrite it after the first edition. It is not the most successful Psmith book or the most successful Blandings book. Its main interest to us in these days is for its attempt, even if not too happy, to develop Psmith as a Raffles and at the same time make him fall in love.

Marriage for Psmith

Was Psmith's a happy marriage? 'Marry someone eccentric,' her friend Cynthia had said to Eve. Psmith was certainly eccentric. How long did he last as Lord Emsworth's secretary? That is one of the expendable jobs in the Blandings saga, and we see several other incumbents in later books: Hugo Carmody, Monty Bodkin, Jerry Vail and even Baxter himself again. Also not a few girls. Presumably Psmith and Eve married soon after the end of *Leave it to Psmith*. Eve was quite a character in her own right, 'straight and slim' with a 'cheerful smile', 'boyish suppleness of body', a 'valiant gaiety', a 'golden sunniness'. She was 'joyously impecunious'. She got £150 a year from a deceased uncle and couldn't touch the capital; but she spent dangerously on buying hats and betting on horses. Did Mr and Mrs Psmith 'live in' at Blandings after she had finished cataloguing the library? That might have been a bit unkind to Freddie Threepwood, who had thought himself so deeply in love with Eve, and who was from time to time incarcerated at Blandings by his infuriated father.

My theory had been that that fish-magnate uncle of Psmith's died and left him a new pile of money, and that Psmith went off somewhere in Shropshire (perhaps buying back his childhood home, Corfby Hall in Lower Benfield) and became a gentleman of easy leisure, like the Infant at the end of the first *Stalky* book. Psmith and Eve would have the Mike Jacksons to stay when Mike could get away from his farm and the claims of Lincolnshire

on his cricket. Psmith would grow grey, but not fat. He would perhaps look more like the Peruvian llama in middle age than he had even in youth, but he would keep his figure and his eyeglass and his smart clothes. Eve would make him resign from five of his London clubs and remain a member of the Drones only. Psmith wouldn't come up to London very often. He would remind you a good deal of the Earl of Ickenham.

In the Preface that Wodehouse wrote for the 1974 omnibus *World of Psmith*, the four novels in one book, he said:

> A married Psmith would not be quite the same. But obviously a man of his calibre is not going to be content to spend his life as Lord Emsworth's secretary. In what direction he branched out I cannot say. My guess is that he studied law, became a barrister, was a great success and wound up by taking silk. If so, I see him as a genial judge like A. P. Herbert's Mr Justice Codd, whose last case, in the book entitled *Codd's Last Case*, is possibly the funniest thing that great humorist ever wrote.

THE SCHOOL STORIES

The Pothunters (1902), *A Prefect's Uncle* (1903), *Tales of St Austin's* (1903), *The Gold Bat* (1904), *The Head of Kay's* (1905), *The White Feather* (1907), *The Luck Stone* (published pseudonymously, as a serial in *Chums*, 1908, and published posthumously in 1997 by Galahad Books), *Mike* (1909) (this has now been divided into *Mike at Wrykyn* and *Mike and Psmith*), *The Little Nugget* (1913).

'THE SCHOOL COMMANDMENTS'

'Behave yourself. Don't make a frightful row in the House. Don't cheek your elders and betters. Wash.' Those were the words of advice that the Gazeka had given the new boy Mike at Wrykyn. Doctrinally you won't find Wodehouse burrowing much deeper into the mystique of the English public school than that. Counting that as a generalised First Commandment, you might construct the rest of the Decalogue as:

2   Thou shalt not put on side.
3   Thou shalt not sneak on other boys.
4   Thou shalt not lie except to get other boys out of trouble.
5   Thou shalt think thine own school the best in England, and thine own House the best in the school.
6   Thou shalt sponge thyself with cold water after a long soak in a hot bath.
7   Thou shalt not smoke: it is bad for fitness. If thou dost smoke, let it be a pipe and not cigarettes.
8   Thou shalt consider games more important than work.
9   Thou shalt not talk about thy parents except in jest.
10 Thou shalt not smarm thy hair with pungent unguents.

And the Eleventh Commandment is for all healthy public-school rule-breakers:

> Thou shalt not be found out. Otherwise you mayest get sacked and have to go into a bank.

NUGGETSDrink

Some of Wodehouse's funniest passages are drunk scenes – and I include parsons plastered on Buck-U-Uppo. He listed, in a Mulliner story, six types of hangover – the Atomic, the Broken Compass, the Cement Mixer, the Comet, the Gremlin Boogie and the Sewing Machine. Bertie Wooster liked a basis of two cocktails, the one drunk fast, the other rather slower. At the Emsworth Arms and similar staging posts for visitors, impostors or no, from London to the big house, the home-brew beer often changed a man's mind conveniently for the plot: he shambled in a timid lover, and strode out a lover-determined-to-declare-his-love-to-the-adored-object-and-no-nonsense. Mr Mulliner's Uncle William had got drunk, slept through the San Francisco earthquake, and won his bride, who worshipped his courage as Desdemona worshipped Othello's. They called their son John San Francisco Earthquake Mulliner, or J.S.F.E. Mulliner for short. There was Gussie Fink-Nottle at the Grammar School prize-giving, Catsmeat Pirbright, Sigsbee Waddington, Lord Worplesdon, Tipton Plimsoll, Mervyn Potter, Motty Pershore, Eggy Mannering, and those two burglars, Ernest and Harold, in 'The Ordeal of Osbert Mulliner'. Memory serves these up as heroic drinkers. Percy Pilbeam as less heroic; but all funny in their cups.

He climbed into the bed as it came round the second time.
As he drained his first glass, it seemed to him that a torchlight procession,
of whose existence he had hitherto not been aware, had begun to march down
his throat and explore the recesses of his stomach. The second glass, though slightly
too heavily charged with molten lava, was extremely palatable. It helped the torchlight
procession along by adding to it a brass band of singular sweetness of tone.
And with the third somebody began to touch off fireworks in his head.

He was in the sort of overwrought state when a fly treading a little too heavily on the carpet is
enough to make a man think he's one of the extras in the film of *All Quiet on the Western Front*.

It just shows, what any Member of Parliament will tell you, that if you want real oratory,
the preliminary noggin is essential. Unless pie-eyed, you cannot hope to grip.

As sober as a teetotal Girl Guide.

You'd remember all right if you'd had a mint julep in America. Insidious things.
They creep up on you like a baby sister and slide their little hands into yours and the
next thing you know the Judge is telling you to pay the clerk of the court fifty dollars.

The barman recommended a 'lightning whizzer', an invention of his own.
He said it was what rabbits trained on when they were matched against grizzly bears,
and there was only one instance on record of the bear having lasted three rounds.

My Uncle George discovered that alcohol was a food
well in advance of modern medical thought.

'Nice day,' said Marlene as she filled the order, for she was a capital conversationalist.
A barmaid has to be quick as lightning with these good things.

Statisticians, who have gone carefully into the figures – the name of Schwertfeger of Berlin is one
that springs to the mind – inform us that of young men who have just received a negative answer to
a proposal of marriage (and with these must, of course, be grouped those whose engagements have
been broken off) 6.08% clench their hands and stare silently before them, 12.02% take the next train
to the Rocky Mountains and shoot grizzlies while 11.07% sit down at their desks and become
modern novelists. The first impulse of the remainder – and these, it will be seen, constitute a large
majority – is to nip off round the corner and get a good, stiff drink. Into this class Packy fell.

Love among the Chickens

A book of laughter by
P.G. Wodehouse who
has been described as
a'National Humorist'.

Ukridge

Love Among the Chickens (1906 and, somewhat rewritten, 1921), ten short stories in *Ukridge* (1924), three short stories in *Lord Emsworth and Others* (1937), three short stories in *Eggs, Beans and Crumpets* (1940), one short story in *Nothing Serious* (1950), one short story in *A Few Quick Ones* (1959) and one short story in *Plum Pie* (1966).

Ukridge is the only arrant rogue among all Wodehouse's public-school immoralists. (Oofy Prosser is an unpleasant immoralist.) Ukridge spans sixty publishing years, starts as a married man, and then goes backwards in time into previous bachelorhood. He is a handier property when he can be single-mindedly selfish, and when the reader's relish of his knavery is not edged with pity for his wife, the adoring little Millie.

In one's memory Ukridge seems to be dressed in one of three garbs or outfits: pyjamas and filthy mackintosh (hurriedly kicked out by Aunt Julia at midnight); filthy grey bags and filthy mackintosh (in pubs, on Battling Billson business); or top-hat, morning coat and all the fixings (temporarily sunning in the gilded Wimbledon cage of Aunt Julia's approval). His socks and shirts are almost always purloined from his friend Corky. His collar is often detached from its back-stud. And he is always wearing his pince-nez attached to his flapping ears with ginger-beer wire. Modern readers will scarcely have heard of pince-nez. Since they have never seen stone ginger-beer bottles with corks held in with wire, the phrase 'ginger-beer wire' will have them guessing. The idea of a young man wearing a top-hat and morning coat in Wimbledon for anything but a wedding or a funeral will seem absurd. But Ukridge himself can be confidently recommended in print to anybody who remembers Tony Hancock, a not dissimilar fantasist, on radio and television. *The Times* wrote thus of Hancock in 1958:

> Mr Hancock is a comedian governed by the basic humours of vanity and greed. The odds are heavily weighted against his satisfying either, but all disasters are effaced from his memory by invincible egoism. Action springs either from his delusions of orientally voluptuous grandeur or from his taste for ludicrously elaborate conspiracy. There is constant alternation between fantasy and realism.
>
> Defeat, indignity, physical cowardice, and moral turpitude are constantly recurring, but they are saved from embarrassment by the aggressiveness of the comedy. Mr Hancock is not a clown to be trampled on: he is a belligerent grotesque who engulfs all surrounding characters, who never descends to pathos, and who

speaks an idiom all his own that is a compound of vehement slang, satirised cliché, and extreme literacy.

It would be a fairly faithful description of Ukridge.

His friend Bill Townend gave Wodehouse, in a letter, the background material – the desperate chicken-farm and its bellowing owner – for *Love Among the Chickens* in 1906. Townend knew the real chicken-farmer, who had been a master at a prep school where Townend had boarded after leaving Dulwich. Wodehouse never met Ukridge's real-life prototype, then or later, and he built up Ukridge's character from several other sources: one school friend in particular, a clothes-borrower, whom he mentions in *Over Seventy*. My guess is that yet another model was James Cullingworth, the amiable villain in Conan Doyle's *Stark Monro Letters*. Cullingworth has a little, timid wife, Hetty, who adores him, and whom Monro (largely Conan Doyle) feels he wants to pick up and kiss. Hetty is not unlike Ukridge's Millie, who has something of the same effect on James Corcoran (largely Wodehouse). Cullingworth calls Monro 'laddie'. Cullingworth is always, he thinks, on the edge of riches, and always, in fact, on the edge of bankruptcy, with duns and county court summonses threatening. Monro's last words on Cullingworth, who was finally planning to make a vast fortune as an eye-surgeon in South America, were:

> 'He is a man whom nothing could hold down. I wish him luck, and have a kindly feeling towards him, and yet I distrust him from the bottom of my heart, and shall be pleased to know that the Atlantic rolls between us.'

Love Among the Chickens

Ukridge appeared in print before Mike Jackson. *Love Among the Chickens* in its first version was on the bookstalls three years before the book *Mike*. In fact, although *The White Feather* came out as a serial in *The Captain* in 1905 (the £60 cheque for it went into Wodehouse's bank in October that year), *Love Among the Chickens* appeared before the book of *The White Feather*. *Love Among the Chickens* came out as a book, without advance serialisation, in August 1906, and had netted £31 5s. 8d. in royalties for its author by January of the next year. *The White Feather* was on the bookstalls in October 1907 (advance royalties £17 10s.). The book, *Mike*, didn't appear till 1909.

It is as well to be a bit bibliographical about this, to establish that Wodehouse wrote a novel about adults and love before he had written his last school book. Put it the other way round: *Mike*, which is his longest and best school novel, was a return to schooldays, written by Wodehouse the novelist. It is as well, also, that, continuing to be bibliographically technical, we should compare the 1906 version of *Love Among the Chickens* with its 1921 successor.

In the dedication at the beginning of the 1921 version, Wodehouse says:

> ...I have practically rewritten the book. There was some pretty bad work in it, and it had 'dated'. As an instance of the way in which the march of modern civilisation had left the 1906 edition behind, I may mention that, on page twenty-one, I was able to make Ukridge speak of selling eggs at five for sixpence.

There wasn't really much original bad work, or much rewriting: only some tidying. And Ukridge himself comes through from 1906 and 1921 with hardly a word altered. He is not the main character in the book, anyway. It is Jeremy Garnet's love, among Ukridge's chickens. In the Blampied drawing on the dust jacket of the second *Love Among the Chickens*, it is Jeremy Garnet in plus-fours chasing the fowls. Of the four charming black and white illustrations by H. M. Brock in the 1906 book, only one showed Ukridge. He was leaning on a gate, between his wife and Garnet, looking at chickens. Ukridge is a much bigger person there than Garnet. But in that book and in those days Ukridge was not specifically a clothes-borrower. In the later stories, when Garnet ('Garny, old horse!') became changed to Corcoran ('Corky, old horse!'), Ukridge and his narrator were about the same size sartorially – which Ukridge made the most of, and Corky regretted.

The main difference between the 1906-21 Ukridge and the Ukridge of the later short stories is that Ukridge is married in the first book, and unmarried ever afterwards. He meets Millie and wins her love, and her aunt's agreement to their marriage, in the last of the ten stories in *Ukridge* (1924). The seven stories that have appeared since then have put Ukridge in the pre-Millie state again. In one of the stories in *Ukridge*, 'No Wedding Bells for Him', Ukridge is trying to oil out of his engagement to fat, giggly Mabel Price, of Balbriggan, Peabody Road, Clapham Common. He says to Corky:

'I was just thinking that, if you were to write them an anonymous letter, accusing me of all sorts of things.... Might say I was married already.'

'Not a bit of good.'

'Perhaps you're right,' said Ukridge gloomily...

But we are used, by 1924, to the blithe clutch-slippings and backfires of Wodehouse's time-machinery. The name of Aunt Julia's butler changes from Oakshott to Barter to Baxter and back to Oakshott again. The Beale of *Love Among the Chickens* turns up again as Bowles, the man who keeps the digs where Corky lives and where Ukridge is given the freedom of the house (by Bowles). But Bowles, in the maturer Wodehouse manner, is now an ex-butler, not an ex-soldier.

Ukridge reborn

Having used Ukridge as a supporting character the first time, Wodehouse found that he was full of 'capabilities'. He gave him star treatment, put his name in lights (the literary equivalent being the titles of the short stories in which he appeared), and built a company round him.

Jeremy Garnet, the narrator of *Love Among the Chickens*, had met Ukridge when they were both masters at the same prep school. But the Ukridge of the later stories was an Old Wrykynian, and Corky, Tupper and Looney Coote had all been at school with him. When Ukridge becomes, or is revealed as, an Old Wrykynian, you realise that he has put down a tap-root. Admittedly he had been sacked from Wrykyn. He broke bounds and rules one night to go to a Fair. He disguised himself in false beard and whiskers, but left his school cap on top of the whole mess, and was easily apprehended. But it is the old-school fellowship that makes Ukridge's limpet-rock, predator-prey relationship with Corky and Tuppy understandable and acceptable; and Corky is able to describe his old school friend with the ruthlessness that (outside a family) only an old-school friendship really warrants. Shared incarceration at a boarding school produces some embarrassing and incompatible acquaintanceships; but, whatever the candour they encourage in the exchange of personalities, they trail inescapable loyalties. None saw this more clearly than Wodehouse, and no author has used and exaggerated the fact more deliberately, joyously and successfully than Wodehouse. But, whereas Bertie Wooster and his Aubrey-Upjohn's-and-Eton friends play the Old School Loyalty gambit for farce (albeit as a convenient hinge in the plot), Wrykyn is a shade more serious. Mike Jackson, Sam Shotter, Ukridge, Tuppy, Looney and Corky are a little closer to Wodehouse's heart and further from his funny-bone. Subliminally, Wrykyn is Wodehouse's own school, Dulwich. When he puts Ukridge at Wrykyn, Ukridge is part of the inner family, and in the long run he will be rescued from his worst idiocies. This gives the reader a rewarding sense of security. He feels able to laugh the louder when Ukridge falls, because he knows Ukridge must be put on his feet again and all will be well, not only with Ukridge (temporarily maybe) but with his own old-school conscience. So one's hope for a fiancially set-fair fade-out for Ukridge is valid. A pity Wodehouse never got round to it.

Ukridge is a thief, a blackmailer, a liar and a sponge. He alternates self-glorification with self-pity, and sometimes has a bout of both in the same paragraph. He is as full of precepts as a preacher in the pulpit and, like a preacher, he swoops from the particular to the general, scattering moral judgements. Ukridge himself is a total immoralist, and he dulls the moral sense in others. He is totally selfish. The most that can be said in his favour is that he has knocked round the world on tramp steamers from Naples to San Francisco, he is good with dogs, Bowles admires him and fawns on him, he is not a snob, and girls sometimes, and for short stretches, like him.

Corky at one point calls Ukridge the 'sternest of bachelors', but his success with girls is curiously believable. Certainly, after the first mendacious build-up, the girls tend to get caught and crushed, with Ukridge, in the machinery of truth and justice. But Ukridge never lets a girl down as he lets Corky and Tuppy and his other male friends down – at the drop, Tuppy might complain, of a top-hat. Ukridge never fascinates in order to speculate. When he gets engaged to Myrtle Bayliss, daughter of the Sussex jute-king, it is through love and not for her money. When he tries to beat the Bart to the favours of Mabel of Onslow Square, it is for love, and not for money or security. Even when he finds himself talked, by her family, into an engagement with Mabel of Clapham Common, he cannot just walk out of the embarrassing involvement, as any strong-minded, sensible rogue would. He is hobbled by the Code. To quote *Jill the Reckless*: when Sir Derek Underhill breaks his engagement to Jill, Wally Mason, the Anglo-American hero, says to Freddie Rooke:

> 'I can't understand you, Freddie. If ever there was a fellow that might have been expected to take the only possible view of Underhill's behaviour in this business, I should have said it was you. You're a public-school man. You've mixed all the time with decent people.... Yet it seems to have made absolutely no difference in your opinion of this man Underhill that he behaved like an utter cad...'

This suggests that Ukridge's attempts to save Mabel Price's fat face, and to get their engagement broken *by her*, may be a last enchantment, a last fleck of a cloud of glory, that Ukridge trails from Wrykyn days.

If the 'bewilderingly pretty' Millie (with whom Ukridge fell in love on an Underground train, at first sight, and without knowing her South Kensington and knightly background) ever reads the stories of Stanley's previous involvements with the two Mabels, 'poor little Dora', and Myrtle Bayliss, she will undoubtedly believe every lying word of Stanley's protestations that he has been traduced by his snake-in-the-grass friend Corky; that these are foul aspersions made by a struggling penny-a-liner just to sell to a magazine; that one of these days he, Stanley, will sue the magazine for slander and everything else

THE LIGHT NOVELS

Wodehouse novels which are not parts of sagas and in which the recurrent characters, if any, are not dominant.

The Prince and Betty (1921), *The Little Nugget* (1913), *Uneasy Money* (1917), *Piccadilly Jim* (1918), *A Damsel in Distress* (1919), *The Coming of Bill* (1920), *The Indiscretions of Archie* (1921), *A Gentleman of Leisure* (1921), *Jill the Reckless* (1921), *The Girl on the Boat* (1922), *The Adventures of Sally* (1922), *Bill the Conqueror* (1924), *Ice in the Bedroom* (1925), *The Small Bachelor* (1927), *Money for Nothing* (1928), *Big Money* (1931), *If I Were You* (1931), *Dr Sally* (1932), *Hot Water* (1932), *The Luck of the Bodkins* (1935), *Laughing Gas* (1936), *Summer Moonshine* (1938), *Quick Service* (1940), *Money in the Bank* (1946), *Spring Fever* (1948), *The Old Reliable* (1951), *Barmy in Wonderland* (1952), *French Leave* (1956), *Something Fishy* (1957), *Ice in the Bedroom* (1961), *Frozen Assets* (1964), *Company for Henry* (1967), *Do Butlers Burgle Banks?* (1968), *The Girl in Blue* (1970), *Pearls, Girls and Monty Bodkin* (1972), *Bachelors Anonymous* (1973).

available and that this is his big chance of achieving the capital which will lead to a stupendous fortune. We get the cosy impression that Millie Ukridge still, after about fifty years of misty marriage, probably thinks Stanley a king among men, and believes he had come to her in that Underground train clean and unsullied by any previous romances.

It is a great tribute to Corky/Wodehouse that he can make such an anti-social menace as Ukridge appealing. There is not a word of sentimentality in the Ukridge stories, but they have a positive charm. They are, in technique of construction and writing, Wodehouse short stories at their springtime best. They are vintage stuff. They are extremely funny, and yet you feel that Corky, the narrator, is not a humorist. He is a dry commentator, incisive and objective. It is his subject, Ukridge, and Ukridge's story, that makes the laughs. You are scarcely conscious that Ukridge is being brilliantly presented and his story brilliantly told: you are so taken with the man in front of the floodlights that you forget the man behind them.

But keep half an eye on Corky. He is really a very interesting background character. He is modest and amusing about his go-anywhere-write-anything trade of Pleasing Editors, but perfectly sure that this is the work he wants to be in. He is fallible and flatterable (he goes and helps Ukridge and Boko at their electioneering largely because he wants to hear the crowds singing the noble election jingle which he has composed for Boko; he falls completely for Ukridge's Millie and her 'Stanley has been telling me what friends you and he are. He is devoted to you'). But he is able to get tough when annoyed. His description of the Pen and Ink Club dance in 'Ukridge Sees Her Through' has, below its alert descriptions of sound, smells, gilt chairs and potted palms, a cold anger. Here for the first time Wodehouse rolls his sleeves up against the Phonies of the Pen. Charlton Prout, the sleek, stout secretary of the club, whose main relish is pushing his own books and excluding from membership authors who lack 'vision', gets Corky's dagger between the ribs. He gets Miss Julia Ukridge's own wrath later, as a blunt instrument on the side of the head. Corky, having stage-managed Miss Ukridge's attack on Prout, tiptoes away, his heart bleeding delightedly.

Ukridge is to some extent a walking parody of careers-thinking by the young, careers-talk *to* the young by headmasters, uncles and self-made business tycoons interviewed by the magazines, and careers-fantasies encouraged by the fiction in the other pages of the same magazines. 'Vision, and the big, broad, flexible outlook' comes from headmasters, uncles and tycoons in print. The rich uncle from Australia, the rich aunt in Wimbledon, the lonely millionaire who needs a secretary, the bright business idea that leads to fortune – these are from the fiction pages. The only young man with a steady profession in the Ukridge stories – George Tupper of the Foreign Office – is treated as a bit of a bore. He had written sentimental poetry in the school magazine, and was always starting subscription lists and getting up memorials and presentations. He had 'an earnest, pulpy heart'. Ukridge could get fivers out of him with a sure touch.

Orwell in his essay on Wodehouse has pointed out that the first object of the Wodehouse hero is to find a soft spot for sitting pretty on financially; anything that brings the security of three meals a day is good enough for him. Ukridge seeks quick opulence, to finance eternal leisure for himself. His friends certainly hope he will find it, so that he will keep his hands out of their pockets. Even George Tupper thinks he has found an answer when he suggests him as secretary to his friend Bulstrode. It never seems to occur to anybody that Ukridge might become a common or garden daily-breader. Did nobody get at him when he was sacked from Wrykyn and try to put him in a Bank? Did Aunt Julia's inheritance loom always, preventing him from learning a trade because he saw the promise of getting her money in the end? If so, why was he so keen, while waiting for her money, to make a fortune for himself?

There are still people who say, sometimes in print, that Wodehouse wrote only about the rich and was, by inference, a snob. It is an absurd criticism, and the answer to it is either short and rude or long and boring. One of the pleasantest things about Ukridge is his complete un-class-consciousness. He is genuinely happy in the company of Battling Billson and the boxing fraternity. He is genuinely knowledgeable about the barmaids in Kennington:

> It appears that Billson has fallen in love with one of the barmaids at the Crown in Kennington. 'Not,' said Ukridge, so that all misapprehension should be avoided, 'the one with the squint. The other one. Flossie. The girl with yellow hair.'

Ukridge can go into criminal partnership with all the servants in his aunt's house while she's away, and treat them as equals. Yet he enjoys from Bowles, the ex-butler, fawning treatment that, by the rules of his guild, a butler only gives to one of the true gentry. Bowles doesn't treat Corky like that. He wouldn't treat Tupper like that. But Ukridge might be the fourth son of an earl as far as Bowles is concerned.

Love Among the Chickens is not the rounded Ukridge or the rounded Wodehouse. The short stories are the thing, and one wonders why Corky, who could write those stories, was still a struggling contributor to *Interesting Bits* at thirty bob a time. There is some beautiful translation of ideas into words in the 1924 collection *Ukridge*. Corky, thrown on to his ear from the pub in the Ratcliff Highway of the East End, is picked up by Billson and, in the process, 'gets a sort of general impression of bigness and blue serge'. And the barman, later ejected by the avenging Billson, 'did a sort of backward foxtrot across the pavement'. Corky, stranded with Flossie the barmaid's ghastly mother with the terrible hat, suggests that they go to Westminster Abbey: 'I had a fleeting notion, which a moment's reflection exploded before it could bring me much comfort, that women removed their hats in Westminster Abbey.' Corky's reaction to the caricature of Boko Lawlor, put up by his enemies in the Redbridge election, is: 'You could see at a glance that here was one who, if elected, would do his underhand best to cut down the Navy, tax the poor man's food, and strike a series of blows at the very root of the home...' Boko himself, towards the end of the electioneering, is speaking 'with a husky confidence' in his success. Finally, in that same story, there is Corky's description of the smell coming up on to the platform at the monster meeting at the Associated Mechanics' Hall – 'a mixed scent of dust, clothes, orange peel, chalk, wood, plaster, pomade and Associated Mechanics'.

In the seven Ukridge short stories that have appeared since *Ukridge*, Corky only narrates one in its entirety. That's 'Buttercup Day'. For the other six, after a page or two of introduction by Corky in the manner of The Oldest Member or Mr Mulliner, Ukridge takes over in double quotes. Ukridge's language and manner of narration are racy and wonderful, but the note of farce is more strongly stressed than in the earlier stories where Corky is the 'I' character. Ukridge has an ebullient style, of forceful parody, injured self-pity, strongly emotional prejudices and cool justification of egregious immorality. Ukridge, that 'human blot'; that 'foe of the human race'; that 'hell-bound'; that giver of false names 'as an ordinary business precaution'; that man with one pair of trousers who spent the night in jail on a plank bed and was – an indignity even for him – forcibly washed by the authorities; that visionary, that manic-depressive, that moralising immoralist ('...I don't know, Corky, if you have ever done the fine dignified thing, refusing to accept money because it was tainted, and there wasn't enough of it, but I have always noticed on these occasions...') – Ukridge is one of the great Wodehouse creations.

NUGGETS Church

No boy can go through fifteen years of English boarding schools, and holidays with uncles at vicarages, without getting the prose of the pulpit, the vocabulary and rhythms of the Bible, Prayer Book and Hymns Ancient and Modern in his memory. Wodehouse owed, and we owe, a great debt to this strand of his education. His use of the Anglican Church – its bishops, vicars and curates – is frequent, hilarious and youthful. I repeat, youthful. The seeds were sown in his boyhood. He went to America first in his early twenties. He lived much of his life in America. He set a number of his novels and short stories in America. But did he ever write about an American church or clergyman? I think not. He hadn't got the subject in his heart and, so, near his funny-bone. In England his curates could steal policemen's helmets, his vicars get black eyes, his bishops get treed by dogs. Wodehouse had total confidence. He knew his stuff and could knock it about for laughs. Irreverence? Plenty of that. Sacrilege? Blasphemy? Bad taste? No, never a breath. He gave the young men of God delectable girls – Stiffy Byng, Gertrude Alcester, Cynthia Wickhammersley, Myrtle Jellaby – you can't ask better than those. He gave their elders strong drink – Buck-U-Uppo Tonic, which tasted bland ('like old boot soles beaten up in sherry'), went straight to the red corpuscles, and brought out bishops and headmasters to paint statues, to dance sarabands at nightclubs, and, in the spirit of true churchmanship, to sock policemen. Verily, Wodehouse ministered well to God's Anglican ministers.

The Rev. Rupert Bingham seemed subdued and gloomy,
as if he had discovered schism among his flock.

England was littered with the shrivelled remains of curates at whom
the Bishop's wife had looked through her lorgnette. He had seen them
wilting like salted snails at the episcopal breakfast table.

'You can't let Harold get it in the neck. You were telling me this afternoon
that he would be unfrocked. I won't have him unfrocked. Where is he going to
get if they unfrock him? That sort of thing gives a curate a frightful black eye.'
(Stiffy Byng defending her fiancé, the Rev. Harold Pinker.)

'Golly, when you admonish a congregation, it stays admonished!'
(Myrtle Jellaby to the Rev. Anselm Mulliner.)

At the top table, with a nasty, vicious look in his eyes, sat a Bishop. Anybody who has ever attended Old Boys' dinners knows that Bishops are tough stuff. They take their time, these prelates. They mouth their words and shape their periods. They roam with frightful deliberation from the grave to the gay, from the manly straightforward to the whimsically jocular. Not one of them but is good for at least twenty-five minutes.

The Rev. 'Stinker' Pinker was dripping with high principles....

She looked like a vicar's daughter who plays hockey and ticks off the
villagers when they want to marry their deceased wives' sisters.

The Bishop of Stortford was talking to the local Master of Hounds
about the difficulty he had in keeping his vicars off the incense.

Lord Emsworth and Blandings

Something Fresh (1915), *A Damsel in Distress* (1919), so nearly a Blandings novel that it should be read in the Blandings sequence, *Leave it to Psmith* (1923), *Summer Lightning* (1929), *Heavy Weather* (1933), *Uncle Fred in the Springtime* (1939), *Full Moon* (1947), *Pigs Have Wings* (1952), *Service with a Smile* (1962), *Galahad at Blandings* (1965), *A Pelican at Blandings* (1969) and *Sunset at Blandings* (1977). Those are the novels. Six short stories set at Blandings occur in *Blandings Castle* (1935), one in *Lord Emsworth and Others* (1937), one in *Nothing Serious* (1950) and one in *Plum Pie* (1966).

A Homer at Blandings

The long entry on Homer in my edition of the *Encyclopaedia Britannica* is by the late Professor Gilbert Murray. In 1957 Murray said: 'When I became ninety, many telegrams came to congratulate or perhaps condone with me. The first was from the Prime Minister of Australia. The second from the Prime Minister of England. The third from P. G. Wodehouse. I have a great admiration for Wodehouse and the sequence gratified me.'

Murray did not bring any references to Wodehouse into his Encyclopaedia article on Homer, but I have heard Oxford dons elaborate a theory that, quite apart from Murray's admiration for both, there is a mystical communion between the two authors so widely separated by the centuries. These Senior Common Room scholiasts (the *Oxford English Dictionary* defines a scholiast as an ancient commentator upon a classical writer, so I have the *mot juste*) say that Homer and Wodehouse write, with deliberate, artistic purpose, about comparable societies, lordly or near-lordly, past, almost timeless, and yet in certain respects engagingly anachronistic; that each author writes a private language, rich in imagery, allusions, repetitions, formulaic expressions and suppressed quotations; that if the subtitle of *The Iliad* was *The Wrath of Achilles*, the subtitle of any *Omnibus* of Bertie Wooster's writings could well be *The Wrath of Aunt Agatha*. And so on.

Personally I would add to the dons' spot passages a quotation from T. E. (Lawrence of Arabia) Shaw's Introduction to his translation of *The Odyssey*. Shaw was writing of the sort of man he deduced, from internal evidence, the author to have been. The italics are mine. The parallels are remarkable:

> ...a bookworm, no longer young, living from home, a mainlander, city-bred, domestic ... dog-lover ... fond of poetry, a great, if uncritical, reader ... with limited sensuous range, but an exact eyesight which gave him all his pictures ... tender charity of heart

and head for serving-men ... the associate of menials, making himself their friend and defender by understanding ... loved the rural scene. No farmer, he has learnt the points of a good olive tree [*for Wodehouse read 'pig' or 'pumpkin' for 'olive tree'*] ... He had sailed upon and watched the sea ... seafaring not being his trade [*Wodehouse had been destined for the Navy as a boy*]. Neither land-lubber nor stay-at-home nor ninny ... He makes a hotch-potch of periods ... pages steeped in a queer naivety ... sprinkled tags of epic across his pages ... very bookish, this house-bred man ... verbal felicity ... recurring epithets ... the tale was the thing...

It is at Blandings Castle that Wodehouse seems to offer his Homeric parallels most noticeably, particularly in the matters of trophies and counters of exchange.

There is no money in Homer, of course. And of course many of Wodehouse's characters have it in plenty. But, especially at Blandings, cash and coin are immanent rather than actual. The counters of exchange at Blandings are generally of the order of the Homeric *keimelia* (the possessions that represented 'prestige-wealth', that changed hands but were never 'cashed': the armour and the trophies; iron, gold, cauldrons and tripods). The plot-making *keimelia* at Blandings are less often amounts of cash than items of prestige-wealth such as pigs, pumpkins, vicarages, manuscripts of memoirs, jobs as secretary, air-guns and scarabs. Most Wodehouse plots are variations of Hunt the Slipper. But there is something about aristocratic Blandings that makes one feel that here is the Lord's or Wimbledon of the game. Freddie Threepwood's sackful of rats was a case in point.

'I have here, Aunt Georgiana,' said Freddie Threepwood, holding up a sack in the amber drawing-room at the after-dinner coffee hour, 'a few simple rats.' This, though Beach removed the sack unopened, was enough to put an end to Gertrude's infatuation with Orlo, the side-whiskered tenor, and make her beefy clergyman fiancé appear in his true lights as a dog-fight-stopper and a king among men. For devious but sufficient reasons, it got 'Beefy' Bingham a vicarage at Much Matchingham too, and thus the ability to marry Gertrude. It got Freddie well placed to land the dog-biscuit contract from Gertrude's mother. It got the plot unravelled and the happy endings. The sack of rats was 'the goods', a typical item of Blandings prestige-wealth.

Blandings and its environs

In shape and size and messuages Wodehouse's Blandings Castle owes a good deal to his boyhood memory of Corsham, the stately home of the Methuens near Bath. The young Pelham, spending school holidays with a clergyman uncle near by, was taken to Corsham to skate on the lake, and the image of the great house remained on the retina of his inward eye. And when, in his early thirties, a resident alien in New York, writing away for dear life and for any American editor who would buy anything, Wodehouse decided to try farce about the English aristocracy, he called his stately home Blandings, his chatelain Lord Emsworth and his story *Something New* (*Something Fresh* in England, 1915).

If Wodehouse studied Corsham only in the skating months, he has been seasonally unfaithful to his memories in the books. Admittedly the weather was cold when Ashe Marson arrived at Blandings in *Something Fresh*. But thereafter, book after book, it seems always to be high summer weather, with tea under the cedars on the lawn, hammocks and deckchairs, the rose garden a glory and the lake calling the ninth earl down for a bathe. Admittedly Wodehouse is not such a knowledgeable gardener as Lord Emsworth, and tulip-time, rhododendron-time, rose-time, hollyhock-time and pumpkin-time are all much the same to him. Admittedly the house party in *Something Fresh* is timed weirdly as 'falling between the hunting and the shooting seasons'. The point is that, apart from hot thunderstorms, Blandings basks and, when Lord Emsworth potters out to commune with his pig, he puts on a hat but never an overcoat.

Emsworth is, in fact, a town on the border of Sussex and Hampshire, in a district rich in place-names that have acquired glory in song or legend. Hilaire Belloc's Ha'naker and Duncton Hill are near by, and Wodehouse has taken from the villages of Bosham and Warblington names for Lord Emsworth's heir (Lord Bosham) and one of his many sisters (Lady Ann Warblington). Blandings Castle in fiction is in Shropshire. Obviously Belpher Castle in Hampshire, the setting for *A Damsel in Distress* (1919), is, in the literary fourth dimension, somewhere on the Emsworth-Corsham-Blandings road. To all intents and purposes *A Damsel in Distress* is a Blandings novel. Lord Marshmoreton in it is an echo of Lord Emsworth, Lord Belpher of Lord Bosham, Lady Caroline Byng of Lady Constance Keeble, Reggie Byng of Freddie Threepwood, Keggs the butler of Beach the butler, and Macpherson the gardener of McAllister the gardener. In fact, Lord Marshmoreton's family name appears to be Bosham. His second son, Freddie Bosham, marries a Phyllis Jackson of 'the Jackson jam-making family'. In the second Blandings novel, *Leave it to Psmith*, you have Mike Jackson married to Phyllis, step-daughter of Lady Constance Keeble.

When an author in a hurry digs down for some names for characters, he will occasionally draw a duplicate. Wodehouse would get his types together before he knew their names, and churn them up into a plot before he knew where the events would happen. He drew his names out of a hat, but in the case of *A Damsel in Distress* forgot that some of these were old ones that had got put back after the last draw. He had not, at the stage of *A Damsel in Distress*, seen saga possibilities in the Blandings set-up of *Something Fresh*. All he knew was that he was happy and at home in an English castle, with a widower earl in the garden, his tough sister as chatelaine, his fat butler in the pantry sipping port, and assorted secretaries, chorus girls and impostors making a plot.

When Blandings assumed saga proportions, the castle became simply a roof under which any member of the Emsworth family could stay and invite friends to stay, where errant sons and nieces were incarcerated (the incarcerated sometimes referred to Blandings as a Bastille, sometimes as a Devil's Island) to make them cool off from love affairs, where detectives were summoned to watch pigs or jewels, brain-specialists were summoned to watch defective dukes, and librarians, valets and secretaries were hired and fired. Blandings is a place where things happen, with lots of time on everybody's hands for things to happen in, lots of bedrooms to put up unlimited *dramatis personae*, lots of corridors, shrubberies, terraces, gardens, pig-sties, water-meadows and parkland for exits and entrances; and the hamlet of Market Blandings two miles away, with plenty of pubs and inns (The Emsworth Arms, The Wheatsheaf, The Waggoners' Rest, The Beetle and Wedge, The Stitch in Time, The Blue Cow, The Blue Boar, The Blue Dragon and The Jolly Cricketers) from which outlying plotters can plan their approaches to the castle stage.

Rather too close is the village of Much Matchingham, home of the dreaded Sir Gregory Parsloe-Parsloe, so often unworthily suspected by Lord Emsworth and his brother Galahad of trying to do harm to Blandings pig or pumpkin that, in the printed synopsis at the beginning of *Pigs Have Wings*, Herbert Jenkins said '...on previous occasions the unscrupulous baronet has made determined attempts to nobble Lord Emsworth's favourite pig.' Not true. Sir Gregory was always innocent of the strategies which the Blandings brothers imputed to him, and Herbert Jenkins ought to have remembered it. Poor Sir Gregory. His only sins (other than overeating) were that, in his hot pre-title youth, he had, or Galahad thought he had, nobbled Galahad's dog Towser before a rat-killing contest and, as a bloated baronet, he had taken on as his pig-man, at higher wages, George Cyril Wellbeloved, who had been guardian, chef and caterer to Lord Emsworth's zeppelin-shaped Black Berskhire sow, the bemedalled Empress of Blandings.

Galahad Threepwood has spoken frankly and sharply to Sir Gregory of his past known, and present suspected, skulduggeries. Lord Emsworth has never yet accused the baronet to his face. But the living of Much Matchingham is in Lord Emsworth's gift, and it was with cunning pleasure that Lord Emsworth gave the Rev. 'Beefy' Bingham the vicarage there, trusting that this ham-handed man of God would be as sharp a thorn in Sir Gregory's flesh as he had been in Lord Emsworth's when he had been infesting the Castle and courting Lord Emsworth's niece, Gertrude.

Lord Emsworth and his clan

Lord Emsworth, euphoric, amiable, but bone-headed ninth Earl, has changed little in the sixty publishing years between *Something Fresh* and the last unfinished novel. He no longer seems to collect things, and his Museum, much in evidence in the first book, is no longer a show-room of the castle. He is no longer a patron of Christie's in London. His younger son, Freddie, formerly a pain in the neck to his father, no longer gets into debt or writes poetry to chorus girls. Marriage to the daughter of an American millionaire (Aggie, *née* Donaldson, was, incidentally, a relative of the Blandings head gardener, McAllister) has made a man of Freddie. In *Full Moon* (1947) Freddie shows his new-found manhood by turning and rending a roomful of tough aunts, uncles and millionaires who are trying to treat him like the worm he had been. It is a great defiance. Freddie is a hard-working and keen Vice-President of his father-in-law's dog-biscuit business now. In fact, Lord Emsworth, who had long despised his son as a drone and a wastrel, in a recent short story ('Birth of a Salesman') was nettled to find his son was now despising *him* for much the same reasons. Lord Emsworth was able to take steps and show himself a salesman and go-getter in America and on American lines.

Lady Constance Keeble is still a threat to her brother's peace. She is the sister (there is a host of them) who most frequently rules the Blandings roost, imports too many literary young men to stay, insists on choosing her brother Clarence's secretaries for him and wants to retire Beach the butler. She is Rupert Baxter's champion. She sees nothing but worth in that gimlet-eyed, lantern-jawed efficiency expert and, if she can't ring him in again as Lord Emsworth's secretary, she rings him in as tutor to Lord Emsworth's schoolboy grandson. Lord Emsworth who, in the first book, was not wholly anti-Baxter, has always since been sure he was potty, a judgement which Baxter reciprocates on Lord Emsworth. Baxter has suffered much indignity at Blandings – the cold tongue, raided from the larder, against the cheek in the dark, and thought to be a corpse; the hail of air-gun pellets against the trousers; the egg, hurled into outer darkness by the Duke of Dunstable, which hit Baxter in the face; the flower-pot episode and the yellow pyjamas; the pig parked in his caravan; the perjured persiflage of Lord Ickenham. But Baxter feels, deep in his lonely soul, I think, that the castle is a shambles and Lord Emsworth needs him as managing director.

Lord Emsworth is stated to have been at Eton in the 1860s. The statement was made at a time when Wodehouse had not learnt to avoid dates. Lord Emsworth comes of a long-lived family. His father, revealed in *A Pelican at Blandings* to have been irascible and domineering, was killed hunting at seventy-seven. His uncle Robert had lived to nearly ninety, his cousin Claude to eighty-four, when he broke his neck trying to jump a five-barred gate (presumably on a horse). Lord Emsworth's age for Wodehouse's purposes is pegged at just short of sixty – not too old for Galahad to be able, for his private ends, to impute to him an infatuation with a young girl; old enough to be psychosomatically deaf and forgetful, so that his sister Connie and other characters can shout the plot and the plotters to him in a way most comforting to the unalert reader. But Lord Emsworth is too old ever to be moulded by Baxter, or made to enjoy his stiff collars, speech-makings, visits to London and other ghastly duties that his sister imposes on him. Give him his flowers to sniff, and his pig loading in her calories; give him Whiffle to read in the evenings, and a glass of port; keep his multitudinous sisters and all other relatives (with the exception of Galahad) away from him. That's all he asks. And that's what he gets, happily, at the end of the last published novel. Lord Emsworth is one of the very nicest lords in literature.

If you come to suspect from the insistence of the Duke of Dunstable and the exasperations of sister Connie that Lord Emsworth is pottier than the normal run of the Wodehouse aristocracy of England, you might reflect on how many members of his family have made him trustee for their sons and daughters. Possibly the Blandings Estate looks after all the family, from Galahad downwards, and Lord Emsworth has, simply by primogeniture, not by merit of brain, to be the final arbiter of who gets what inheritance and when. Potty or not himself, Lord Emsworth had married a wife with insanity in her own family. She herself appears to have had delusions of poverty. Her only recorded words are 'Oh dear, oh dear, on dear', spoken when she had given birth to her second son, and occasioned by her fear that his education would be a great expense. An uncle of hers had thought he was a loaf of bread, and had first announced the fact (or fancy) at Blandings. Lord Bosham, heir to Blandings and the Emsworth title, is pretty potty in his turn. He has had a breach of promise case in his day, he has bought a gold brick, he has lent Lord Ickenham his wallet, and he talks almost total drivel. With Lord Emsworth, Lord Bosham, the Duke of Dunstable and Lord Ickenham all together at Blandings (*Uncle Fred in the Springtime*), the castle becomes an inferno of potty peers. But Wodehouse holds by the cheerful view that there is pottiness in all the most aristocratic English families, and he is frank and fearless about mentioning its incidences among the forebears of his favourites. (He also indicates that pottiness occurs in the best American families, too: the millionaire Baileys in *The Coming of Bill* and the millionaire Stokers in *Thank You, Jeeves*.)

The potty Threepwood genes have gone more to the males of the young generation than to the females. Except for Veronica Wedge, that lovely dumb blonde who might have come out of an Evelyn Waugh novel, all the Emsworth nieces are girls of mettle, and they tend to marry the nice young men of their own choice, rather than the vapid peers of their Aunt Connie's. Ronnie Fish may have, in his Uncle Galahad's words, looked like a minor jockey with scarlatina, but he married Sue Brown, the charming chorus girl daughter of Dolly Henderson, who had charmed Galahad and Lord Emsworth when she had been singing at the Tivoli in pink tights. Sue is one of the best in the longish line of nice Wodehouse chorus girls, and Ronnie is lucky to have won her, and to have kept her against all the slings and arrows operated by his disapproving mother. I forget now what typically Wodehouse future Ronnie and Sue face together. Ronnie is going to be a bookmaker, or run a road-house or a nightclub, or keep an onion soup bar, or start a gymnasium, or breed dogs, or farm. He has got his girl. He has got his capital out of Uncle Clarence. He has got his eye on a job somewhat more life-enhancing than working for Lord Tilbury. He has driven off in the two-seater towards the happiness-for-two reserved for most of the young, however blah, in the last pages of a Wodehouse novel.

At any stately home the size of Blandings there is an interesting life teeming behind the green baize doors. You should reread *Something Fresh* to see this described from a servant's-eye view. Ashe Marson (a detective story-writer) and Joan Valentine (a journalist) represent the main young-love interest. They are both visiting Blandings, for shady reasons, as servants. Ashe is valet to Mr Peters, a dyspeptic American millionaire, and Joan is taken on as lady's maid to Aline Peters, the millionaire's daughter. It is through Ashe's eyes that we get our first close-up view of Sebastian Beach, the Blandings butler, with his appearance of imminent apoplexy, his dignified inertia, his fat hands, his fruity voice 'like tawny port made audible', his fear of Socialism, his corns, his ingrowing toenails, his swollen joints, his nervous headaches, his blurred vision and weak stomach. Most of these complaints are forgotten in subsequent books, possibly because Beach never again has the opportunity to talk about them to another servant. In *Something Fresh* we first meet Mrs Twemlow, the housekeeper, and we count the heads of Merridew, the under-butler, James and Alfred the footmen, a flock of male guests' gentlemen and lady guests' ladies. We hear of the chef, the groom of the chambers, Thorne the head gardener (McAllister doesn't come on till a later book), the chauffeur, the boot-boy, and a whole host of laundry maids, housemaids, parlourmaids, scullerymaids, kitchenmaids and between-maids. And the ordering of their lives is described with as much detail and ten times as much humour as in Victoria Sackville-West's *Edwardians*, George Moore's *Esther Waters* or anywhere in Dornford Yates. In later books we shall take the servants' hall for granted, and go only to Beach's pantry for port. In *Something Fresh* is a survey of the servants' hall which shows us that Wodehouse knew his stuff about below-stairs grandeur, loved the grandees and sympathised with the whole company, from butler to buttons.

Blandings footmen come and go in later books; the office of attendant to the Empress, pig-man or pig-girl, is apt to change hands dramatically; Beach rounds out into being a force for good in every plot, even if he does have to put a green baize cloth over his bullfinch's cage when young lovers talk, or bribe, him into stealing his master's pig. Beach possesses the finest library of thrillers in Shropshire, having inherited Freddie Threepwood's collection when Freddie went West. Beach is no innocent. In really critical moments (such as when Lord Emsworth decides to grow a beard) Beach will regretfully decide to resign his long-held post. Sometimes, tried just short of resignation, he will drink brandy in his pantry instead of port.

His physical ailments forgotten in the later books, Beach remains a rock, a stately procession of one, a sportsman and a sentimentalist. For the people he likes he will do anything. For Lord Emsworth and his niece Angela, Beach chants 'Pig-hoo-o-o-o-ey!' to the Empress. He brings Galahad a whisky and soda all the way to the Empress's sty. He gets kissed by Sue Brown for all the help he has given her and her Ronnie in their troubled wooing. It's a pity that the autograph manuscript of Galahad's memoirs was consumed by the Empress, because there were mentions of Beach in its chapters. Beach, and Beach's mother in Bournemouth (or was it Eastbourne?), would have been pleased to see the family name honoured in print. It was good, though, that Beach had time to read in the manuscript the story of Gregory Parsloe and the prawns. It is possibly the only time in Wodehouse that we see a butler really laugh. 'HA ... HOR ... HOO!' he roared, admittedly believing himself alone and unobserved. (Wodehouse died without telling *us* the story of those prawns, or of Lord Ickenham and Pongo at the dog races.)

Is the Gutenberg Bible still in the Blandings Library? A copy, described as probably the last in private hands, was, in 1974, being offered by a dealer at a sum of Swiss francs equivalent to £1 million sterling. Does Galahad still wind clocks when time hangs heavy? Is Blandings now frequently open to the public? There are bedrooms in it so magnificent that they have never been slept in since the first Queen Elizabeth's day. Is Jno. Banks still the Market Blandings hairdresser? At the Emsworth Arms (G. Ovens, Propr.) is the 'large, pale, spotted waiter' still waiting, and is there still the smell of 'cold beef, beer, pickles, cabbage, gravy soup, boiled potatoes and very old cheese' in the coffee-room? Does the boiled turbot still come up as a 'rather obscene-looking mixture of bones and eyeballs and black mackintosh'? And does the inkpot still contain that 'curious sediment that looked like black honey'? Does Blandings still run the old Hispano-Suiza car? And what are the trains to and from Paddington these days? Wodehouse was constantly changing their times, and it is a constant astonishment to me that so many impostors managed to catch them and arrive safely to get down to their plottings at the castle.

Sunset at Blandings

Wodehouse was more than half-way through a new Blandings novel when he died. Sixteen chapters are fairly complete in typescript, and Wodehouse's autograph notes take it, in scenario, to the end – a total of twenty-two chapters. He had not given it a title.

A walk round the deserted workshop shows the tools bright and sharp, even if the product itself is taking a recognisably old (see *Service with a Smile*, published in 1962) shape. Galahad Threepwood and Frederick Lord Ickenham have long been nearly interchangeable. Both can 'tell the tale' or 'deviate from the truth' with fluency and the full approval of the author and his readers. Lord Ickenham was rampant at Blandings in *Service with a Smile*. Here it is Galahad slogging it out, across Lord Emsworth's limp body, with their sister Florence ... a new sister, which, with the other new one, Diana, in this book, gives them ten sisters in all, and all menaces except Diana. Diana's first husband, a big-game hunter, far too handsome and a bit of a rotter (as most handsome men are in Wodehouse), has been eaten by a lion. Now she is going to marry an old adorer who has, since abandoning the chase of Diana to the lion-hunter, become Chancellor of the Exchequer. As usual, the job of being secretary to Lord Emsworth is open, and, as usual, that leaves the door open to an impostor, whom Galahad is instantly ready to usher in through it. The Empress's portrait is to be painted for the Gallery. (Who will paint her? That's another door open for an impostor.) Hammocks, deckchairs and their required weather are all there, all the time. Blandings now has, or it is now revealed that Blandings has, a croquet lawn, and Galahad refers to it in the same sort of erotic terms as the rose garden ... a strong attraction for young lovers.

So far, so good: sixteen out of twenty-two chapters. In his notes Wodehouse communed with himself on work done and work to be done. When a chapter seemed to him ripe and ready, he marked it 'Aziz', i.e. to remain as is. Most of the first sixteen chapters are marked 'Aziz'. In his notes for the remaining six it looks as though he had a stolen necklace as a strong plot-twister in an earlier scenario. But he hadn't needed the necklace up to the end of Chapter 16, and we can assume that it had been counted out. There is a suggestion, marked with a query in Wodehouse's scribbled notes, that Beach the butler might be made the uncle of nice Jeff Bennison, who captures the love of nice young Vicky Underwood, the step-daughter of this new Threepwood sister, Florence. Florence is now a widow, but she had married Vicky's father, an American newspaper millionaire.

Jno. Robinson's station taxi is still chugging along. Beach's bullfinch is still in his cage in the pantry, and Beach still dispenses port there to his friends. At the pub near the station Ovens's home-brew is still a mocker for the thirsty after the long train journey from Paddington. There is a Bentley in the castle garage. Galahad is ever the old Pelican. Lord Emsworth's son Freddie is rather the old silly ass of *Something Fresh* days than the go-getting dog-biscuit tycoon of the more recent novels and short stories.

The last chapter of *A Pelican at Blandings* (1969) had been a very happy requiem. The Empress in her bijou residence had turned in for the night. Voules the chauffeur was playing his harmonica somewhere. Beach brought Lord Emsworth and Galahad their dinner (leg of lamb, boiled potatoes and spinach, followed by well-jammed roly-poly pudding) in the Library. Lord Emsworth was wearing his old shooting coat with the holes in the elbows, and his feet were sensuously comfortable in bedroom slippers. Through the open window came the scent of stocks and tobacco flower. Constance, the Duke of Dunstable, assorted godsons, impostors and pretty girls had all paired off and gone away. It seems a pity that Wodehouse should, five years later, get them all stirred up again in a further book. But perhaps Chapter 22 of the unfinished novel – posthumously published as *Sunset at Blandings* – would have been an even better ending to the Blandings revels and provided an even fonder last look at its cloud-capp'd towers. Evelyn Waugh in his tribute to Wodehouse on his eightieth birthday wrote 'For Wodehouse there has been no fall of Man: no "aboriginal calamity" ... the gardens of Blandings Castle are the original gardens from which we are all exiled.' Well, yes.

NUGGETSChildren

*T**he Coming of Bill* (1920) was almost a serious novel, and The White Hope – Bill, child of Kirk and Ruth Winfield – was a fine specimen, eugenically born, and rescued from over-hygienic nursery upbringing by his father, his nineteen-year-old nannie and an ex-prize-fighter. I think that Bill was the last child of an age in single figures to whom Wodehouse was even distantly civil. Children thereafter were monsters, fiends, thugs, blackmailers, objects of derision at best, but more often of boots and whacks on the back-side, slaps across the head, the nose pushed sideways (a threat by his mother to Braid Bates), the eyebrows burnt off. Such correctives (except the burnt-off eyebrows, an act of God) were acts of well-meaning adults if they could get the little snurges in reach. When Bingo Little, hoping for a loan, took his baby son Algernon Aubrey to visit his godfather Oofy Prosser (who was temporarily in the fireplace sleeping off a binge), Oofy's valet 'started back, his arms raised in a rudimentary posture of self-defence'. Bonzo Travers, Young Thos Gregson ('Aunt Agatha's loathly son') and Edwin Craye, cousins of Bertie's – all menaces. Oswald Glossop, Little Seabury Chuffnell, Dwight Stoker, Wilfred and 'Old Stinker' in 'The Passing of Ambrose' – excellent little horrors.

Wodehouse didn't make much use of pre-teens girls, did he? But Ambrose's simple creed was Wodehouse's in his farce fiction.

Like so many young men Ambrose Wiffen was accustomed to regard small boys with a somewhat jaundiced eye. It was his simple creed that they wanted their heads smacked. When not having their heads smacked, they should be out of the picture altogether.

Young Thos leaned across and slipped a penny in my hand, saying 'Here, my poor man' and urging me not to spend it on drink. At any other moment this coarse ribaldry would have woken the field that sleeps in Bertram Wooster and led to the young pot of poison receiving another clout on the head, but I had no time now for attending to Thoses.

Every impulse urged me to give the little snurge six of the best with a bludgeon. But you can't very well slosh a child who has just lost his eyebrows. Besides I hadn't a bludgeon.

A spectacled child with a mouth that hung open like a letter-box.

He was ten years old, wore a very tight Eton suit and had the peculiarly loathsome expression which a snub nose sometimes gives the young.

The sweetest triumph of an assistant master's life is the spectacle of one boy smacking another boy's head because the latter has persisted in making a noise after the master has told him to stop.

Young Thos, poising the bucket for an instant, discharged its contents. And old Mr Anstruther received the entire consignment. In one second, without any previous training or upbringing, he had become the wettest man in Worcestershire.

A small boy with a face like a prune run over by a motor bus.

The infant was looking more than ever like some mass-assassin who has been blackballed by the Devil's Island Social and Outing Club as unfit to associate with the members.

'One of my unswerving rules in life is never to go to a film if I am informed by my spies that there is a child in it.'

It was one of those bulging babies. It looked a little like Boris Karloff and a little like Winston Churchill.

UNCLE FRED

The story 'Uncle Fred Flits By' in *Young Men in Spats* (1936), *Uncle Fred in the Springtime* (1939), *Uncle Dynamite* (1948), *Cocktail Time* (1958), *Service with a Smile* (1962).

A sort of elderly Psmith

Lord Ickenham leads the dance in four novels and a short story. He is an excellent invention, and worth a short, sharp look.

Wodehouse in *Performing Flea* refers to this sprightly old earl as 'a sort of elderly Psmith'. 'Don't *talk* so much!' said Freddie Threepwood to Psmith in *Leave it to Psmith*. 'Don't *talk* so much, Uncle Fred!' said Myra Schoonmaker in *Service with a Smile*. Lord Ickenham referred to himself in *Uncle Dynamite* as 'one of the hottest earls that ever donned a coronet'. He emerged, a rounded character, fully fledged and fully armed to deceive, in a short story, and it shows Wodehouse's pleasure in him that, though his next appearance was in a Blandings novel, he had his name in the title. He is a whirring dynamo of misrule. As a boy he was known as 'Barmy' and now, in what should be the autumn of his days, he plays the giddy goat with an irrepressible springtime frivolity. He is extremely kind at heart and, for his own amusement as much as anybody's, very funny. He is a sort of performing flea himself, and something of an analogue of Wodehouse the writer.

Frederick Altamont Cornwallis, fifth Earl of Ickenham, is in his middle sixties, with iron-grey hair, a slim, youthful figure, an American wife (always off-stage) who tries to keep him under control ('American girls try to boss you. It's part of their charm'), and a stately home, with far too many nude statues in it, at Bishop's Ickenham in Hampshire. Luckily for Barrie & Jenkins, Lady Ickenham occasionally let the fifth earl go to London, for reputable reasons like the Eton and Harrow match, though threatening to skin him with a blunt knife if he didn't return on the dot. And occasionally she herself departed for the south of France or the West Indies to tend an ailing mother; which gave Lord Ickenham his freedom to go A.W.O.L.

It is Lord Ickenham's nephew and heir, Pongo Twistleton-Twistleton, who suffers most acutely from his Uncle Fred's enlargements. Lord Ickenham claims that London brings out all the best in him and is the only place where his soul can expand like a blossoming flower and his generous nature find full expression. Pongo has rooms in Albany – or had until Uncle Fred saw to it that he married Sally Painter. Uncle Fred descends on Pongo and, sooner or later, the trouble starts. The first time, often referred to, but never reported in detail, Uncle Fred had lugged Pongo to the dog races, they had been in the hands of the constabulary in ten minutes. Lord Ickenham complained that they were letting a rather neurotic type of man into the Force these days, and that on this occasion a better stamp of magistrate would have been content with a mere reprimand. But, as he had given his name in court as George Robinson, of 14 Nasturtium Road, East Dulwich (the first recorded of his many impersonations), Lady Ickenham presumably never heard about it.

That his dear wife should hear about him is about the only thing Lord Ickenham fears in this world. One must suppose that the fine he had to pay in court, for himself and Pongo, was not big enough to require a cheque. Lady Ickenham believes in a strong centralised government and handles the Ickenham finances. She gives her husband enough for golf balls, tobacco and self-respect. No more. Pongo, loyally or spinelessly, doesn't sneak on his Uncle Fred to his Aunt Jane; but Pongo's sister Valerie, a girl of spirit, is quite prepared to threaten these reprisals when she finds her Uncle Fred interfering in her love-life. Uncle Fred is a keen matchmaker, and, in bringing A and B together, he generally has to bust up their existing unsuitable engagement to C and D respectively. 'Help is a thing I am always glad to be of,' says this splendid old nuisance: his mother had been frightened by a Boy Scout.

Anyone but Gina Lollobrigida

Lord Ickenham is an intrepid impersonator. As a dissimulator he has, when young, like all good Wodehouse elders, worn false moustaches and whiskers to baffle creditors. (Lord Ickenham says the Archbishop of Canterbury probably had to do the same when he was a young man.) But today he prefers simulation, or at least simply passing himself off as somebody else. He says, in fact, that he never feels comfortable going to stay at houses under his own name. It doesn't seem sporting.

Lord Ickenham is a card, a joker ready to stand in for anybody in a full house. He has claimed that the only people he wouldn't be able to impersonate are a circus dwarf and Gina Lollobrigida. In the story 'Uncle Fred Flits By' he was driven to seek shelter from the rain in a suburban house, and he pretended to be (*a*) a vet come to clip the parrot's claws (Pongo was to be his deaf and dumb assistant. 'Tap your teeth with a pencil, and try to smell of iodoform!'), (*b*) a Mr Roddis and (*c*) a Mr Bulstrode – in that order as the plot developed, in the space of about one hour. In *Uncle Dynamite* he went down to the house of an old school acquaintance, pretending, to one and all, to be Major Brabazon Plank, the famous explorer from Brazil. This worked easily and well until he met (*a*) the policeman who had arrested him at the dog races, and who knew him therefore to be George Robinson of East Dulwich, and (*b*) the real Major Brabazon Plank. The old school acquaintance whom Lord Ickenham, then 'Barmy' Twistleton, had beaten with a fives bat as a boy, for bullying, was too dazed by all this imposture to matter much. Anyway, as so often in later Wodehouse books, the old school acquaintance was preparing to stand for Parliament, which left him wide open for blackmail to keep his mouth tight shut. On general principles Lord Ickenham doesn't like to meet his old school contemporaries. They tend to wear beards and be toothless, and this makes Lord Ickenham feel he must be forty if a day.

In *Uncle Fred in the Springtime* Lord Ickenham is not only himself impersonating Sir Roderick Glossop, but he takes with him to Blandings Polly Pott, a bookmaker's daughter, who has to pretend to be his (Lord Ickenham's) daughter, and his nephew Pongo, who has to pretend to be his secretary. In *Cocktail Time* Lord Ickenham becomes Inspector Jarvis of Scotland Yard. If impersonation fails temporarily, he has a smooth technique with knock-out drops. 'It is madness to come to country houses without one's bottle of Mickey Finns,' he says. He used these tranquillisers with effect at Blandings ('Pongo lit a reverent cigarette; he did not approve of his Uncle Fred, but he could not but admire his work'), and wished he had had them handy in *Uncle Dynamite*. He was in the Home Guard round Ickenham in the Second World War, and would probably have been a baffling underground fighter in the English Resistance had the invasion happened.

Lord Ickenham was a younger son who came into the title unexpectedly after twenty years in America, as a soda-jerker and cow-puncher among other pastimes. In a set piece of excellent buzzing dialogue with Sally Painter at Barribault's restaurant, he has told of his early struggles as a mere Hon., and how he later deservedly won through to being a haughty earl. You can't keep a good man down, is his opinion. And he is frank in his further opinion that he is a good man, *capable du tout*, especially in the springtime. He admits that he sometimes feels like a caged skylark at Ickenham, with Lady I. forbidding his sweetness-and-light-spreading excursions. 'There are no limits, literally none, to what I can accomplish in the springtime,' he says. In the noble sentence from the first story, repeated for reminder and emphasis in the later books, a Crumpet at The Drones says to his guest: 'I don't know if you happen to know what the word "excesses" means, but these are what Pongo's Uncle Fred from the country, when in London, invariably commits.' Since Wodehouse demands a country-house setting for most of his novels, Lord Ickenham commits excesses also at Blandings, Ashenden Manor and Hammer Hall.

Lord Ickenham provided the mature Wodehouse with some good new outlets. In his determination to whack amusement out of any situation that could be stood on its head and made to kick its heels in the air, he paralleled the unrepentant frivolity of his senescent author. A lifetime friend of Galahad Threepwood, Lord Ickenham is more of a practical joker than Gally, more of a licensed loony. He is the grown-up-schoolboy-slightly-inebriated-undergraduate who inebriates himself especially with the exuberance of his own buzzing verbosity. He is the best buzzer in all Wodehouse. His joy in impersonation, lying and blackmail, his manic generation of muddle and mayhem as a challenge to his own powers of Houdini-like escape – these enabled Wodehouse to ravel his plots into webs apparently hopelessly tangled, and then, in magical dénouement, to shake them out into happy endings, with all the right couples paired off. And, although one must at all times and at all costs avoid accusing Wodehouse of offering us messages, Lord Ickenham in his middle sixties is a high-stepping proof that, for the elderly as for the young, the brow should be worn low and unfurrowed, the hat should be perched on the side of the head and the shirt should not be stuffed.

What girls want: The Ickenham System

Lord Ickenham gave the autumnal Wodehouse a chance to air a technique of love-making pleasantly at variance with the formulas established hitherto. The Ickenham System, as recommended to the laggard male, is to grab the adored object by the wrist, waggle her about a bit, clasp her to the bosom like a stevedore heaving a sack of coals, breathe hot words of romance into her ear (e.g. 'My mate!') and shower passionate kisses on her upturned face. This, says Lord Ickenham, is what many girls want, and it brings very good results. (Lord Uffenham had much the same ideas, and gave similar advice to Jeff Miller in *Money in the Bank.*) Lord Ickenham's nephew, Pongo, a romantic youth who has been falling in love ever since his boyhood dancing-class days, represents (at least in one book) the technique against which the Ickenham System is a revolt. Pongo yearns to win a girl's love by sacrifice – by saving her from a burning house, by finding opportunity to help her in her troubles – and then to kiss her gently on the forehead and fade off, *preux* to the last drop, into the sunset. In some of the bilge-literature he has been reading, such selflessness is rewarded not only with a saintly feeling of heroism, but with the girl running after him and saying 'Take me, I am yours, my shy king among men!'

Lord Ickenham scorns such goings-on, largely on the grounds that the girl is insensitive to them; what she wants is to be flung across a saddle-bow by an Elinor Glyn or Ethel M. Dell demon lover, and galloped off with into the burning desert. Anyway, though there has been a good deal of Pongo-esque renunciation, with Wodehouse's apparent approval, in some of his earliest heroes, his late-flowering Lord Ickenham firmly insists on the whirlwind embrace, the reckless declaration and the risked slap in the face and angry 'Unhand me, sir!' He successfully eggs Bill Oakshott on to apply the System to Hermione Bostock, and he successfully eggs Peasemarch on to apply it to Phoebe Wisdom. (He less successfully eggs on the diffident policeman to apply it to Johnny Pearce's formidable old Nanny. It gets him a box on the ear, but he wins her in the end.) Did Lord Ickenham himself try it in his youth with Lady Ickenham? She broke off their engagement six times before she married him. Now, in his not-so-sere sixties, he is not given any purposeful courting to do. But he agonises Pongo with the amount of hand-patting, waist-encircling and easy osculation that he achieves in quick time with the beautiful girls with whom he is so easily on avuncular terms. Pongo automatically falls in love with them, speechlessly, at first sight. Lord Ickenham gets his arm round them, and Pongo resents this.

A man of learning

In one other small way Lord Ickenham may have been a spokesman for his past-middle-aged author more coeval than any of his other characters. Wodehouse gave him a wider background reading, and memory of reading, than he gave even to Jeeves. Lord Ickenham shows familiarity, in reference and quotation, with all the stock Wodehouse sources, the Bible, Shakespeare, Tennyson, Gilbert, *et al.* But he also shows his converse with Pierre Louÿs's *Le Roi Pausole*, Walter Pater, Damon Runyon, Hemingway, the Sitwells, Sinclair Lewis, Fenimore Cooper, Newbolt, Evelyn Waugh, Proust and Kafka. And he once dives into the deep end of *Pickwick* with all the aplomb of a Bernard Darwin and in a way which must have made his current hearers wonder what on earth he was talking about.

We are never exactly told at what public school Lord Ickenham was educated: where he lent 'Bimbo' Brabazon Plank the two shillings that were for so long outstanding, and where he beat 'Muggsy' Bostock with a fives bat. The fives bat suggests Winchester or Rugby, not Eton. But 'Barmy' Twistleton, now Earl of Ickenham, still trails clouds of schoolboy frivolity from whatever prison-house he attended, and if he ever speaks in a debate in the Upper Chamber of the Palace of Westminster, may I be there in the gallery to hear him. I expect there'll be a catapult visible on his hip.

In *Service with a Smile* he meets Lord Emsworth in Moss Bros. Both had been attending the opening of Parliament, and both are now bringing back their suitcases full of hired finery.

> 'Were you at that thing this morning?' said Lord Emsworth.
>
> 'I was indeed,' said Lord Ickenham, 'and looking magnificent. I don't suppose there is a peer in England who presents a posher appearance when wearing the reach-me-downs and comic hat than I do. Just before the procession got under way, I heard Rouge Croix whisper to Bluemantle "Don't look now, but who's that chap over there?", and Bluemantle whispered back, "I haven't the foggiest, but evidently some terrific swell."'

When Peter Fleming wrote fulsomely of Wodehouse's *Louder and Funnier* in the *Spectator*, he received a letter from the Alpes Maritimes:

> Dear R.P.F.,
>
> Thanks awfully for your kind review. The local peasants as I pass whisper to one another '*Il me semble que Monsieur Vodehouse est satisfait de lui aujourd'hui.*'

Uncle Fred, Lord Ickenham, was '*satisfait de lui*' all the time. And can one blame him?

INSULTINGTHE WODEHOUSEWAY

'Forget that I called you a dish-faced moron.'
'You didn't.'
'Well I meant to.'

She has about as much brain as a retarded billiard ball.

He had just about enough intelligence to open his mouth
when he wanted to eat, but certainly no more.

Even at the Drones Club, where the average of intellect is not high, it was
often said of Archibald that, had his brain been constructed of silk, he would have
been hard put to it to find sufficient material to make a canary a pair of cami-knickers.

She gave me the sort of look she would have given a leper she wasn't fond of.

The Duke of Dunstable had one-way pockets. He would walk
ten miles in the snow to chisel a starving orphan out of tuppence.

'If ever there was a pot-bellied little human louse who needed to have
the stuffing knocked out of him and his remains jumped on by strong men in
hobnailed boots, it is you, Mr Pott. The next time I see a mob in the street
setting on you, I shall offer to hold their coats and stand by and cheer.'

'He says my moustache is like the faint discoloured smear left
by a squashed black-beetle on the side of a kitchen sink.'

He's one of those men whose legs you have to count to make sure they aren't mules.

Oofy, despite his colossal wealth, had always been a man who would walk ten miles
in tight shoes to pick up even the meanest sum that was lying around loose.

'As a sleuth you are poor. You couldn't detect a bass drum in a telephone booth.'

As ugly a devil as you would wish to see outside the House of Commons.

'You poor sap ... if you had another brain, you'd just have one!'

'Alf Todd,' said Ukridge, 'has about as much chance of winning the
heavy-weight championship, as a one-armed blind man in a dark room trying
to shove a pound of melted butter into a wild-cat's left ear with a red-hot needle.'

'There's another thing about you that I don't like. I've forgotten
what it is at the moment, but it'll come back to me soon.'

She wrinkles her nose at me as if I were a drain that had got out of order.

'Have you ever tasted such filthy coffee?'
'Never,' said Joe, though he had lived in French hotels.

Mr Butterwick had left his hat with the hat-check girl, but if it had
been on his head, Monty would have accused him of talking through it.

CARRY ON, JEEVES

When the jolly old storm-clouds rolled up,
Bertie Wooster turned instinctively to
his man, Jeeves. Bertie's friends likewise.
Jeeves's judgment was infallible, likewise his
taste in neckwear.   By P.G.Wodehouse.

BERTIE WOOSTER

The story 'Extricating Young Gussie' in *The Man with Two Left Feet* (1917), four stories in a collection of eight entitled *My Man Jeeves* (1919), *The Inimitable Jeeves* (1923), a loosely stitched novel of eighteen chapters which make ten separate stories in *The Jeeves Omnibus*, *Carry On, Jeeves* (1925), a collection of ten stories, four of them from *My Man Jeeves*: a fifth which, in *My Man Jeeves*, had been told by and about Reggie Pepper and is here tailored to make a Bertie Jeeves story 'Fixing It For Freddie' (in this Aunt Agatha's name is still apparently Miss Wooster: so it should strictly ante-date the lot): one describing Jeeves's arrival from the Agency: and a last one narrated by Jeeves himself, *Very Good, Jeeves* (1930), a collection of eleven stories. *The Jeeves Omnibus* (1931), collects and re-collects thirty-one stories; Wodehouse distinctly edited and tidied the old material for this new collection. In *A Few Quick Ones* (1959) is 'Jeeves Makes an Omelette', a rewrite of another old Reggie Pepper story in *My Man Jeeves*. There is one short story in *Plum Pie* (1966). The first proper novel is *Thank You, Jeeves* (March 1934). *Right Ho, Jeeves* followed the same year (October 1934), *The Code of the Woosters* (1938), *Joy in the Morning* (1947), *The Mating Season* (1949). *Ring for Jeeves* (1953) is the only Jeeves novel not told by Bertie; he is mentioned in it, but does not appear. *Jeeves and the Feudal Spirit* (1954), *Jeeves in the Offing* (1960), *Stiff Upper Lip, Jeeves* (1963), *Much Obliged, Jeeves* (1971) and *Aunts Aren't Gentlemen* (1974).

'Providence looks after the chumps of this world; and personally I'm all for it,' said Bertie Wooster in 1925. Providentially he was with us to the end, as delightful a young chump as ever.

A reviewer in *The Times Literary Supplement* once condemned 'the sort of insensitive souls who see nothing but a vapid wastrel in Bertie Wooster, that kind, chivalrous and, on the whole, eminently sensible Englishman'. It seems to me that to call Bertie Wooster eminently sensible is not only wrong; it underrates by a mile Wodehouse's aims and achievements in handling Bertie as a character. Bertie is not a vapid wastrel, agreed (by all except Aunt Agatha). He is kind and chivalrous, agreed. He is an Englishman, agreed. But as far as brain is concerned, he is as near to being null and void as makes very little differ-ence. The *Lit. Supp.* reviewer (*Lit. Supp.* reviewers were anonymous in those days) would presumably have amplified his judgement by saying that Bertie's eminence was that of a half-wit among nit-wits. Well, Wodehouse could have pulled that off easily enough. In fact, though, he pulled off something much more difficult. He made Bertie a nit-wit among half-wits, a super-fool among fools. He is, to me, one of the most charming innocents in print. My heart aches for him in his enormous agonies and rejoices with him in his puny exaltations. But Jeeves is right – Bertie is mentally negligible.

And Wodehouse made him his medium in more than a dozen books. They are tales told by an idiot, but Bertie proves to be an unselfconsciously brilliant narrator. This has needed very careful handling. As a character in the books, Bertie's only claim to literary achievement (and he is outspokenly proud of it) is the 'piece' he once contributed to his Aunt Dahlia's magazine, on 'What the Well-dressed Man is Wearing'. But as Wodehouse's medium, Bertie has written all those stories and novels, and this fictional dichotomy does not grate for a moment. As a story-teller Bertie is his own central character, and he has to narrate strictly from the first-personal point of view, often writing scenes in such a way that Bertie-the-character must not realise the purport of what Bertie-the-narrator is narrating, but his readers must. Very difficult, and he does it very smoothly. But still Bertie the writer must project his fictional self as a man capable of being mightily proud of a single incursion into print, in *Milady's Boudoir*.

Wodehouse's other recurrent mouthpieces tell their stories with themselves standing on the side-lines, and with narrator's licence. They may start in double quotes, stating the facts from personal experience. But soon the double quotes disappear, the voice of the specified narrator fades out, and narrator Wodehouse takes over. We are told what a man and a girl say, declaring their love, in a golf-bunker or a two-seater, and we do not ask 'How do you know they said that if you were not there?' Author Wodehouse/Oldest Member is a fly in the wall of the bunker; author Wodehouse/Mulliner is a fly on the windscreen of the two-seater. But Bertie is the core of his own stories, and he has to be there throughout, or fill in with reported speech, delivered to himself. One or two other narrators sustain this technique for a single book (Jeremy Garnet for the second edition of *Love Among the Chickens* and Reggie Havershot in *Laughing Gas*). Bertie has done it for ten novels and fifty-odd short stories.

At his preparatory school, Bertie was known as 'Bungler' Wooster. This nickname may not have had associations with the Conan Doyle Sherlock Holmes stories ('Scotland Yard bunglers') in the minds of Bertie's masters and friends. It certainly had those associations in Wodehouse's mind. I seem to keep finding, or I keep seeming to find, trace elements of Doyle in the Wodehouse formulations. I sense a distinct similarity, in patterns and rhythms, between the adventures of Jeeves as recorded by Bertie Wooster and the adventures of Sherlock Holmes as recorded by Dr Watson: Holmes and Jeeves the great brains, Watson and Bertie the awed companion-narrators, bungling things if they try to solve the problems themselves; the problems, waiting to be tackled almost always in country houses, almost always presented and discussed at breakfast in London; the departure from London, Holmes and Watson by train, Jeeves and Bertie by two-seater; the gathering of the characters at the

country house; the gathering of momentum, Holmes seldom telling Watson what he is up to, Jeeves often working behind Bertie's back; the dénouement; the company fawning on Holmes or Jeeves; the return trip to 'the rooms' in town; possibly Holmes's '...and I pocket my fee' paralleled by Bertie Wooster's 'How much money is there on the dressing-table, Jeeves? ... Collar it all. You've earned it!'

The high incidence of crime in the Wodehouse farces, especially the Bertie/Jeeves ones, may be an echo of the Sherlock Holmes stories, too – blackmail, theft, revolver shots in the night (*Something Fresh*), airgun shots by day ('The Crime Wave at Blandings'), butlers in dressing-gowns, people climbing in at bedroom windows, people dropping out of bedroom windows, people hiding in bedroom cupboards, the searching of bedrooms for missing manuscripts, cow-creamers and pigs. I am not accusing Wodehouse of having concocted his stories deliberately on Doyle's lines; I am saying that, of all the authors to whom Wodehouse's debt shows itself, Doyle is second only to W. S. Gilbert. And Wodehouse would gladly have acknowledged both debts.

On another level you may see Bertie Wooster as a modern Don Quixote, constantly setting out on adventures to help his friends and constantly making an endearing ass of himself. Don Quixote has a wiser *vade mecum* in Sancho Panza; Bertie has the wiser Jeeves. Bertie, like Don Quixote, has his brain curdled with romance. Don Quixote's romance came from books of knight-errantry; Bertie's from Edwardian fiction and a regular diet of detective novels. Don Quixote's enchanting books were burnt, but he carried the gist of them always in his mind; Bertie has an ever-ready memory of the plot-clichés of the Rosie M. Banks writers of his boyhood. When he tries to disentangle his friends' problems along Rosie M. Banks's lines, he gets those lines crossed and the entanglements made worse. He is a prime bungler. A good-natured romantic, but a bungler. One comes back to the Doyle word.

Bertie's magpie babble

The important thing, if you study Bertie, is not so much the width of his reading of bilge literature as the depth to which he absorbs the stuff. His little mind keeps a gooey sludge of words, phrases and concepts from what he has read, and it gives him a magpie vocabulary of synonyms and quotations. It contributes largely to his Code. He is a fantasist. Even, perhaps specially, in moments of tension and peril, his attention seems to wander, and he gets beside himself, watching himself, aligning himself with the heroes of his reading, adopting their attitudes, blurting out their clichés of speech. Bertie shares his escape route with Mr Pooter, Walter Mitty, Billy Liar, Catherine Morland, Emma Bovary and other literary dreamers. So far Bertie has only encountered Sir Roderick Glossop, the loony-doctor, socially. Never in the consulting room. But Sir Roderick may still be waiting for Bertie fairly confidently as a patient.

In *Right Ho, Jeeves*, Bertie, while nobly, if cautiously and anonymously, pleading Gussie's cause with Madeline Bassett, makes it appear to Madeline that he is brokenly and shyly pleading his own love for her. It was an old Wodehouse plot-shape; indeed much older than Wodehouse. For a brief, climactic moment Bertie finds that Madeline has received his words as a proposal. And his book-bred Code says that no gentleman can break off his engagement to however disastrous a girl. You'd expect, if you didn't know Bertie, that in this crisis his brain would either cease to function or, ice-cold in an emergency, would attend to the matter in hand with single strictness. Not so. Bertie, clenching his fists in agony, is wondering whether his knuckles are, or are not, standing out white under the strain. And when, seconds later, Madeline tells Bertie that she is sorry, the thing's impossible, you'd expect that the relief would clarify Bertie's mind wonderfully, and pinpoint his attention on the facts. Again not so. The relief is great, yes. But Bertie the fantasist lets his mind wander and is instantly beside himself again, seeing the event in homely images:

> 'I am sorry...' said Madeline...
>
> The word was like one of Jeeves's pick-me-ups. Just as if a glassful of meat sauce, red pepper and the yolk of an egg ... though, as I say, I am convinced that these are not the sole ingredients ... had been shot into me, I expanded like some lovely flower blossoming in the sunshine. It was all right, after all. My guardian angel had not been asleep at the switch.

If you say that this is Bertie the narrator, remembering in tranquillity and with a trained literary mind events which allowed no such mental gymnastics at the time, I am not convinced. Bertie's mind drifted *during the crisis* into mazes of metaphor and meat sauce. He was carried off on a stream of semi-consciousness and free association, with time for a parenthesis stating his doubts about the Jeeves pick-me-up recipe. Then he sees himself in the guise of some lovely flower blossoming in the sunshine. He is back to his books.

Bertie hops through the looking-glass and stands beside himself very often and at slight provocation. His memory is so full of the words and music of heroic action that he can find a phrase to fit almost any situation. His narrative and conversation are larded with second-hand alternatives to direct description. By mixing his soiled metaphors and colliding his clichés, he fabricates a burbling language of evocative innocence. Quite often in narration he drops into the Bertie-beside-himself third person singular:

> Those who know Bertram Wooster best are aware that he is a man of sudden, strong enthusiasms and that, when in the grip of one of these, he becomes a remorseless machine, tense, absorbed, single-minded. It was so in the matter of this banjolele-playing of mine...

and

> 'Yes, Jeeves?' I said. And though my voice was suave a close observer in a position to watch my eyes would have noted a steely glint...

and

> When I wore it (the white mess jacket) at the Casino at Cannes, beautiful women nudged one another and whispered: 'Who is he?'

and

> He quivered like a mousse. I suppose it must always be rather a thrilling experience for the novice to watch me taking hold...

In his last book of all, Bertie is still watching himself in a mirror, hearing himself talk and ready with self-applause when it is earned.

> 'Hullo, old ancestor,' I said, and it was a treat to hear me, so full of ginger and loving kindness was my diction.

Bertie laughing down from lazy eyelids and flicking specks of dust from the irreproachable Mechlin lace at his wrists; Bertie answering an angry questioner 'with a suavity that became me well'; Bertie inspecting his imagination and finding that it boggled; Bertie saying 'Oh'

and meaning it to sting – with Bertie, we are dealing with a young man whose boyhood reading has been wider than a church door, and whose memory of it is deeper than a well. Bertie is a shining example of a magpie mind cherished whole into adult life.

Shakespeare had a magpie mind, too. It is only the fine, imaginative, noticing mind, like Shakespeare's and Bertie Wooster's, that dares wander down the garden path without losing its way back. Your lawyer and chartered accountant would feel naked and lost so far from home. If they look wistfully out into the garden, and to the perilous seas and faery lands beyond, they take good care to keep the magic casement shut, lest they start climbing through. Shakespeare equates the lunatic, the lover and the poet – types who can't keep their feet on the ground or their minds on the subject under advisement. Bertie is three parts lunatic. He sometimes loves. In his wild imagery he is not far off from being a poet.

Bertie asked Pauline Stoker to marry him. It was in New York, at the Plaza. Bertie relates the incident only in a flashback, as a necessary starting point for *Thank You, Jeeves*, necessary because it gives an excuse for a good jealousy-teeth-grinding-let's-see-the-colour-of-his-insides menace to Bertie from his old friend Chuffy, who is now, three months later, in love with Pauline. The green-eyed Chuffy questions Bertie keenly about what went on when he and Pauline were engaged. He grills Bertie into revealing that, during the two days' betrothal, he never kissed the adored object even once:

'I hope you will be very, very happy [says Bertie to Chuffy]. I can honestly say that I always look on Pauline as one of the nicest girls I was ever engaged to.'

'I wish you would stop harping on that engagement.'

'Quite.'

'I'm trying to forget that you were ever engaged to her.'

'Quite, quite.'

'When I think that you were once in a position to...'

'But I wasn't. Never lose sight of the fact that the betrothal only lasted two days, during both of which I was in bed with a nasty cold.'

'But when she accepted you, you must have...'

'No, I didn't. A waiter came into the room with a tray of beef sandwiches and the moment passed.'

'Then you never...?'

'Absolutely never.'

'She must have had a great time, being engaged to you. One round of excitement. I wonder what on earth made her accept you?'

That engagement was broken up by Pop Stoker, abetted by Sir Roderick Glossop. But, although Wodehouse frequently juxtaposed sentiment and food, romance and greediness, as incongruities to make comic bathos, for the moment I want to put the lights on that tray of beef sandwiches at the Plaza in New York.

When Bertie recalls those beef sandwiches, is he babbling the free associations of a mind permanently loose in the socket? Or is he half-way to poetry? Shakespeare, as we know, was all for free association. Take Juliet's nurse, her woolly old mind swithering about trying to pinpoint Juliet's age. She remembers, she remembers ... yes, she'll get it soon. Yes, she had weaned Juliet ... yes, she had put the wormwood to her dug,

> Sitting in the sun under the dove house wall;
> My lord and you were then at Mantua.

Forty years ago I wrote in a note against those two lines in my Temple *Romeo and Juliet*: 'cf. Bertie W's beef sandwiches'. Juliet's nurse, under Shakespeare's guidance, remembers the sun and the dove house and the wall. Bertie, earthier, remembers the beef sandwiches.

Bertie admits that he has a tendency to babble in moments of tension. In a burst of sympathy for the cloth-headed newt-fancier, Gussie, who, terrified by the arrival of the mood, the moonlight and the expectant Madeline all together, started talking about newts, Bertie remembers how, in the dentist's chair, he had, through sheer nerves, held up the man behind the forceps with a silly story of an Englishman, an Irishman and a Jew. But often in a crisis he repeats sounds without knowing their meaning. He refers to someone in an advanced state of gloom looking like a cat in an adage. When Tuppy Glossop is reaching for Bertie's neck in the garden, to wring it for (as Tuppy believes) having traduced him (Tuppy) to the girl (Angela) whom he (Tuppy) loves, Bertie says:

> 'I have always regarded you with the utmost esteem. Why, then, if not for the motives I have outlined, should I knock you to Angela? Answer me that. Be very careful.'
>
> 'What do you mean, be very careful?'
>
> Well, as a matter of fact, I didn't quite know myself. It was what the magistrate had said to me on the occasion when I stood in the dock as Eustace Plimsoll, of The Laburnums; and as it had impressed me a good deal, at the time, I just brought it in now by way of giving the conversation a tone...

If Bertie wrenches logic and language into perilous distortions, it is not entirely through vapidity. It is partly a genuine hankering for the *mot juste*, the vivid phrase, the exact image. At another moment of acute crisis he can pause to express his shock at discovering that Uncle Tom's second name is Portarlington, or to ask Jeeves to check a quotation for him. Referring to Aunt Dahlia and her weekly magazine, *Milady's Boudoir*, he writes:

Seeing it go down the drain would be for her like watching a loved child sink for the third time in some pond or mere...

That 'or mere' comes with the pride of a magpie which has collected a gold ring *and* a silver paper milk-bottle top; it is the poet hoarding an alternative for rhyming; it is the pin-head who lets his feeble mind wander in word-associations when an aunt is in peril. This one may be a Tennysonian evocation. Bertie's sources may be anything from the Psalms (frequently) to Scott's last message from the Antarctic (once). He hasn't the discrimination to be a snob about his sources. To go to the Old Vic with his cousin, Young Thos, at Aunt Agatha's orders, to witness Shakespeare or Chekhov, is torture, to him as to Thos. But once a literary phrase has got tamped down in his memory, it becomes a fiery particle of his vocabulary. In Jeeves he has a walking lexicon and dictionary of quotations, which he adds to his simmering brew of tosh and tag-ends, thin on reason but often producing a sweet poetry.

> Reason has moons, but moons not hers
>   lie mirror'd on her sea,
> confounding her astronomers,
>   but O! delighting me.

Bertie hardly ever tries to be funny and he is not a bit witty. He will use a piffling phrase for a lofty sentiment or a lofty phrase for a piffling sentiment. He bubbles and burbles, innocent and vulnerable. Fantasist, schizo, duffer, do-gooder, hungry for praise. Bertie has a mind that is a tape-recorder for sounds and rhythms, but has no discipline or control in playing them back. This is the quintessence of the highly disciplined and tightly controlled Wodehouse burble. Bertie is its chief executant. But, make no mistake, 'Bertie Wodehouse' language has power, suppleness and great speed of communication. When Hilaire Belloc wrote that Wodehouse was the best writer of English alive, he was paying tribute not only to his control of schizophrenic imagery, but to his discipline in telling a complicated story quickly and clearly. Wodehouse can, in Bertie's artificial language, get from A to B by the shortest route and still litter all sorts of flowers at your feet as you follow it.

> Tuppy Glossop was the fellow, if you remember, who, ignoring a lifelong friendship in the course of which he had frequently eaten my bread and salt, betted me one night at the Drones that I wouldn't swing myself across the swimming baths by the ropes and rings, and then, with almost inconceivable treachery, went and looped back the last ring, causing me to drop into the fluid and ruin one of the nattiest suits of dress-clothes in London.

Try altering or cutting a word in that sentence. You can't. Every *mot* is *juste*. When Bertie describes the warning note of an angry nesting swan as being 'like a tyre bursting in a nest of cobras', it shows Bertie, again at a moment of tension, day-dreaming into a poetic image even as his adrenal reflexes (fight or flight) send him skimming up the wall of the summer-house. But it is a glorious image, expressed in words which themselves, of their structure, menace and explode with sibilants.

Bertie Wooster's age stays put at about twenty-four, but you can spot certain changes in his slang styles as the publishing years advance. He stopped saying 'chappie', 'dear boy' and the parenthetical 'don't you know' in the 1920s. He stopped saying 'rattled' (meaning pleased), and 'rotten' as a universal pejorative, in the 1930s. By the middle 1930s he had virtually made his own language, and it became frozen and time-less to the last. A great number of people have tried to parody the 'Bertie Wodehouse' style in print. Rather fewer have tried to imitate it without parody. None has succeeded. The best parodies of Bertie's style are by Wodehouse himself when he let a page go to the printer without quite the necessary polish. Then you are probably reading the sixth draft, rather than the tenth. At his polished best the burble that Wodehouse put into Bertie's mouth is beautiful stuff.

> It is pretty generally recognised in the circles in which he moves that Bertram Wooster is not a man who lightly throws in the towel and admits defeat. Beneath the thingummies of what-d'you-call-it his head, wind and weather permitting, is as a rule bloody but unbowed, and if the slings and arrows of outrageous fortune want to crush his proud spirit, they have to pull their socks up and make a special effort.
>
> Nevertheless, I must confess that when, already weakened by having to come down to breakfast, I beheld the spectacle which I have described, I definitely quailed. The heart sank, and, as had happened in the case of Spode, everything went black. Through a murky mist I seemed to be watching a negro butler presenting an inky salver to a Ma Trotter who looked like the end man in a minstrel show.
>
> The floor heaved beneath my feet as if an earthquake had set in with unusual severity. My eye, in fine frenzy rolling, met Aunt Dahlia's, and I saw hers was rolling, too.

Twelve Woosterisms in seventeen lines: the general clash of jargon phrases, the Bertie-beside-himself third person singular of the whole first paragraph, a botched quotation from Henley, and two, less botched, from Shakespeare, the babu interposition of the presumably nautical 'wind and weather permitting' inside the botched Henley, the boxing image, the good old Wodehousian elaboration of the 'everything went black' cliché, the good old Wodehousian 'earthquake had set in with unusual severity' (that's generally 'Judgement

Day', not 'earthquake'), the medical use of 'the' heart instead of 'my' heart, the medical 'weakened' to emphasise that Bertie had breakfasted downstairs that day for once, the enforced use of the single eye, forgivable in the first case, because Bertie is quoting Shakespeare, but foolishly cyclopean when transferred to Aunt Dahlia in the second.

Since Wodehouse wrote in his Bertie Wooster voice more, much more, than in any other, it is reasonable to suppose that he put it on more comfortably than any other. Is it also reasonable to suppose that we find more of the Wodehouse personal identity hidden in Bertie than in any other of Wodehouse's puppets? I think so.

The self-derogatory first person singular has been a staple of English language humour over the last seventy-five years. If 'He slipped on a banana skin' is funny, 'I slipped on a banana skin' is conceivably funny and charming. This is not the only technique of whimsy, but it is a very frequent factor in whimsy. 'Whimsy' and 'whimsical' are rude words in literary criticism these days. But three-quarters of a century ago, and through the majority of Owen Seaman's years on *Punch*, the value-judgement in the words was for the most part kind and appreciative. Seaman's *Punch* catered for, and then overfed, the taste for whimsy. The magazine of his day was full of self-derogatory first person singular pieces. Admittedly one's suspension of disbelief in *Punch* was made more unwilling by the magazine's weird habit of having, in an issue containing, say, ten 'I' pieces, three signed by initials, three by pseudonyms and four not signed at all. But the fact remains that the 'I' piece has been, for three-quarters of a century of English humorous writers, a favourite stand-by. Its main laws have remained unaltered since Thackeray and Burnand.

Wodehouse, whose *floruit* spanned much of the whimsy era of *Punch*, wrote very little direct 'I' stuff. In *Louder and Funnier* and *Over Seventy* he showed that he could do it expertly. But if you suppose that any good funny writer with a taste for editorial cheques would use a profitable technique for all it was worth to him, you may be surprised that Wodehouse did not cash in more on his opportunities.

Bertie and Plum

Subliminally, I believe, Bertie Wooster was, and increasingly became, Wodehouse's main surrogate outlet for the self-derogatory first person singular mood. The name Wooster is significantly close to Wodehouse. Bertie, in portions of his background and many of his attitudes (though not in his Eton and Oxford status), is the young Wodehouse that the older Wodehouse remembered with amusement, candour, modesty and (a sixth-form tag that Wodehouse himself used in several of his youthful books) *pothos* and *desiderium*. The identification in ages is between Bertie at an eternal twenty-four and Wodehouse in that *annus mirabilis* of mental age at which most Wodehouse farce is played – fifteen.

A doctor has told me that when a patient is coming out from under anaesthetic, the anaesthetist needs some test of the stages of his re-emergence. So the anaesthetist starts saying to the patient 'How old are you?', 'How old are you?' And (the doctor told me), however advanced the age of the patient, his first mumbling answer is frequently 'Nineteen'. He may say 'nineteen' two or three times till adequate consciousness returns, and then he gets it right at fifty-five, or sixty-five or seventy-five.

Belloc wrote of the unchanging place where all we loved is always near, where we meet our morning face to face and find at last our twentieth year. Nineteen is (according to the doctor) the usual *annus mirabilis*. Fifteen was Wodehouse's, and Wodehouse, significantly, often let Bertie take him back to the green pastures of that irresponsible period, the last moment at which he could see himself unselfconsciously.

Bertie's manner of life, his money, his personal servant, his riding, shooting (once), rackets (once), squash, darts and tennis, his clubs, his idleness, his love for fancy dress balls, his contemptible cunning, risible ruses and puny piques, his overweening optimism and his babu burble of clashing clichés and inattentive images – these are creations of Wodehouse the story-teller. Bertie, the kind, the chivalrous, the greedy, the aunt-ridden, the Code-ridden, the girl-fearing, the pal-helping, the tag-quoting, the slug-abed – he is a poetic, middle-voice throwback to the dewy, pie-faced schoolboy romantic that Wodehouse saw himself as having been before he struck out into the world for himself. Bertie, in two separate senses, is more of an 'I' character than anyone else in the books. On some spiritual, astral plane, Bertie Wooster and P.G. Wodehouse, their dross shed, may have now met as twin souls.

Bertie is the only one of Wodehouse's heroes or protagonists for whom the mere release from terror and pain is always a sufficiently happy ending. This modest sufficiency is very much in the formula of the technique of 'I' humour. Reggie Havershot, narrator and hero of Wodehouse's light novel, *Laughing Gas*, survives ten chapters of bewilderment, indignity and bullying by an 'aunt' figure. But he is rewarded in the end by winning a jackpot and a Wodehouse heroine in marriage. It is sufficient for the first-personal Bertie that others get the jackpots and girls, and that he be simply released from bewilderment, indignity, bullying by aunts and other circumambient menaces. Bertie, indeed, almost always actually pays for his releases by some kind of atonement-forfeit (Old Etonian spats) or punishment (the great midnight bicycle ride from Brinkley and back). It is acceptable to the reader as a minor, but regular, nemesis for Bertie's earlier hubristic certainty that he can settle his friends' problems, either better than Jeeves can, or at all. Wodehouse allows such forces of misrule as Uncle Fred and Aunt Dahlia to go scot-free from the debt of their immoralities. But not first-personal Bertie. Bertie suffers, and, through suffering, he is kept in place. The addition of punishment to the massive terrors and embarrassments that Bertie gets into through his desire to please is artistically supportable, and indeed rewarding, to the reader only because the story is being told by someone cordially underwritten by the author whose name appears on the spine of the book.

Wodehouse autobiography, chopped small, drifts like thistledown into Wooster fiction. The novel, *The Mating Season*, published in 1949, contains an interesting collection of the sort of memory-accretions, many of them anachronistic, which give strength to the theory that, consciously or unconsciously, Wodehouse used his own nineteenth-century childhood as a general source of Bertie's twentieth-century youth. Bertie is stuck in a house full of aunts – not his own in the book, but giving him frequent cause to philosophise about aunts. Bertie recalls boyhood dancing classes, boyhood recitations, boyhood pimples, a boyhood Little Lord Fauntleroy suit, and a boyhood nannie. He is made to help at a village concert, and he is wise in the ways of village concerts, as Wodehouse doubtless was when he lived with aunts-married-to-clergymen in his school holidays. Village concerts as a regular threat to country life must have been severely hit by the arrival of radio, and killed stone-dead by television. But there, in 1949, is Bertie in the midst of one. Nobody sings 'The Yeoman's Wedding Song', but Muriel Kegley-Bassington comes across with 'My Hero' from *The Chocolate Soldier* followed by 'Oh, who will o'er the downs with me' as an encore. Except for the Christopher Robin verses, every turn has an 1890-ish date to it. The vicar's niece, who organises the concert, is Corky Pirbright, now a Hollywood star. Her brother, Catsmeat, though a member of The Drones, is an actor. There is much talk of the low esteem in which the respectable gentry holds members of the acting profession – an Edwardian, not later Georgian attitude. Bertie in this book is unusually full of stage jargon, and is deft to compose a lyric for the squire (who loves Corky) to sing at the concert. This surely is the young Wodehouse, whose dabbling in, and success at, writing for the theatre must have caused his own flock of aunts to think he was getting into bad company in his twenties, much more dangerous than the friends he would have made if he had stayed in the bank.

For the length of *The Mating Season*, and the date still being 1949, Bertie stays at Deverill Hall, a house more or less run by these strict aunts, but where champagne is served without question at dinner; a house full of modern conveniences, but where all sudden announcements from the outside are made by telegram, not by telephone. Bertie meets the butler, Silversmith (Jeeves's uncle), and is reminded of the old-fashioned, sixteen-stone butlers who made him feel insignificant and badly dressed as a young man. But Bertie *is*, for the purposes of the story, a young man. Aged twenty-four in 1949, he would have been born in 1925, a good fifty years too late for him to have been bothered by Little Lord Fauntleroy suits, childhood recitations of 'Mary Had a Little Lamb' and 'Ben Battle', and the sort of village concert that this one turned out to be. Wodehouse was giving his own stripling memories to Bertie, in spite of a difference of fifty years in period. In another book Bertie remembers his Little Lord Fauntleroy suit again, and this time he also remembers that he wore his hair in ringlets to match. I don't know if the boy Wodehouse was made to wear his hair in ringlets. Nor do I know for sure (though I would make a bet) that Bertie was speaking for his ninety-three-year-old author in *Aunts Aren't Gentlemen* when he said 'When I was a child, my nurse told me that there was One who was always beside me, spying out all my ways, and that if I refused to eat my spinach I would hear about it on Judgement Day.'

John Hayward in *The Saturday Book* of 1942 made the point that Wodehouse had 'a wide knowledge of English literature and Shakespeare's plays'. He may have had, but the knowledge that he exhibited is essentially schoolboy stuff. Bertie and Jeeves between them bandy quotations from the poets freely. But where these are not from Shakespeare and the classical poets (and an A-level schoolboy of today might have the same stock), they are from such minor Victorian sources that a boy might have learnt them for Repetition at school in the late 1890s, but not in the 1920s. And a significant number of Bertie's images (the tiger and his breakfast coolie, the Pathan sneaking up on the *sahib* across the *maidan*) seem to jump right out from illustrations in *Chums* and similar magazines of the 1890s. This again is Wodehouse giving his memories to Bertie. Bertie once or twice looks back to the days of Covent Garden balls, fights with costermongers and nights spent at the hammams, almost like the original, eighteenth-century William Hickey. Bertie is an ageless young man, spanning the ages.

Bertie started life as a type, and he became a character. He remains the Knut, the Piccadilly Johnny and the playboy bachelor. But, because Wodehouse liked him and wrote through his eyes so often, Bertie became more three-dimensional than any other character in these highly artificial books. In *Performing Flea* Wodehouse says: 'I go off the rails unless I stay all the time in a sort of artificial world of my own creation. A real character in one of my books sticks out like a sore thumb.' Bertie comes alive in the sense that he is predictable. He dictates his own terms for plot and characterisation. While other cardboard characters walk into the soup and displace hardly a spoonful, Bertie displaces it in credible waves. We go in there with him and suffer with his suffering. When Freddie Widgeon, Bingo, Ukridge or a Mulliner go into the soup, we stay on the rim of the tureen and laugh. With Bertie we share the agony and the wetness. His mental deficiency is such that our own brains feel powerful. But we love Bertie and identify ourselves with him, as Wodehouse did to the limits of his own very rigid modesty and self-esteem.

Bertie looks back to a childhood and boyhood of normal rowdiness. When, in 'The Love that Purifies', he sees a septuagenarian asleep in the garden in a deckchair, he tells Jeeves that, in his boyhood, he would certainly have done something drastic to such a septuagenarian, probably with a pea shooter. He stole and smoked one of Lord Worplesdon's cigars at the age of fifteen. He may not have been as fiendish a young gangster as his cousin Thos when he was Thos's age, but he wasn't a prig, like Edwin

Craye, or a sissy, like Sebastian Moon. He went through Malvern House, Eton and Oxford at the proper pace. But, somewhere about the age of twenty-four, Bertie stopped ageing.

Very occasionally in the last few publishing decades twenty-four-year-old Bertie indicates that he is not such a young young man as he was. He no longer envies the all-night undergraduate energy of Claude and Eustace. As late as *Jeeves and the Feudal Spirit* (1954) Bertie is saying: 'I'm not much of a lad for the night clubs these days. Age creeping on me, I suppose.' But he is still a member of half a dozen in London. And when, after a nightclub raid, the magistrate at Winton Street comes to sentence 'the prisoner Gadsby' (Bertie's alias) he says: 'In consideration of your youth I will exercise clemency.' So Bertie gets only a fine, not the jug. And in the 1960 novel, *Jeeves in the Offing*, Bertie shows signs of age, I think, in that he accepts, for the first time without protest, the two frightening jobs that 'Kipper' Herring and Bobbie Wickham push him into in order to advance their own loves. They are both jobs that Bertie has been pushed into before, in earlier books, by other friends. And in those books Bertie entered *nolle prosequi*s for several recusant paragraphs before the Code of the Woosters got the upper hand. Now, in *Jeeves in the Offing*, he is told to shove the Rev. Aubrey Upjohn into the lake and, when that fails, to go into the study and call him names so that Kipper can come in and take Upjohn's side against the frightful Wooster, and thus get Upjohn to call off the libel suit etc., etc. Bertie, aged in experience if not in years, does as he is told, without a yip, knowing that resistance has always proved useless in the past and will do so again this time. He is getting trained.

There is some doubt about which college Bertie was in at Oxford. He says Magdalen, but he also says that he bicycled (in the nude, after a Bump Supper) round his college fountain, and that could only mean Christ Church. But there is no doubt that it was in his schooldays, not at Oxford, that he acquired the main commandments of his eternal Code.

The Code

The Code of the Woosters is part public school, part novelette. Its two main commandments are: (1) Thou shalt not let down a pal; and (2) Thou shalt not scorn a woman's love. Most of the plots of Bertie's stories hinge on one or the other, or both, of these commandments. Bertie has a genuinely kind heart, and, though Palmanship forces him to undertake terrible exploits, he really is made happier when he can do a good turn for a friend, and especially for two friends, a man and a girl with a lovers' tiff to be tidied up.

John Aldridge sees Bertie as the eternal adolescent set between the warring factions of mother and father surrogates. Aunt Dahlia and Jeeves are the main mother surrogates, Aunt Agatha and Sir Roderick Glossop are representative father surrogates. The menaces

of the latter (Aldridge's argument runs) 'demand from Bertie an abandonment of the boyhood state and the prompt assumption of deadly adulthood'. But 'with Jeeves to protect him Bertie is free to pursue a way of life exactly suited to his retarded needs and desires. The boyhood world can be preserved intact.'

This seems to me a just psychological analysis. But it needs expansion. What does authority mean to someone with a family, social and educational background such as Bertie's? I think it is based on the public-school system. In public schools, both of fiction and of fact, headmasters, housemasters and their lackeys, the prefects, represent authority in a highly undemocratic state. The serfs and proles of the lower and middle schools have no say in who bosses them. Authority is always elected from above. Prefects are not, in any school that I know of, chosen by an electorate of juniors saying 'Please govern us.' The housemaster nominates the prefects, the headmaster nominates the housemaster and the governing body nominates the headmaster. Young Johnny's parents pay large sums for young Johnny to live in this hieratic discipline, subdued until the time comes for him, as a prefect, to subdue.

Bertie Wooster's relationship with Jeeves seems to me a public-school arrangement, easy for Bertie, though surprisingly accepted by Jeeves. Bertie sometimes berates Jeeves like a prefect berating a fag, not like a master berating a servant. And as Bertie is always wrong on these occasions, and Jeeves knows it, Bertie is extremely lucky to have a servant who understands his master's Code and forgives it. But in the wider Wodehouse social set-up, though authority does not specifically employ the public-school indignification of beating grown-up people on the 'billowy portions', it does, in the public-school manner, work to a set of sanctions, checks and balances of great power, but, almost all of them, non-valid in, and beyond the reach of, common law. You can't have the law on an aunt when she makes you steal pearl necklaces for her, but you know that, if you don't comply, the cooking of the best chef in England will be wiped from your greedy lips in indefinite punishment. Call it blackmail, but can you tell it to the magistrate? You can't have the law on a ghastly girl when she says she's going to marry you, but you'll put yourself in peril of the law by pinching a policeman's uniform in order to set in motion a series of events which will culminate (if Jeeves is working them out) in your quasi-honourable release from the engagement. When Stiffy Byng makes her fiancé, the sainted Rev. 'Stinker' Pinker, prove his love for her by bringing her policeman Oates's helmet, he can do nothing but wail 'If the Infants' Bible Class should hear of this!' When Florence Craye makes her fiancé, Stilton, grow a moustache, he is powerless except to grind a tooth or two. When an ex-London magistrate, a maniac collector of old silver, puts a rival maniac collector out of the running for the acquisition of a rare antique by, with cunning aforethought, feeding him cold lobster at lunch and so confining him to quarters with writhing indigestion, the second maniac's ever-loving wife knows that the law cannot help. Bertie must go and steal the cow-creamer back for its 'rightful' owner. In Wodehouse's farces everybody is playing cops and robbers in a law-free society.

Bertie, the most innocent of do-gooders temperamentally, has no inborn authority of his own. He never uses his money to buy authority and, apart from money, what is he? He has accepted the position of being a 'Hey-you' to aunts, uncles and quite a lot of girls. But Wodehouse was in Bertie's corner, and Wodehouse gave Bertie Jeeves. With certain reservations about white mess jackets, Old Etonian spats and banjoleles, Jeeves is completely and self-effacingly pro-Bertie. All three, Bertie, Jeeves and Wodehouse, are transparently anti-prefect (Aunt Agatha), anti-fag (Edwin) and pro the status of the fifteen-year-old public-school boy.

But watch Bertie when he suddenly does get the moral cosh of authority into his hands. He knows all the prefect's manner of speech. Though he is properly the bossed, the chivvied, the man in the ranks, the man on the receiving end of orders and objurgations, Bertie can snap, with absurd ease, into the jargon of authority. Listen to him come the headmaster over terrible Spode, when he has blessedly remembered the magic word 'Eulalie', and thus has the goods on this pestilential amateur dictator:

> 'I shall be very sharp on that sort of thing in the future, Spode.'
>> 'Yes, yes, I understand.'
>> 'I have not been at all satisfied with your behaviour since you came to this house. The way you were looking at me during dinner … and calling me a miserable worm.'
>> 'I'm sorry I called you a miserable worm, Wooster. I spoke without thinking.'
>> 'Always think, Spode. Well, that is all. You may withdraw.'

Macaulay wrote of the 'arrogant humility' of the younger Pitt. Bertie's humble arrogance is a much more touching thing.

The Wooster clan

Who was Bertie Wooster, and what was his family background? It has to be pointed out, and then quickly forgotten, that in the first story in which Bertie appeared, 'Extricating Young Gussie' in *The Man with Two Left Feet*, his surname was undoubtedly Mannering-Phipps. Also that in three short stories, which you can find in earlier Wodehouse books, related, and acted in, by one Reggie Pepper, Bertie took over, for later books, with little more than the names changed and Jeeves injected. Perhaps also that when, for the length of a novel (*Ring for Jeeves*, 1953), Wodehouse removed Bertie from the scene and lent Jeeves to Lord Rowcester, Lord Rowcester could, with disturbing accuracy, take over Bertie's lines in the hitherto supposedly sacred stichomyth between master and man.

Make a face-sized oval in white cardboard, put two dark smudges for eyes, and hold it above the cot of a very young baby. Up to the age of seven weeks the baby, if he has started to smile at all, will smile just as regularly at the cardboard face as at his mother's. Bertie has cardboard beginnings.

In a literary sense Bertie and Jeeves were both born in America. 'Extricating Young Gussie' was first published in America. All the four Jeeves stories in *My Man Jeeves* (1919) are set in New York. The original miscue at Bertie's surname was probably caused itself by over-anxiety to please America. In Wodehouse's early New York days the resounding and seemingly aristocratic English name was something of a joke. Americans liked to think that Courtney de Vere-Vere was a typical English name. We liked to think that Silas Q. Higgs was a typical American name. Wodehouse mentions the business of English names in America in one or two of his essays, and, in 'In Alcala', the somewhat autobiographical English hero in New York gets his name cut down by the American heroine from Rutherford Maxwell to George. Mannering-Phipps was at that period a typical English name for Wodehouse's American purposes and was acceptable without a smile to English readers. Gussie himself says he feels a fearful ass in New York when he has to sign his name as Augustus Mannering-Phipps. He starts calling himself George Wilson.

So Bertie was Mannering-Phipps as a pupa. He had a chrysalis stage as Reggie Pepper. And he finally emerged as Wooster. He seems to have become an orphan at eight or nine. He hardly ever mentions his father, still less his mother. For the period of one story only he has a widowed sister with three daughters, but they are soon forgotten. He has a number of Wooster uncles. One of them surprisingly becomes Lord Yaxley, obviously through no damned merit, since he is fat, idle, foolish and slightly pickled in alcohol. He eventually marries an ex-barmaid. Another Wooster uncle, father of Claude and Eustace, died in some sort of a home, 'more or less off his onion', with rabbits in his bedroom. Another uncle, at the age of seventy-six and under the influence of crusted port, would climb trees. The Wooster family has its full quota of loonies to qualify it for Wodehouse's upper classes.

Bertie's aunts are more interesting than his uncles.

'The whole trouble is due to your blasted aunt,' said young Bingo.
'Which blasted aunt? Specify, old thing. I have so many.'
'Mrs Travers. The one who runs that infernal paper.'
'Oh, no, dash it, old man,' I protested. 'She's the only decent aunt I've got...'

Bertie's Aunts Agatha and Dahlia are sisters. It is difficult to dream up a joint childhood that could have produced two such different types, but there it is. Dahlia used to hunt incessantly in the Shires when young. There is no history of the hunting field, or even of youth, in the Agatha archives. She was engaged at an early stage to Percy Craye who was, or later became, the Earl of Worplesdon. But he got into a disgraceful dust-up after a Covent Garden ball, and Agatha gave him back his ring when she read his press notices in the evening papers. She married a stockbroker, 'a battered little chappie', whose name is variously given as Spenser, Spenser-Gregson and Spenser Gregson. He had made a fortune in Sumatra rubber. He never made a live appearance, and he died conveniently to allow Aunt Agatha to marry Lord Worplesdon for *Joy in the Morning* (1947).

Aunt Agatha strongly advised Florence Craye not to marry Bertie, because he was a spineless invertebrate. And for exactly the same reason she was most anxious that Honoria Glossop *should* marry him. Aunt Agatha is the only person who has ever suggested that Bertie should have a job. Although Bertie does once crush her ('Pearls Mean Tears') and splendidly defy her (end of *The Mating Season*), he is really terrified of her. She has been his scourge and evil conscience from the first. It is comforting in a way to know that Bertie is not her only target. She makes Lord Worplesdon give up smoking, and his agonies are frightful.

Aunt Agatha was tall, grey and beaky, and must have made a convincing Boadicea in that historical pageant at Woollam Chersey. She once started to go in for politics, but retired hurt when rude fellows heckled her speeches.

Bertie's splendid Aunt Dahlia married Tom Travers 'the year Bluebottle won the Cambridgeshire'. It was her second marriage, her first husband having been a drunk. I think her Angela and Bonzo are both children of the Travers marriage. In the earliest references Aunt Dahlia was Bertie's aunt only by marriage, and Uncle Tom was described by Bertie as 'between ourselves, a bit of a squirt', and not good enough for his wife. At that period, too, Uncle Tom refused to live in the country, and Aunt Dahlia had to compensate for hunting by running *Milady's Boudoir*, a weekly magazine. But soon Aunt Dahlia becomes established as being sister to Bertie's father, and a true Wooster. (She had saved Bertie's life, to her outspoken regret in later years, when, as a baby, he nearly swallowed his rubber comforter.) Uncle Tom forgets his dislike of the country. He develops into a pleasant old silly, very fond of Dahlia, in an income-tax-ridden sort of way. And he lives perfectly happily at Brinkley (as in Charles Street) so long as too many poets and other pests don't come to stay. He has a lot of money and a bad liver, both made in the Far East, a good collection of old silver, a yacht, mild insomnia and a face like a walnut. Most first generation rich men in Wodehouse pay the price in dyspepsia. Uncle Tom's pays dividends in a literary sense, because it heightens the importance of Anatole, the fabulous chef whom Aunt Dahlia lured away from the Bingo Littles. Anatole, and only Anatole, can cook food that soothes Uncle Tom's alimentary tract, and enables him to be a plentiful, if not very willing, provider of cheques for *Milady's Boudoir* (which he always refers to as 'Madame's Nightshirt'). If Anatole were to cease to cook for him, Uncle Tom's digestion would play up again, and it would follow, as the night the day, that he would think taxes were crippling him and that the revolution was setting in. The result would be no money to pay Aunt Dahlia's baccarat debts, and general misery.

Five times, so far as I can count, has Aunt Dahlia been in danger of losing Anatole, once as a gambling debt to Lady Snettisham, twice to Sir Watkyn Bassett, once to the frightful Liverpudlian Trotters, and once when Gussie Fink-Nottle made faces at the skylight of Anatole's bedroom at Brinkley. The possible loss of Anatole has been a good plot-maker. Bertie once offered to take a rap to the tune of thirty days in prison to prevent Aunt Dahlia losing Anatole, and Aunt Dahlia can always bend Bertie to her will by the threat that, if he disobeys her, he will not be asked to her *cordon bleu* table any more.

Brick-red and brazen-voiced from the hunting fields of earlier days, a devout blackmailer, able to slang and chaff an opponent with schoolboy pith the relish, Aunt Dahlia is Bertie's all-time favourite relative of any sort, let alone aunt. Their dialogue is some of the best stuff in Wodehouse. They understand each other very well. Aunt Dahlia is a middle-aged version of Wodehouse's best girls, Stiffy Byng, Nobby Hopwood, Bobbie Wickham *et al*. She is an excellent creation.

There was plenty of money in the Wooster family. Bertie's uncles were all comfortably unemployed. His Aunt Dahlia was intermittently short of cash, but both she (at least once) and Agatha (twice) married 'into trade'. Bertie refers to himself as being 'stagnant with the stuff'. He lives in Berkeley Mansions, and there is enough in the petty cash float, to which Jeeves had access, for Jeeves to be able to buy two round the world cruise tickets at the end of *The Code of the Woosters*. (Did they ever go on that cruise?) The Wooster class is upper, without being of the county. Its nesting territories are London W.1. and the country. I wonder why Aunt Agatha's son, the tough young Thos, is down to go to Pevenhurst, not to Eton.

Love and marriage

Bertie has still not suffered that 'fate worse than death – *viz.* marriage'. But he has run it pretty fine with eight or nine girls at one time or another. Bertie is no wolf. If Jeeves finds Bertie's bed unslept in, he assumes, and correctly, that Bertie has spent the night in jug somewhere, not with any girl. Aunts and friends break in on Bertie's bedroom before breakfast, with never a suspicion that he may have company there. When Bertie, by mistake, climbs into Florence Craye's bedroom window at Brinkley, Florence, to whom he has been engaged once or twice already, assumes that, still yearning, he has come to kiss her while she sleeps. Bertie (who possibly hasn't read Kipling's 'Brushwood Boy') is pained by such advanced modern thought. When Pauline Stoker, to whom Bertie has also once been engaged, is revealed in Bertie's bed, in Bertie's pyjamas, unchaperoned, in Bertie's little seaside cottage at midnight, Bertie is shocked to his foundations. Bertie is pure as driven snow, if not purer. He refers to himself as a 'reputable bachelor who has never had his licence so much as endorsed'.

But, sucker as he is for getting embroiled with, and engaged to, brainy girls like Honoria Glossop and Florence Craye, soupy girls like Madeline Bassett and festive little squirts like Bobbie Wickham, Bertie does from time to time take positive steps as a lover. He had, at the age of fourteen, written to Marie Lloyd for her autograph. He had, when they were kids, let his cousin Angela call herself his own little sweetheart. He had asked Cynthia Wickhammersley to marry him. (This was rash, because she was full of ideals, and would probably have required Bertie to carve out a career and what-not. Bertie had distinctly heard her speaking favourably of Napoleon. But it all worked out well. When Bertie proposed, Cynthia nearly laughed herself into permanent hiccups.) Bertie had given Pauline Stoker a rush in New York, and was engaged to her within a matter of days. Bertie had been in love with Corky Pirbright. He was in love with Gwladys Pendlebury, the artist. Then there was Vanessa Cook, the protest-marcher. He twice thought he wanted to marry Bobbie Wickham, and twice Jeeves had to show him what a heartless little red-head she was. Once (*Jeeves in the Offing*) Bobbie announced her engagement to Bertie in *The Times*. But that was only to scare her mother into giving her approval to her (Bobbie's) marrying 'Kipper' Herring. On the evidence of *My Man Jeeves*, but suppressed when the same story was included in *Carry On, Jeeves* and the *Jeeves Omnibus*, Bertie had once 'tried to marry into musical comedy'. The family had objected – Bertie's family, that was.

Pauline Stoker put it well when she said there was a 'woolly-headed duckiness' about Bertie. 'Mentally negligible, but he has a heart of gold,' says Jeeves of the young master. When Bertie is old and grey and full of sleep, he will look back on his romantic youth and probably decide that the greatest compliment he was ever paid was from Pauline's father. Pop Stoker, an incandescent American millionaire, hearing that his daughter had spent the night in Bertie's cottage, captured Bertie in his yacht and proposed to keep him there till he had married the errant girl. Pop Stoker, at any rate, believed Bertie had passions that he could unbridle, and Pop Stoker had a nasty Victorian sense of etiquette to deal with the situation as he guessed it.

Pauline would not have been too bad a wife for Bertie. But, when the smoke has cleared away, we accept Jeeves's judgement that Bertie is one of nature's bachelors. We're glad that Bertie lasted the course in single strictness, with Jeeves to look after him and to bring tea for one to the bedroom in the mornings.

NUGGETS Manservants

I have known no footmen, no valets and only two or three butlers. In Wodehouse's books they are numerous, and he does honour to their calling. I am content to base my knowledge of their habits, duties, shapes, diet and language entirely on Wodehouse and his illustrators.

There are plenty of butlers in the stories Wodehouse set in America, but all of them, even the crooks, are transplanted English, aren't they? I saw a film advertised outside one of those small cinemas near Piccadilly Circus, entitled 'What the Swedish Butler Saw'. I didn't see the film, alas. But I bet you the butler was English by birth. There is a tombstone in the churchyard at Battle in Sussex: HERE LIES ISAAC INGALL, born 1658, died 1778, AGED 120 YEARS. He had been in service with the Websters of Battle Abbey for more than a hundred years and ended as Head Butler. The chronicles say that, when he was aged a hundred, the Lady Webster of the day had ticked him off for – well, one chronicle says being untidily dressed, the other for not opening a gate quick enough – and he had walked the seven miles into Hastings to find another job, failed to find one, and walked the seven miles back. I wish I had thought of telling Wodehouse about Isaac Ingall.

Beach, informed that there was a gentleman asking for him and finding that
the person thus described was a pig-man whom he had never liked and who
in his opinion smelled to heaven, was at his most formal. He might have been a
prominent Christian receiving an expected call from one of the troops of Midian.

It is a very impoverished butler in Beverly Hills who does not own a natty little roadster.

I found Oakshott in his pantry. Dismissing with a gesture the
housemaid who was sitting on his knee, I unfolded my proposition.

Bowles, like all proprietors of furnished rooms in the Sloane Square
neighbourhood, is an ex-butler, and even in a plaid dressing gown he
retained much of the cold majesty which so intimidated me by day.

'I found that Vosper was willing to come to us in America. He had been eighteen years with
the Duke, and he told me that he couldn't stand the sight of the back of his head any more.'

Slingsby loomed in the doorway like a dignified cloudbank.

'What-ho, Jeeves!' I said, entering the room where he waded knee-deep in
suitcases and shirts and winter suitings, like a sea-beast among rocks. 'Packing?'
'Yes, sir,' replied the honest fellow, for there are no secrets between us.

Jeeves lugged my purple socks out of the drawer as if he
were a vegetarian fishing a caterpillar out of his salad.

Jeeves entered – or perhaps one should say shimmered into – the room ...
tall and dark and impressive. He might have been one of the better class
ambassadors or the youngish High Priest of some refined and dignified religion.

Parker made no comment. He stood in the doorway, trying to look as
like a piece of furniture as possible – which is the duty of a good butler.

'I have no desire to be a deputy,' said the butler, with the cold subtinkle in his voice which
had once made the younger son of a marquess resign from his clubs and go to Uganda.

Jeeves let his brain out another notch.

JEEVES

(The only book in which Jeeves appears without Bertie Wooster is *Ring for Jeeves* (1953).)

The Times obituary of Eric Blore, the film-actor, in 1959, ended:

> He made a speciality of that most English of all professions ... the gentleman's gentleman or manservant, the very epitome of Jeeves. Indeed, he and another English actor, Mr Arthur Treacher, may be said to have made a virtual corner in butler parts in Hollywood during the thirties, and no study of an upper-class English or American household was complete without one or other of them. Treacher, tall and thin, was haughty and austere, a man with a permanent smell under his nose. Blore, who was shorter and slightly tubby, was a trifle more eccentric in manner, but equally capable of registering eloquent but unspoken disapproval of any untoward behaviour. But he could yet suggest a taste for a lower life, and it was Blore who introduced into an American film *It's Love I'm After* the eloquent line: 'If I were not such a gentleman's gentleman I could be such a cad's cad.'

It is just tribute to Wodehouse that *The Times* could already use 'Jeeves' like that, without quotation marks and without acknowledgement. To some extent it was due to Wodehouse's glorification of the English manservant that Treacher and Blore could live their prosperous lives in Hollywood. Butlers had always been useful in plays, to come on and explain the set-up, in dialogue with a dusting housemaid or into a telephone while the audience settled down. But Hollywood's cameras could wander around and show direct what a stage butler had to get across in speech. Hollywood used the stately and funny butler because he was a fat part and he paid dividends. Wodehouse had put butlers on the map. Hollywood used them where they stood, and paid Wodehouse scant thanks.

Origins of Jeeves

Wodehouse wrote a good deal, for him, about writing about butlers and gentlemen's gentlemen. He told us that his love for the tribe on the other side of the green baize door started when he was a boy and used to be lugged round by aunts and clergymen uncles to call on the great houses. Young Pelham was a bust as a conversationalist in the drawing-rooms over the cucumber sandwiches, so his uncles and aunts often sent him off with the butler to have his tea in the servants' hall. And there young Pelham kidded back and forth with footman and housemaid and everybody was very happy – the boy showing off, the servants encouraging him in a way his uncles and aunts never did.

Doubtless even then Wodehouse was awed by the majesty of the butlers. Ukridge's visual description of Oakshott really stands for all butlers: 'Meeting him in the street and ignoring the foul bowler hat he wore on his walks abroad, you would have put him down as a Bishop in mufti or, at the least, a plenipotentiary at one of the better courts.' The first sentence of 'The Good Angel' in the book of short stories *The Man Upstairs* (1914) is: 'Any man under thirty years of age who tells you he is not afraid of an English butler, lies.' Lord Ickenham, for all his insistence that Earls had a right, and almost a duty, to be haughty, was equally at home in castle and cottage. But, though he was at least sixty, his affection for his butler, Coggs, was tempered by awe. Bertie Wooster himself, who normally treats servants as to the manor born, was overawed by Silversmith, butler at Deverill Hall in *The Mating Season*. This was one of those flickers of Wodehouse-Wooster autobiography.

In an unrepublished *Strand* story, in 1914, 'Creatures of Impulse', Wodehouse told of a perfect servant, Jevons (the name Jeeves may have been taking shape even then), who, on an impulse, put ice down the neck of his Baronet master at the dinner table. The Bart sacked him. But then, later, the Bart got an air-gun in his hands in the country, and, on an impulse, shot a gardener in the trouser-seat with it. He couldn't think what had come over him, but he realised he had wronged Jevons, and he summoned him back by telegram. Obviously bits of this story went into the making of 'The Crime Wave at Blandings'. Wodehouse gives us good butlers and bad butlers. Julia Ukridge's butler Oakshott was called 'inky-souled' by no less a rogue than Ukridge himself. It is pleasant to see Oakshott taking off his coat to cuddle a housemaid on his knee in his pantry. It is pleasant to see Oakshott, in a moment of panic, dive into a wardrobe when he thought the police were after him. Another butler preached Socialism in Hyde Park. Another played the fiddle. Beach of Blandings kept a bullfinch and stole pigs. And what about the bank-burgling butler? These are good grace-notes.

You will find fine Wodehouse butlers in fifty books, Attwater, Barlow, Barter, Bayliss, Baxter, Beach, Benson, Blizzard, Bowles (ex-butler), Bulstrode, Chibnall, Coggs, Ferris, Gascoyne, Keggs, Oakshott, Pollen, Ridgway, Silversmith, Slingsby, Spenser, Sturgis,

Swordfish, Vosper and Watson being the names that spring to the mind. Swordfish (the name that Sir Roderick Glossop took when pretending to be the butler in Brinkley in *Jeeves in the Offing*) was indeed a name that sprang to the mind of that scheming young menace, Bobbie Wickham. But there is virtually only one gentleman's personal gentleman in the books, and that's Jeeves. You will find a few other valets or what passed for valets, including Archie Mulliner's Meadowes and that other Meadowes, Jeeves's predecessor in Bertie's service (he sneaked Bertie's socks), and Jeeves's substitute in *Thank You, Jeeves*, who got tight, trolled hymns and went after Bertie with the meat knife. But Jeeves is supreme.

'There is none like you, none, Jeeves,' says Bertie, thereby showing a knowledge of Tennyson's *Maud*, but a number of gaps in his reading. The *débrouillard* manservant was a staple of Greek and Roman comedy. Chesterton described Sam Weller as 'something new – a clever comic servant whose knowledge of the world is more than that of his master, but who is not a rascal'. Barrie's Crichton follows Weller. The stately, orotund manservant, often called Jeames, was in and out of *Punch* as early as the 1860s. John Buchan's Sir Archie Roylance had an encyclopaedic manservant who 'patently educated' him.

In Cynthia Asquith's memoir of Barrie is a description of Barrie's own butler, Thurston, who read Latin and Greek while polishing the silver, and would correct Barrie's literary guests when they got their quotations wrong. Frank Thurston became Barrie's manservant in 1922, at a time when Jeeves was already coming out serially in print. If you read Chapter 4 of Cynthia Asquith's *Portrait of Barrie*, you'll see how the factual Thurston resembled the fictional Jeeves:

> Dictionaries and various learned tomes cluttered up the pantry ... I discovered him poring over a Spanish book. 'Is that a difficult language, Thurston?' I asked. 'No, My Lady, it presents little difficulty if one has a fair knowledge of Latin and French.' ... He could supply any forgotten date or quotation ... Barrie would counsel guests that, if they must take a 'thriller' to bed, they had better 'hide it in between a Pliny and the latest theory of Ethics', or they might feel abashed when Thurston came to draw

their curtains in the morning ... 'You are inimical to your apparel, Sir,' said Thurston to Barrie, who used to burn his clothes with sparks from his pipe ... 'I still haven't found out,' Barrie said one day, 'what it is that Thurston doesn't know, but I don't give up hope.' ... From Italy he wrote to me, 'The beauty of Venice is almost appalling, and so was Thurston's knowledge of it as we entered it.' ... Thurston, uncommunicative, inscrutable, puma-footed ... no one ever heard him enter or leave a room ... was so unusual, indeed, so mysterious a being that he might almost have been written by his master ... A man who inspired not only instantaneous respect, but – for his heart was as good as his head – growing affection. In the last letter Barrie wrote (it was to Thurston) Barrie said 'I want you besides the monetary bequest to pick for yourself a hundred of my books. Few persons who have entered that loved flat have done more honour to books.'

This is a remarkable consonance with Jeeves. Denis Mackail, a good friend and great admirer of Wodehouse, and author of a fine *Life* of Barrie, said there was no need to think there is any link, in any dimension, between Thurston and Jeeves. Wodehouse didn't know Barrie well and never went to the Adelphi flat. It is probable that Cynthia Asquith, when she came to write about Thurston, had herself come to equate him with Jeeves and unconsciously to use some of the Wodehouse brushwork for her portrait of Thurston.

Bring On the Girls suggests a factual origin for Jeeves, but it post-dates Jeeves's arrival and naming by at least ten years and must be ignored. More likely as germ-carriers for the idea of Jeeves are two fictional manservants in the books of Conan Doyle (once more), Ambrose, the cravat-tying, coffee-making valet to the Regency buck, Sir Charles Tregellis in *Rodney Stone*; and Austin, Professor Challenger's servant in *The Poison Belt* (1913).

'I'm expecting the end of the world today, Austin.'
'Yes, sir, what time, sir?'
'I can't say. Before evening.'
'Very good, sir.' The taciturn Austin saluted and withdrew.

Compare with this the Bertie/Jeeves dialogue in the first story of all, 'Extricating Young Gussie':

'Jeeves,' I said, 'we start for America on Saturday.'
'Very good, sir. Which suit will you wear?'

There is a difference between a gentleman's personal gentleman and a butler, but it is only that the former is thin and the latter fat, and they have different spheres of duties.

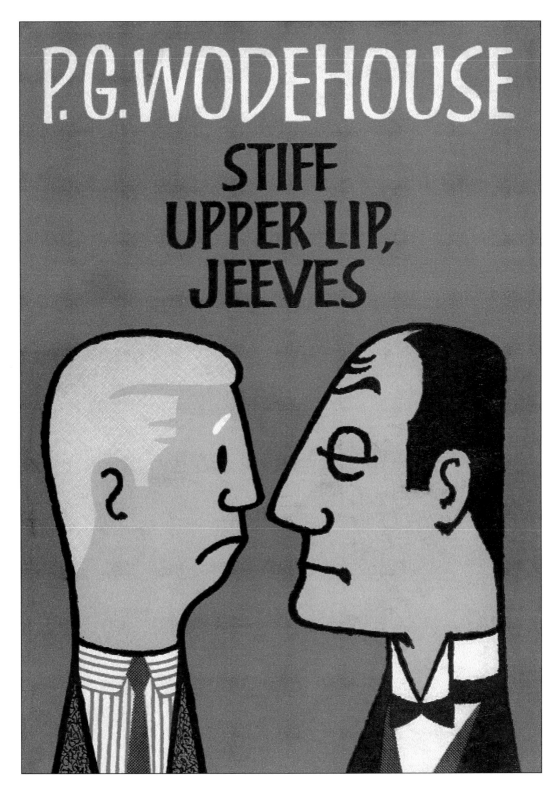

P.G.WODEHOUSE

STIFF
UPPER LIP,
JEEVES

Wodehouse would have claimed no originality for Jeeves as a broad type. What Wodehouse could have claimed as his own patent with Jeeves was his successful use of him as a recurrent, charming, funny and credible agent in plot-making.

Plots and forfeits

The Wodehouse farce plots are highly complicated, and Wodehouse took immense trouble in handling them ingeniously. Other good authors, having achieved plots one stage less involved, would feel perfectly justified in their artistic consciences to allow their dénouements to start through a coincidence or act of God. Wodehouse, in the Jeeves stories, used Jeeves as an extra dimension, a godlike prime mover, a master brain who is found to have engineered the apparent coincidence or coincidences. When Bingo Little was sorely harassed by his wife Rosie's old school chum, it would still have been a good story if the picnic basket had been put in the wrong car in error, and if Bertie's car had run out of petrol in the wilds at tea-time by chance. That would have sufficed to cause the flaming row between Rosie and her chum and to have restored sanity to the way of life of the Little household. But Jeeves had engineered it all. There was no error, no chance.

Jeeves in most stories is the rim of the wheel and the hub, the plotter and the plot. Bertie sometimes insists on handling problems his own way. Jeeves, in his background planning, can not only allow for Bertie's mistakes; he can estimate their extent in advance and make them a positive part of the great web he is himself spinning. And he is so confident of his success that he will often take his reward before his success has actually happened and before his reward has been offered. 'Jeeves, you may give away those plus-fours of mine you dislike so.' 'Thank you, sir, I gave them to the under-gardener yesterday.'

Jeeves has a genuine fondness for Bertie, and enjoys helping him and his friends. He likes them to appeal to him, and is not annoyed to be summoned by telegram back from the middle of his summer seaside holiday to rescue them from their idiocies. He takes their side calmly. He remains perfectly polite, and seems quite impartial to the current opposition. He simply out-generals it. If Bertie, through asininity, sets up an unexpected diversion, Jeeves doesn't let that crimp his style. He envelops it and out-generals Bertie, too. He usually makes Bertie pay a forfeit. But, godlike in this too, Jeeves chastens and still loves, loves and still chastens. He accepts Bertie's sacrifice (in the case of the banjolele, a burnt offering), and the score is settled.

Bertie does not bear his grudges against Jeeves for long. Jeeves does not bear grudges against Bertie at all. There is nothing maudlin about their association, either. Bertie can be demanding and even rude. Jeeves can be cold and non-cooperative. Bertie sacked Jeeves twice in a single story and would be silly enough to do it again if there were a major clash of wills. Jeeves has resigned twice and he would do it again at the drop of a bowler hat if

Bertie continued in some absurd course. Jeeves means it when he resigns. Even he could not plot the happy end of Bertie's banjolele. It was a menace and Jeeves would not be in the same cottage with it. So he resigned and was immediately snapped up by Lord Chuffnell. As it happened, Chuffy, thanks largely to Jeeves's machinations, was able to woo and win Pauline Stoker, which meant that Jeeves did not propose to stay on as his servant. In Jeeves's experience, when a wife comes in at the front door, a valet goes out at the back. As it happened, Bertie's cottage went up in flames and the banjolele was burnt. The *casus belli* between master and man was removed and, on Bertie's assurance that banjolele-playing was a thing of the past for him, Jeeves gladly consented to team up with him again. Honour was preserved on all fronts, though Bertie had had to forfeit a good deal of face (with bootblack on it most of the time) as punishment for his diversionary activities in the middle chapters.

When, in Kipling's *First Jungle Book*, Mowgli is flattered by the *bandar-log* and whisked off by them terrifyingly to the Cold Lairs, Baloo and Bagheera, his fond mentors, have their work cut out to rescue him. But Mowgli had disobeyed their instructions in having anything to do with the *bandar-log* in the first place, and Mowgli has to be punished, when the night's alarms and excursions are over. Baloo and Bagheera give him a beating. The principle of Bertie's punishment (not by any means always inflicted by Jeeves) is the same as the principle of Mowgli's, and of Greek tragedy, and of the Old Testament. Hubris not only gets its nemesis. It requires it, especially with such a childlike character as Bertie. Otherwise, childlike, he would go on swanking. Childlike, he would not have the sense to understand the small print on the social contract. He would not renounce his silliness without punishment. And, for the readers, he would not start the next story with the required clean-slate innocence. The slate would carry an unsettled score. We wouldn't mind about that with Ukridge, Aunt Dahlia or Uncle Fred. We would mind with Bertie.

Considering the tough eggs that Jeeves has to out-general, it is no small part of his superhumanship that he does it without (except in *Ring for Jeeves*) loss of his impeccable servant status. Sir Roderick Glossop, Aunt Agatha, Sir Watkyn Bassett, Spode, Pop Stoker, Florence and Stilton probably to this day do not realise that Jeeves pulled the strings to nullify their menaces to Bertie. Aunt Agatha and Honoria objected to Jeeves because Jeeves's influence on Bertie was too strong. Jeeves seemed to them an outward and visible sign of Bertie's inward and spiritual spinelessness. Aunt Agatha and Honoria never knew just how much Bertie's escape from their clutches had been engineered by Jeeves. This is a situation that Jeeves has to handle carefully, because aunts go on for ever, and Honoria is apt to pop up in Bertie's life whenever there's a lull. Many of Bertie's friends (Aunt

Dahlia, Gussie, Bingo and Co.) do realise Jeeves's omnipotence, and this makes Bertie temporarily piqued and jealous, so that, to show his own cleverness, he concocts silly plans which complicate the plots, increase the pity and terror and laughter, and add to Jeeves's laurels in the end.

Why Jeeves, with that brain, and that confidence in his own brain, should remain a gentleman's personal gentleman is fairly mysterious. He is a keen and shrewd gambler. He could make a fortune in the City, and have all the time he wanted for fishing, shrimping, sea-travel and reading. You can't suspect Jeeves of snobbish motives in staying in service with the nobility and gentry; nor of timidity in not wanting to better himself. I am sure he has read Karl Marx and has been exposed to all the dialectic that might persuade lesser valets to work only for the Red Dawn, or to try to collar the means of production and thus become a master rather than a serf. Jeeves just isn't a lesser valet. He lets the foolish Bertie pull rank on him and call him an ass. A lesser valet of spirit wouldn't allow that. Jeeves takes it in the spirit (public school) in which it is dished out. Which is pretty superb. But Jeeves is a pretty superb person. Bertie calls him an ass occasionally. Bertie snubs him and tells him to put a sock in his reminiscences and poetic analogies. Bertie tells him his brain is softening. Bertie treats him, in fact, not like a social inferior, but like an equal. And Jeeves calmly goes on treating Bertie like an employer first, and like a mentally negligible favourite child second. It is a delicate balance to maintain. Jeeves maintains it.

Jeeves gets his way, and Bertie pays his forfeits. The forfeit is always necessary for Bertie's atonement, but often it is also part of the way Jeeves gets. As story succeeds story, so do Bertie's young enthusiasms and items of swank. He maintains them as long as he can against Jeeves's disapproval, but in the end he gives them up or hands them over. Jeeves had contributed eleven pages about Bertie to the book at the Junior Ganymede Club in which all members had to file the facts about the gentlemen to whom they are personal gentlemen. Probably one of the eleven pages under WOOSTER B. lists all the things that Bertie has loved and lost. The Old Etonian spats, the purple socks, the loud plus-fours, the Alpine hat, the cummerbund, the white mess jacket as worn at Cannes, the soft silk shirts for evening wear, the banjolele, the vase with dragon designs on it and the two moustaches (be it remembered that the first time Bertie lost his moustache to Jeeves, Jeeves himself shaved it off). The list may also include the things that Jeeves has wanted, Bertie has refused, and Jeeves has finally got, such as the trip on Aunt Dahlia's yacht, the Christmas at Monte Carlo and the round the world cruise (if they ever did go on that cruise).

Life beyond Bertie

There must be a lot of entries over Reginald Jeeves's by-line in the Junior Ganymede book, in addition to the eleven pages on WOOSTER B. Jeeves has served at least nine employers since his first job as page-boy at a girls' school. He was with Lord Worplesdon for nearly a year, and resigned because his master insisted on dining in evening trousers with a flannel shirt and a shooting coat. He was with Mr Digby Thistleton, now Lord Bridgnorth, the financier who marketed a product unsuccessfully as a depilatory, and then changed its name to Hair-O and marketed it successfully as a hair-growing unguent. He was with Mr Montague Todd (is this a subliminal memory of Dickens's Montague Tigg?), another financier, but who did less well, and was, at the moment of Jeeves's mention of his name, in the second year of his sentence. He was with Lord Brancaster, who fed his lethargic parrot with seed-cake steeped in '84 port, and was bitten in the thumb for his kindness. He was with Lord Frederick Ranelagh, who was swindled in Monte Carlo by a confidence trickster called Soapy Sid, the same man who nearly swindled Bertie and Aunt Agatha at Roville. He was with Lord Rowcester for the length of *Ring for Jeeves*. He was with Lord Chuffnell for a week, and Pop Stoker for less. He was with Gussie Fink-Nottle for a few days in *The Mating Season* (Gussie was pretending to be Bertie). At the end of *Stiff Upper Lip, Jeeves* he accepted service with the ever-predatory Sir Watkyn Bassett, but only as a ruse for getting Bertie released from prison.

Jeeves was such a good servant, so much pursued by poachers, that one wonders how on earth he came to be unemployed and on an agency's books at that happy, star-skipping moment when Bertie's man, Meadowes, had to be fired. Bertie went up to London, contacted the agency, had a night out with the lads, and a hangover when Jeeves rang his bell. Jeeves shimmered in and mixed Bertie his since-famous pick-me-up, and was hired with no further questions asked.

Private Jeeves

Jeeves's origins were 'of the people', and he seems to have had a pattern of aunt-uncle-cousin-ridden orphanhood that mirrored Bertie's own. There was the aunt who tried Walkinshaw's Supreme Ointment for her swollen limbs and was so jaunty about seeing her photograph in the advertisements. (James, the footman at Blandings in *Something Fresh*, had done the same with the same results.) There was the other aunt who paid someone five shillings to bring a movie actor to tea at her house. There was the third aunt in S.E. London who had a passion for riding in taxi-cabs, often breaking into the children's savings boxes to get the money for such outings. The family used to get the parson to talk her out of this craze when they saw an attack coming on. There was Aunt Annie whom the family invited to stay when there was a family quarrel. The whole family so detested Aunt Annie that they became friends again when they other-directed their hatreds at Annie. There was the aunt who owned nearly all Rosie M. Banks's novels. There was that final aunt at the village of Maiden Eggesford.

Jeeves mentions one uncle, and we meet another. His Uncle Cyril had a favourite story which amused his nephew, but amused Bertie less when Jeeves told it to him just before he set out on that midnight bicycle ride from Brinkley. The story was of two men, called Nicholls and Jackson, who rode a tandem bicycle, ran into a brewer's van and were considerably fragmented. In fact, when the accident squad came to collect the bits, they could only find enough for one person, and they buried this under the name of Nixon. Jeeves's Uncle Charlie Silversmith is butler at Deverill Hall and quite in the whirl of the plot of *The Mating Season*. His daughter, Jeeves's cousin Queenie, marries the local consta-ble Dobbs – a church wedding presumably, because by the happy ending of the book Constable Dobbs has been cured of his atheism.

Jeeves has a cousin who is a constable at Beckley-on-the-Moor in Yorkshire, and another cousin who is a jeweller, who taught Jeeves all (and it is considerable) that he knows about pearls and diamonds. He has a third cousin of whom we know nothing because Bertie made Jeeves dam up a flood of reminiscence that was just starting intempestively. And he has that niece who is now Mrs Biffen. She married Bertie's forgetful friend, and £15,000 a year into the bargain.

Of Jeeves's early love-life we know very little, and he doesn't seem to have one at all in the later books. He had an 'understanding' with the present Lady Bittlesham, the then Jane Watson who was Bingo Little's uncle's cook. But the uncle decided to marry his cook to make sure that nobody lured her away from his kitchen. This was, in the story, something of a relief to Jeeves, because he had already got his eye on a young lady called Mabel whom he had met at a subscription dance in Camberwell. This was the Mabel with whom Bingo Little had for a short while been in love, and to whom Bingo introduced Bertie at that dreadful tea-shop near the Ritz. We do not know what became of Mabel. She does not appear in Jeeves's later life, and he does not seem to be mourning her absence or her loss. Jeeves was kissed by a twelve-year-old schoolgirl, Peggy Mainwaring, who sounded nice, but got Bertie into a lot of trouble at Miss Mapleton's school. Jeeves had read Peggy's father's (Professor Mainwaring) philosophical treatises, but he found the opinions expressed in them somewhat empirical. Stiffy Byng once proposed to kiss Jeeves, but she didn't make contact.

Before we study, and theorise about Jeeves's reading and education (he plays bridge and can type and do shorthand), we should perhaps gather what little else of his history has been revealed. Jeeves says he 'dabbled in' the First World War to a certain extent. It seems generally accepted that he feeds largely on fish, and that fish supplies phosphorus to the giant brain. Himself, he has said that he eats 'little or no' fish, but Bertie keeps forgetting this. (A prep school headmaster whom I knew, a Wodehouse addict, in the summer term took groups of his top form boys to sit for public school scholarships and, a tribute to Jeeves, it was fish for breakfast at the hotels each morning for all his young hopefuls. That was an order.) Alcohol has a sedative, not a stimulating effect on Jeeves. He says once that he smokes only gaspers, though he has been seen enjoying a cigar and, when Bertie asked

Jeeves's mother had thought him intelligent as a child, and in adult years he reads Spinoza, Nietzsche and Professor Mainwaring. Also Dostoevsky and the great Russians. I have made a cursory count of the sources from which he has ready quotations, and can establish Lucretius, Pliny the Younger, Whittier, Fitzgerald, Pater, Shelley, Kipling, Keats, Scott, Wordsworth, Emerson, Marcus Aurelius, Shakespeare, Browning, Rosie M. Banks, Moore, Virgil, Horace, Dickens, Tennyson, Milton, Henley, the Bible, Stevenson, Gray, Burns, Byron and whoever it was who wrote 'The Wreck of the Hesperus'. Wodehouse has clearly siphoned off into Jeeves all his tags of sixth-form reading, and Jeeves speaks copperplate *Times* Augustan to Bertie's *Sporting Life* vernacular.

'The scheme I would suggest cannot fail of success, but it has what may seem to you a drawback, sir, in that it requires certain financial outlay.'
'He means,' I translated to Corky, 'that he has got a pippin of an idea, but it's going to cost a bit.'

him, in *Thank You, Jeeves*, if he had such a thing as a cigarette on his person, Jeeves offered him a choice of Turkish and Virginian. Bertie describes Jeeves as 'tallish, with one of those dark, shrewd faces' and reiterates that his head sticks out at the back. When he wears a hat, it is a No. 8 bowler. He probably wears it for shrimping at Bognor.

Jeeves gives the impression of never being amused or rattled. When he is disapproving to Bertie, he looks something like a governess, something like an aunt. He has a silent walk and, when attacked about the ankles by a Scottie, can do a smooth high-jump on to a dresser. On the other hand he can deal with an infuriated nesting swan on an island in a rainstorm with total efficiency. Bertie passes on the Jeeves technique to his readers:

Every young man starting life ought to know how to cope with an angry swan, so I will briefly relate the proper procedure. You begin by picking up the raincoat which somebody has dropped: and then, judging the distance to a nicety, you simply shove the raincoat over the bird's head; and, taking the boat-hook which you have prudently brought with you, you insert it underneath the swan and heave. The swan goes into a bush and starts trying to unscramble itself; and you saunter back to your boat, taking with you any friends who may happen at the moment to be sitting on roofs in the vicinity. That was Jeeves's method, and I cannot see how it could have been improved upon.

Jeeves had said: 'In the presence of the unusual, Mr Wooster is too prone to smile weakly and allow his eyes to protrude.' There has been hardly anything unusual enough to rock Jeeves. When he first saw Boko Fittleworth, Bertie's untidy author friend, Jeeves blenched and retired to the kitchen 'doubtless to pull himself together with cooking sherry'. And he clutched at a table when Bingo Little turned up at the flat wearing a beard. Otherwise he has remained calm and dignified, with an occasional twitch of the lip or eyebrow. No more.

Bertie's friends, Reggie Foljambe and Alistair Bingham-Reeves, have tried to lure Jeeves away for gold, but he is bribe-proof so long as Bertie behaves, and doesn't marry. He runs his 'big Mayfair consulting practice' from Berkeley Mansions and Bertie is quite used to finding people consulting the oracle direct, without coming to him first. 'Jeeves isn't the only onion in the hash,' says Bertie, piqued. But in his calmer moments Bertie knows that that is just what Jeeves is. Jeeves's motto is 'Resource and Tact', and he knows that employers need managing. He managed Bertie for sixty happy years.

Hilaire Belloc singles Jeeves out as Wodehouse's prime contribution to

that long gallery of living figures which makes up the glory of English fiction.... In his creation of Jeeves he has done something which may respectfully be compared to the work of the Almighty in Michelangelo's painting. He has formed a man filled with the breath of life.... I should like the foreigner or posterity (much the same thing) to steep themselves in the living image of Jeeves and thus comprehend what the English character in action may achieve. Talk of efficiency.... If in, say, fifty years Jeeves and any other of that great company – but in particular Jeeves – shall have faded, then what we have so long called England will no longer be.

I would not put so nationalistic a label on Jeeves as Belloc does in this trumpet-tongued peroration. And I am sure that Bertie Wooster is a greater (and more difficult) creation than his manservant. As a pair they are much more than the sum of their single selves. I see Bertie as a marvellously constructed model ship inside the protecting and encompassing bottle that is Jeeves. And I see Wodehouse less as the Almighty passing life to a single Adam through his finger-tip, more (and equally respectfully) as a microscopic craftsman of highly ingenious *trompe l'il* puppets confined in ingenious artificial settings.

Bertie suggested to Jeeves that when he died he should bequeath his brain to the nation. I'd be more interested, if I were the nation, or a brain specialist, in studying Wodehouse's brain: the brain that fabricated Jeeves's great one and Bertie's tiny one.

NUGGETS The Female of the Species

It was a surprise to read, in the novel that Wodehouse left unfinished when he died, now *Sunset at Blandings*, the advice given to the timid Chancellor of the Exchequer by his dominant sister: 'If you want to marry Lord Emsworth's sister Diana, you must dominate her. The Threepwood girls abominate weakness.' I thought all the Threepwood 'girls' – Constance, Hermione, Julia, Georgiana, you name them – dominated, or had dominated, their husbands; Constance indeed two husbands. *Sunset at Blandings*, in this way, cancelled the 'teaching' of all the previous ninety-one books – that, although a girl approves of a bit of cave-man dominance in wooing, when she is won she does the dominating for the rest of married life. In the many plots that hinge on husband/wife joint bank accounts, is it ever the husband who keeps the cheque-book? No. In *The Girl on the Boat* Jane Howard, the big-game hunter, positively looks for a weak man to marry, and catches the ideal chap, mother-dominated Eustace Hignett. In *Money in the Bank* it's another Eustace and another big-game huntress: little Eustace Trumper, a Balliol man, positively flaunts his littleness, meekness and weakness to win the love and protection of Mrs Cork. Rosie rules the Little roost, Agatha rules Lord Worplesdon, Stiffy rules Stinker, Bobbie won't stand any nonsense from Kipper, nor Honoria from Blair. And I bet Veronica has Tipton under her thumb by now and may even have forbidden him drink. Even Sue probably bosses Ronnie. It really is odd about *Sunset at Blandings*.

Honoria Glossop was one of those large, strenuous, dynamic girls with the physique of a middle-weight catch-as-catch-can wrestler and a laugh resembling the sound of the Scotch Express going under a bridge. The effect she had on me was to make me slide into a cellar and lie low till they blew the All Clear.

Bobbie Wickham, a one-girl beauty chorus.

I was compelled to remind myself that an English gentleman does not swat a sitting redhead.

He and Rosie had always been like a couple of turtle doves, but he knew only too well that when the conditions are right, a female turtle dove can express herself with a vigour which a Caribbean hurricane might envy.

Dinty took over the conduct of affairs with the quiet, efficient smoothness so characteristic of women when they are about to embark on a course of action not scrupulously honest.

She was feeling like a mother who, in addition to having to notify him that there is no candy, has been compelled to strike a loved child on the base of the skull with a stocking full of sand.

She gave a sniff that sounded like a nor'easter ripping the sails of a stricken vessel.

Like so many of these big muscle-bound men, he was a mere serf in the home.

The exquisite code of politeness of the Woosters prevented me clipping her one on the ear-hole.

The whole wheeze in married life, Bingo had come to learn, was to give the opposite number as few opportunities of saying 'Oh, how could you?' as possible.

It is a curious fact, and one frequently noted by philosophers, that every woman in the world cherishes within herself a deep-rooted belief, from which nothing can shake her, that the particular man to whom she has plighted her love is to be held personally blameworthy for practically all of the untoward happenings of life.

Few things in life are more embarrassing than the necessity of having to inform an old friend that you have just got engaged to his fiancée.

58 OTHER MEMORABLE PEOPLE AND A MEMORABLE PIG

Arnold Abney, M.A.

Headmaster of the boys' private school, Sanstead House in Hampshire: 'quite a small school, but full of little dukes and earls and things.' He is long and suave, with an air of hushed importance: a great snob and a runner-up-to-London. As the action of *The Little Nugget* hots up, he recedes into the background. He is mentioned again, by mistake, in *Much Obliged, Jeeves*, where Bertie Wooster says he was *his* prep school HM.

Adair

He is not given a Christian name. He is not the sort of boy anybody at school would try to call by his Christian name. He is that rare (this is Wodehouse speaking) being, the boy who loves his school passionately. He is captain of Sedleigh, cricket and football. He is in the Shooting VIII, good at fives, had won the Mile two years running, and would have boxed at Aldershot if he hadn't sprained his wrist. Serious, dedicated and a bit of a bore, he disapproves of Mike Jackson and Psmith, elderly and scornful new boys, especially when Mike, whom he knows to be a star cricketer, refuses to play.

Anatole

The great chef. Anatole (he is not given a surname), 'God's gift to the gastric juices', is in the employ of Bingo and Rosie Little in 'Clustering Round Young Bingo' in *Carry on, Jeeves*. But Rosie needs a housemaid, and Bertie's Aunt Dahlia needs a good cook. Rosie is writing, for Aunt Dahlia's magazine, *Milady's Boudoir*, a piece titled 'How I Keep The Love of My Husband-Baby'. This, wails Bingo, must be stopped at all costs. And the cost is Anatole. Jeeves plays both ends against the middle. Rosie gets her housemaid and loses her chef. Aunt Dahlia gets a chef and loses Rosie's piece for her magazine.

Anatole settles into the Travers kitchens – Brinkley Court, Charles Street and the yacht – without any threats of reprisals from the Littles. Uncle Tom Travers's liver is at peace, and this means peace in the home and willing subsidies from Uncle Tom's wealth to pay Aunt Dahlia's debts on the magazine. Also Aunt Dahlia can always get her greedy nephew Bertie to obey her hair-raising demands by threatening to forbid him Anatolian meals unless he does what he is told. And when Sir Watkyn Bassett J.P., catches Bertie in a theft instigated by Aunt Dahlia, and proposes to jug him for thirty days without the option, what a meal that is which he and his aunt sketch out to celebrate his eventual enlargement!

He is a tubby little man, Anatole, with an outsize moustache which sticks up at the ends if he is happy and droops if he is not. Before being with the Littles, he had two years in Nice, with an American family who also had a Brooklyn-Irish chauffeur. From him Anatole had picked up some strange and wonderful English, but not much. He is volatile. He is mercenary. Sir Watkyn tries to lure him away from the Travers kitchens to his own (*The Code of the Woosters*). Mrs Trotter of Liverpool tries to get him in *Jeeves and the Feudal Spirit*. Mr Runkle covets him in *Much Obliged, Jeeves*. Uncle Tom is at one stage prepared to trade him to Sir Watkyn in return for a silver cow-creamer. Aunt Dahlia herself bets him against Jane Snettisham's kitchenmaid in 'The Love That Purifies'. With such transfers threatened, Aunt Dahlia has to keep Anatole's salary in the topmost bracket.

Anatole, who presumably cooks for himself and other Travers staff, gets an occasional *mal au foie* and retires to his bed. Butler Seppings gets a *mal au foie* (in English) from, or in spite of, Anatole's cooking. Such luxury! Those *Timbales de ris de veau Toulousaine*! Those *Sylphides à la crème d'écrevisses*! Bertie tells us that Anatole is at his best in the pheasant season. As it is always tea-on-the-lawn/bathe-in-the-lake high summer in the books in which Anatole is part of the plot, we must take Bertie's word for it that the best, in any year, is still to come.

Mr Anstruther

'A rather moth-eaten septuagenarian', this old friend of Aunt Dahlia's late father was at Brinkley when Bertie and Jeeves arrived in 'The Love That Purifies' story in *Very Good, Jeeves*. Caught in the firing line in a quarrel between two small boys, he gets a bucket of water midships. 'In one second, without any training or upbringing, he had become the wettest man in Worcestershire.' Mr Anstruther wins a place among Wodehouse's important characters on that sentence alone.

Bassett, Sir Watkyn and Madeline

One Boat Race Night Bertie Wooster had, as was his custom, tried to part a London policeman from his helmet. And that's what brought him first to the attention of Sir Watkyn Bassett, then magistrate at the Bosher Street court. He fined Bertie £5 and, though Bertie was on several occasions engaged, however briefly, to be married to Sir Watkyn's daughter, Madeline, his relationship to his threatened father-in-law was never cordial.

Sir Watkyn retired having, allegedly, inherited a fortune. Bertie always assumed this was just a cover story for his having trousered the fines in his court. At all events Totleigh Towers, the considerable Bassett spread in Gloucestershire, was an ill-omened place for Bertie and Jeeves to visit, and Sir Watkyn not a cheery host. He was a collector of old silver and *objets d'art* generally, and a rival in this of Bertie's uncle, Tom Travers. Sir Watkyn, and especially his crony Roderick Spode, later Lord Sidcup, generally suspected Bertie of having designs on some *objet*. And they were generally right.

A widower and courting a widow (a Mrs Wintergreen), Sir Watkyn is, in two books, a threat and a hindrance to men and women of good will. He nobbles Tom Travers by feeding him cold lobster for lunch at his club. He tries to steal Mrs Travers's great chef Anatole. He covets, and does briefly employ, Bertie's Jeeves. As a country J.P., he dispenses prison or punishment to suspected malefactors at whim and without trial. He is a bad man, a heavy, one of Wodehouse's best.

His daughter Madeline is beautiful, but soupily and squashily sentimental (she thinks that the stars are God's daisy-chain). She is a threat, too, certainly to Bertie. Originally Bertie's friend Gussie Fink-Nottle, the newt-fancier, had fallen in love with her, but did not dare to declare himself. So Bertie stupidly tried – the old plot – to break the news to Madeline. She deduced that shy, hesitant Bertie was really voicing his own love for her, and for ever afterwards, when she and Gussie broke their engagement, she rounded on Bertie and took him for her future-wedded husband. After many books she will be marrying Roderick Spode, now Lord Sidcup, who has loved her silently since her childhood.

Right Ho, Jeeves, The Code of the Woosters, The Mating Season (Madeline doesn't come on stage here, but she is engaged, off, to Gussie who is on stage centre), *Stiff Upper Lip, Jeeves* and *Much Obliged, Jeeves* are the novels in which the chronicles of Madeline Bassett and her father are written.

Rupert Baxter

The Efficient Baxter with gleaming spectacles – in the beginning (*Something Fresh*) he is a good secretary to Lord Emsworth, duteous, an authority on scarabs, appreciated. He becomes a menace and a bogey-man in the later Blandings books, suspecting nice impostors of being impostors, disliked by the staff and filling Lord Emsworth with dread. Lady Constance would like her brother to take Baxter back as secretary.

It is at the end of *Leave it to Psmith*, when Baxter, shut out of the castle in yellow pyjamas in the dawn, throws flowerpots at Lord Emsworth's bedroom windows, that Lord Emsworth decides that Baxter is 'mad as a coot', and sacks him. And although his later employment with Mr Jevons, the Chicago tycoon, is profitable, Baxter still hankers to apply his efficiency to Lord Emsworth's affairs and domain. It is only when, in 'The Crime Wave at Blandings' (*Lord Emsworth and Others*), as prospective holiday tutor to young George the grandson, Baxter gets a fusillade of airgun pellets on his hinder parts that he is convinced that he is better off with Mr Jevons.

He has had no luck at the castle: his love spurned by Sue Brown (he thinks she is the rich Miss Schoonmaker); his caravan filled with the Empress of Blandings; his face hit by an egg hurled by his (then) employer the Duke of Dunstable – and always Lord Emsworth remembering back to the flower-pots. See also *Summer Lightning* and *Uncle Fred in the Springtime*.

Sebastian Beach

Eighteen years in service at Blandings Castle, risen from the footman ranks, once, in *Something Fresh*, with an under-butler, Merridew, to boss, Beach is our favourite of, at final count, sixty-one Wodehouse butlers. He has been a friend of all the Blandings nephews and nieces, pretending to be a bear or a hippopotamus to amuse them as children, serving them port and comfort when they have come to port-drinking age and, for Master Ronald, who, even when at Eton, had given him profitable racing tips, positively assisting in the hijacking and maintenance of his master's champion pig.

In those *Something Fresh* days Beach was a hypochondriac, having corns and an interesting stomach as conversation pieces. But in the later books, though he is fat, he is not an invalid. He is a bachelor, but he had been one for the girls in his footman days. He keeps a scrapbook and pastes into it items from the press about the Threepwood clan. Long ago (like Bertie Wooster) he had won a choirboys' bicycle race. Just recently he won the Market Blandings Darts Tournament. He inherited the library of thrillers that Freddie Threepwood collected before his marriage. His bullfinch bursts into song when he hears his master's tread approaching in the passage. He has gone briefly to prison on the orders of the Justice of the Peace who will later become his nephew-in-law.

The castle could not run without Beach. And now that his niece has become Lady Parsloe at Matchingham Hall nearby, she may heal the breach between those two old sillies, her husband and her uncle's employer.

Remember Beach singing 'Pig-hoo-o-o-o-ey!' with Lord Emsworth and niece Angela outside the Empress's sty? Remember Beach putting the green baize over the bullfinch in his pantry when Master Ronald was persuading him to help hijack the Empress? Remember the roar of laughter from Beach when he read, in the manuscript of Gally's Reminiscences, the story of Sir Gregory and the prawns? Remember Beach, beyond the call of duty, reading *The Care of the Pig* aloud to Lord Emsworth when the latter's eyes got tired? Remember how, when angry Baxter had left the castle in a hurry, the great front door had been closed behind him 'with a soft but significant bang – as doors close when handled by an untipped butler'?

Beach is eminent or immanent in twelve books. In the first of them, which has a wintry start, he has a fire, a kettle and whisky to make a hot toddy for a visiting valet. In those that follow it is always port and the castle is bathed in summer. He has resigned once, fearing the sack for shooting at Baxter with the air-gun. He was on the point of resigning over the ghastly beard that Lord Emsworth grew. Lady Constance has called for his retirement on pension. But these crises blew over. Beach remains, cornerstone of a great house.

George Bevan

By the date, 1919, of *A Damsel in Distress*, Wodehouse was deep, and profitably, into the theatre world.

George Bevan is American and a composer – Jerome Kern rather than P.G. Wodehouse. But one feels that there's more of the latter than of the former in this tall, well-knit, Harvard-educated, golf-playing composer, who is taking three per cent of the gross of the smash hit 'Follow The Girl'. He will marry Lord Marshmoreton's daughter, Lady Maud Marsh, who has a tip-tilted nose and goes round the golf course in the low 80s. *A Damsel in Distress* is one of Wodehouse's best contributions to Anglo-American entente.

Monty Bodkin

Montague (or Montrose – Wodehouse plays it both ways) Bodkin, tall, lissom, amiable, is the second richest man at the Drones. But the father of the girl he loves, hockey international Gertrude Butterwick, insists on his holding down a job, any job, for a year to show his worthiness to be his son-in-law. In *Heavy Weather* Monty is employed by Lord Tilbury, Lord Emsworth and Percy Pilbeam in that order. In *The Luck of the Bodkins* he is, for devious reasons, given a job in Hollywood by Ivor Llewellyn of Superba-Llewellyn. Travelling to America in the same ship as Gertrude, he becomes perilously involved with film-star Lottie Blossom. Gertrude, encouraged by her father, is always quick to suspect her fiancé of infidelity. There had been trouble about that 'Sue', with a heart round it, tattooed on Monty's chest.

In *Pearls, Girls and Monty Bodkin* Monty very sensibly rejoices in being given his freedom by Gertrude. He will marry young, shrimp-sized American, Sandy Miller. Sandy had long longed to stroke his hair, and you know what that means – pure girlish love.

Jno. Bodmin

His shop is in Vigo Street and over its door you may read 'Bespoke Hatter to The Royal Family'.

'That means, in simple language adapted to the lay intelligence, that if the King wants a new topper, he simply ankles round to Bodmin's and says "Good morning, Bodmin, we want a topper". He does not ask if it will fit. He has bespoken Jno. Bodmin and he trusts him blindly.'

Well, in that classic story 'The Amazing Hat Mystery' (*Young Men in Spats*) two Dronesmen, one very large the other very small, get their new Bodmin toppers switched. And this brings about a happy switch of fiancées.

Joe Boffin

Droitgate Spa, like any other, was a hot-bed of invalid snobbery. In the Pump Room a duke with asthma might always be high-hatted and snubbed by a commoner whom the doctors had twice given up for dead. Major General Sir Aylmer Bastable suffered from a gouty foot and the inferiority that this negligible ailment entitled him to. But he was eagerly courted by the aritocrats the moment they learnt that his nephew was going to marry the niece of 'Boffin of St Luke's', a cad and an eyesore, but a famous invalid who had spent most of his life in hospitals, had had a temperature of 107.5 once and had been interviewed for the Christmas number of *The Lancet*.

'Romance at Droitgate Spa': one for the anthologies, in *Eggs, Beans and Crumpets*.

Brinkley/Bingley

In *Thank You, Jeeves* Jeeves gave notice and Bertie hired a new man from the agency. Brinkley was a communist, got drunk and, thinking Bertie (who was blacked up as a minstrel just then) to be the Devil, pursued him with a carving knife. He also set fire to the cottage where Bertie was staying. Bertie sacked him.

But he turned up again as Rupert Bingley in *Much Obliged, Jeeves*. Wodehouse doesn't explain the name change. But, as most of the events of *Much Obliged, Jeeves* centre on Bertie's Aunt Dahlia's place, Brinkley Court in Worcestershire, the reason seems clear. By this time Bingley has become a man of property, with a butler of his own. But he is still a country member of the Junior Ganymede and he called Jeeves 'Reggie'. He seems to have given up his communism. Possibly drink, too. One wonders how many other members of the Junior Ganymede have butlers of their own.

Sue Brown

Sue is the best and most important chorus girl in all Wodehouse, and Gally, by hook, crook, blackmail and self-sacrifice, gets her into the Blandings family. He is prejudiced in Sue's favour when he learns, first, that she is at the castle under an assumed name – an impostor, no less. And then, she turns out to be the daughter of the only girl Gally has ever loved, dear, departed Dolly Henderson of the Tivoli and old Oxford.

Sue is engaged, secretly so far, to Ronnie Fish, small, pink, jealous son of Lord Emsworth's tough sister Julia. She had been engaged to Monty Bodkin once, and that upsets Ronnie. She is being pursued, with flowers and proposals, by the loathsome Percy Pilbeam, and that upsets Ronnie. And Ronnie's mother is doing her best to kill her son's proposal to marry a chorus girl. That upsets Ronnie. Lord Emsworth is Ronnie's sole trustee (a plot-hinge in so many of the Blandings-based romances) and, under the batterings of two such sisters as Lady Julia and Lady Constance, he can't bring himself to release Ronnie's money so that he can marry Sue. There is a moment when Ronnie and Sue have the Empress in the back of the two-seater and are going to take her away until her owner redeems her with his signature on the money and blessing on the marriage.

Sue is Mrs Ronnie Fish now. Hats off to Gally!

'Sue Brown appears in *Summer Lighting* and *Heavy Weather*.

Stephanie ('Stiffy') Byng

She is now Mrs Pinker, wife of Bertie Wooster's Oxford friend, boxing Blue and rugger international the Rev. Harold ('Stinker') Pinker, vicar of Hockley-cum-Meston. But it took Stiffy two whole novels to get there, *The Code of the Woosters* and *Stiff Upper Lip, Jeeves*. She lived at Totleigh Towers with her ankle-chewing Aberdeen terrier, Bartholemew, and her guardian and honorary uncle, Sir Watkyn Bassett. Quick-tempered and ruthless, she had a feud on with the local constable of police, Oates, whom Bartholemew had seen bicycling without hands and had tipped into a ditch. And her beloved, the sainted Harold, was instructed to steal the enemy's helmet to teach him a lesson. Which Harold, whose love for Stiffy overpowered his clerical scruples, did.

Harold couldn't marry her on a curate's stipend, so she was always promoting schemes to get Uncle Watkyn to give the vacant vicarage of Totleigh to Harold. Jeeves finally fixed things for the young couple. A great girl, Stiffy.

The Carlisles, the Molloys and Chimp Twist

I do not think Soapy Sid and Aline Hemmingway, in 'Aunt Agatha Takes the Count', were married; nor Edward Cootes and Aileen Peavey in *Leave it to Psmith*. But Wodehouse had two husband-and-wife crook teams who served him well in seven hunt-the-treasure novels: Thos G ('Soapy') and Dolly Molloy and Gordon ('Oily') and Gertrude ('Sweetie') Carlisle. The Molloys operate in *Ice in the Bedroom*, *Money for Nothing*, *Money in the Bank*, *Ice in The Bedroom* and *Pearls, Girls and Monty Bodkin*. The Carlisles are in *Hot Water* and *Cocktail Time*.

There's not much to choose between these two twosomes. Oily sells dud copper-mine shares; Soapy sells dud oil stock, and both are at the top of their specialist trees. Both are bossed by their cleverer wives. When Dolly and Soapy first appear, in *Ice in the Bedroom*, they have just got married. When Gertie and Oily first appear, in *Hot Water*, they have married, quarrelled and separated. She had hit him on the head with a vase containing glad-ioli, which had almost spoiled the honeymoon. They met again in the French holiday resort of St Rocque. She was now 'Medway', maid to rich American Mrs Gedge, and he was 'M. le duc de Pont-Andemer'. He had started life as a 'lumberer', that is, a man who has found a ruby ring in a gutter and will sell it dirt cheap to a sucker. Oily always keeps a ruby ring on him as a reminder of those early innocent days at the bottom of the ladder.

Dolly is the Molloy with the more exciting past. She had been Dora Gunn, known to her friends as 'Fainting Dolly' because she was adept at fainting into the arms of rich-look-ing customers in the street and picking their pockets while being revived. She is an accom-plished shoplifter still. She and Soapy always carry knockout drops to settle arguments. If the Carlisles do (they probably do), it is not specified. All four are American. For Wodehouse they operate only in England.

The Molloys are the more interesting pair: not only because they are given greater scope – five novels against the Carlisles' two. But they're really a threesome. Where there's treasure to be found or stolen and the Molloys close in, there's always Chimp Twist to be reckoned with. The three of them have been friendly partners in a few jobs, we understand, but in these novels the partnership isn't friendly at all.

> 'I'll tell you, honey,' says Soapy to his Dolly. 'I'm not so darned sure that I sort of kind of like bringing Chimp into a thing like this. You know what he is – as slippery as an eel that's been rubbed all over with axle-grease. He might double-cross us.'
> 'Not if we double-cross him first.'
>
> *Money for Nothing*

Alexander ('Chimp') Twist 'has the face of an untrustworthy monkey'. In *Money for Nothing* he is Dr Alexander Twist, 'the well-known physician and physical culture expert' and he is running 'Healthward Ho', where rich clients pay big fees to be exercised by a sergeant major and forbidden food, drink and smoking. For subsequent books he is Sheringham Adair, Private Investigator, of Halsey Chambers, Mayfair. He gets hired to protect treasures or to watch a butler, or to find a missing husband, or (as a valet) to watch a greedy, fat husband and see that he doesn't diverge from the strict diet his wife has put him on to. But there's a treasure in all these stories, and always the Molloys come in to get their hooks on it when Chimp is preparing to get *his* hooks on it.

They all three fail, again and again. And they retire hurt and cursing: the Molloys cursing Chimp and Chimp the Molloys. They have given very good value, for nil reward, in all the books.

D'Arcy ('Stilton') Cheesewright

He had been at Eton and Oxford with Bertie and had rowed in the Oxford Eight. Huge, strong and a jealous lover, Stilton was a menace to Bertie in two novels, *Joy in the Morning* and *Jeeves and the Feudal Spirit*. In the former he is a country policeman, bicycling his beats, bathing in the river, at Steeple Bumpleigh, where his fiancée, Lady Florence Craye, lives in the big house with her father, Lord Worplesdon, and her step-mother (whom she calls 'Mother'), Bertie's Aunt Agatha. Stilton, although he has a rich uncle prepared to finance him into Parliament, stubbornly insists on starting on the bottom rung of policemanship and lifting himself by his own bootlaces to, he proposes, great heights in the Force.

He finds out that Bertie was once engaged to Florence (what man in Wodehouse hasn't been at some time?) and is steamed up with jealousy thinking Bertie is still in love with her and waiting his chance. Not so, but far otherwise. But Bertie's evisceration seems inevitable. Enter, then, fortunately, litterateuse Daphne Dolores Morehead, beautiful blonde bombshell best-seller. Stilton falls for her like a ton of bricks and hand in hand they walk out of Florence's life. And Bertie's.

James Orlebar Cloyster

He is the hero (of sorts) in that strange early novel, *Not George Washington*, which Wodehouse wrote in collaboration with his wayward friend Herbert Westbrook. That said, one's only interest in Cloyster, a journalist, is that he does things that we know the young Wodehouse did and lived in digs at the Walton Street address where the young Wodehouse had lived. Any glimpse of Wodehouse through Wodehouse's eyes is interesting, and it is interesting that he could have put his name to such an incompetent novel.

James Corcoran

He is the narrator of, and listener to, all the Ukridge short stories in *Ukridge* and one other of those scattered through *Lord Emsworth and Others*, *Eggs, Beans and Crumpets*, *Nothing*

Serious, *A Few Quick Ones* and *Plum Pie*. Corky is a reasonable self-portrait of the young, struggling Wodehouse. He is a journalist, prepared to go anywhere, write anything for which an editor will pay, careful with his hard-earned money.

The Ukridge stories, whether told by the long-suffering Corky or by Corky's only begetter, are fast, spare and funny.

Mr Cornelius

If you find yourself in Mulberry Grove, Valley Fields, London SE21 on a weekend, and if you see a man with a long white beard feeding his rabbits, tending his flowers or sitting under a tree reading a Leila Yorke novel, you're looking into the garden of The Nook, and the man with the beard is Mr Cornelius. He's half of Matters and Cornelius, House Agents, of Ogilvy Street. He is writing, in his spare time, a History of Valley Fields. He was born here, was at school here and has lived all his life here. He wouldn't want to live anywhere else, and he's apt to tell you so, and to quote at you twelve lines on the trot of that 'Breathes there a man with soul so dead...' bit of Walter Scott. He quoted it to Sam Shotter in *Sam the Sudden* and again to Dolly Molloy in *Ice in the Bedroom*.

Don't tell his wife, but Mr Cornelius is very rich. You see, Mr Cornelius's brother Charles left England years ago, under something of a cloud, went to America and did very well, with an apartment in Park Avenue, houses on Long Island and in Florida, an aeroplane and a yacht. That all sounds good, but Mr Cornelius of Valley Fields has a reservation. Brother Charles couldn't have been entirely happy because he didn't live in Valley Fields. Well, brother Charles is dead now and he left his money to Mr Cornelius. Mr Cornelius has not told dear Mrs Cornelius that, because she is happy as she is and, if she knew they were rich, she'd make Mr Cornelius live up to it, like going to the opera and playing polo. But if Freddie Widgeon wants a mere £3,000 to marry Sally Foster and go coffee-farming in Kenya, Mr Cornelius will lend it to him readily. But – not a word to the wife.

Valley Fields is the West Dulwich of Wodehouse's schooldays. The silver-voiced clock on the big tower over the College still strikes the quarters as it did for schoolboy Wodehouse (P.G.) and in *Sam the Sudden*. Wodehouse comes back to Valley Fields in novel after novel, always with affection.

Mr Cornelius has rented houses to most of the Valley Fields residents we meet, and he knows, who better?, that Mon Repos and San Raphael were once a single house – information which helps Sam Shotter locate the two million dollars stolen from the New Asiatic Bank and stashed away by the late 'Finky' Finglass. So Chimp Twist and Dolly and Soapy Molloy are foiled.

Mr Cornelius is in *Sam the Sudden*, *Big Money* and *Ice in the Bedroom*: Valley Fields is in these and many more.

Craye, Lady Florence and Edwin

Only daughter of Percy, Earl of Worplesdon, Lady Florence Craye was Bertie Wooster's first recorded fiancée ('Jeeves Take Charge' in *Carry On, Jeeves*). She is, much against his wishes, his fiancée in *Jeeves and the Feudal Spirit*, and again in *Aunts Aren't Gentlemen*. She is a platinum blonde and has a terrific profile, but she is domineering and 'steeped to the gills in serious purpose', and she plans to mould Bertie and improve his mind. She is author of the novel *Spindrift* which another fiancé, Percy Gorringe, dramatises and which closes after three nights at the Duke of York's – so Percy is dismissed as a loser. 'England is strewn with ex-fiancés whom she bounced because they did not come up to her specifications.' Other than the recurrent Bertie and Percy Gorringe, the bounced fiancés include Stilton Cheesewright (*Joy in the Morning* and *Jeeves and the Feudal Spirit*), Ginger Winship (*Aunts Aren't Gentlemen*), Boko Fittleworth and a gentleman jockey, unnamed, whose fault it had been to take a spill at the Canal Turn in the Grand National. Her re-engagement to Bertie in *Aunts Aren't Gentlemen* lasts for a single page and she then accepts someone's word (as Madeline Bassett in *Stiff Upper Lip, Jeeves*) that Bertie is a kleptomaniac. She remains unmarried to the end of the canon. She has given Wodehouse great mileage.

Her young brother, ferret-faced Edwin, might be a viscount. As only son, however pestilential, of an earl, he is entitled to the precedence of a viscount, surely. But in the chronicles, related by his (sort of) cousin Bertie, he is 'young ruddy Edwin' or worse. He is about fourteen, of no known schooling, a keen Boy Scout, but always behind the calendar with his daily good deed. He gets considerably savaged in *Joy in the Morning*: having mistakenly set Bertie's cottage alight, he loses his eyebrows in the flames. Bertie boots him into a garden bed, and this endears Bertie to Edwin's sister (he has made a mess of her precious press-cuttings book) and his father (whom he has biffed, hard and low, with his Scout staff in a night-time fracas). Edwin had appeared first in the short story 'Jeeves Takes Charge' in *Carry On, Jeeves*, grassing to Bertie's Uncle Willoughby that Bertie has hijacked the manuscript of his memoirs on its way to the publishers.

Alaric, Duke of Dunstable

A real old brute, this duke. He invites himself, alone or with his secretary Baxter, or with his niece, Linda, to Blandings for three separate visits – *Uncle Fred in the Springtime*, *Service with a Smile* and *A Pelican at Blandings*, and Lady Constance can't say No to him. She does tell him once that he has the manners of a pig, but he thinks she's potty. He thinks practically everyone is potty – that his father had been potty, that both his nephews are potty. Certainly he thinks Lord Emsworth is potty, about his pig and in an absolute sense.

Arrogant, bald, with a prominent nose and a cascade of white moustache, he is vastly rich and vastly mean. He had inherited wealth with the title and then had married a very rich girl from the North. She died and left him all her money. He was engaged to Connie once, and it is no surprise to learn that he broke it off because her father wouldn't provide her with a big enough dowry. She is very glad now that she never married him, but somehow she can't say No when he inflicts himself on the castle for extended visits.

He had been a bit of a bounder, apparently, when young, already rich and a Guardee. There had, earlier, been a girl who had had to be bought off when he was at Oxford. Gally's friend Stiffy Halliday had knocked the Duke out with a cold turkey at Romano's. Such things were certainly no bar to membership of the Pelican. But when the Duke came up for election, Gally remembers, the top-hat burst with blackballs against him.

Heloise, Princess von und zu Dwornitzchek

A most surprising Wodehouse character, a man-eating wicked step-mother in an otherwise cheerful novel, *Summer Moonshine*. She probably started life in a script for play or film written with a more worldly collaborator such as Guy Bolton. Her husbands have been a Mr Spelvin (in the fish-glue business), Franklin Vanringham (Joe Vanringham, her step-son, says she bullied him to death) and the Prince, whom she divorced. She is very rich and mean; has a yacht, a house in Berkeley Square, a butler, one of the best chefs in Mayfair and, as her current gigolo/fiancé, the ornamental heiress-hunter, Adrian Peake. She doesn't sound like a Wodehouse concept, does she?

Empress of Blandings

She is a splendid great fat Black Berskhire sow and, after his pumpkin phase, Lord Emsworth became happily obsessed with her, and he is still obsessed. He goes to her sty at night, just to listen to her breathing. She has won the Silver Medal, the highest honour, in the Fat Pigs Class at the Shrewsbury Agricultural Show three years running. Previously no pig had won it more than once.

For various and nefarious reasons she gets hijacked out of her sty from time to time. She goes off her feed when she misses George Cyril Wellbeloved (jugged for fourteen days for drunk and disorderly). She eats a carelessly dropped, still lighted cigar-end of Lord Emsworth's. She bites young Huxley Winkworth's finger. She eats a bit of pig-man Pirbright's Sunday hat. She eats the manuscript of Galahad's memoirs.

She has had a succession of custodians. The 'superbly gifted', but squint-eyed Wellbeloved was lured away for higher wages by Sir Gregory Parsloe of Matchingham Hall up the road. Wellbeloved came back to the castle for a period, but later was left a public house in Wolverhampton and now presumably gets all the drink he wants – which is a lot. Pirbright took over from Wellbeloved when he went to Matchingham. Pirbright is tall, thin, scraggy and (as all of them) niffy. Then Edwin Pott, a small gnome of a man with no roof to his mouth. He won a football pool and was last heard of in Canada. He was succeeded by Monica Simmons, niece of Sir Gregory, one of six daughters of a rural vicar, all of whom played hockey for Roedean. She has large feet and has referred to the Empress in Lord Emsworth's agonised hearing as 'the piggy-wiggy'. She will marry little Wilfred Allsop. To get up courage to propose to her he had got a flask of strong drink. But it fell into the Empress's trough and produced her one recorded bout of drunkenness. Monica Simmons was succeeded at the sty by Cuthbert Price. Who serves the Empress's meals now? We do not know. There is no pig-man or girl mentioned in *Sunset at Blandings*, though Lord Emsworth in that last, unfinished, novel is still trying to find an artist to paint the Empress's portrait for the Portrait Gallery at the castle.

Wodehouse's typescript for *Sunset at Blandings* reminds us of another problem: how much food did the Empress get? Lord Emsworth had always insisted on the Wolff-Lehmann diet as recommended by his favourite book, Whiffle's *The Care of the Pig* (or *On the Care of the Pig*) – a daily intake of 57,000 or more calories. In three separate passages in earlier books Wodehouse had given it as 57,800 calories, in one passage 57,500 and in the others 57,000. But in *Galahad at Blandings* he gave it twice as 5,700 calories, and this figure is repeated in the *Sunset at Blandings* typescript. I am assured by the Agricultural Press Ltd Information Service that 5,700 is a far more realistic figure than 57,800, and that the Lehmann pig feeding system was essentially one in which boiled or steamed potatoes were used to replace barley meal on a 4 to 1 basis. The Berkshire was once a numerous breed: now, however, it is a 'minor fancier's pig'. All Berkshires are black, though some-times white round the feet. Wodehouse refers to the Empress as a black Berkshire, but no illustrator took his word for it till after his death.

The Empress spans nine novels and a short story: *Summer Lightning*, *Heavy Weather*, 'Pig-Hoo-o-o-o-ey!' in *Blandings Castle*, *Uncle Fred in the Springtime*, *Full Moon*, *Pigs Have Wings*, *Service with a Smile*, *Galahad at Blandings*, *A Pelican at Blandings* and *Sunset at Blandings*.

Augustus Fink-Nottle

Gussie had been at school with Bertie Wooster. He lived in Lincolnshire, kept and studied newts, and was a teetotal bachelor with a face like a fish. Then he met Madeline Bassett. Too shy to declare his love, he let Bertie deliver the message for him, and Madeline was sure that Bertie was speaking for himself. But she accepted Gussie. Thereafter one of Bertie's preoccupations was to keep Gussie and Madeline happy and engaged and, if possi-ble, to hurry them to the altar. Otherwise Madeline might turf Gussie out and round on Bertie with, 'I will marry you, Bertie, and try to make you happy.'

A constant threat to Gussie is the enormous and angry Roderick Spode. A friend of Madeline's father, he has always loved Madeline (without telling her) and is prepared to pound to pulp any fiancé who does her wrong, breaks her heart or even neglects her. He assaults Gussie several times in the two novels in which they are opposed. Gussie finally elopes with the daughter of an American millionaire. Madeline is now the Countess of Sidcup. Spode had inherited the title.

Right Ho, Jeeves (in which Gussie is required to present the prizes at Market Snodsbury Grammar School and, to give him courage, Bertie and Jeeves lace his orange juice with gin with hilarious results). *The Code of the Woosters*, *The Mating Season* and *Stiff Upper Lip, Jeeves* all include Gussie.

Ogden Ford

Most of Wodehouse's boy characters are fiends (Young Thos Gregson, Bonzo Travers, Sebastian Moon, Braid Bates, Edwin Craye *et al.*). But Wodehouse loved them and we do, too. Not Ogden Ford. He's a real little stinker. A fat, undisciplined, spoiled, chain-smoking American boy, he is sent to a snobbish little English preparatory school, from which several people are trying to kidnap him for gain (*The Little Nugget*). He turns up again, equally odious, home in America, in *Piccadilly Jim*.

Sir Roderick Glossop, his daughter Honoria and his nephew Tuppy

Sir Roderick is one of the few major characters who commute between the worlds of Wooster and Blandings. Bald with big black eyebrows, a Harley Street loony-doctor and, when we first meet him in *The Inimitable Jeeves*, President of the West London branch of the Anti-Gambling League, he is a heavyweight heavy. Bertie Wooster's Aunt Agatha, a friend of Lady Glossop, thinks Honoria, the Glossops' daughter, would make Bertie a good, disciplinary wife ('The Pride of the Woosters is Wounded' in *The Inimitable Jeeves*, but 'Scoring off Jeeves' in the omnibus *World of Jeeves*). Later Sir Roderick suffers at the hands of Bertie's twin cousins, Claude and Eustace, and he decides that Bertie would be more suitable as a patient than as a son-in-law. Sir Roderick breaks up Bertie's engagement to the beautiful American Pauline Stoker by informing her father that Bertie is not the right son-in-law for him, either (*Thank You, Jeeves*). He appears in two stories in *Carry On, Jeeves* and, in 'Jeeves and the Yuletide Spirit' (*Very Good Jeeves*), he finds Bertie puncturing his hot water bottle in the small hours and once again pencils him in as a half-wit.

By the time of *Thank You, Jeeves* Sir Roderick must have lost the wife who had invited Bertie to Ditteridge Hall in the first place, because he is now courting Lord Chuffnell's Aunt Myrtle. He and Bertie, for different reasons, black their faces up as minstrels and they suffer together through the night from lack of butter to remove their blacking. Little Seabury, Aunt Myrtle's son, had made a butter-slide for Sir Roderick and that's where all the butter had gone. Little Seabury gets Harley Street treatment, free, on the seat of his pants.

Sir Roderick started his printed life as an angry elder threatening Bertie. In his last few appearances his forgiving author has made him rather a pa-man, blacking his face as a minstrel, padding up as Father Christmas, serving as butler with the name Swordfish, exchanging Christian names in the vocative with Bertie, the secrets of his schooldays revealed (he was nicknamed 'Pimples' and he stole the headmaster's biscuits) and medical student days (poverty, hunger and pushing someone into a lake in order to win merit by a rescue). But one still wonders what a Harley Street specialist charges for a week-long professional visit to a country house, disguised as, and with the duties of, a butler: or, for that matter, for a visit to America to treat a millionaire (millionaire J. Washburn Stoker's brother) for a tendency to walk on his hands.

There are difficulties about dates, publishing v. real times. For instance, in 'Jeeves and the Greasy Bird', in *Plum Pie* published in 1965, Aunt Dahlia is still running *Milady's Boudoir*, though in *Jeeves and the Feudal Spirit* (1954) she had sold it to the Leeds publisher, Lemuel Trotter. But who cares about such literary cruces? They passed Wodehouse by like the idle wind which he regarded not. In the cosy hereafter that we legitimately visualise for Wodehouse's characters, Sir Roderick and his Myrtle are man and wife, Little Seabury is less of a fiend, at a good boarding school with long terms and short holidays, Honoria is Mrs Blair Eggleston, and nephew Tuppy, enriched by the money long owed by L. P. Runkle (*Much Obliged, Jeeves*), has married Angela Travers. If Bertie ever got even with Tuppy after that dunking in the Drones swimming bath, the telling of it must join the others for which the world was still not ready when Wodehouse died: the arrest of Uncle Fred and Pongo at the dog races, Parsloe and the prawns, Young Thos and his liver pad and Anatole and the unwanted wedding present.

Mrs Spenser Gregson/Lady Worplesdon
Bertie Wooster's Aunt Agatha

Her first husband, Spenser Gregson, was a stockbroker who had made a fortune in Sumatran rubber. She had been engaged before that to Lord Worplesdon, or Percy Craye if he hadn't then inherited. But he had got his ring back smartly when she had read in the papers of his behaviour at a Covent Garden ball.

Agatha is totally unlike her sister Dahlia, Bertie's good aunt. Aunt Agatha, Bertie alleges, chews broken bottles, kills rats with her teeth and wears barbed wire next to the skin. She thinks Bertie is practically an idiot, tells him so and treats him like one. She comes on strong in early short stories, but recedes into being an off-stage threat in the novels: the aunt whose loathly son, Young Thos, Bertie has to board, lodge and take to the Old Vic (*Macbeth, Hamlet, Patience* and *The Seagull*) in exeats from school; the aunt who would be terrible in her wrath if she found out (about Lord Worplesdon, her husband, in *Joy in the Morning*, about Bertie impersonating Gussie Fink-Nottle in *The Mating Season*). In *Much Obliged, Jeeves*, published in 1971 when Wodehouse was ninety, we find that Bertie's main fear about the Junior Ganymede Book of Revelations is still (see *The Code of the Woosters*, 1938) that his Aunt Agatha shall somehow get to read what his manservants have written about him there.

Nobby (Zenobia) Hopwood

She appears in only one novel, *Joy in the Morning*. She is Lord Worplesdon's ward. Her father, too fond of pink gin, nearing his end, had begged his friend Percy Worplesdon (or perhaps still Craye) to look after her and see she didn't marry a blot on the landscape. Bertie's writer friend Boko was the lucky man who got her and she is now Mrs Boko Fittleworth in Hollywood. Partly because of 'young pipsqueak' Nobby, scheming, lying, blackmailing, raging, forgiving, loving, *Joy in the Morning* is a gem of a novel.

Mike Jackson

In the one-volume *Mike*, the last, longest and best of the public school novels, Mike is the coming Test cricketer. He has his problems as such as a new boy, with the head of his House, with his elder brother, with his form-master and with his father. After three years of bad form-reports and just when Mike is due to be captain of cricket, his father removes him from Wrykyn and sends him to Sedleigh, a smaller school, but with a reputation for making boys work. At Sedleigh, an elderly new boy with a grievance, he meets another elderly new boy, similarly removed, from Eton.

This is Psmith, and Wodehouse now lets Mike recede into the shadow cast by this premature adult. (Besides, Wodehouse had his foot in the door of the American market now, and cricket is not a subject that appeals to the American masses.) Mike's father, in the Argentine ranching business, loses a lot of money and Mike can't go to Cambridge. He starts work in the City at the New Asiatic Bank. And who should turn up as a fellow slave there but Psmith? The title of the book is *Psmith* (not *Mike*) *in the City*. Mike and Psmith go to America and the book's title then is *Psmith Journalist*. The last, of the two of them, is *Leave it to Psmith*. Here we find that Mike has eloped with and married Phyllis, step-daughter of Joe Keeble, millionaire husband of Lady Constance of Blandings. Mike is in a schoolmastering job. Psmith gets him out of that and into farming in Lincolnshire, which he will enjoy.

Mike had been, first and foremost, the public schoolboy, serious, rather solemn, modest, not a talker, not a brain – just a great batsman. And Wodehouse's chapters on cricket matches are some of the best in the fiction of the game. Wrykyn School was, to all intents and purposes, Wodehouse's own school, Dulwich. The New Asiatic Bank was the Hong Kong and Shanghai where Wodehouse himself had been a trainee.

The Littles – Bingo, Rosie and Algernon Aubrey

Bertie Wooster's friend, Richard ('Bingo') Little was a bachelor Drones Club romantic, living on an allowance from his uncle, Lord Bittlesham: a good vehicle for short stories of idiocy and confusion. He was always falling in love, promoting wild schemes, losing his money on the racecourse and generally making an ass of himself and needing Jeeves's help to get him out of the soup. After seven unsuitable courtships, Bingo meets and marries a best-selling novelist, Rosie M. Banks, and fathers Algernon Aubrey Little.

In the Little marriage Rosie is, of course, the boss. In the story 'Jeeves and the Old School Chum' Bingo has inherited Bittlesham money and a Norfolk property. But then, without explanation, he reverts to dependence on, and enslavement to, a job as editor of *Wee Tots* and to housekeeping hand-outs from Rosie when she goes on lecture tours and such. Ruthlessly professional, in one piece, commissioned by Bertie's Aunt Dahlia but, thank Jeeves, never published, Rosie refers to her husband as 'half god, half prattling, mischievous child'.

The arrival of Algernon Aubrey lets in Bingo's old Nannie for 'The Shadow Passes' in *Nothing Serious*, and enables Wodehouse to write the ultimate in 'ugly babies' stories, 'Sonny Boy' in *Eggs, Beans and Crumpets*.

Seven stories of *The Inimitable Jeeves*: in the last of these Bingo meets and will marry Rosie. Twelve more stories with the Littles married, in *Carry On Jeeves*, *Very Good, Jeeves*, *Lord Emsworth and Others*, *Eggs, Beans and Crumpets*, *Nothing Serious*, *A Few Quick Ones* and *Plum Pie*.

Ivor Llewellyn

Mr Mulliner tells five stories in *Blandings Castle* and one in *Plum Pie* about Hollywood, its tycoons and some of his own relations who worked, as serfs, assistant serfs and under-serfs, for the tycoons in the movie business there. The tycoons were Jacob (Jake) Schnellenhamer, Sigismund (Sam) Glutz, Jacob Glutz, Isidore Fishbein and Ben Zizzbaum. The corporations they controlled, before and after takeovers and mergers, were Colossal-Exquisite, Perfecto-Wonderful, Zizzbaum-Celluloid, Perfecto-Zizzbaum and Medulla-Oblongata-Glutz. Jacob Glutz also appears in *The Old Reliable*.

Ivor ('Ikey' to some, but he prefers 'Jumbo') Llewellyn, President of Superba-Llewellyn of Llewellyn City, is a more substantial and long-lasting proposition, with important parts in four novels, *The Luck of the Bodkins, Frozen Assets, Pearls, Girls and Monty Bodkin* and *Bachelors Anonymous.* He is fat, with three chins. He is bad-tempered: he throws porridge at his manservant. He is unreliable: he has made a film about English society life, with fox-hunting in July. He is gullible: he hires Ambrose Tennyson, the novelist, at $1,500 a week for five years, believing he is *the* Tennyson. His first wife had been a weight-lifter in pink tights in vaudeville. His fifth wife, Grayce, had been one of the best-known panther-women of the silent screen, and she keeps her husband under her thumb, with threats and a joint bank account.

Under the benificent influence of alcohol, he rounds on Grayce and she gets a divorce. *Bachelors Anonymous* is largely concerned with the efforts of his Hollywood friends

to keep Llewellyn from marrying again, for a sixth time. Like so many of Wodehouse's elderly heavies, Llewellyn gets partial redemption when he reveals, proudly, that he had been a rowdy young man, often in trouble with the police and once in prison for drunk and disorderly. He becomes quite an old softie in *Pearls, Girls and Monty Bodkin*, and in *Bachelors Anonymous* more so. There Wodehouse needs him to indulge in racy dialogue and to throw educated quotations about. So Llewellyn reveals that, when he was a boy in Wales, he had come under the influence of a schoolmarm who had hammered Shakespeare and other good stuff into his memory. An improvement on the early Llewellyn to whom Tennyson and Dante were not even names.

Rutherford Maxwell

Another wisp of Wodehouse autobiography in an early, and painfully sentimental, long short story, 'In Alcala' in *The Man Upstairs*. Rutherford Maxwell is the young Englishman sent to the New York branch of the London bank that employs him. In cheap digs in a big cheap apartment house, Alcala, in the evening he sits at a table and writes stories, hoping to make a mark and a living this way and get out of the bank. An actress, Peggy, with a room upstairs, introduces herself, laughs at his long English name, calls him George and rather falls in love with him. But there's a photograph on his mantelpiece of The Girl Back Home in Worcestershire. Peggy kisses George on the forehead. It is goodbye. It has all been 'a Broadway dream'.

Mr Mulliner

He is a mouthpiece for some of Wodehouse's tallest and best stories. A fisherman, though none of his stories is about fishing, he holds court nightly in the bar parlour of the Anglers' Rest (Ernest Biggs, landlord; Miss Postlethwaite, barmaid). Mr Mulliner is a bachelor, with an unlimited number of nephews, nieces and cousins. It is mostly stories about them that he tells. His audience at the Anglers' Rest is identified not by their names, but by their drinks. Mr Mulliner's preferred drink is hot Scotch and Lemon. The others are the Whisky and Splash, the Small Port, the Sherry and Bitters, the Stout and Mild and you-name-them. Their conversations and discussions, when they can get a word in edgeways and stop Mr Mulliner, change subject with great rapidity.

'Cats are not dogs!'

There is only one place where you can hear good things like that thrown off quite casually in the general run of conversation, and that is the bar parlour of the Anglers' Rest.... Although the talk up to this point had been dealing with Einstein's

Theory of Relativity, we readily adjusted our minds to cope with the new topic ... In our little circle I have known an argument on the Final Destination of the Soul to change inside forty seconds into one concerning the best method of preserving the juiciness of bacon fat.

Some of Mr Mulliner's nephews are in the Church and one of them introduces us to Buck-U-Uppo Tonic. Buck-U-Uppo produces the euphoria of instant alcohol without the sin, the hangover or the remorse. It leads one bishop to go out at night with a headmaster and paint a statue in the school close; another to fell a policeman in a night-club raid.

Mr Mulliner is well connected in the socio-snob sense. Bobbie Wickham's mother, Lady Wickham, is one of his cousins (hence three stories of that charming, red-haired heart-breaker Bobbie, who later counted Bertie Wooster's among her scalps). And he walks straight on to Mr Jacob Schnellenhamer's yacht at Monte Carlo as a guest with state-room: Schnellenhamer being President of the Perfecto-Zizzbaum Motion Picture Corporation of Hollywood and a big cheese ('George and Alfred', a variant of, and a great improvement on, an old Reggie Pepper story, 'Rallying Round Old George', in the American edition of *The Man with Two Left Feet*).

Montrose Mulliner, a distant cousin, gives Mr Mulliner the entrée to distant Hollywood, good, very good for six stories. And one of the Devonshire Mulliners had married a man named Flack and their girl, Agnes Flack, is a beefy expert on the golf course: this putting Mr Mulliner temporarily into the shoes or guise, of the Oldest Member, telling of a golf story, 'Those in Peril on the Tee'.

I am imprinted with the mental picture of Mr Mulliner on the dust jacket of the first volume of Mulliner stories, *Meet Mr Mulliner*. But, though there is little evidence that Wodehouse noticed, still less criticised, illustrations that editors and publishers obtained for his stories and books, I know, from a letter to Bill Townend that's not in *Performing Flea*, that Wodehouse disliked this particular portrayal of his new story-teller. 'God may have forgiven Herbert Jenkins for the picture of Mr Mulliner on the dust jacket, but I never shall.'

It is nice to know, from Wodehouse's Preface to *The Mulliner Omnibus* that the Mulliner stories came out of the old typewriter with a minimum of birth-pangs: 'It was like finding money in the street ... the stuff came pouring out as if somebody had turned a tap. I am, as a rule, a thousand-words-at-a-sitting man, but with Mulliner it was more like half a story before lunch.'

Meet Mr Mulliner, *Mr Mulliner Speaking* and *Mulliner Nights* are collections made after the first three turns of the tap. Other stories appear in *Blandings Castle*, *Young Men in Spats*, *Lord Emsworth and Others*, *Eggs, Beans and Crumpets*, *A Few Quick Ones* and *Plum Pie*.

THE INIMITABLE JEEVES

CARRY ON, JEEVES

NUGGETS Writers

A large proportion of Wodehouse's young heroes are writers of novels of suspense – about baronets found with daggers of oriental design between the shoulder-blades, squint-eyed Chinese lepers, and corpses, with or without gash in throat. Although any literary critic will tell (and often does tell) serious novelists that they write about writers at their peril, a writer is useful as a character because he doesn't have to keep office hours, he can be poor or rich, he can travel and he can always take his golf clubs with him. Anyway Wodehouse used a lot of writers and only the 'serious' ones, Charlton Prout, Florence Craye, Blair Eggleston, Raymond Parsloe-Devine, were, like the 'Great Russians' they admired, pilloried as phonies. His Bokos, Jeffs and Jerries were fools, badly dressed, their faces spotted with ink, yes. But not phonies. And the female best-seller – she was one of Wodehouse's special loves: Rosie M. Banks, Leila Pinckney, Lady Wickham, Leila Yorke. Splendid old girls all of them. All glory to them.

It has been well said that an author who expects results from a
first novel is in a position similar to that of a man who drops a rose petal
down the Grand Canyon of Arizona and listens for the echo.

She wrote novels: and that instinct of self-preservation which lurks
in every publisher had suggested to him that behind her invitation
lay a sinister desire to read those to him one by one.

'The moment my fingers clutch a pen, Widgeon, a great change comes over me. I descend to depths of goo which you with your pure mind wouldn't believe possible. I write about stalwart men, strong but oh so gentle, and girls with wide grey eyes and hair the colour of ripe wheat, who are always having misunderstandings and going to Africa. The men, that is. The girls stay at home and marry the wrong bimbos. But there's a happy ending. The bimbos break their necks in the hunting field and the men come back in the last chapter and they and the girls get together in the twilight, and all around is the scent of English flowers and birds singing their evensong in the shubbery. Makes me shudder to think of it.' (Leila Yorke)

Rodney Spelvin was in for another attack of poetry. He had once been a poet, and a very virulent one, too: the sort of man who would produce a slim volume of verse bound in squashy mauve leather at the drop of a hat, mostly on the subject of sunsets and pixies.

...that inevitability that was such a feature of the best Greek tragedy. Aeschylus once said to Euripides 'You can't beat inevitability,' and Euripides said he often thought so, too.

She often asked him if he thought it was quite nice to harp on sudden death and blackmailers with squints. Surely, she said, there were enough squinting blackmailers in the world without writing about them.

Poets, as a class, are business men. Shakespeare describes the poet's eye as rolling in fine frenzy, from heaven to earth, and giving to airy nothing a local habitation and a name, but in practice, you will find that one corner of that eye is generally glued on the royalty returns.

Ambrose isn't a frightfully hot writer. I don't suppose he makes enough out of a novel to keep a midget in doughnuts for a week. Not a really healthy midget.

'What a curse these social distractions are. They ought to be abolished. I remember saying that to Karl Marx once, and he thought there might be an idea for a book in it.'

'I didn't know poets broke people's necks.'
'Ricky does. He once took on three simultaneous costermongers in Covent Garden and cleaned them up in five minutes. He had gone there to get inspiration for a pastoral, and they started chi-iking him, and he sailed in and knocked them base over apex into a pile of Brussels sprouts.'
'How different from the home life of the late Lord Tennyson.'

The Oldest Member

Wodehouse gives him no name. He sits on the terrace of the golf club, English or American, and waits to capture an audience for his golfing stories: not his own golf – he gave the game up long ago – but stories of young men and maidens, goofs and experts, poets and novelists, children and spavined septuagenarians, all addicts of the game.

He tells nine out of the ten stories in *The Clicking of Cuthbert*, all nine of *The Heart of a Goof*, five in *Nothing Serious* and one in *A Few Quick Ones*.

Sir Gregory Parsloe-Parsloe

(*Wodehouse only seldom gives his name both barrels*)

Much Matchingham is a village in Shropshire, a few miles from Blandings Castle. At Matchingham Hall lives Sir Gregory Parsloe, J.P., seventh baronet. Also, if they are married by now, Maudie, his wife, once Maudie Montrose of the Criterion bar. Lady Constance at the castle is always hoping that Blandings and Matchingham can be friendly neighbours, but to her brothers, Lord Emsworth and Galahad, Parsloe is bad news, an enemy, a rival in the competitive world of pigs.

In his earlier phase of enthusiasm for pumpkins, Lord Emsworth's entry had won against Sir Gregory's at the show, putting a stop to the sequence of three first prizes that Sir Gregory had won for pumpkins till then. And Sir Gregory had behaved like a gentleman and congratulated the winner.

> There was the right stuff in Sir Gregory. He was a gentleman and a sportsman. In the Parsloe tradition there was nothing small or mean.

That was before Galahad had appeared as a character, let alone as a remembrancer of young Parsloe's behaviour in London when he was poor and untitled. Parsloe nobbling Gally's dog Towser in the ratting contest against his own Banjo – that was the memory that rankled with Gally. And when his brother's Empress was going for her second Fat Pigs medal, and Sir Gregory had Pride of Matchingham and Queen of Matchingham in training against her, with George Cyril Wellbeloved as his new pig-man, then Galahad persuaded Lord Emsworth that Parsloe would nobble the Empress somehow.

'Tubby' Parsloe had been told to diet by his lissom fiancée Gloria Salt, and he sent his butler to the village chemist to buy some bottles of Slimmo for him. This news came to Gally and the inference was clear: Parsloe was going to feed it privily to the Empress. That sort of thing. No nice, neighbourly trust. Earlier Lord Emsworth had been much harassed by the Rev. Rupert Bingham, a clumsy clergyman whom his niece, Gertrude, wanted to marry. The vicarage of Matchingham was in Lord Emsworth's gift and it lacked a vicar at the time. So he gave the incumbency to the clumsy, harassing clergyman with his blessing for the wedding, and hoped that he would harass the local squire from then on – viz Sir Gregory Parsloe. Not nice, neighbourly behaviour.

One comes to feel rather sorry for Sir Gregory matched against such dedicated and quick-thinking opponents as Lord Emsworth and Gally.

The pre-pig rivalry over pumpkins, Blandings v. Matchingham, is told in 'The Custody of the Pumpkin' in *Blandings Castle*. The first mention of the Empress and her then guardian, George Cyril Wellbeloved, is in another story in that book, 'Pig-Hoo-o-o-o-ey!'. The events of *Summer Lightning* are really post-'Pig-Hoo-o-o-o-ey!'. So are the events of *Heavy Weather*. And as the Empress's silver medals were won in three consecutive years, *Pigs Have Wings* is closely linked in real time with the two earlier Blandings novels. But we know what publishing dates are, compared to real time, with Wodehouse. The polite word is 'misleading'.

Percy Pilbeam

A recurrent snake in the grass, Pilbeam appears in six books. At the age of twenty-three, having started on *Pyke's Home Companion*, answering correspondents as 'Aunt Ysobel' (*Bill the Conqueror*), Pilbeam becomes editor of *Society Spice*. The proprietor of Mammoth Publishing, Sir George Pyke, soon to be Lord Tilbury, sets store by Pilbeam as an expert in grubby journalism.

Pilbeam is small, with black marcelled hair, pimples and a horrible small moustache which he tries to train upwards with a pen-nib. He wears a cricket club blazer as a working coat in the office and plays for the club on Saturdays in summer. He also wears paper cuffs. He has mean little eyes and has been kicked downstairs when doing detective work on a juicy story. For some reason he is also a Fellow of the Royal Zoological Society.

Pilbeam is upstaged in *Sam the Sudden* by another recurrent slithy tove, crookeder, creepier Chimp Twist. In *Summer Lightning* Pilbeam is running his own business, the Argus Enquiry Agency, and pursuing Sue Brown, chorus girl. Sir Gregory Parsloe, for whom Pilbeam had acted in the confidential matter of some indiscreet letters, had earlier recommended Pilbeam to Lord Emsworth. At one stage at Blandings Pilbeam is serving four clients simultaneously: Lord Emsworth to find his missing pig, Millicent Threepwood to keep an eye on her fiancé Hugo Carmody, Hugo to get the Memoirs for Lord Tilbury to publish, and Sir Gregory to get the Memoirs and destroy them.

He is still at Blandings in *Heavy Weather* and his is the historic hand that feeds the precious manuscript to the Empress in her sty – well, hides it there with the result that she eats it. It was not strictly on the Wolff-Lehmann diet for her, but consumable.

Pilbeam turns up again in *Something Fishy* and *Frozen Assets*. Lord Tilbury still admires him and employs him on tactful jobs, and wishes he had not let him leave the editorship of *Society Spice*. In *Frozen Assets* we meet, surprisingly, Pilbeam's father, a resident of Valley Fields, in 'his moth-eaten middle fifties', a sidesman in church, a gardener and a total abstainer (his son, Percy, had twice, by then, got drunk at Blandings Castle). Jerry Shoesmith, hero of *Frozen Assets* and once himself editor of *Society Spice* – he had hated it and was sacked – thought Pilbeam, 'like something unpleasant out of an early Evelyn Waugh novel'.

Roderick Spode, later Earl of Sidcup

The Code of the Woosters was published in 1938 and Sir Oswald Mosley must have recognised himself in Roderick Spode, amateur dictator, founder of The Saviours of Britain, the Black Shorts if not necessarily as

> a breath-taking cove. About seven feet in height, and swathed in a plaid ulster which made him look about six feet across, he caught the eye and arrested it. It was as if Nature had intended to make a gorilla, and had changed its mind at the last moment...

Spode had been in love with Madeline Bassett since she was so high, but he regarded himself as a Man of Destiny and thought he would travel faster if he remained a bachelor. On the other hand he was ready to beat up any man he thought was playing fast or loose with Madeline, e.g. Gussie Fink-Nottle, her fiancé, or Bertie Wooster when he seemed to be trying to detach Madeline from Gussie.

Jeeves found the quencher, the Dark Secret, on this man of wrath. In the Book of Revelations about employers kept by Jeeves's club, the Junior Ganymede, it was written, by an ex-valet of Spode's, that Spode designed ladies' underwear and was the power behind the Bond Street shop, Eulalie Soeurs. If that news were to be spread abroad, what price the Man of Destiny? Spode came to heel.

He menaced again, briefly, in *Jeeves and the Feudal Spirit*, yet again, more so, in *Stiff Upper Lip, Jeeves*, and again, slightly, in *Much Obliged, Jeeves*. He has inherited the earldom of Sidcup and £20,000 a year, and Madeline will, after many chops and changes between Gussie and Bertie, be Lady Sidcup soon. But in the interim we have had the pleasure of seeing the man felled for the count three times, once by Stinker Pinker, the curate, with an expert blow to the jaw, once by Emerald Stoker, temporary cook, with a china basin, once by Aunt Dahlia with a cosh. He has also been hit in the eye with a potato at an election rally.

He came in like a lion and he goes out like a chastened lamb. We feel that soupy Madeline will not allow any of that amateur dictator stuff from Roderick at the Sidcup castle in Shropshire.

The Hon. Freddie Threepwood

Freddie is Lord Emsworth's second son. After minimal mentions in *Something Fresh* and *Leave it to Psmith*, Lord Bosham, heir to the earldom, takes a minor part in *Uncle Fred in the Springtime* and shows himself to be the silliest ass in all the books. His younger brother Freddie gets much fatter parts.

In *Something Fresh* Freddie is described as heavy, loutish-looking, with prominent eyes and mouth always open. Expelled from Eton, sent down from Oxford, two years at a crammer, failed for the Army, he had fallen for a chorus girl, whom he had not met, and had written poetry to her. There was talk of his going into the Church, but he resisted that. He was engaged to Aline, daughter of an American millionaire, but didn't mourn much when she went off with a brighter suitor. His betting was a failure, and his father paid £500 of his debts, but insisted that he come and live at the castle where he could keep an eye on him.

By the time of *Leave it to Psmith* Freddie has become slim. Joe Keeble, Lady Constance's husband, said of him that he had only once shown any initiative, and that was when he had parted his hair in the middle when all the members of his club, the Bachelors, were wearing theirs brushed straight back. In that book, largely through Psmith's machinations, Freddie got the money to set himself up in the bookmaking business.

Bookmaking forgotten, we find him back at the castle and getting on his father's nerves again in a big way in 'The Custody of the Pumpkin' in *Blandings Castle*. And Lord Emsworth, playing on the roof with his new toy, a telescope, spots Freddie embracing a girl down in the water-meadows beyond the lake. Lord Emsworth had always feared Freddie would get entangled with an unsuitable girl. But this ends happily, as the girl is American, Aggie Donaldson, and her father, a dog-biscuit magnate.

Marriage to Aggie is Freddie's salvation. He becomes an enthusiastic dog-biscuit salesman, a go-getter – so much so that his father feels that Freddie looks down on him for being a drone and a wastrel. Lord Emsworth is still apprehensive that something may cause a rift between Freddie and Aggie and that Freddie will come back and moon round the castle again. With the Atlantic between himself and his son, distance makes Lord Emsworth's heart much fonder.

The Hon. Galahad Threepwood

When, in the first chapter of *Summer Lightning* Lord Emsworth's younger brother, Galahad, walked from the castle across the sunlit lawn to the tea tables, carrying a whisky and soda, he had a spot of ink on his nose – always Wodehouse's way of denoting the Life Literary. He had been introduced to us already, a man at work on his Reminiscences – and what reminiscences they were likely to be!

Galahad in his day had been a notable lad about town. A beau sabreur of Romano's. A Pink 'Un. A Pelican. A crony of Hughie Drummond and Fatty Coleman; a brother in arms of the Shifter, the Pitcher, Peter Blobbs and the rest of an interesting but not straight-laced circle. Bookmakers had called him by his pet name, barmaids had simpered beneath his gallant chaff. He had heard the chimes at midnight. And when he had looked in at the Old Gardenia, commissionaires had fought for the privilege of throwing him out. A man, in a word, who should never have been taught to write and who, if unhappily gifted with that ability, should have been restrained by Act of Parliament from writing Reminiscences.

So thought Lady Constance, his sister.

He walks into the books a fully fledged major character, and he keeps the character and amplifies it in seven more books. He was calling the tune in the novel Wodehouse was writing when he died. Battling his sisters, protecting his brother, unsundering hearts young and old, 'telling the tale', blackmailing where necessary, using Mickey Finns where advisable, infiltrating impostors, chaffing Beach and drinking port in his pantry; he lived at a pace and was never defeated.

One of the Old Brigade, Musketeer of the 90s, last of the Pelicans – he is variously described. 'My deplorable brother' (Lady Constance), 'That old image' (Sir Gregory Parsloe), 'Somewhat wild as a young man' (Beach). He was the pride of the servants' hall, his sisters were afraid of him, he was a fairy godfather – not with his own money ('I subsist on a younger son's allowance from the estate') – to a long list of godsons. Their fathers had been his drinking companions once, and several of them, as they died of cirrhosis of the liver, had said to Gally, 'Look after the boy', or words to that effect.

There had been one tragedy in his life. He had loved Dolly Henderson, singer, in pink tights, at the Old Oxford and the Tivoli. But, before he could marry her, his angry father shipped him off to South Africa. You do not have to read much Wodehouse to realise that he thought the dominant sex was female. Bertie Wooster is a rabbit and he remains a bachelor largely because he is a rabbit. All the strong men and heroes are house-tamed sooner or later willingly or unwillingly, by wives or sisters. Gally himself, had he married Dolly, would have been a dutiful husband surely. As it is he remains triumphantly his own man. Knee-deep in blondes, ballet dancers and barmaids he may have been when he had the energy. But in the best and truest sense, he is a bachelor; unique, I think, in Wodehouse.

Black-rimmed monocle on a black ribbon, thick grey hair now, a scar on his leg where a ballet dancer of mixed Italian and Spanish descent had stabbed him with a hat-pin, he spends most of his time at the castle. He used to prefer London and although he has a headquarters on the fourth floor on Berkeley Mansions, W1 (it had been in Duke Street,

St James's) the castle is probably the best address for him if you want to ask him for the whole story of Sir Gregory Parsloe and the prawns. Wodehouse died without telling us.

Summer Lightning, Heavy Weather, Full Moon, Pigs Have Wings, Galahad at Blandings, Plum Pie, A Pelican at Blandings, Sunset at Blandings all include Gally.

George Pyke, Viscount Tilbury

He is Sir George Pyke, and he has just been offered a peerage, in *Bill the Conqueror*. He is Viscount Tilbury next year in *Sam the Sudden*, and in *Heavy Weather, Service with a Smile* and *Frozen Assets*. He is founder and proprietor of the Mammoth Publishing Company – newspapers and magazines. He is rich, short, fat and Napoleonic. He had married a wait-ress in a café, who had produced a son, Roderick, and died. Lord Tilbury bosses his son, as he does everybody except (in *Bill the Conqueror*) his sister. Roderick, limp-wristed and highbrow, has published, at his own expense, a book, bound in limp purple leather, on the prose of Walter Pater. Now he wants his father to acquire *The Poetry Quarterly* and let him edit it. He is not happy as editor of *Society Spice*. He is not happy proposing marriage to the girl whom his father wants him to marry. The girl is happy to be rid of him. Roderick, the son and heir, disappears after the first book.

Lord Tilbury pursues his money-making ends in four more novels. He has his trousers forcibly removed in *Sam the Sudden*. And, poor chap, coming into *Frozen Assets*, which is largely a rerun of *Sam the Sudden*, he has his trousers forcibly removed again. But he marries a beautiful girl, Gwendolyn Gibbs, who has been his secretary. Although she is a cousin of Percy Pilbeam, she is a very nice girl. And that's the sort of benison Wodehouse gives, even to this undeserving autocrat.

Travers – Dahlia, Tom, Angela, Bonzo

Mrs Tom Travers is Bertie Wooster's good aunt, in sharp contradistinction to her sister, Agatha. Bertie's father had been their brother. Aunt Dahlia's first husband had been a drunk – only mentioned in passing and retrospect. He had drowned himself, not intentionally, when drunk. When 'Uncle Tom' Travers first appeared, in 'Clustering Round Young Bingo', Bertie was thinking him 'a bit of a squirt' and not half good enough for his aunt; and, as Uncle Tom refused to live in the country, Aunt Dahlia had to give up her hitherto incessant hunting.

In later books Uncle Tom seems equally at home in their country house, Brinkley Court in Worcestershire, as in their Mayfair house in Charles Street. In *Much Obliged, Jeeves* he has galloped off to the south of France to avoid the house party that Aunt Dahlia has collected for the Market Snodsbury parliamentary by-election. And he had presumably gone out in the yacht to Cannes with Aunt Dahlia and Angela in *Right Ho, Jeeves*. But Aunt Dahlia doesn't hunt any more, though she keeps the brick-red complexion and the long-distance voice she acquired in the field with the Quorn and Pytchley. She now runs a sixpenny weekly paper in London, *Miladay's Boudoir*. This she sells to L. G. Trotter of Liverpool (*Jeeves and the Feudal Spirit*).

Uncle Tom had made a 'colossal pile' of money in the Far East, but it had put his digestion on the blink. Jeeves found the great French chef, Anatole, for the Travers kitchen, and Uncle Tom could forget his digestive troubles. And we must forget that Uncle Tom was ever 'a bit of a squirt'. In the background, rattling his keys, trying to avoid his wife's guests, fussing over his collection of old silver, cursing the Inland Revenue men, forking out to pay Aunt Dahlia's everlasting debts on *Milady's Boudoir*, Tom Travers is a good uncle.

Aunt Dahlia and Uncle Tom have two children: Angela, engaged on and off to Tuppy Glossop (and once, as a gesture of defiance, to Gussie Fink-Nottle), and Bonzo, a tough youngster of seven or eight. Aunt Dahlia is fond of Bertie, though she frequently berates him, and occasionally she reminds him that, when he was a baby, he swallowed his comforter and she had rescued him from death by asphyxiation – which perhaps she had better not have done. Her dialogues with her nephew are among the best exchanges of badinage in Wodehouse. And her relationship with her husband is cordial.

She is Governor of the Market Snodsbury Grammar School. She loses her shirt at baccarat in the south of France. She knocks Spode out with a cosh. She is a great admirer of Jeeves's brain and annoys Bertie by often appealing to her nephew's man for help before appealing to her nephew. She reads detective fiction and is still puzzling over the *Observer* crossword puzzle well into the week.

She comes into five novels and seven short stories. A splendid lady, and a pleasant family. It looks as though, after *Much Obliged, Jeeves*, Tuppy will have money sufficient to end his long engagements to Angela and marry her.

Lady Constance Threepwood/Keeble/Schoonmaker

There is always a sister-boss darkening Lord Emsworth's life at Blandings, and Connie is the most persistent of the ten (well, count Diana out: she's a sister, but not bossy, in the unfinished *Sunset at Blandings*). Lady Constance appears in seven novels and five short stories. Like all the sisters except Hermione, who looked like a cook, she is handsome.

She served Wodehouse well as a representative of the forces of disturbance in Lord Emsworth's life – people who make him wear stiff collars and top-hats on baking summer afternoons, people who bring nieces to the castle in order to disengage them from unsuitable love affairs, people who don't want the Empress's portrait in the Gallery, people who talk airily of getting rid of the pig and, once even, of Beach the butler.

In spite of her disapproving role, the kindly Wodehouse gives her two successive nice millionaire husbands. And, hypnotised by the sight of her grand-nephew's air-gun, she remembers that as a girl she had been a keen air-gunner and had shot her governess in the bustle. But when, in 'The Crime Wave at Blandings', she takes a sitting shot at Beach in his deckchair near the shrubbery, she misses.

Sir Derek Underhill Bart, MP

He had everything, good looks, money, a future. He was about thirty, dark, lean, very popular with women. He was a Wykehamist, and Freddie Rooke, who had been his fag there, worshipped him still. He was a fine shot and played polo 'superlatively well'. He had fallen in love with Jill Mariner (*Jill the Reckless*) at first sight, and he was afraid his mother would disapprove of her.

He was afraid of his mother, full stop. And she did disapprove of Jill. And, just when Jill lost all her money and got involved in a fracas rescuing a parrot, Derek broke the engagement. And later, when he wanted to make it up and start again, he learnt that she was a chorus girl in New York, and that put the lid on it.

It is *not* done in Wodehouse for a man to break an engagement. Wodehouse was serious about it in 1921, though he made it a staple of his comic plots with Bertie Wooster and others later and to his dying day. Sir Derek was a cad, a disgrace to his class, his school, his clubs, his career. And Freddie Rooke finally told him so: 'You're a tick. If we meet again, do not claim my acquaintance.'

Derek Underhill appears only in *Jill the Reckless*, though there is a distinct echo of him with Henry Blake-Somerset in *Frozen Assets* forty-three years later.

Augustus Whiffle or Whipple

There is a problem about the name of the author of Lord Emsworth's favourite book, *The Care of the Pig*. Is he Whiffle or Whipple? Until *Galahad at Blandings* he was always Whiffle. But in that book he becomes Whipple, Augustus Whipple, member of the Athenaeum. He is the same pig-expert, and he has written to Lord Emsworth and asked to be allowed to come down and photograph the Empress, of whom he has heard so much. Lord Emsworth gives Gally a telegram to send, saying 'Come and stay. Very welcome.' And Gally gets an idea. He sends Whipple a telegram saying 'Don't come yet. Lord Emsworth has German measles,' and he infiltrates his godson Sam Bagshott into the castle, saying *he* is Whipple.

Not only that, but he pitches his brother a heart-rending tale of this (which?) Whipple having lost £1,000 at poker at the Athenaeum – a sum Lord Emsworth is delighted to pay off for the man whose book he admires so much – the cheque to be made out to Gally, who will save Whipple's blushes in accepting the money by cooking up a story about it. This is one of the wilder patches of Gally's tale-telling to help Wodehouse to end the book. In fact the 'oblong strip of paper with its invigorating signature' (Lord Emsworth's cheque) is going to pay for several other happy endings that Gally is engineering. And Whipple, the real Whipple, is last heard of corporeally at the Emsworth Arms. Never, in print, are we to have that great meeting of souls – Lord Emsworth's, the Empress's and that of the author of the book which has directed her feeding through the years.

When typing out the early chapters of what became *Sunset at Blandings* Wodehouse put the name as Whipple and then, in his own recognisable handwriting, changed it to Whiffle. We can take that as the last word. The name is Whiffle, and *Galahad at Blandings*, though right on the Wolff-Lehmann calories, was wrong on the author of *The Care of the Pig*.

A British television personality, James Hogg, recently made an interesting discovery. In a second-hand bookshop in Eastbourne he found *The Pig – Breeding, Rearing and Marketing*, by Sanders Spencer, published by C. Arthur Pearson in 1919. Opposite page 32 is the picture of a magnificent sausage-shaped sow, black except for the white under-belly and white last few inches of each leg. Underneath is printed *A BERKSHIRE SOW* and *From a Painting by Wippell*. Is it conceivable that Wodehouse saw the picture, its title, the pig's colour and the ascription to 'a painting by Wippell'? And could this have given birth to his idea of having Lord Emsworth trying, novel after novel, to find someone to paint the Empress's portrait?

Dame Daphne Winkworth

She is a heavy, and one of the few characters who bridge the gap between Bertie Wooster's world and Lord Emsworth's. In *The Mating Season* she is widow of a historian, a friend of Bertie's Aunt Agatha, and Madeline Bassett's godmother.

She had been, before this first appearance in a book, proprietor and headmistress of a fashionable girls' school in Eastbourne. And in *Galahad at Blandings* she is that again, somehow, and invited to the castle, with her unpleasant young son, Huxley, because Lady Constance remembers that, a long time ago, Lord Emsworth, after his wife had died, had been quite attached to Daphne Littlewood, as the Dame had then been. So why not promote her now as a possible second Countess of Emsworth? Dame Daphne leaves the castle angry and disappointed.

She is still the headmistress, and another young man's aunt, in *Sunset at Blandings*. And her voice on the telephone from Eastbourne blows the gaff on the hero-impostor. She remains a heavy, unredeemed.

Percy Earl of Worplesdon

You must ignore, or rise above, the Lord Worplesdon of 'Extricating Old Percy' in *The Legion Book* and even of 'Jeeves Takes Charge' in the 1967 omnibus *World of Jeeves*, and take him as he is in *Joy in the Morning*: father of Florence and Edwin Craye, and married now (second marriages for both of them) to Bertie's Aunt Agatha. Address: Steeple Bumpleigh. You may also want to discredit, or forget, that Jeeves said that he had been Lord Worplesdon's valet for about a year once. There is no mention or recognition of this earlier employment in *Joy in the Morning*, though Lord Worplesdon clearly knows about Jeeves's wisdom, his discretion and his consultative practice.

Lord Worplesdon is now a shipping magnate, head of the Pink Funnel Line. When his wife is away, and not making him give up smoking, he is quite a cheery soul. Wodehouse gave him, as to so many other forgiven heavies, a rowdy youth. He was arrested at a Covent Garden fancy dress ball. He was engaged to Bertie's Aunt Agatha at the time, and when she read the reports of the arrest in the papers she broke the engagement. It was only years later, after each had married and had children elsewhere, that they married, widow to widower.

It's odd the way men in Wodehouse go to fancy dress balls without their ladies. In *Joy in the Morning* there is that fancy dress dance at East Wibley, to which, in various guises, go Boko, Bertie, Lord Worplesdon and J. Chichester Clam. There was no suggestion that Nobby should go with her beloved Boko; nor that Florence should partner her father or Bertie. These men went to dance. With whom *did* they dance?

NUGGETS Animals, Mostly Dogs

Wodehouse and his wife had many dogs, and, latterly, many cats. And they adored them all. Their decision in 1935 to live at Le Touquet had been strongly influenced by their dogs and the English quarantine restrictions. And their failure to escape to England from Le Touquet when the Germans invaded France in 1940 was partly due to their inability to face the idea of their dogs going into quarantine for six months when they arrived.

Wodehouse himself was a Peke man. He dedicated his *Louder and Funnier* to: 'GEORGE BLAKE, A SPLENDID FELLOW AND VERY SOUND ON PEKES, but he should guard against the tendency to claim that his Peke fights Alsatians. Mine is the only one that does this.' In *Money in the Bank* Jeff falls in love with Anne when he hears her laugh. That laugh 'conjured up visions of a cosy home on a winter's night, with one's slippers on one's feet, the dog on one's lap, an open fire in the grate and the good old pipe drawing nicely.' Wodehouse wrote *Money in the Bank* in Tost Civilian Internment Camp in Upper Silesia during the war, when there were plenty of winter nights, no open fires in grates and people sometimes smoked a mixture of straw and tealeaves. Certainly no dog, and no Anne.

There's a good deal about hunger in *Money in the Bank* – hunger for pork pies in a vegetarian health farm. That is significant. But the dog on his lap, in Jeff's mind, was surely the Peke, Wonder, whom Wodehouse had left behind with Ethel at Le Touquet, and who would come to Berlin with Ethel to greet him on his release nearly a year later.

It was one of those hairy, nondescript dogs, and its gaze was cold, wary and suspicious,
like that of a stockbroker who thinks someone is going to play a confidence trick on him.

(A dog working up to a fight) To the ears of those present there came, faintly at first,
a low, throaty sound, like the far-off gargling of an octogenarian with bronchial trouble.

It looked something like a pen-wiper and something like a piece of hearth-rug.
A second and keener inspection revealed it as a Pekinese puppy.

Now, just before the tiger of the jungle springs upon its prey,
I am told by chaps who know tigers of the jungle, there is always a
moment when it pauses, flexes its muscles and rubs its feet in the resin.

He had just that expression of peeved surprise that one of those
sheep's head fish in Florida has when you haul it over the side of the boat.

Beach's bullfinch continued to chirp reflectively to itself,
like a man trying to remember a tune in his bath.

Any dog will tell you what these prize-ribbon dogs are like.
Their heads are so swelled they have to go into the kennel backwards.

The word is divided into those who can stop dog-fights and those who cannot.

The Aberdeen terrier gave me an unpleasant look
and said something under his breath in Gaelic.

Too often, when you introduce a ringer into a gaggle of Pekes,
there ensues a scrap like New Year's Eve in Madrid: but tonight, after a
certain amount of tentative sniffing, the home team issued their OK, and he
left them all curled up in their baskets like so many members of the Athenaeum.

GALLY'S OLD FRIENDS AND ENEMIES

Lord Emsworth's younger brother Galahad had been a gay spark and dedicated man-about-town in his younger days. A member of the Pelican Club and frequenter of the Old Gardenia, Romano's, the Café de l'Europe and other night spots, the music halls and racecourses. He was proud to recall that bouncers had fought for the privilege of throwing him out when things got rough, and that it generally took two or three of them, with one more behind carrying his topper.

When Gally let it be known that he was writing his Reminiscences, a shudder went round the best houses in London and the country. Admirals, generals, cabinet ministers, bishops, masters of fox-hounds – they were afraid Gally would remember what they remembered (with regret) about themselves.

In fact Gally sacrificed his Reminiscences – promised not to publish them – on the altar of his long-ago love of Dolly Henderson, the music hall singer.

But nothing stopped him prattling about some of the old friends, old enemies and old scandals he would otherwise have brought to book. This is a collection of names and hints of the stories that Gally tells in Wodehouse's books.

Friends (and some enemies) of Galahad's Younger Days

Boko Bagshott: 'One of the brightest brains at the Old Pelican', but died of cirrhosis of the liver. Father of Sam Bagshott, who loved Sandy Callender in *Galahad at Blandings* (1965). Sam had been named from Sam Bowles the jockey, and given a second name, Galahad, in the hopes that he would acquire his godfather's skill at picking winners. Old Boko frequently saw faces at windows. He used to get free medical check-ups by pretending to be about to buy big insurances, and being vetted free for them.

Plug (Major Wilfred) Basham: To cure a fit of his depression Gally and Puffy Benger put old Wivenhoe's pig, painted in phosphorus, into Plug's bedroom at Hammer's Easton. It cured him. 'The Bashams have always ordered quarts,' he said. Plug had once seen what looked like two brides at one wedding reception in a hotel, and he decided to give up drink. He took to absinthe, which he was convinced was harmless. He once laid out 'Stinker' Pyke, later Lord Tilbury, with a side of beef at Romano's. Jerry Vail, Lord Emsworth's secretary in *Pigs Have Wings*, was Plug's nephew.

Stiffy Bates: A Pelican. He had broken his leg stepping off a bus. Silly ass, he should have taken a cab. Thinking a man was a butler, Stiffy had given him ten shillings and a note for the daughter of the house. The butler turned out to be the girl's father and he chased Stiffy out with a garden fork. Gally also told this story about Bill Bowman.

Jack Bellamy-Johnstone: He had the name Esmeralda Parkinson-Willoughby tattooed on his wish-bone, then quarrelled with her and got engaged to a May Todd.

Blinky Bender: A Pelican and a bilker of bookies.

Puffy Benger: Had helped Gally steal old Wivenhoe's pig at Hammer's Easton and put it in Plug Basham's bedroom. His niece, an expert typist, could, he said, also play the piano very fast – Chopin's Funeral March in forty-eight seconds. When he said that, the house was struck by lightning and Puffy thought the Almighty might have let that story pass.

Fruity (Admiral George J.) Biffen: He had worn a false beard, mustard coloured, Assyrian shape, at Newmarket to baffle the bookies to whom he owed money. Did it again at Hurst Park where it fell off in Tattersall's ring. Took a small house furnished, Sunnybrae, just down the road from Blandings Castle, but he couldn't stand the noises of the country – birds, gnats, butterflies, etc. Went back to London. He is still alive and well.

Bishop of Bognor: There was some scandal about him when he was an undergraduate at Oxford.

Bill Bowman: Gally tells the same story, about the gardener turning out to be the father, as of Stiffy Bates above.

Alaric Duke of Dunstable: Once a stinker, always a stinker. It pleases Gally to remember that Johnny Halliday's father, Stiffy Halliday, had floored him with a cold turkey at Romano's in the good old days. He had also filled the top-hat with blackballs when the Duke's name came up for membership of the Pelican.

Lord Emsworth: There was one occasion when Gally took him to the Pelican. Lord Emsworth was not a great brain, but he was very good at mixing salads, and, chopping and adding, chopping and adding, he had mixed a great one for the table at the Pelican, consumed to the last morsel. He then discovered that his finger-stall was missing.

Miles Fish: Later Major General Sir Miles Fish of the Guards, married to Gally's sister Julia and, according to Lord Emsworth, the biggest fool in the Brigade. In the late summer of 1897 he had ridden a bicycle down Piccadilly in sky-blue underwear. On New Year's Day 1902 he had tried to shoot a coal-scuttle.

Stiffy Halliday: Father of Johnny Halliday, Gally's godson. He had once stunned a man named Percy Pound with a cold turkey at Romano's, and did the same apparently (see above) for the Duke of Dunstable. Perhaps Gally was misremembering one occasion and giving two protagonists.

Dolly Henderson: She had sung in pink tights at the Old Oxford and the Tivoli, and she was the love of Gally's life. He was shipped off to South Africa by a stern father before he could marry her. Sweet Sue Brown, who married Ronnie Fish, Gally's nephew, was really Sue Cotterleigh, Dolly's daughter.

Beefy Muspratt: Had smashed a billiard table in 1898.

Sir Gregory Parsloe-Parsloe: An old enemy of Gally's. In a ratting contest he nobbled Gally's dog Towser with a vast meal of steak and onions, so that he was too sleepy to kill rats, and the Parsloe entry, Banjo, won. He stole Lord Burper's false teeth in 1896 or so and pawned them in the Edgware Road. At the Café de l'Europe he had raffled his trousers in an attempt to raise the price of a bottle of champagne. There was a story about Parsloe and the prawns which went into the manuscript of Gally's Reminiscences, but was read only by Beach before the manuscript was eaten by the Empress. We shall never know the story.

Legs Ponderby: The nickname was a shortening of 'hollow legs'. He had been engaged to a girl who had a snake act on the Halls. One night at supper at the Bodega one of her troupe escaped and climbed up Legs's legs, and Legs hit it on the nose with a bread stick and lost the love of his girl.

Freddie and Eustace Potts: Two brothers, Freddie an alcoholic, Eustace a teetotaller. At Eustace's villa near Grasse in the south of France they sent the chef out to buy a chicken for a casserole. The chef found a dead hedgehog in the road and brought that back (charging for the chicken) and casseroled it. Eustace got hedgehog poisoning, but Freddie was not affected, and he ate the rest of the casserole cold next day. So much, Gally says, for teetotalism.

George 'Stinker' Pyke: later Lord Tilbury, the publishing tycoon. Plug Basham had laid him out cold at Romano's with a side of beef.

Buffy Struggles: Drank too much. Was shown how an earthworm could be killed by alcohol. So he went out and bought ten pounds of tea and was run over by a cab in Piccadilly. Just shows you, thinks Gally, what tea can do. Earlier Buffy had been engaged to a girl, but got the ring back because he used to poach in mixed doubles with her at tennis. He was killed before he could effect a reconciliation with the girl.

Chet Tipton: Rich American. He liked to get his drinks free by waiting for the moment when he should be paying and then saying, 'I've got smallpox.' This cleared the bar and the barman, so Chet didn't have to pay. He was enormously fat. Someone recommended that he wear one of those abdominal belts: very uncomfortable. He did so and a friend came up to him and said, 'You've got very fat. What you should do is wear one of those abdominal belts.' Fond of buttered rums at the Criterion bar.

Gladys Twistleton: Later married a man called Harringay. She was known to have a compulsion, during thunderstorms, to kiss men. Men used to get near her when they thought thunderstorms were coming.

Stiffy Vokes: Called himself Orlando Maltravers to baffle bookies to whom he owed money.

NUGGETSAunts

Wodehouse's father's work was in Hong Kong. Young Pelham came back from Hong Kong at the age of two, went to school in England and saw his parents only when his father got his leaves – which were few, far between and, as the journeys took six or seven weeks, that much shorter. So, like thousands of other middle-class children in the days of the British Empire, Pelham was much in the care of aunts, and he said that when he did get to know his mother, she had become, through absence, an aunt-like figure. He was always grateful to his own aunts in memory, but he got a lot of mileage in his books out of aunts as boss-figures, quick with disapproval, commands, threats and curses.

His aunt still affected him as of old. That is to say she made him feel as if he had
omitted to shave and, in addition to that, had swallowed some drug which had
caused him to swell unpleasantly, particularly about the hands and feet.

This aunt made a hobby of collecting dry seaweed, which she pressed and pasted
in an album. One sometimes thinks that aunts live entirely for pleasure.

It isn't often that Aunt Dahlia lets her angry passions rise, but when
she does strong men climb trees and pull them up after them.

For some moments there was nothing to be heard but
the sloshing sound of an aunt restoring her tissues.

Her words did not appear to me to make sense. They seemed the mere aimless
vapourings of an aunt who has been sitting out in the sun without her hat.

'My dear Ronald, that tie!'
Ronnie gazed at her lingeringly. It needed, he felt, but this. Poison was running through his
veins, his world was rocking, green-eyed devils were shrieking mockery in his ears, and along
came blasted aunts babbling about ties. It was as if somebody had touched Othello on the
arm as he poised above the pillow and criticised the cut of his doublet.

Her niece Millicent was to be united with a young man who, besides being penniless,
had always afflicted her with a nervous complaint for which she could find
no name, but which is known to scientists as the heeby-jeebies.

Aunt Agatha's demeanour now was rather like that of one who, picking daisies
on the railway, has just caught the down express in the small of the back.

Many a fellow who looks like the dominant male and has himself photographed
smoking a pipe curls up like carbon paper when confronted by an aunt.

I believe that Aunt Dahlia in her prime could lift fellow-members of the
Quorn and Pytchley out of their saddles with a single yip, though
separated from them by two ploughed fields and a spinney.

92 BOOKS

P.G. Wodehouse's fiction, with English titles and publication dates.

1902	*The Pothunters*		1924	*Ukridge*
1903	*A Prefect's Uncle*		1924	*Bill the Conqueror*
1903	*Tales of St Austin's*		1925	*Carry on, Jeeves*
1904	*The Gold Bat*		1925	*Sam the Sudden*
1904	*William Tell Told Again*		1926	*The Heart of a Goof*
1905	*The Head of Kay's*		1927	*The Small Bachelor*
1906 1921	*Love Among the Chickens*		1927	*Meet Mr Mulliner*
			1928	*Money for Nothing*
1907	*The White Feather*		1929	*Mr Mulliner Speaking*
1907	*Not George Washington*		1929	*Summer Lightning*
1909	*The Swoop*		1930	*Very Good, Jeeves*
1909	*Mike*		1931	*Big Money*
1910	*A Gentleman of Leisure*		1931	*If I Were You*
1910	*Psmith in the City*		1932	*Doctor Sally*
1912	*The Prince and Betty*		1932	*Hot Water*
1913	*The Little Nugget*		1933	*Mulliner Nights*
1914	*The Man Upstairs*		1933	*Heavy Weather*
1915	*Something Fresh*		1934	*Thank You, Jeeves*
1915	*Psmith Journalist*		1934	*Right Ho, Jeeves*
1917	*Uneasy Money*		1935	*Blandings Castle*
1917	*The Man with Two Left Feet*		1935	*The Luck of the Bodkins*
1918	*Piccadilly Jim*		1936	*Young Men in Spats*
1919	*My Man Jeeves*		1936	*Laughing Gas*
1919	*A Damsel in Distress*		1937	*Lord Emsworth and Others*
1920	*The Coming of Bill*		1938	*Summer Moonshine*
1921	*Jill the Reckless*		1938	*The Code of the Woosters*
1921	*Indiscretions of Archie*		1939	*Uncle Fred in the Springtime*
1922	*The Clicking of Cuthbert*		1940	*Eggs, Beans and Crumpets*
1922	*The Girl on the Boat*		1940	*Quick Service*
1922	*The Adventures of Sally*		1946	*Money in the Bank*
1923	*The Inimitable Jeeves*		1947	*Joy in the Morning*
1923	*Leave it to Psmith*		1947	*Full Moon*

1948	*Spring Fever*	1962	*Service with a Smile*
1948	*Uncle Dynamite*	1963	*Stiff Upper Lip, Jeeves*
1949	*The Mating Season*	1964	*Frozen Assets*
1950	*Nothing Serious*	1965	*Galahad at Blandings*
1951	*The Old Reliable*	1966	*Plum Pie*
1952	*Barmy in Wonderland*	1967	*Company for Henry*
1952	*Pigs Have Wings*	1968	*Do Butlers Burgle Banks?*
1953	*Ring for Jeeves*	1969	*A Pelican at Blandings*
1954	*Jeeves and the Feudal Spirit*	1970	*The Girl in Blue*
1956	*French Leave*	1971	*Much Obliged, Jeeves*
1957	*Something Fishy*	1972	*Pearls, Girls and Monty Bodkin*
1958	*Cocktail Time*	1973	*Bachelors Anonymous*
1959	*A Few Quick Ones*	1974	*Aunts Aren't Gentlemen*
1960	*Jeeves in the Offing*	1977	*Sunset at Blandings*
1961	*Ice in the Bedroom*		

THE POTHUNTERS 1902

It is the Sports term at St Austin's College (600-plus boys; cricket, rugger, fives, racquets). But we start with the Public Schools Boxing at Aldershot. Tony Graham of St Austin's knocks out his cousin, Allen Thomson of Rugby, in the final of the Middleweights. This is a novel, though the episodes hang together loosely as though they started as short stories. The silverware sports prizes disappear from the Pavilion and are cached in a hollow tree in Squire Sir Alfred Venner, MP's pheasant-coverts, out of bounds to the boys. Inspector Roberts comes down from Scotland Yard. In the boys' Houses there are plenty of study frowsts and teas. Charteris ('the Alderman') who talks rot pleasantly, as though he might develop into a Psmith, shares a study with Welch, the all-rounder. Charteris edits *The Glow-Worm*, an anonymous and jovial school monthly magazine.

A PREFECT'S UNCLE 1903

The summer term at Beckford College. Alan Gethryn is head of Leicester's House, in the Sixth, the XI and the XV. A new boy arrives at Leicester's, Reginald Farnie, who reveals himself to be Gethryn's uncle. Farnie is a bright lad, but an embarrassment to the nephew set in authority over him. Farnie gets into money trouble (not his fault) and disappears. Gethryn leaves a cricket House Match to go and find him, and Leicester's lose the match without him. There is a poetry prize, entry mandatory to the whole of the Upper Fifth. Lorimer of the Upper Fifth has a kid sister, Mabel, and Pringle, who shares a study with Lorimer, is 'gone on' her. Sex had not reared its innocent head in *The Pothunters* (1902) at all.

TALES OF ST AUSTIN'S 1903

Back to St Austin's College for twelve short stories, eleven of which had appeared in *The Captain* and *The Public School Magazine*. Charteris appears again. In fact 'The Manoeuvres of Charteris' (forty-three pages) may have been the start of a notional novel, with the Headmaster's twelve-year-old niece Dorothy as heroine to Charteris's hero. The book ends with five essaylets from *The Public School Magazine*. 'The Tom Brown Question' asks, in dialogue, who can have written the utterly feeble second half of that classic public school novel. (In fact it was still Hughes. But later biography has shown that he wrote the second half after the loss of a beloved daughter, which had badly affected his skill as a novelist.)

THE GOLD BAT 1904

We are at Wrykyn School now, in the rugger term. The statue of Sir Eustace Briggs, Mayor of Wrykyn, in the recreation ground has been tarred and feathered in the night. And a small gold bat, of the type given to school cricket colours to hang on watch-chains, is found at the scene of the crime. There is a fight in a fives court, and a couple of the boys keep (illegal) ferrets. Clowes, left wing three-quarter, is a solemn wit, lazy – another potential Psmith.

WILLIAM TELL TOLD AGAIN 1904

How tiny Switzerland threw off the yoke of horrid Austria, thanks to William Tell. Hermann Gessler, the Governor, was, with the help of a Lord High Executioner and his attendant oil-boiler, taxing the poor (but honest) Swiss down to the nub. But Hermann Gessler got an arrow where it did most good, in the heart. A short, cheerful narrative by Wodehouse, excellent colour pictures by Philip Dadd and excellent verse captions to the pictures, by John W. Houghton – very much the sort of expert verse Wodehouse himself was already writing, in *Punch* and elsewhere.

The pictures (and perhaps the verse) were done a year and more before Wodehouse was asked to supply the narrative.

THE HEAD OF KAY'S 1905

Now we are at Eckleton School, at the end of the summer term and into the autumn term, with some chapters of a Schools Corps Camp between. Mr Kay is an unpopular house-master and Kay's has gone downhill. Kennedy, 2nd prefect of Blackburn's House, and in the school cricket XI, is transferred, not too willingly, to be head boy of Kay's, with encouragement to make it a decent House again. He has to fight a dissident Kayite to assert his authority. House matches at cricket and rugger, and a five-mile run which Kennedy just wins for Kay's. Jimmy Silver, head of Blackburn's House and captain of cricket, is a near-Psmith talker.

LOVE AMONG THE CHICKENS 1906

The first five chapters are narrated about, the last eighteen by, Jeremy Garnet, Old Wrykynian, struggling author, verse-writer, ex-prep-schoolmaster, golfer. He is persuaded to join his feckless ex-school, ex-schoolmastering colleague, Stanley Featherstonehaugh Ukridge and his adoring wife Millie, in Lyme Regis where they are setting up a chicken farm that is supposed to be going to make fortunes for all of them. In the train from Paddington, Garnet meets a girl, Phyllis Derrick, who is actually reading one of his own (two) novels. She is going to join her father, Professor Derrick, at Lyme Regis. The Ukridge chicken-farm founders. The Professor quarrels with Ukridge and forbids his daughter the house. To win Phyllis's favour Garnet arranges to have her father upset from a boat in the harbour so that he, Garnet, can rescue him. But the Professor only gives his approval to the marriage after Garnet has let him win the final of the local golf tournament. The wedding is told as a short stage play. This book gives us our first view of Ukridge, that great dreamer, idler, schemer, borrower of money and clothes, and general menace.

Wodehouse revised the book and it was reissued in 1921. Now it was all told by Garnet, and the playlet of the wedding was removed. For some reason Lyme Regis was changed to Combe Regis. And the price of eggs was changed to allow for inflation.

THE WHITE FEATHER 1907

Back to Wrykyn School, in the spring term. A mayoral election is pending in the town. St Jude's, a school in the High Street, has a feud against Wrykyn. There is a mix-up fight in the street, and Sheen, head of Seymour's House, a scholar and a pianist – no boxer – is faced by Albert, a red-haired toughie of St Jude's. Sheen funks fighting him. This gets Sheen despised and virtually cut by the whole school – difficult when you have a House to run as head prefect. Sheen takes to going, illegally, to the Blue Boar where Joe Bevan, ex-world lightweight champion, failed actor, great quoter of Shakespeare, teaches and trains boxers. Sheen, with Joe's training behind him, eventually gets permission from a surprised sports master to enter for the lightweights at the public schools meeting at Aldershot. He beats Peteiro of Ripton in the final.

NOT GEORGE WASHINGTON 1907

A very poor novel, written in collaboration with Herbert Westbrook, who was more than half in Wodehouse's mind for the character of Ukridge, in *Love Among the Chickens* and many later and more expert short stories. James Orlebar Cloyster is engaged to Margaret Goodwin in Guernsey, and the arrangement is that she shall join him and they'll get married as soon as Cloyster has made a position for himself in London as a writer. Later he tries to conceal his successes so that Margaret won't hear of them and demand marriage. Later still they do marry – or rather, they are left, apparently happy, on the brink of marriage.

I do not understand the title of this book. I do understand why it is such a rarity, and why collectors of Wodehouse pay very high prices when copies emerge at auction sales.

THE SWOOP 1909

There had been novels in England foreseeing enemy invasion as far back as *The Battle of Dorking*, serialised in *Blackwood's Magazine* in 1870. From 1902, when Germany had decided to build a battle-fleet to equal England's, the idea of a blitz invasion across the North Sea, before the English battleships could get back from the Mediterranean, was a best-selling subject for the popular press, from 'Chums' to the Harmsworth journals.

Wodehouse's *The Swoop* is a short squib, taking off these invasion-scare writings as well as the recently formed, and popular, Boy Scouts. England is invaded by the armies of a multitude of enemies: Saxe-Pfennig, Russia, Afghanistan, China (under General Ping Pong Pang), Turkey, Morocco, Monaco and the distant isle of Bollygolla. England's defences crumble – it's August and everybody is away on holiday. Only the Boy Scouts resist the invaders. Clarence Chugwater, aged fourteen, and a junior reporter on an evening paper, is in command of a troop on the Aldwych site, and he leads his men in with catapults and hockey sticks. Eventually the music halls offer the invading generals and princes vast weekly salaries to appear nightly on their stages, Clarence himself topping the bills with £1,150 a week. Some real names occur. Edgar Wallace is a war correspondent, as he was at that time. Charles Frohmann is a theatrical producer, Baden Powell is head of the Scouts.

In 1915 Wodehouse adapted the book to signal an invasion of America by Germany and Japan in 1916, and sold it for serialisation to the smart New York monthly magazine, *Vanity Fair*.

Writing to George Orwell in June 1948 (*The Letters of Evelyn Waugh*, edited by Mark Amory, 1980), Waugh seems to ascribe importance to *The Swoop* in the context of the broadcasts Wodehouse made to neutral America from Berlin in 1941. Waugh also says 'This book is very much funnier than *The Head of Keys* (sic) which preceded it, and in fact forms an important literary link with *Mike* published next year.'

The Head of Kay's is not a funny book in that sense, and there were three books of Wodehouse's published after that one and before *The Swoop*. It is anybody's guess what Waugh thought the important literary link was between *The Swoop* and *Mike*.

MIKE 1909

Of the five Jackson brothers one plays cricket for England, two others for counties. But Mike, the youngest at fifteen, shows signs of being the best batsman of them all. He goes to Wrykyn School as a new boy. His elder brother Bob is in his last term and they both get their First XI colours that summer. Mike, in the Ripton match, turns disaster into victory with a heroic innings. But two years later Mike's school report is so bad that his father removes him from Wrykyn, when he is just about to be cricket captain, and sends him to a minor school, Sedleigh, where they make boys work.

At Sedleigh Mike meets, and becomes friends with, another elderly new boy, similarly displaced from Eton, and similarly scornful of his new school – Psmith. The two 'lost lambs' share a study, and decide not to take cricket seriously, but to rag. The Sedleigh cricket captain, Adair, dislikes Mike's lack of keenness and it takes a fist-fight (which Mike wins by a knock-out) to cure his antagonism to Adair and to Sedleigh.

A GENTLEMAN OF LEISURE 1910

Jimmy Pitt, rich, generous, popular American bachelor, has fallen in love with an unknown girl on a transatlantic liner. He bets a friend at the Strollers Club in New York that he can break into a house like any Raffles. He does so and it happens to be the apartment of a crooked New York policeman (English originally, sacked from Eton, and has now changed his name: a bad hat), John McEachern, whose daughter is/was the girl on the boat. The scene changes to Dreever Castle in Shropshire, where 'Spennie', Earl of Dreever, is bossed around by his self-made millionaire uncle, Sir Thomas Blunt, MP. Lady Julia Blunt has a £20,000 'diamond' necklace (it proves to be valueless white jargoon). Spennie is being sharked at billiards, poker and picquet by one of the house party. Among the guests are John McEachern, who has made his pile by New York graft and spends it bringing his beloved daughter into good English society. He now hopes to marry her to the 12th Earl of Dreever. Spennie's uncle and aunt also hope this will be a match because they think

Molly McEachern is an heiress. Jimmy Pitt is of the house party too. He wins the love and hand of Molly.

Dreever Castle, a massive grey pile in Shropshire, built against raiders looming over the Welsh border, is a forerunner of Blandings, and perhaps Lady Julia and her 'diamonds' are forerunners of Lady Constance and her diamonds in *Leave it to Psmith*.

In the two stage versions of this novel Douglas Fairbanks Sr. and John Barrymore, neither well known at the time, played the Jimmy Pitt part.

PSMITH IN THE CITY 1910

Mike Jackson's father has lost 'a very large sum of money' and Mike now can't go to Cambridge. So Mike goes into the New Asiatic Bank in the City. Psmith's rich and eccentric father thinks that Psmith should go into commerce, so Psmith turns up at the bank too.

Psmith has a comfortable flat in Clement's Inn to which Mike goes to live. Psmith belongs to the same club, the Senior Conservatives, as Mr Bickersdyke, crusty manager of the New Asiatic Bank, who is also running for Parliament for the Conservatives. Psmith decides to harass Bickersdyke and discovers that he had once been a rabid Socialist.

Mike is paid £4 10s a month. He and Psmith are both bored by the bank. They 'bunk' it together on the same day, Mike because he gets a sudden call to play for his county at Lord's (he makes 148), Psmith to go and watch. They are both sacked, joyfully, by Mr Bickersdyke.

Now Psmith's father wants him to go to Cambridge and read Law. And he offers Mike a future agency of his estates, after three or four years at Cambridge which Mr Smith will finance. (Mike's brother Joe, an All England batsman, is already the agent of a sporting baronet, keen on cricket.)

A good worm's eye view of City life in banking, and some amusing excursions into politics and political meetings where you can 'rag' by heckling.

THE PRINCE AND BETTY 1912

Betty Silver, twenty-four, is step-daughter of millionaire-tycoon Benjamin Scobell, the nephew and sole male relative of Mrs Jane Oakley, multi-millionairess miser. Some years ago Betty had met a John Maude when he was at Harvard, and he has been her *prince loin-tain* ever since. Benjamin Scobell virtually owns the Mediterranean island of Mervo and he runs it as a gambling property. He discovers that John Maude's late father had been Prince and ruler of Mervo, deposed when the island elected to be a republic. Scobell decides, for business reasons, to bring John Maude in as Prince and – to keep him in the family – to marry him to his step-daughter Betty. Betty goes out to Mervo, meets John Maude again, but thinks he is courting her simply because her step-father has ordered him to. She runs away to New York. Her aunt, Mrs Oakley, likes her, tells her to dry her tears and get a job. As 'Betty Brown' she goes as a typist to *Peaceful Moments*, a sleepy weekly. Rupert Smith, ex-Harvard newspaperman, is deputy editor, but, when the editor is ordered away for three months for health reasons, Smith takes over and peps the magazine up. Rupert Smith is clearly a clone of Psmith: very tall, thin and dark, with a solemn face; immaculately dressed, monocle in left eye and calls people 'Comrade'. Helped by good researching, muck-raking and writing by Betty 'Brown', the paper attacks the anonymous owners of the Brosher Street slum tenements in New York. Meanwhile John Maude has quit Mervo, not liking the Scobell methods, and he gets a job at *Peaceful Moments* through his old friend Rupert Smith. Betty, thinking he is pursuing her, disappears and takes a job as cashier in one of Bat Jarvis's (a nice cat-loving gangster) cafés. It transpires that Benjamin Scobell is owner not only of *Peaceful Moments* all the time, but of the Brosher Street tenements also. He repents and says he will repair them and run them properly. John Maude, reunited with Betty, wants to marry her. Mrs Oakley gives them enough money for them to buy a farm out west and make the happy ending.

THE LITTLE NUGGET 1913

'The Little Nugget' is the kidnappers' name for Ogden Ford, a fat, chain-smoking, rude and badly spoilt American boy, aged thirteen or fourteen. Ogden's mother and father (she rich, he richer) are divorced, and each trying to get the boy away from the other. Meanwhile professional kidnappers are trying to get him, for ransom from either parent. Elmer Ford, the father, pays double fees for Ogden to go to a snobbish little English preparatory school (boarding) where he thinks the boy will be fairly safe and may even learn some discipline. Peter Burns (rich, a cricket and rugger Blue) is persuaded by his fiancée, who is in the pay of Mrs Ford, to go as an assistant master to this school and kidnap Ogden so that his mother can get him on to a yacht and out of his father's reach. But who is White, the new school butler? A professional kidnapper. And others prowl and prowl around. Peter Burns tells the story (except the first twenty-five pages of it) and it makes an excellent thriller, set mostly in the grounds and house of the prep school.

THE MAN UPSTAIRS 1914

Nineteen early short stories, some fairly good, some fairly bad. Most of them were written in America for the American pulps. 'Archibald's Benefit' is Wodehouse's first golf story. 'The Good Angel' is the first story with a strong butler part (and some very ill-informed comings and goings of a shooting party at an English country house). Rollo and Wilson in 'Ahead of Schedule' are a foretaste of Bertie Wooster and Jeeves. Sally, who, in 'Something to Worry About', feuds with a policeman and asks her fiancé to pull the man's helmet down over his eyes, is a foretaste of Stiffy Byng in *The Code of the Woosters*. 'In Alcala' has strands of autobiography in it; its sentimentality is remarkably gooey, but is there, anywhere else in Wodehouse, a heroine who admits to having been a man's mistress?

SOMETHING FRESH 1915

The first of the Blandings saga. Aline Peters, daughter of dyspeptic American millionaire scarab-collector J. Preston Peters, is to marry the Hon. Freddie Threepwood, and there is to be a fortnight-long house party at the castle, 'a gathering together of the Emsworth clan by way of honour and as a means of introduction to Mr Peters and his daughter'. Lord Emsworth has pocketed one of Mr Peters's valuable scarabs, thinking it a gift. And Mr Peters is determined to get it back, offering a reward, too. Ashe Marson, writer of thrillers (*Gridley Quayle, Investigator*), signs on as Mr Peters's valet with instructions to steal back the scarab. And Joan Valentine signs on as Aline Peters's lady's maid with the same quest, and reward, in mind. Ashe and Joan (who are in the same London digs to start with) are to get married in the end and Aline rejects Freddie to elope with George Emerson, of the Hong Kong Police, whom Freddie has asked down casually for the party.

There is more about what goes on below stairs the other side of the green baize door here than in any other book of Wodehouse's.

PSMITH JOURNALIST 1915

Originally published as a serial in *The Captain* in 1909, Mike Jackson goes to America to play for an MCC side, with his friend Psmith accompanying him 'in a private capacity'. While Mike goes off to Philadelphia to play cricket, Psmith stays in New York and becomes the hero of this novel.

There is no heroine. In a New York restaurant Psmith meets the acting editor of the weekly *Cosy Moments*, and, through him and the office boy, the cat-loving leader of the Groom Street Gang, Bat Jarvis. As the real editor is away and out of contact, and the proprietor in Europe, Windsor (the acting editor) and Psmith (amateur sub-editor) decide to jazz up the paper and, amongst other campaigns, to attack the unknown landlord of some dreadful New

York slum tenements. The anonymous landlord threatens reprisals to Windsor, Psmith and the paper. With the help of Bat Jarvis and his gang they fight the gangs that the landlord hires to beat them up. There is some shooting and Psmith has to get a new hat as a result.

Psmith, with the help of a legacy from an uncle, and his father in Switzerland, buys *Cosy Moments* from its proprietor. The owner of the slum property turns out to be a politician running for City Alderman. He is made to repent and to make great improvements in the houses for his tenants.

Psmith calls back the old stagnant staff and hands the paper back to them, while remaining owner (apparently) after he and Mike go back to Cambridge.

UNEASY MONEY 1917

Bill (Lord) Dawlish, twenty-four, is a good footballer, boxer and golfer, has good health, many friends, a beautiful (though hard) fiancée, minor actress Claire Fenwick, and no money except the £400 a year he gets as secretary to exclusive Brown's Club. Claire refuses to marry him on £400 a year. Then Bill hears he has been left a million pounds by an eccentric American whose golfing slice he had cured. He also hears that the eccentric's niece, Elizabeth Boyd, who farms bees on Long Island, had expected to inherit the million pounds. Bill, without telling Claire, goes to America (as Bill Chalmers) to see that Elizabeth gets at least half of the inheritance. Claire, separately and unknown to Bill, also goes to America, to stay with her ex-chorus-girl friend who is now a successful barefoot dancer calling herself Lady Pauline Wetherby. Claire meets an American millionaire on the boat and makes him propose to her, and she accepts. Then, hearing of Bill's new wealth, she breaks with her American and expects to be taken back by Bill. But Bill now is in love with Elizabeth, though she refuses to marry him with no money of her own.

Well, the eccentric old millionaire had made a later will, and so...

This novel has the common early Wodehouse Anglo-American pattern, with Anglo-American marriages. There is some untidy gun-play near the end and Claire's millionaire accidentally shoots a pet monkey.

THE MAN WITH TWO LEFT FEET 1917

Thirteen early short stories, written in America. One, 'Extricating Young Gussie' is important because it introduces Bertie (though his surname seems to be Mannering-Phipps), Jeeves and Aunt Agatha. Gussie Mannering-Phipps, head of the 'very old and aristocratic' family now that his father, Bertie's Uncle Cuthbert, keen drinker, unsuccessful gambler, big spender, has died, has gone to America and is involved with a girl on the New York vaudeville stage. Aunt Agatha sends Bertie over to extricate Gussie. Bertie is unsuccessful, and all ends happily, with Gussie marrying the vaudeville girl, his mother, herself ex-vaudeville, remarrying, this time to an old vaudevillian adorer, and Bertie staying on in New York with Jeeves for fear of meeting Aunt Agatha's wrath.

Otherwise mostly sentimental apprentice work. One story, 'The Mixer', is told by a dog, another is about a cat; one, 'One Touch of Nature', is about a rich American forced by his society-minded wife to live in England, but longing to see baseball games again. One, 'The Romance of an Ugly Policeman', is about a pretty cook in London courted by the milkman, falsely accused of theft by the lady of the house, being marched off by a policeman and, after doing her thirty days, finding the policeman, not the milkman, waiting for her. 'The Making of Mac's' could almost have been written by 'Sapper'.

PICCADILLY JIM 1918

Even in Lloyd George's premiership would a second-rank American actor, married to an American millionairess forging ahead in London society, be given an English peerage? No, but it's important to the plot of this comedy-thriller that the American millionairess is aiming at just that – to spite her millionairess sister who has said she married beneath her. Bingley Crocker is the suffering peer-hopefully-to-be, a baseball fan stuck in London with an ambitious, snobbish wife, an English butler who is a cricket fan and a son, Jimmy, who is now 'Piccadilly Jim', playboy. Jimmy Crocker, like Jimmy Pitt in *A Gentleman of Leisure*, had, before he became cushioned by money, been a newspaperman and had written a hurtfully ribald review of a volume of heart-felt poetry by Ann Chester – not a good start because he later finds he wants to marry her.

Here comes young Ogden Ford again, and his mother, widowed, and now remarried to, and making life hell for, Peter Pett, New York financier and baseball fan. Ann Chester is Peter Pett's niece and comforter, also governess and supposed to be in charge of Ogden, whom she rightly detests mainly because he adds to the hell of his step-father's life. The whole family, Peter Pett, Nesta Pett, Ogden and Ann come over to England to persuade Mrs Pett's sister, Mrs Crocker, to let them take her step-son Jimmy back, to work in New York, rather than be 'Piccadilly Jim', the joy of the columnists (he has had two breach-of-promise cases against him – a barmaid and a girl in a flower shop) in London.

There is far too much disguising and false-naming for even faint credibility. At one stage Jimmy Crocker, pretending to be son of English butler Bayliss, has to *pretend* to be Jimmy Crocker to fool his father. There is a sub-plot about the Secret Service and a new explosive, partridgite.

Jimmy Crocker gets Ann in the end, both agreeing that his hurtful review of her poems five years ago had reformed and toughtened her hitherto soppy outlook; and anyway a fellow like him needs a tough wife.

MY MAN JEEVES 1919

Four Jeeves stories told by Bertie Wooster staying in New York to avoid the wrath of his Aunt Agatha: four stories told by Reggie Pepper. Six of these eight stories turn up again in *Carry on, Jeeves* (1925), two of them, which had been told by Reggie Pepper, now recast as Bertie/Jeeves stories, set in England.

If your textbook is *The World of Jeeves* omnibus, the stories that belong in essentials to *My Man Jeeves* are 'The Artistic Career of Corky', 'Jeeves and the Chump Cyril', 'Jeeves and the Unbidden Guest', 'Jeeves and the Hard-Boiled Egg', 'The Aunt and the Sluggard' and 'Jeeves Makes an Omelette'.

In fact Jeeves had first appeared – though only two lines of him – in 'Extricating Young Gussie' in *The Man with Two Left Feet*.

A DAMSEL IN DISTRESS 1919

This is almost a Blandings novel. Belpher Castle is in Hampshire, but it has an amber drawing-room, a terrace below and a rose garden. Its widower châtelain is the Earl of Marshmoreton. He is a great gardener, he is bossed by his sister, he has a butler who looks like a saintly bishop and a foolish son and heir. He marries, at the end, a charming (American) chorus girl, a felicity never allowed to Lord Emsworth – only to his nephew Ronnie Fish.

The hero of this book is American composer George Bevan. The heroine is Lady Maud Marsh, the Earl's daughter, a good golfer, with tilted nose. She is a captive at the castle under aunt's orders because of her 'ridiculous infatuation' for an impossible American. That's not, in fact, George Bevan. Bevan is eminently possible: nice, a golfer, with a good line in Psmith talk, and he makes $5,000 a week in a theatre season in a good year, which is not hay even with $5 to the £1. (Italian restaurants in Soho serve *table d'hôte* lunches for 1s 6d and you get your top-hat ironed in your shaving parlour.)

A good deal of good theatre stuff here and a two-weeks house-party with a ball at the castle for the son and heir's twenty-first birthday. The impossible American who has been a threat to George Bevan's courtship of Maud only comes on stage briefly at the end. When she had fallen for him he had been a 'slim Apollo'. Then he had gone out of her life, but not heart, for a year – during which he had, incidentally, been toying, under an assumed name and the nickname 'Pootles', with the affection of a nice chorus girl (is there ever a nasty chorus girl in a story or novel of Wodehouse's?) to the tune of £10,000 for breach of promise – and now he returns, thirty pounds overweight and talking about food, not love. It is easy for Maud to make the big decision and say Yes to George.

THE COMING OF BILL 1920

It was all the fault of Lora Delane Porter, rich American widow, eugenist, writer and lecturer. When Kirk Winfield, an unsuccessful artist but with a small private income and a fine physique, fell in love with Ruth Bannister at first sight, and she with him (she being Mrs Porter's niece and the daughter of a Wall Street millionaire), Mrs Porter said, 'Marry, for the good of the race.' They marry. It is not too happy. Kirk's income isn't enough for two. Ruth objects to his sponging friends and to the friendly model who is sitting for his 'Ariadne in Naxos' and calls him Kirk. Ruth suggests that Kirk go in for landscape painting, and, if he must, finish Ariadne with herself as model. She faints on the dais and there's going to be a b-a-b-y. Enter Bill, nine pounds and with a fine physique. He is instantly, and without much fuss from Ruth, brought up on Mrs Porter's lines of eugenic untouchability. Kirk, in the hope of making money, goes off gold-prospecting in Colombia with his old friend Hank Jardine. Ruth's father dies and she inherits money and becomes a prominent New York hostess, pursued by a rich ex-boyfriend. Kirk returns, having failed to find gold and having lost his friend Hank Jardine (fever). Kirk, with the help of Steve Dingle, the ex-pug gymnasium instructor, and Mamie, Bill's nursemaid, kidnaps Bill and whisks him off to a mountain fastness. Ruth loses her money in the crash of her silly brother's firm, inherited from father, on Wall Street, and she returns to her own family, poor but happy. It's *that* for Aunt Lora. Young Bill *shall* get dirty sometimes, he *shall* fight the neighbour bully child, he *shall* have an Irish terrier puppy to hug. It's happy endings for the Winfields, reunited, and not so happy for Aunt Lora.

All American, except for an English butler in the Bannister house.

JILL THE RECKLESS 1921

Jill Mariner, pretty, young, with plenty of money, lives in Ovington Square (and owns the house) with her raffish uncle, Chris Selby. She is engaged to Sir Derek Underhill, Bart., MP, a rich, handsome, athletic stuffed shirt who is dominated by his mother, Lady Underhill. At a first night of a very bad play the theatre catches fire and Jill, who is with

'Mr. Wodehouse is a national humourist'
Manchester Guardian

The
COMING OF BILL

by P.G.WODEHOUSE
author of 'Piccadilly Jim'
and 'A Damsel in Distress'

FOR
SUMMARY
OF THIS STORY
SEE
BACK OF
WRAPPER

Jill
the Reckless

P. G. WODEHOUSE

By the way did you read Piccadilly Jim,
and do you know A Damsel in Distress? This
is by the same author, the ever-amusing
WODEHOUSE

Derek and his mother, escapes with the help of the man in the next seat, who is Wally Mason. He happens to be the author and backer of the play and to have known Jill in childhood and to have loved her since. Jill and Wally go to the Savoy and there they meet Derek and his mother. Uncle Chris loses Jill's money for her, as her trustee, and at the same time Jill gets arrested in London for fighting with a man who is teasing a parrot. Derek, under pressure from his mother, breaks off the engagement (because of the arrest) and everybody thinks he has done it because Jill's no longer rich. She goes in poverty, to America, to the place on Long Island of a dour uncle (her father had been American). She joins the chorus of a play being prepared for Broadway. She acquires money and buys the play, which is foundering. Wally Mason doctors it and it is a hit. Jill will marry Wally. Derek has come over to New York to ask her, again, to marry him, but the answer is No. Even Freddie Rooke, Derek's ex-fag (Winchester) and hero-worshipper, turns on him in the end and calls him a rotter.

Good, with knowledgeable chapters about the theatre. Freddie Rooke, Winchester, Bachelors Club, Albany, moneyed (but goes down on Amalgamated Dyes), gets happily engaged to Nelly Bryant, American chorus girl.

INDISCRETIONS OF ARCHIE 1921

The silly ass Englishman, Eton and Oxford, in America during Prohibition, married to the daughter of an American millionaire. Hardly a novel. A stitching together of a series of episodes which started as short stories.

An ex-bankrupt who has married Lucille Brewster without her father's knowledge and coming to seek his blessing, Archie has a row with the manager of the Hotel Cosmopolis in New York and finds that he is the proprietor, also his father-in-law. A bad start, but at the end Daniel Brewster accepts his daughter's marriage, and even her husband, because they are going to make him a grandfather.

In Chapter 12 there is a very good, long newspaper report of a pie-eating contest *in verse*.

THE CLICKING OF CUTHBERT 1922

Nine stories of golf told by the Oldest Member, and one Christmas Number fantasy, 'The Coming of Gowf'. Reverent mockery of the game and its votaries in the days when the clubs had proper names – baffy, cleek, mashie and so on. There is generally a pretty girl to play for. In the story that gives the collection its title Vladimir Brusiloff, the great Russian writer, turns out to be, behind the beard, handicap 18 at Nijni Novgorod and as mad keen a golfer as Cuthbert Banks who had won the French Open and often played with Abe Mitchell.

THE GIRL ON THE BOAT 1922

Sam Marlowe, English, six foot, broad-chested, a stopper-of-dog-fights, a romantic and a buzzer, has been in America to play in the amateur golf championship (beaten in the semifinals). Wilhelmina (Billie) Bennett, American, is a very pretty redhead, with a freckle on the tip of her nose, a Peke, Pinky-Boodles (who bites everybody), and a rich, fat father. Sam and Billie meet on the SS *Atlantic*, heading for England and, although Billie has one, if not more, other adorers or courtiers, and though Sam makes a damnfool of himself at the ship's concert, he wins Billie in the end. Some other characters are Mrs Adeline Horace Hignett, Sam's formidable aunt, a writer and lecturer on Theosophy, a dominant dame who, to prevent her coddled son, Eustace, from going out to get married, steals all his trousers; Jane Howard, the big-game hunter who takes her elephant gun and cartridges with her on a country house visit in England and is longing to find a nice *weak* man to marry and fuss over – so what about Eustace? And Montague Webster, Billie's father's stately, ambassadorial 'personal gentleman's gentleman', a flamboyant and haughty sort of Jeeves. The last chapter evokes the midnight scene at Blandings Castle in *Something Fresh*. And Sam boning up on Tennyson's to impress the girl will be repeated in the Freddie Widgeon story 'Trouble at Tudsleigh'. Long quotations from poets written as prose – quite a habit in this book. A very yeasty light novel.

THE ADVENTURES OF SALLY 1922

Like *Jill the Reckless*, an Anglo-American novel largely about the theatre. American Sally Nicholas has inherited $25,000. She is engaged to a very good-looking English unsuccessful artist, who is a would-be playwright too, Jerry Foster. Her brother Fillmore has also inherited, but his new money makes him fat and pompous. Sally is forgiving of his faults and foolishnesses and encourages the good-hearted and simple Gladys Winch, show girl, to marry Fillmore and look after him. Jerry, like almost all good-looking young men in Wodehouse, is a heel. He married, behind Sally's back, a girl friend of Sally's who has become a rising star in the theatre. The marriage is headed for failure, and Jerry for the bottle. Sally, a game little friend of all the world, has Ginger Kemp as a constant adorer. Ginger is English. He was doing well at Oxford – boxing and rugger blues – when his father 'failed' in business and Ginger had to go and work for his uncle. That was a failure; then schoolmastering, also failure. He meets Sally on the beach at Roville, and stops a dog-fight and asks her to marry him. He follows her to America, and does eventually marry her, when she has lost her money. They set up, happily, a sort of dog-farm which is enjoyable and is going to be successful. Sally rumples Ginger's hair, a sure sign of connubial love and contentment in Wodehouse.

A jerky, choppy book. Mrs Meecher's lodging house in New York is Dickensian. Several short story themes are tied up untidily together, and there is a scrambling of loose ends to finish up.

P.G.WODEHOUSE

The Adventures of Sally

THE INIMITABLE JEEVES 1923

Ten short stories, eight set in England, one in New York, one in Roville-sur-mer. Seven of them feature Bertie's friend Bingo Little, in love successively with a tea-shop waitress, Honoria Glossop, Daphne Braythwayt, Charlotte Corday Rowbotham, Lady Cynthia Wickhammersley, Mary Burgess and, for marriage and keeps, Rosie M. Banks, the best-selling novelist. We also meet Claude and Eustace, Bertie's twin cousins, reading for, at, or sent down from, Oxford. 'The Great Sermon Handicap' is one for the anthologies.

LEAVE IT TO PSMITH 1923

Psmith's father has died and the estate has been broken up. Mike Jackson, married to Phyllis, step-daughter of Joe Keeble, husband of Lady Constance of Blandings, is a schoolmaster and not liking it. Lady Constance had wanted Phyllis to marry rich Rollo

Mountford, with 'horrid swimmy eyes', but she had eloped with Mike. Mike wants to buy a farm in Lincolnshire. Psmith advertises himself to go anywhere, do anything, and Freddie Threepwood asks him to come to Blandings Castle to help him help Joe Keeble to steal Connie's £20,000 diamond necklace. Freddie wants, as a reward from Uncle Joe, money to set himself up in a bookmaking business. Psmith goes after the reward in order to help Mike. He goes down to Blandings Castle pretending to be Ralston McTodd, Canadian poet, author of *Songs of Squalor*. Cataloguing the Library at Blandings Castle is Eve Halliday. Psmith pursues her for marriage, and succeeds. Freddie has been pursuing Eve too. A crook, Eddie Cootes, turns up intending to pass *himself* off as Ralston McTodd. There is some minor gun-play. The necklace is stolen successfully and hidden – by whom? The efficient Baxter is locked out of the castle in his pyjamas, throws flowerpots at Lord Emsworth's windows and is sacked. Connie will get another nice necklace (she and Joe have a joint bank account: she won't mind seeing £20,000 on the debit side for a new necklace – but she has refused to have Joe spend money helping Phyllis Jackson). Mike Jackson gets the money for his farm. Eddie Cootes finds his old card-sharping partner, Aileen Peavey, at Blandings Castle and they are going to team up again. Psmith will marry Eve Halliday and take the job of Lord Emsworth's secretary.

This is the first of many times that Wodehouse uses the husband-and-wife joint bank account as a way to stop even a millionaire (Joe Keeble) from writing a £3,000 cheque when his wife says No.

N.B. Wodehouse and his wife Ethel had a joint bank account, with Ethel in total control.

UKRIDGE 1924

We first met Ukridge in *Love Among the Chickens*, 1906 and 1921. He was then married to his beloved and loving Millie. In these ten stories he has gone back to bachelorhood and he only meets Millie and gets engaged to her in the last story.

These stories are told by 'Corky' Corcoran, who had been at Wrykyn with Ukridge and to whom Ukridge was always a threat – borrowing money and clothes. Here we meet 'Battling' Billson, the soft-hearted heavyweight boxer whom Ukridge is promoting; Ukridge's rich Aunt Julia; George Tupper of the Foreign Office, another school friend of Ukridge's; Evan Jones, a Welsh revivalist whose preaching makes Battling Billson think fighting is wicked; Bowles, Corky's ex-butler landlord in Ebury Street; Flossie, the barmaid, Billson's fiancée; and Mabel Price of Clapham Common to whom Ukridge becomes perilously engaged. And finally Lady Lakenheath, Millie's Aunt Elizabeth with a multilingual parrot, Leonard.

These are some of the best stories that Wodehouse ever wrote.

BILL THE CONQUEROR 1924

Bill West is an athletic young American living on an allowance from a millionaire uncle. The uncle sends him to London to see why his, the uncle's, business interests are going downhill. Bill takes with him his best, but hard-drinking, friend Judson Coker, to whose beautiful sister Bill aspires to be engaged. She had wanted Bill to take Juddy away and keep him off the drink.

In London Felicia ('Flick') Sheridan, twenty-one, is engaged to Roderick Pyke, son and heir of Sir George Pyke, founder and proprietor of the Mammoth Publishing Company. Flick had, as a schoolgirl in America, fallen in love with a Harvard footballer who had dragged her out of a lake in which she was foolishly beginning to drown. This was Bill West, and Bill and Flick meet again in London just when Flick had broken her engagement to Roderick and, fearing reprisals, has run away from home and disapproving elders. Flick goes to America. Bill's uncle comes to London. Flick helps Bill find the man who is robbing his uncle's London till, Wilfred Slingsby. So...

Here is Wodehouse's first use of Mario's Restaurant where Society dines and has fracas and where – as at the old Café de Paris – diners downstairs (Must Dress) cannot see the diners upstairs (Needn't Dress) who *can* see *them*.

CARRY ON, JEEVES 1925

This collection of ten short stories contains five that appeared first in *My Man Jeeves*. 'Jeeves Takes Charge' goes back in story-time to Jeeves arriving from the agency at Bertie's flat, curing his hangover and being instantly taken on, soon sacked and soon re-taken on. Bertie is engaged to Florence Craye here, not for the last time in the annals. We meet for the first and last time Bertie's Uncle Willoughby of Easeby, Shropshire, and, for the first time, Florence's disastrous kid brother, Edwin the Boy Scout. We find that Jeeves had once worked for their father, Lord Worplesdon. Bertie's forgetful friend Biffy is engaged to Honoria Glossop in 'The Rummy Affair of Old Biffy'. We meet Bertie's Aunt Dahlia Travers ('Clustering Round Young Bingo') and her paper *Milady's Boudoir* for which Bertie has written a 'piece'. And here are Bingo and Rosie Little, whose chef Anatole joins the Travers staff for many books and excitements to come. The last story 'Bertie Changes His Mind' is the only one in the canon told by Jeeves.

SAM THE SUDDEN 1925

Sam Shotter (Old Wrykynian, his father English, mother American), roughing it in a log-hut in Canada, has fallen in love with a girl in a picture – a photograph from an English weekly that his predecessor in the log-hut had stuck up. Sam comes to England with his

SAM THE SUDDEN

P. G.
WODEHOUSE

FRANK
MARSTON

disreputable friend, and servant, Hash Todhunter, late cook on the tramp-steamer *Araminta*. Sam's American uncle, in process of a business negotiation with Lord Tilbury (as he now is – Sir George Pyke as was) gets Lord Tilbury to give Sam a job in Mammoth Publishing. He now writes the 'Aunt Ysobel' page ('Chats with my Girls') in the *Home Companion* magazine, and finds that the girl in the picture is the niece of his editor and that she lives with her uncle in the bungalow in Valley Fields next to the one that he himself has rented. And one of those semi-detacheds contains a $2 million stock of bearer bonds that had been stolen from a bank and hidden away by a thief who had died before he could cash them. So here come Soapy and Dolly Molloy and Chimp Twist (alias J. Sheringham Adair). This is our first meeting with this crooked trio. Also horrible Percy Pilbeam, now editor of *Society Spice* for Mammoth. And this is our first visit to Wodehouse's beloved Valley Fields, the West Dulwich of his boyhood.

Sam Shotter is a good specimen of the Wodehouse buzzer hero: no laggard in love and quick to rescue kittens stuck up in trees. He kisses the heroine at their first meeting and gets a furious rebuff. But she is ruffling his hair enjoyably in the last chapter. Sam had found the missing bonds and will get the ten per cent reward from the bank. He has also had the privilege of calling Lord Tilbury 'you pompous little bounder!'

THE HEART OF A GOOF 1926

Nine more golf stories told by the Oldest Member. In two of them, set in America, we meet a fine couple of fat multi-millionaires who are rivals at golf (both very bad, and arrant cheats) and rivals as collectors of golf treasures (such as J. H. Taylor's shirt stud). They play each other for high stakes. Bradbury Fisher has a baffy Bobby Jones had used in the Infants All-In Championship of Atlanta, Georgia, and he is prepared to trade it for Gladstone Bott's English butler, Blizzard, the finest on Long Island. And then back from England comes Mrs Bott, with Vosper, the butler supreme lured from the Duke of Bootle's establishment. In two stories we watch the romance of William Bates and Jane Packard, golfers, result in marriage and the birth of young Braid Vardon Bates. We meet this lot again in *Nothing Serious*.

THE SMALL BACHELOR 1927

George Finch, shy young man from Idaho, inherits money and goes to New York to try to be a painter. He is a rotten painter. He goggles with love at a cuddly girl. She turns out to be Molly Waddington, daughter of a 'synthetic Westerner', Sigsbee Waddington, who is tied to New York by his snobbish and rich second wife, but dreams of the open-air life as depicted by Zane Grey's novels and Tom Mix's films. To get money for an investment

which he thinks will make him rich and free of dependence on his bossy wife, Sigsbee Waddington has stolen the pearls from his daughter's valuable necklace, sold them and replaced them with fakes. George Finch has a 'man', Mullett, a reformed (?) convict. Mullett is engaged to Fanny Welch, pickpocket, and both are trying to go straight. Place, New York. Time, Prohibition. There is a poetical policeman, Garroway, a phony English Lord ('Willie the Dude') Hunstanton, J. Hamilton Beamish, incorrigible writer of advice booklets, and a displaced English butler looking back wistfully from service with the Waddingtons in New York to Brangmarley Hall in Shropshire where he had been footman and then butler in his day.

The whole thing is a farce, as near a Ben Travers imbroglio as any of Wodehouse's books, and its plot and dialogue show that it started as a play. The first good Wodehouse drunk scene – Sigsbee drunk on alcohol and George Finch drunk on love.

MEET MR MULLINER 1927

Wodehouse's first outing with Mr Mulliner, teller par excellence of non-fishing fisherman's tales. Over a few hot Scotch and Lemons at his regular haunt the Anglers' Rest pub, Mulliner captivates the locals with tales about his cousins, nephews, uncles, brothers and various other relatives who all seem to be perennially in the soup. We're told of George Mulliner for whom being chased by a mob through the English countryside is a cure for a bad case of stammering. Then there's Augustine Mulliner and his rise through the ranks of the Anglican Church thanks to a trusty flask of his uncle Wilfred Mulliner's experimental Buck-u-Uppo tonic. Throw in the odd film star, society photographer and bishop facing disgrace and you have the perfect recipe for comic mayhem. Most of the subjects of Mulliner's tales eventually find the love and success they desire, but only after running the gauntlet of high farce. A wonderful nine-story start for a classic Wodehouse mouthpiece that came easily to his pen.

MONEY FOR NOTHING 1928

A very good light novel. In the sleepy Worcestershire village of Rudge-in-the-Vale John Carroll is in love with Pat Wyvern. But John's uncle, fat, rich, miserly Lester Carmody, squire of Rudge Hall, and Pat's damn-your-eyes father, Colonel Wyvern, long friends, are now feuding. Lester Carmody's other nephew, and heir, Hugo Carmody, wants his uncle to unbelt £500 for him to go shares in a London nightclub with Ronnie Fish, Eton and Cambridge friend.

Dr Alexander Twist (it's Chimp again, the crook) is now running an expensive health farm not far from Rudge. And enter Soapy Molloy and his 'daughter' Dolly. Lester

Carmody can't sell his Rudge Hall heirlooms, so why not fake a burglary and diddle the insurance? (The first heirlooms/burglary plot.) Lester Carmody, Chimp, Soapy and Dolly collude to do so. Everything goes wrong. John Carrol and Chimp are given knock-out drops. Briefly Hugo is engaged to Pat. But it ends happily, of course, with John and Pat engaged, Hugo released, Lester Carmody and the Colonel friends again and Chimp, Dolly and Soapy foiled and ejected.

MR MULLINER SPEAKING 1929

Nine more 'stretchers' told by Mr Mulliner, about relatives near and far. In 'Those in Peril on the Tee' Mr Mulliner becomes, to all intents and purposes, the Oldest Member, and introduces us to Agnes Flack and Sidney McMurdo, stalwart golf addicts. And 'Something Squishy' (a snake in the bed), 'The Awful Gladness of the Mater' (poor Dudley Finch!) and 'The Passing of Ambrose' (two splendidly repulsive schoolboys) are about the heartless and delightful Bobbie, redhead daughter of novelist Lady Wickham, who is, of course, a Mulliner cousin.

SUMMER LIGHTNING 1929

The third Blandings novel. The Hot Spot nightclub, run by Ronnie Fish and Hugo Carmody, has failed and Ronnie has got Hugo the job of secretary to Lord Emsworth at Blandings Castle. Ronnie is in love with sweet chorus girl Sue Brown, but what are Ronnie's mother and aunts going to say about a chorus girl, even if her father had been an officer in the Irish Guards? If Ronnie is to marry Sue, he must get his trustee, Lord Emsworth, to unleash the money required. Then there's this rich American girl, Myra Schoonmaker, whom the aunts want Ronnie to marry. And the loathsome Percy Pilbeam is sending Sue flowers and mash notes to the theatre. And Hugo (secretly engaged to Millicent, Lord Emsworth's niece) had known Sue for years – one of his favourite dancing partners. Small, pink, jealous – poor Ronnie. On an impulse he makes Sue come to the castle *as* the rich Myra Schoonmaker. And Sue meets Galahad Threepwood who finds she is the daughter of his long-ago dearly beloved Dolly Henderson. So he is determined to get Sue into the family, even if it means her marrying his pink little nephew – nothing like good enough for her. Meanwhile the efficient Baxter surfaces in a caravan, and the Empress disappears and neighbour and rival pig-enthusiast Sir Gregory Parsloe is suspected of having abducted her.

Lord Emsworth sends to London for a detective, and that's how Percy Pilbeam, now proprieter of the Argus Agency, joins the guests at the castle.

Ronnie gets his money and is set to marry Sue. Galahad sees to that. This is our first meeting with that *beau sabreur* of the Threepwood clan.

VERY GOOD, JEEVES 1930

Eleven short stories. Jeeves saves Bertie from being secretary to a cabinet minister, and saves both from a nesting swan on a lake-isle in a rainstorm. He destroys an offensive vase that Bertie has bought, and takes away an offensive suit of plus-fours new from his tailors. He knocks out Oliver Sipperley with a putter to the back of the head, annuls Bertie's love for Bobbie Wickham, ditto for Gwladys Pendlebury, rescues Bingo Little and Tuppy Glossop twice each, and saves Bertie's Uncle George from a mésalliance.

We're into the long *floruit* period of Wodehouse's enormous output – every story a winner. In this lot, if Bertie's worst predicament was the cabinet minister and the swan, his next worst was having, on his Aunt Agatha's orders, to go to East Dulwich to buy off a young girl at whose feet foolish old Uncle George was throwing his superfatted heart and unexpected title. Lady Yaxley now is that far, far better thing, the young girl's aunt, widowed ex-barmaid at the Criterion (see, later, Maudie Stubbs, Beach's niece, now Lady Parsloe).

BIG MONEY 1931

Berry Conway, saddled with his ex-nannie, now over-motherly and gossipy housekeeper, Mrs Wisdom, lives in Valley Fields and works in the City as secretary to dyspeptic American millionaire (Torquil) Paterson Frisby. Berry's school friend Biscuit (Lord Biskerton) is engaged to Frisby's niece, beautiful, rich Ann Moon. To baffle his creditors Biscuit goes to live in the house next to Berry in Valley Fields, and calls himself Smith. To prevent his fiancée from following and Discovering All, he pretends he has mumps. Next door, on the other side of Berry's house, is staying a diminutive American girl, Kitchie Valentine. Biscuit falls for her across the fence. Meanwhile Berry has fallen for Ann Moon and she for him.

Berry has, from an aunt, inherited a lot of worthless-looking shares including the ownership of the Dream Come True copper mine, next door to the Horned Toad mine owned by Frisby. After a lot of good legal and financial skulduggery the Dream Come True justifies its name.

All very fizzy. Biscuit is an amiable buzzer, Berry a nice simple hero. And they are going to marry delightful American girls. Extra dividends are: Biscuit's indigent and sponging father, man-about-town sixth Earl of Hoddesdon; a fine conference between sharp financiers and their lawyers; an Old Boys' dinner; and Lord Hoddesdon's visit to Valley Fields in a grey topper, which causes derision, disgust and a chase up Mulberry Grove.

This book is a *locus classicus* for Valley Fields.

IF I WERE YOU 1931

Obviously fleshed out from a play-script. Act 1 Country House, 2, Barber shop in Knightsbridge, 3, Country House. This time the old nannie is chief trouble-maker and flywheel for the plot. Mrs Price, something of a drunk, sister of Slingsby the butler, had been nannie to the fifth Earl of Droitwich and is mother of Syd who runs a successful hairdressing establishment in Knightsbridge. Or is it the other way round? Was there a cradle-swap? Is cockney Syd the rightful earl and charming aristo Tony the rightful barber? Ma Price knows the answer and Tony's relatives have, behind Tony's back, bribed and pensioned her to keep her mouth shut. But alcohol opens it and Syd is going to take his case – backed by a strong likeness to one of the early earls in the portrait gallery – to the House of Lords. Tony is happy enough to lose the earldom because it will free him of his engagement to Violet, haughty daughter and heiress of Waddington's Ninety-Seven Soups. He has fallen in love with sweet Polly Brown, American, manicurist in Price's Hygienic Toilet Saloon of Mott Street, Knightsbridge.

Well, who is the fifth earl of Droitwich today? And who's the countess? And who's making a million out of Price's newly patented Derma Vitalis Hair Tonic?

DOCTOR SALLY 1932

This is a novel made from the play 'Good Morning, Bill', adapted by Wodehouse from the Hungarian. Doctor Sally Smith is an American apparently practising in London, with hospital rounds too. Small, pretty and with handicap 6 at golf. She doesn't realise till the end that Bill Bannister, who has fallen for her in a big way from the first moment, works hard at his farming in Woollam Chersey. When she discovers that he does, she is able to respect him and to respond to his love. She will now be an American country gentlewoman in England, who plays very good golf and practises medicine on the side.

HOT WATER 1932

It is mid-July, fête-time at the French seaside resort of St Rocque. The château up the hill has been rented by the Gedges from America: she rich from a previous marriage, ambitious and dominant, he downtrodden and poor. Her plan is to get him (whether he likes it or not, and he does *not*) made the next American Ambassador to France. She is blackmailing Senator Opal, the great 'Dry' campaigner, to exert his influence. By muddling envelopes he had posted to her a letter to his bootlegger. News has also got around to 'Oily' Carlisle, ace con-man, and to 'Soup' Slattery, ace safe-blower, that Mrs Gedge has some good diamonds which make St Rocque worth a visit.

Packy Franklyn, young American athlete and millionaire, is engaged to Lady Beatrice Bracken who, wanting him to become cultured, orders him to consort with Blair Eggleston, the Bloomsbury novelist. Blair somehow gets taken on as Senator Opal's valet, and Packy falls in love with Senator Opal's daughter Jane, who is secretly and foolishly engaged to Blair. Packy rents a yawl and sails it across to St Rocque. There, too, is Old Etonian French playboy, Vicomte de Blissac ('Veek'). Almost all the males, in the absence of their ladies, get plastered at the fête. Mrs Gedge's maid and her secretary turn out to be under aliases, and Mrs Gedge herself – well, she never did become wife of the Ambassador to France, that's for sure. But Packy got Jane, who has promised never to make him go to lectures or meet Bloomsbury novelists again.

MULLINER NIGHTS 1933

Nine short stories, two of them about the bishop's cat, Webster, whose whole outlook and life has been changed by alcohol and who rescues the bishop from marrying an unsuitable widow. Augustine Mulliner's Buck-U-Uppo helps another bishop, dressed as Sinbad the Sailor, to hit a policeman, raiding a nightclub, in the eye. Well, the bishop had, when younger, two years in succession won the Curates' Open Heavyweight Championship. Yet

another bishop, once a headmaster, cures hitherto timid young Sacheverell Mulliner of offensive self-confidence produced by a correspondence course.

But the other five stories are of the laity. There is evidence that Wodehouse had difficulties with 'The Knightly Quest of Mervyn', but that's the only one here that possibly scores less than an alpha.

HEAVY WEATHER 1933

It is ten days after the events of *Summer Lightning*. Ronnie Fish is engaged to chorus girl Sue Brown, and his mother, Lady Julia, is determined to prevent the marriage. Sue was once briefly engaged to Monty Bodkin. When she hears that Monty is to come to the castle as Lord Emsworth's secretary she is very worried that dear Ronnie will get to know and squirm with jealousy. She rushes up to London to tell Monty they must meet as strangers, and Ronnie's mother sees them lunching at the Berkeley before all three take the train to Market Blandings.

Gally has undertaken not to publish his Reminiscences. But Lord Tilbury had a contract with him and is determined to publish them if he can get at them by hook (Monty) or crook (Pilbeam). Sir Gregory Parsloe is worried silly that Gally's book will tell about his scandalous younger days, and he wants to be the Unionist candidate for the local election to Parliament. Ronnie's mother is considerably jolted to learn that Gally will tell about her late husband's scandalous younger days. Lord Tilbury comes down to reason with Gally and, a pig-enthusiast himself, he covets the Empress.

The book becomes a fast and complicated doubles game – Hunt the Reminiscences and Steal the Pig – with Beach the butler involved much more than he likes on both counts. Pilbeam gets drunk and makes an ass of himself. Lord Tilbury is rolled in the Empress's sty. Gally's manuscript adds healthy paper-weight to the omnivorous pig. Ronnie and his Sue drive off into the night with a big cheque from Lord Emsworth for honeymoon expenses, and they will be married in the morning. It is Gally's finest hour. Sue is the heroine. The villain is Pilbeam. The enemy is mothers and aunts. It is a very good book.

N.B. Lord Emsworth and Gally still think it was Baxter, working for Sir Gregory, who stole the Empress in *Summer Lightning*.

THANK YOU, JEEVES 1934

This, the first full-length Bertie/Jeeves novel, starts with a clash of wills about Bertie's banjolele, and Jeeves gives notice. The banjolele has produced complaints from the neighbours in Berkeley Mansions, so Bertie proposes to take a country cottage somewhere and devote himself to mastering the instrument. His friend Lord Chuffnell (Chuffy) has a large

country house (which he would like to sell) near the sea and lots of cottages. He rents one to Bertie (with his new 'man', Brinkley) and snaps Jeeves up as his own 'personal gentleman'. At Chuffnell Regis there arrives off-shore a large yacht containing American J. Washburn Stoker, multi-millionaire, his beautiful daughter, Pauline (to whom Bertie was once, in New York, engaged; but Sir Roderick Glossop had easily convinced the girl's father that Bertie was a near-loony) and his young son, Dwight. Chuffy thinks Stoker may buy the house to be a clinic for Sir Roderick's patients. Chuffy and Pauline fall in love, but Chuffy, 'penniless', cannot, by the code, speak his love to heiress Pauline – to her fury. Chuffy's aunt lives at the Dower House near the hall. Sir Roderick is courting her. Pauline's father thinks Pauline is still pining for Bertie and he tries to keep her on board the yacht. In order to see Chuffy she swims from the yacht at night and arrives at Bertie's cottage (Bertie and Brinkley are both out) and gets into Bertie's pyjamas and his bed. Chuffy discovers her and there is a great quarrel between them. Pauline's father, thinking that Bertie has done her wrong, decides that they must marry quickly. He kidnaps Bertie on to the yacht. There is a birthday party for Dwight on board, with minstrels. Jeeves does heroic work as a treble-agent, to release Bertie from the yacht, blacked up as a mintrel, to bring Chuffy and Pauline together and to quench Pauline's domineering father. At one stage both Bertie and Sir Roderick are going round with blacked-up faces and unable to find butter or petrol to clean up with. Brinkley sets fire to Bertie's cottae. The banjolele dies with it. Jeeves agrees to come back to Bertie if he gives the instrument up for lost for ever. (We shall meet Brinkley, the communist valet, again in *Much Obliged, Jeeves*. There he becomes Rupert Bingley, a sort of propertied squire in Market Snodsbury.) Bertie sacks Brinkley. It looks as though Sir Roderick and Myrtle, Lady Chuffnell are going to marry and Chuffnell Hall will become a clinic after all.

Two nice, silly policemen – Sergeant Voules and his nephew Constable Dobson – also appear.

RIGHT HO, JEEVES 1934

Jeeves disapproves of the white evening mess jacket that Bertie has brought back from Cannes. Bertie disapproves of all his friends taking their troubles direct to Jeeves, bypassing him. Newt-loving teetotaller Gussie Fink-Nottle is in love with soupy Madeline Bassett and fears to speak. Tuppy Glossop has quarrelled with his fiancée Angela Travers. Aunt Dahlia has lost, at baccarat, money that Uncle Tom gave her to pay the bills of her magazine, *Milady's Boudoir*. And she has to find someone to give the prizes at Market Snodsbury Grammar School of which she is a governor. Bertie, funking it himself, persuades her to make Gussie do the prize-giving, and he and Jeeves lace Gussie's orange juice with gin, and more gin, to get his courage up. The prize-giving is a riot, probably the best-sustained and most anthologised two chapters of Wodehouse. Bertie's attempt to tell Madeline of Gussie's love for her convinces her that he is pleading his own cause. Bertie's recommendation to Gussie, Tuppy and Aunt Dahlia to seek sympathy from their loved ones by going off their feed, causes Anatole to give notice. Bertie's idea of ringing the fire-alarm bell at Brinkley (in order to get Tuppy to rescue Angela and thus show his love) results in the whole household being locked out in the small hours and Bertie's having to bicycle eighteen miles without lights to get the key.

Not Bertie's finest hours, these. But Jeeves solves all the problems in his own ways and Bertie forfeits the mess jacket.

You can feel a three-act plot and pattern here similar to that of *Thank You, Jeeves*. Wodehouse, knowing he's got it right, will do it again and again, with only minor variations of names, places and time, in the five or six subsequent Bertie/Jeeves novels. It's vintage Wodehouse. What bounty!

BLANDINGS CASTLE 1935

The six Blandings stories that make the first half of this book were, with one exception, published in magazines before the publication of *Summer Lightning* (1929). 'The Custody of the Pumpkin' appeared in 1924, 'Lord Emsworth Acts for the Best' in 1926, 'Pig-Hoo-o-o-o-ey!' in 1927, 'Company for Gertrude' and 'Lord Emsworth and the Girl Friend' in 1928. 'The Go-Getter' first appeared in 1931. Not that this strict chronology matters much. But 'The Custody of the Pumpkin' shows Lord Emsworth, in Wodehouse's words, 'passing through the brief pumpkin phase which preceded the more lasting pig seizure'. And, until (between 'Pig-Hoo-o-o-o-ey!' and 'Company for Gertrude') Sir Gregory Parsloe basely lured – with a higher salary – the gifted pig-man Wellbeloved away from the castle sties to tend his Matchingham competitors, Sir Gregory was a friendly fellow-J.P. of Lord Emsworth's, and dined at the castle. In *Summer Lightning* Sir Gregory starts as an enemy and is prime suspect in the disappearance of the Empress.

The other half of *Blandings Castle* contains one Bobbie Wickham story, told straight, not by Mr Mulliner (an uncle of hers) or by Bertie Wooster (an admirer, once ardent). In fact this Bobbie Wickham story, 'Mr Potter Takes a Rest Cure', is more than a little reminiscent of 'Saki'. The last five stories here are told by Mr Mulliner in the bar parlour of the Anglers' Rest, but they are all about Hollywood.

THE LUCK OF THE BODKINS 1935

The central character here is a stuffed Mickey Mouse doll, the head of which screws off in case you want to fill it with, say, chocolates. Monty Bodkin bought it in the shop of the SS *Atlantic*, as a *douceur* for his on-again, off-again fiancée, Gertrude Butterwick. Gertrude had cut up rough when, seeing, in a snapshot Monty had sent her from Antibes, a spot on his chest, she had had the photograph enlarged and the spot spelt 'Sue' with a heart round it: a tattoo. Gertrude (centre forward) is travelling to America with an All-England ladies hockey team. Also aboard are Ivor Llewellyn, President of Superba-Llewellyn Motion Pictures of Hollywood, who has been, to his horror, ordered by his wife to smuggle a pearl necklace for her past the New York Customs; Reggie and Ambrose Tennyson, brothers, Reggie an amusing drone of the type that the ravens feed, Ambrose a serious spare-time novelist, who has been hired away from his job at the Admiralty to write for Superba-Llewellyn for $1,500 a week (Llewellyn had been told that he was *the* Tennyson, who had written *The Boy Stood on the Burning Deck*, which of course was by Shakespeare). Ambrose is engaged to Lottie Blossom, Hoboken Irish redhead movie star with a pet alligator, the most turbulent of all Wodehouse's hell-raising heroines. The staterooms (or 'sheds') of all these passengers are served by steward Albert Eustace Peasemarch, tubby, talkative and, if, as seems likely, this was once a play or film script, a fat part for Eric Blore.

Another Anglo-American novel, ninety per cent of it afloat, long and one of the best.

YOUNG MEN IN SPATS 1936

Eleven short stories, three of them told by Mr Mulliner, all eleven about Dronesmen (Freddie Widgeon, Archibald Mulliner, Pongo Twistleton-Twistleton, Barmy Fotheringay-Phipps and such). Two of the best ('The Amazing Hat Mystery' and 'Uncle Fred Flits By') were based on ideas supplied to Wodehouse by his friend Bill Townend.

It's our first meeting with Pongo's irrepressible Uncle Fred, Lord Ickenham, least haughty of earls. He will get star billing in *Uncle Fred in the Springtime* (1939), *Uncle Dynamite* (1948), *Cocktail Time* (1958) and *Service with a Smile* (1962).

In another of the best stories, 'Tried in the Furnace', there is a heart-breaking girl, a country vicar's daughter, Angelica Briscoe, loved at first sight by two Dronesmen, engaged to somebody else, who turned up again, still young and inexplicably unmarried, thirty-eight years later in the last Bertie/Jeeves novel *Aunts Aren't Gentlemen* (1974).

LAUGHING GAS 1936

Reggie (Earl of) Havershot, twenty-eight, ugly, boxing blue at Cambridge, goes to Hollywood to rescue his cousin Egremont (Eggy), a souse, and bring him back unmarried. Reggie had been engaged once to Ann Bannister, an American newspaper girl. He finds that she is now engaged to Eggy and has a job looking after Joey Cooley, child film-star with golden curls, idol of American motherhood, pride of the Brinkmeyer-Magnifico Motion Picture Corp. T. P. Brinkmeyer is a simple, globular multi-millionaire who is bossed by his sister, Beulah, and wishes he was back in the cloak and suit business. The Brinkmeyers have an English butler, Chaffinch. All the servants in the household are hoping to be star actors if they can only get a start by impressing Brinkmeyer.

Reggie meets April June, film-star, very keen to be a countess. He is just about to propose to her when his wisdom tooth gives him gyp. At the I. J. Zizzbaum/B. K. Burwash dentist's surgery, his identity passes, under gas, into the patient under gas in the next room, Joey Cooley. They wake up with swapped personalities.

Joey, now fourteen stone, six foot one inch, and a good boxer, enjoys his new-found ability to poke his former enemies (e.g. Beulah Brinkmeyer whom he chases into the swimming pool, April June and Orlando Flower and Tommy Murphy, rival film-stars) in the snoot, to eat pancakes, drink and smoke cigars. He paints the nose of a statue of T. P. Brinkmeyer red and misbehaves generally.

Reggie Havershot, now a boy with golden curls, gets a kick in the pants from April June, and she kidnaps him so that she can hit the headlines by rescuing him. Chaffinch sells Joey's tooth for $5,000. Eggy Mannering gets engaged to a girl who is an enthusiast for the Temple of the New Dawn and teetotalism. And, when the identity switch-back comes (a motorbike accident with Joey and Reggie thrown together), Reggie will make nice Ann Bannister his countess.

Wodehouse does not bother much about language and accent differences between Reggie and Joey. But he is always funny about Hollywood, and Joey must be the only boy with golden curls in all the books of whom Wodehouse approves.

LORD EMSWORTH AND OTHERS 1937

Nine short stories, 'The Crime Wave at Blandings', more than twice as long as the usual P.G.W. short story, is the only Blandings one in this collection. Three others are about Ukridge. Three are told by the Oldest Member about golf, one by Mr Mulliner and one about Freddie Widgeon, by a Crumpet at the Drones. In 'The Crime Wave at Blandings' the efficient Baxter returns to the castle, much to the annoyance of a) Lord Emsworth, who had hoped never to see this, his first secretary, again and b) Lord Emsworth's grandson George, who finds himself threatened with an unexpected tutor plum spang in the middle of his holidays. But Baxter leaves, and hurriedly, after being shot at, unerringly, with an air-gun by a) George b) Beach the butler and c) Lord Emsworth himself, twice. Meanwhile Lord Emsworth's pretty niece Jane gets the man of her choice, poor, nice George Abercrombie, and rejects the man of Aunt Connie's choice, rich, boring Lord Roegate.

SUMMER MOONSHINE 1938

Sir Bucktone Abbott, Bart., has no money and is saddled with a large, ugly and impossible Victorian country house, Walsingford Hall. He is taking paying guests and hopes to sell the house to a very rich and horrid Princess Heloise von und zu Dwornitzchek. Joe Vanringham is the Princess's step-son and they have parted brass rags. Joe, a good buzzer and obviously the hero, works for a dishonest publisher, Mortimer Busby, who has published Sir Buckstone's *My Sporting Memoirs* at Sir Buckstone's expense (£500) and is now trying to charge him an extra £96 3s 11d for 'incidental expenses'. Joe has written a play in which his step-mother is the scarcely concealed villainess. It has got good notices for its first night in London and Joe is going to leave Busby's. Sir Buckstone's daughter Jane (obviously the heroine) has gone up to London to plead with Busby's to reduce the bill. Joe meets her, falls in love, gets the bill cancelled and takes her to the Savoy for lunch and proposes marriage. Jane is foolishly engaged (secretly) to wet Adrian Peake who thinks she will inherit a lot of money. He is the Princess's gigolo currently and secretly engaged to her too. The Princess sees Joe's play, recognises herself and has it taken off. This leaves Joe without a play, without a job and without money. Sir Buckstone's easy-going (American) wife has an unexpected brother, Sam Bulpitt, a retired 'plasterer' (process-server). His last job is to plaster Tubby Vanringham (Joe's foolish younger brother) for breach of promise and heart-balm to Prudence Whittaker, Sir Buckstone's secretary – very Knightsbridge ('quate').

The Princess goes off with Adrian and won't buy the hall. Joe and Jane will marry. Then Sam Bulpitt turns out to be very rich and a fairy godfather. He buys the hall and gives Jane $500,000 as a wedding present – *Pecunia omnia vincit*.

Bulpitt the plasterer is a rather surprising Wodehouse character. The Princess, wicked step-mother and not a bit funny, is the most un-Wodehousian character in all the books. The rest of the cast here are from Wodehouse stock and Joe Vanringham is a really good buzzer.

THE CODE OF THE WOOSTERS 1938

The Code says that if a girl says to a man, 'I'm going to marry you,' he can't say, 'Oh no, you're not!' So here's poor Bertie *twice* having to face Sir Watkyn Bassett as a prospective relation-by-marriage: once when his daughter Madeline gives Gussie the air and claims she will marry Bertie: and once when his ward Stiffy Byng uses Bertie as a shock-absorber in her determination to get Sir Watkyn to approve her marriage to the Rev. 'Stinker' Pinker. And Sir Watkyn, as the Bosher Street magistrate, had recently fined Bertie £5 for trying to steal a policeman's helmet on Boat Race Night.

Sir Watkyn has treacherously bought a silver cow-creamer that Aunt Dahlia insists ethically belongs to her husband, rival collector, Bertie's Uncle Tom. So, on threat of his never getting another meal of Anatole's cooking, she tells Bertie to go to Totleigh Towers and steal the cow-creamer for Uncle Tom. Gussie Fink-Nottle, scared at the thought of having to make a speech at his wedding breakfast, in front of such people as Sir Watkyn and Spode, the amateur dictator (Sir Watkyn is hoping to marry Spode's aunt), takes Jeeves's advice and makes notes, in a little book, of all the despicable points about Sir Watkyn and Spode; the idea being that this will enable him to face them calmly, despising them for, e.g. the way they eat asparagus. Well, of course, Gussie loses this explosive notebook and of course it gets into the hands of Sir Watkyn and Spode. Meanwhile Sir Watkyn wants Anatole, and Uncle Tom is briefly prepared to trade the super chef for the cow-creamer, and Aunt Dahlia is briefly prepared to trade him for Bertie's release from a likely thirty days in prison. And Stiffy is feuding with the local policeman and gets her curate fiancé to pinch his helmet. And Jeeves learns Spode's dark secret from the Junior Ganymede Book of Revelations. It's our first meeting with this man of wrath, leader of the Black Shorts, and

we wonder what Oswald Mosley made of the loud and sustained raspberry this book delivered to him and his movement.

A Wodehouse plot more complicated than any yet, clockwork with a hundred moving parts, interdependence absolute and a patter of verbal felicities, five or six to a page. Stiffy Byng is possibly the fizziest of all Wodehouse's fizzy girls, quick to anger, tears and revenge – deplorable, adorable. We assume that Jeeves got Bertie off on that world cruise – he had bought the tickets, though the young master had said No. A reverse forfeit.

UNCLE FRED IN THE SPRINGTIME 1939

The Duke of Dunstable has invited himself, plus secretary Rupert Baxter, to stay indefinitely at Blandings Castle. Notorious for laying about the furniture with a poker if thwarted, he demands eggs for throwing at whichever gardener keeps singing or whistling 'The bonny, bonny banks of Loch Lomond' outside his window. And he tells Lord Emsworth that his pig (twice in succession winner in the Fat Pig class) needs exercise and diet. He says, 'Give her to me. I'll have her slimmed down and you'll be less potty without her.' And Lady Connie insists that the dangerous Duke be given anything he asks – or else.

Lord Emsworth must take steps to save the Empress and decides to rope in Lord Ickenham, his brother Gally's friend, to help him. Lady Connie, thinking that the dangerous Duke is going round the bend, has told Lord Emsworth to go to London and get Sir Roderick Glossop, the loony-doctor, to come and keep the Duke under observation.

There are bustling sub-plots. Lord Ickenham's nephew Pongo owes a vindictive bookmaker £200. He tries to borrow it off Horace Davenport, who is engaged to his sister, Valerie. Horace, unable to go to the Drones Le Touquet golfing weekend, has sent 'Mustard' Pott, private investigator, to tail Valerie up in case she becomes enmeshed in licentious Drones males at golf or casino. Meanwhile Polly, 'Mustard''s pretty daughter, is engaged to Ricky Gilpin, poet, boxer, nephew of the Duke of Dunstable. He needs £500 to buy into an onion soup bar and marry Polly.

Sir Roderick won't come to Blandings. Lord Ickenham seizes his chance and comes *as* Sir Roderick, and he brings Pongo as his secretary and Polly as his own daughter. The idea is that Polly shall fascinate the Duke so that he will provide the £500 for an onion soup bar and marriage. But Baxter sees through the impersonations. For his pains, he gets orders to steal the Empress for the Duke. He also gets, literally, egg on his face and a Mickey Finn in his drink.

Uncle Fred Ickenham is in his element. He brings the right couples together and a proper redistribution of other people's wealth. A masterly mix-up, suavely sorted out.

This is our first and only close view of George Viscount Bosham, Lord Emsworth's son and heir. He is, triumphantly, the most blithering idiot in the whole rich Wodehouse canon.

EGGS, BEANS AND CRUMPETS 1940

Nine short stories: four, told by a Crumpet, about Bingo Little, editor of *Wee Tots*, his wife, Rosie M. Banks, the best-selling novelist, and his overlord, Purkiss, proprietor of *Wee Tots*. There are three Ukridge stories, and one about Freddie Fitch-Fitch getting caught up in, and getting a fiancée out of, the fearful snobberies of well-to-do invalids at a fashionable spa. The gem of the collection is the solitary Mulliner, 'Anselm Gets His Chance'. Anselm Mulliner is a country curate whose selfish vicar always praches at Sunday Evensong in summer, prime time for maximum audience appreciation, as every selfish country vicar knows. But the vicar in this case gets a juicy black eye in a midnight scuffle with Joe the ex(?)-burglar who sings in the choir. So Anselm preaches his long-hoarded 'Brotherly Love' sermon that Sunday evening, and he preaches as he has never preached before. Result – his engagement to a financier's daughter, and a £10,000 cheque from said financier (who is also a philatelist) for a stamp album for which his first shrewd bid had been £5.

QUICK SERVICE 1940

J. B. Duff, dyspeptic head of Duff and Trotter, London's classiest provision-merchants, was once in love with a girl called Beatrice, who gave him the air because he could only talk about Duff and Trotter's Paramount hams. Joss Weatherby, second-rate artist and first-rate buzzer, is on Duff's staff, designing advertisements for the hams. He recently did a portrait of the above Beatrice, now Mrs Chavender, widow. The portrait hangs in Claines Hall in Sussex, where Mrs Chavender lives with her rich sister-in-law, Mabel Steptoe, who is  married to an ex-pug, small-time Hollywood actor whom she is still trying to civilise, hiring valets to make him dress properly etc. Mrs Chavender's pretty secretary, Sally, is engaged to Lord Holbeton, who sings 'Trees' but can't marry her unless he can get some of the money held in trust for him. And who's his sole trustee? Dyspeptic J.B. Duff, of whom he is much afraid. Sally says she will go and tackle J.B. Duff for him.

Mrs Chavender, revolted by slices of a new ham at breakfast at Claines Hall, learns that it's a Duff and Trotter Paramount, so she goes up to London, with a box of slices, to show Jimmy Duff, her erstwhile courtier, how disgraceful his product is. Joss instantly falls in love with Sally. Duff decides that Joss's painting of Mrs Chavender would make a good advertisement, saying, 'Take this stuff away.

Bring me a Paramount ham!' Duff fires Joss, and tells Sally he'll give Lord Holbeton his money if Lord Holbeton will steal that portrait and bring it to him at an inn near the hall where he is going to stay, wearing a false moustache. Sally hires Joss as the new valet for Steptoe. He ('Mugsy') wants to raise enough money to get himself back to Hollywood.

Duff eats sticky cakes and mixes them with brandy and hell breaks loose inside him. So Mrs Chavender cures him (most nice male dyspeptics in Wodehouse are cured by nice women) and love re-burgeons. There is an all-night scrambling of people trying to cut the painting out of its frame in order to get money from Duff. Also two suspects locked in the coal cellar by the butler.

Lord Holbeton gets enough of his money to go to Italy to have his voice trained. Duff rehires Joss, to be head of the Duff and Trotter Art Department. Joss will marry Sally. Mrs Steptoe, loathing English weather (which has ruined her garden party), is happy to go back to California with her husband. Perhaps this is Wodehouse admitting that the weather he has always given England is Californian and here now he is trying to tell the truth.

MONEY IN THE BANK 1946

Lord Uffenham, sixth earl, is pear-shaped, with huge feet and a tendency to go on about his gallant youth, Boat Race Nights revelry and being thrown out of Victorian music halls. He has rented his ancestral Shipley Hall to rich, big-game-huntress widow Mrs Cork, and she is running it as a vegetarian, teetotal health farm. Lord Uffenham stays on in the guise of butler, Cakebread. He has hidden some diamonds away and cannot remember where. He worries because they are all he can give his niece Anne as dowry. If he can't find the diamonds, he will have to make the supreme sacrifice for Anne's sake, and marry Mrs Cork for her money. It turns out that the diamonds, which have given the book its treasure-hunting, with Chimp Twist, Dolly and Soapy Molloy at it again, are in the bank at the other side of the pond.

Jeff Miller, like Romeo, and so many Wodehouse heroes, is engaged to the wrong girl at the start. Anne Benedick, heroine, is likewise engaged, to handsome, silky-moustached, feet-of-clay Lionel Green, interior decorator. Anne, at the end, says 'I never want to see another beautiful man as long as I live.'

Wodehouse wrote this novel while interned by the Germans. Probably all-male camps account for the use of words such as 'fanny', 'bloody awful', 'too bloody much' and 'lavatory inspector'. Such modernisms must be balanced against Wodehouse's dreamy return to an England where telephones hardly exist. At one stage in this story Jeff goes up to London from the hall to send a message to Chimp at Halsey Court, Mayfair, by district messenger. The Cork Health Farm, filled with clients longing for square meals, may have got an impetus from internment camps.

Here Jeff Miller is a buzzer. Not the first, but it's the first time Wodehouse has used the word for the type. Chimp says here that he wishes he had thought of starting a health farm, forgetting that in the earlier *Money for Nothing* he had been running one.

JOY IN THE MORNING 1947

Bertie's friend Boko Fittleworth, the popular writer, had been engaged to Florence Craye, as had Bertie in his day. Now Boko wants to marry Nobby Hopwood. Florence being his daughter and Nobby his ward, Lord Worplesdon objects to Boko as a flitter-and-sipper, half dotty and financially unsound, and won't give his OK to Nobby's marrying him. Lord Worplesdon is on the edge of a big shipping deal with American Mr Clam and wants a private place in which to meet him for final talks. On Jeeves's advice Lord Worplesdon provides a cottage on his Steeple Bumpleigh estate for Bertie. It is here that Clam is to nest for the secret pourparlers. Boko has a cottage nearby and Stilton Cheesewright is the local policeman, and now engaged to Florence. Edwin the Boy Scout, trying to catch up on his good deeds, burns Bertie's cottage to the ground. Luckily Bertie's Aunt Agatha, now Lady Worplesdon, is away, ministering to young Thos at prep school: he has mumps.

Stilton is furious with jealousy when he hears that Florence was once engaged to Bertie. Boko locks Clam in the potting shed thinking him to be a burglar. There is a fancy dress dance at a neighbouring village. Lord Worplesdon goes as Sinbad the Sailor, with ginger whiskers, Clam goes as Edward the Confessor, Bertie goes in a policeman's outfit pinched by Jeeves from the river bank where Stilton is bathing. Boko, not knowing that Lord Worplesdon is asleep, tight, at the back of his car, locks him in the garage overnight. But Jeeves organises forgiveness and some happy endings. Boko and Nobby are off to Hollywood with Lord Worplesdon's hard-won blessing. Jeeves rescues Bertie from his second (but by no means last) engagement to the dread Florence. Lord Worplesdon, his business deal completed at great profit, is relieved that his wife has been away and may never hear of the dire doings of the last forty-eight hours.

The idiocies of Boko here, the vituperations he gets from his beloved Nobby and the head-shakings of his friend Bertie – 'You can never trust a writer not to make an ass of himself' – may remind us that Wodehouse finished his novel after he had made an ass of himself, with those talks on the radio from Berlin in 1941.

FULL MOON 1947

Two new Emsworth nieces need help towards the altar. Veronica, daughter of Lord Emsworth's cook-like sister Lady Hermione Wedge, is the dumbest and most beautiful of the tribe, and she, and her parents, long for a rich suitor. (All three are staying at the castle.)

American Tipton Plimsoll, friend of Freddie Threepwood, could fill that bill. Prudence, small, pretty daughter of another sister, Lady Dora Garland in London, is caught trying to elope with big, ugly Bill Lister, a rather bad artist and a godson of Galahad. Prue is sent to the castle to cool off. Lord Emsworth is trying to find an artist to paint the Empress's portrait for the gallery. Thanks to Galahad, Bill Lister infiltrates the castle three times, in three guises: Messmore Breamworthy, an artist (Lord Emsworth sacks him as soon as he sees his rough for the Empress's portrait), an under-gardener (McAllister has been bribed to silence) and Landseer, another artist. The portrait is never done, but, largely as a result of the Empress being shoved in her bedroom, Veronica and Tipton are paired off successfully. And, under threat that his son Freddie's marriage will come unstuck and he, Lord Emsworth, will be stuck with Freddie haunting the castle again, Lord Emsworth gives the green light and a cheque for £5,000 to Prue and Bill to get married and take over The Mulberry Tree pub near Oxford.

This novel is too episodic for comfort, and unevenly paced. In patches Gally, its real hero, acts and talks more like Lord Ickenham than himself. 'Spreading sweetness and light' is Lord Ickenham's specific role, but at the end of Chapter 7, part 3 here, Wodehouse, seeming to forget, applies these words to Gally. It strikes an odd note.

NB 'Sweetness and light' is a phrase from Matthew Arnold, who was related by marriage to the Wodehouse family.

SPRING FEVER 1948

Another impecunious widower earl (of Shortlands, family name Cobbold) with a money-eating stately home, Beevor Castle. His ambition is to raise £200 somehow, marry Mrs Punter his cook and buy her the pub on which she insists. He has three daughters, two bossy, one nice. One of the bossy daughters, Adela, is married to a very rich American, Desborough Topping. But they have a joint bank account and Adela is in charge of it, so her father gets no £200 from her. Ellery Cobbold is another very rich American, distantly related. His son Stanwood has fallen for a Hollywood star, Eileen Stoker. To distance Stanwood from Eileen, Ellery sends him over to England where, as it happens, Eileen Stoker has just arrived to make two pictures. Sent over by Ellery Cobbold to keep an eye on his son is manservant Augustus Robb, cockney ex-burglar, 'saved' by attending a revivalist meeting. He is a snob and a Bible quoter.

Lord Shortlands looks like a butler. His butler, Spink, looks like an earl, and is also courting Mrs Punter. The question is, which suitor will first get the £200 for the pub? Courting Lord Shortlands's nice daughter Terry (Lady Teresa Cobbold) is American Mike Cardinal, very good-looking, prosperous Hollywood agent and a good natural buzzer. Terry, having once been in love with, and let down by, a very good-looking musical comedy juvenile lead, refuses very good-looking Mike for that reason. But Mike gets involved in a fracas with drunk ex-burglar Robb and his face, much bashed about, then looks very good to Terry. Spink gets Mrs Punter. Stanwood gets Eileen Stoker. Mike takes Terry and her father to Hollywood, the latter to play in butler roles.

The novel splits obviously into three acts and must have been a play script on its way to hard-back print. Once again Wodehouse uses the rich man's joint bank account with a dominant wife for sour comedy. Once again he makes the hero ugly, by force this time.

UNCLE DYNAMITE 1948

Dotty doings in distant Hampshire. His Uncle Fred (Lord Ickenham) wants Pongo to marry American Sally Painter, a not very successful sculptor in Chelsea. They had been engaged, but she had broken it off when Pongo refused to smuggle jewellery into America for a friend of hers. Now he has got engaged to Hermione Bostock, a bossy, bookish beauty whom Bill Oakshott, just returned from Brazil, had hoped to marry. Bill is the real owner of Ashenden Manor, but his uncle, Sir Aylmer Bostock, ex-Colonial Governor, is a short-tempered cuckoo in the nest, proposing to stand for Parliament. As a JP he sentences Pongo and Sally to thirty days jug without the option, her only tort being pushing the local cop into a duck-pond.

Pongo is *not* a success with Hermione's parents. And Bill Oakshott, disappointed lover, sees Pongo kissing the housemaid, who is engaged to the local policeman, who is bossed by his sister. Wouldn't you know it – Potter the policeman had arrested Pongo and Uncle Fred that day at the dog-races and remembered them by sight and their false names.

Since Lady Ickenham is away, Lord Ickenham wades in gratefully to spread sweetness and light. He had been at school with 'Mugsy' Bostock and had given him six with a fives bat then for bullying. Blackmail, lying, impersonation, knock-out drops, arrests: stealing, breaking and substitution of busts, one of which contains jewellery for smuggling. Preparations for the Ashenden fête, and a Bonny Baby Competition. The curate gets measles, and spreads it around.

This is our first meeting with the eccentric Major Brabazon Plank, leader of the Brazilian expedition of which Bill Oakshott was a member. (Here Plank is a cricketer: in *Stiff Upper Lip* (1963) he is a rugger fanatic; in BBC Radio 4's adaptation of that book he is a soccer fanatic.) He had been at school with 'Barmy' (Uncle Fred) and 'Mugsy' and his name had been 'Bimbo'. Barmy and Bimbo talk Mugsy into dazed humility and repentance, and the right couples kiss and make up: policeman Potter and housemaid Elsie Bean, Pongo and Sally, Bill and Hermione. Uncle Fred had taught Bill the 'Ickenham Method' of wooing (polite violence and sex) and when Bill sees a man kissing Hermione and goes into action, Hermione gives the memorable yowl, 'Don't kill him, Bill. He's my publisher!'

A brilliantly sustained rattle of word-perfect dialogue and narrative topping a very complicated and well-controlled plot.

THE MATING SEASON 1949

Gussie Fink-Nottle goes wading for newts in a Trafalgar Square fountain at 4 a.m. and is sentenced to fourteen days in prison. This is awkward because he, as Madeline Bassett's fiancé, is due to present himself at Deverill Hall, where Madeline's godmother, Dame Daphne Winkworth, lives and wants to meet him. Bertie is due there too, to star in a village concert organized by the Vicar's niece, Corky Pirbright, Hollywood star, sister of 'Catsmeat'. Corky is in love, and vice versa, with the squire, rich, handsome Esmond Haddock. Deverill Hall is his home, but full of his disapproving aunts, Dame Daphne being one. Corky says she won't marry Esmond until he defies his aunts and tells them to get off his back.

Bertie must at all costs prevent Madeline knowing that her fiancé is doing time, since, whenever she rejects Gussie, she reaches for the man who can't say No, Bertie Wooster. So Bertie goes to Deverill Hall saying he *is* Gussie. Then Gussie's sentence is remitted and he arrives saying he is Bertie Wooster, and Corky ropes him, too, into the concert. He falls in love with her. Madeline, who could explode this double imposture, announces that she is coming to the Hall, and she must be kept away. Aunt Agatha, who could also blow all gaffs, threatens to come. Jeeves goes to her son, Young Thos's, prep school and easily lures him into doing a bunk and coming to stay with Corky at the Vicarage – so that his mother will go safely to Bramley-on-sea to join the search for him in Sussex.

Jeeves's uncle, Charlie Silversmith, is butler at Deverill Hall. And there is an atheist village policeman who harrasses the Vicar and who's in love with the housemaid at the hall. Jeeves converts Constable Dobbs to theism with a cosh. Catsmeat elopes with his beloved Gertrude, daughter of Dame Daphne.

The big scene is the village concert, at which Esmond comes out strong and poor Bertie, alias Fink-Nottle, has to recite Winnie-the-Pooh verses.

Two pinpricks and a mild raspberry here could remind the alert that Wodehouse was remembering three people who had attacked him for his wartime broadcast talks to America from Berlin. Gussie, up before the beak after his newt-hunt in the Trafalgar Square fountain, gives his name as Alfred Duff Cooper. Duff Cooper had been the Minister of Information who had sponsored William 'Cassandra' Connor's attack on Wodehouse on the BBC National Service. One of the (bad) performers in the King's Deverill village concert was Miss Eustacia Pulbrook. Sir Eustace Pulbrook, an eminent old boy of Dulwich, had spoken or written something derogatory about eminent Old Boy Wodehouse at the time. And A.A. Milne, whose Winnie-the-Pooh verses struck such terror (of being given the bird with vegetables in the air) into Bertie's heart when he found he had to recite them in public, had written a sly and damaging letter about his 'old friend' in the *Daily Telegraph*.

NOTHING SERIOUS 1950

Ten short stories, five of them about golf, told by the Oldest Member. But in three of them the O.M., the club and the course are American. 'Rodney Has a Relapse' pulls A. A. Milne's nose again. 'Birth of a Salesman' has Lord Emsworth temporarily in America and jealous of his son Freddie's success as a mini-magnate in the dog-biscuit business. 'How's that, Umpire?' is the story of the salvation of Conky Biddle, obliged to go to cricket matches (which he loathes) with his uncle Lord Plumpton, who provides his allowance and is dotty about the game. A beautiful American girl with a millionaire father rescues Conky from unemployment and cricket. Two stories are about Bingo Little, and one of them brings back, to be nanny to young Algernon Aubrey, the nanny who had nannied Bingo in infancy: a resurrection that Bingo would not recommend now, to any pater-familias. The other Bingo story brings the disruptive Freddie Widgeon into the Little family's lives. 'Success Story' is Ukridge at his best, outlying and outsmarting his aunt's crooked butler Oakshott. But Corky still has to pay the bill for the lordly celebratory lunch.

THE OLD RELIABLE 1951

This is *Spring Fever* (1948) again, put through the theatrical mincing machine and emerging in Hollywood as a second novel. The only English characters are the ex-safe-blower butler, Phipps (see Augustus Robb in *Spring Fever*) and Lord Topham, scrounging hospitality from the aristos of the film colony.

Ex-silent-films star Adela Shannon Cork's late millionaire husband had said 'Take care of my brother Smedley', so Smedley gets board and lodging at the big house in Beverly Hills, and nothing more. He longs to go on a toot and tries to borrow the wherewithal from Adela's butler. Adela's sister, 'Bill' Shannon, loves Smedley and lends him $100 and he goes on a bender and invites to stay *chez* Adela for several weeks Joe Davenport, who is in love with the Shannon niece Kay.

Adela's house once belonged to Carmen Flores, passionate Mexican film-star now dead. Everybody is looking for the diary she must have written and left somewhere in the house. It's sure to be red-hot property for a publisher. 'Bill' Shannon is ghost-writing her sister's memoirs. She had been on a jury which had sent Phipps to prison. She has been a crime reporter, sob sister, press agent, minor actress. She quotes a lot from Shakespeare and explains that she had been a stewardess on a fruit-boat and *The Plays of Shakespeare* had been the only book on board. (N.B. Wodehouse in 1940 had packed only one book, *The Works of Shakespeare*, when he went off to internment camps.)

Pretty Kay Shannon, the niece, works on a New York magazine. She calls her Aunt Wilhelmina 'The Old Reliable'. Writer Joe Davenport has been blacklisted in Hollywood because he once threw a heavy book at Ivor Llewellyn. But he has recently won a radio jackpot. He is a good buzzer. He wants to marry Kay. Kay says No, thinking he is not serious about her. But when she sees him lying on the floor, knocked out apparently by a bottle by the drunk Phipps, she showers kisses on his upturned etc., etc. In fact 'Bill' had slipped Joe a Mickey Finn to achieve exactly this effect. Joe will marry Kay. 'Bill' will marry Smedley and Phipps will play butler parts for Medulla-Oblongata-Glutz.

BARMY IN WONDERLAND 1952

'Wonderland' is the American theatre world. Cyril ('Barmy') Fotheringay (pronounced Fungy) Phipps, Eton, Oxford and Drones Club, is attracted by Dinty Moore, secretary of a Broadway producer, Joe Lehman. Film-star, buzzer and boozer Mervyn Potter, due to appear in a Broadway play, burns his cottage down and is rescued by Barmy. He persuades Barmy to put his little all, $22,000, to buy twenty-five per cent of his play, 'Sacrifice', producer Joe Lehman. Potter is engaged to Hermione (page 55) or Heloise (page 128) Brimble, daughter of a tycoon.[1] She swears him off drink and puts a detective on to report if he drinks. Potter owns a Tanganyika lion-dog, Tulip, dangerous when Potter is drunk and argumentative.

Potter will *not* marry Miss Brimble. Barmy Phipps will marry Dinty. The play is 'fixed' to be a success. Lehmac Productions buy Barmy out for $100,000.

It's a return to the backstage world of *A Damsel in Distress*, *Jill the Reckless*, and *The Adventures of Sally*. It is loosely adapted from George Kaufman's play, 'The Butter-and-Egg Man'. Some critics said Wodehouse's American dialogue, especially the slang, was all wrong, but he said that he took it verbatim from the Kaufman script. So there!

Fanny, wife of Joe Lehman of Lehmac Productions, 'a man of the great indoors', had been a great juggler. She is a very good wisecracker.

Peggy Marlowe, show girl, is based, surely, on Marion Davies, mistress of William Randolph Hearst, American newspaper tycoon, owner of, and host at, San Simeon.

PIGS HAVE WINGS 1952

Gally, Beach and others have bet their savings on the Empress for a third win in succession in the Fat Pigs Class at the Shropshire Show. Now Sir Gregory Parsloe, having already lured Wellbeloved away from Lord Emsworth for higher wages as pig-man, has *bought* a super-fat pig, Queen of Matchingham – legally, but unethically – to run against the Empress. Monica Simmons, Lord Emsworth's new pig-girl, turns out to be Sir Gregory's

[1] There is another Hermoine Brimble, English and daughter of a bishop, in 'The Right Approach' in *A Few Quick Ones*

niece. Gally and Lord Emsworth are sure Sir Gregory will try to nobble the Empress so that the Queen may win the Silver Medal. Beach's widowed niece, Maudie Stubbs, once barmaid at the Criterion, had been going to marry young 'Tubby' Parsloe, but they had missed each other at the wedding. Now Sir Gregory is engaged to Gloria Salt, a lithe tennis player who has ordered him to diet drastically, or else ... Penny Donaldson, younger sister of Freddie Threepwood's wife, Aggie, is at the castle. Lady Constance wants her to marry Orlo, Lord Vosper, handsome, serious, rich, a tennis player (who had been engaged to Gloria Salt, but they had quarrelled about poaching on court). Penny is in love with Jerry Vail, writer of thrillers, and they need £2,000 for Jerry to take over a health farm. Gloria, asked by Lady Constance to find Lord Emsworth a secretary, produces Jerry Vail, who used to be something of a boyfriend of hers.

Sir Gregory's butler goes to the village chemist to buy half a dozen bottles of Slimmo for his master. Gally hears of this and is sure it is meant for thinning the Empress. The battle-lines are drawn and it develops into snatch and counter-snatch of pigs, the castle commando being Gally, Penny and Beach. They bring Maudie Stubbs, who has inherited a detective agency from the late Stubbs, down to watch over the Empress's cause, and they infiltrate her into the castle as being a friend of Penny's millionaire (American) father. Lord Emsworth's foolish heart goes out to Maudie in a letter (which has to be retrieved quick when Lord Emsworth discovers she is an ex-barmaid and ... more embarrassing ... niece of his butler – he'd have to call his butler 'Uncle Sebastian'). Well, Lord Emsworth, thinking that Jerry has restored the Empress to her sty, writes the necessary £2,000 cheque for him and Penny to start in on the health farm. Orlo Vosper and Gloria Salt become a mixed double again and Sir Gregory proposes again to dear Maudie, who will become Lady Parsloe, and will work on the principle that the way to a Bart's heart is through his stomach. Beach, having been in the Market Blandings police lock-up for half an hour, gets £500 hush-money from Lady Constance for his pains. The Queen consumes six bottles of Slimmo and the Empress wins the Silver Medal for the third time running. The local newspaper celebrates the event in expert verse.

RING FOR JEEVES 1953

Guy Bolton 'borrowed' Jeeves from Wodehouse for a play. He is now a butler who helps his master, 9th Earl of Rowcester, make the money he badly needs for white elephant, leaky, 147-room stately home, Rowcester Abbey. They set up as bookies – Honest Patch Perkins (Lord Rowcester disguised) and his clerk (Jeeves disguised). This is a novel shaped out of a play. And Bertie Wooster is explained away as having gone off to a post-war school that teaches the aristocracy to fend for itself 'in case the social revolution sets in with even greater severity'.

The bookie firm is in trouble and has to welsh over a flukey double pulled off (£3,005 2s 6d) by Captain Biggar, white hunter, in love with Mrs Rosie Spottsworth, widow of two multi-millionaire Americans. (But she is nice. She had written *vers libre* in Greenwich Village before she started marrying millionaires.) Biggar's code says 'A poor man mustn't make advances to a rich lady' but he ends up satisfactorily engaged to marry Rosie.

Bill (9th Earl) Rowcester will marry small, pretty Jill Wyvern, freckled, local vet, ex-hockey outside right. Her father is Chief Constable of Southmoltonshire. Bill sells the Abbey to Mrs Spottsworth who, not liking its dampness, will have it transported brick by brick and rebuilt in California, to dry out at last.

There is something badly wrong, in print anyway, about Jeeves as a butler, in disguise, acting as a bookie's clerk and hamming it up. He overdoes the quotation thing ... Pliny the Younger, The Psalms, Whittier, Kipling, Omar, Tennyson, Shakespeare (eighteen times), Maugham, Marcus Aurelius, Milton, Byron, Congreve and (slightly inaccurately) Montrose. Languages: *'fons et origo mali'*, *'ne quid nimis'*, *'rem acu tetigisti'*, *'retiarius'*. And French *'faute de mieux'*. It is odd that this should ring so false. But it does.

JEEVES AND THE FEUDAL SPIRIT 1954

Once more Bertie grows a moustache, and again Jeeves disapproves. But Florence Craye thinks it's beautiful, and that infuriates Stilton Cheesewright who is engaged to her (he is no longer a policeman). Florence orders Stilton to grow a moustache, too. Stilton would beat Bertie up in his jealousy, but he has drawn the Wooster ticket in the Drones Darts Tournament sweep, and Bertie's tipped to win. Naturally Stilton does not want to have his man throwing darts with bunged-up eyes and a twisted neck.

Florence, needing atmosphere for her next novel, gets Bertie to take her to a low London nightclub, the Mottled Oyster. Of course it is raided by the cops. The magistrate next morning happens to be Stilton's uncle, and Stilton finds out. Stilton has to lie low in London while his moustache is growing, so Bertie gratefully drives, with Jeeves, to Brinkley Court, where Aunt Dahlia is entertaining the ghastly Trotter couple from Liverpool. She wants L. G. Trotter to buy *Milady's Boudoir* for his stable of magazines. She hopes that a week or two of Anatole's cooking will soften Trotter up to sign for a generous price.

The ghastly Mrs Trotter is trying to get her husband knighted, so that she, 'Lady Trotter', may queen it over Mrs Alderman Blenkinsop, her rival in Liverpool society. The Junior Ganymede Book of Revelations reveals to Jeeves that Mr Trotter has actually been offered a knighthood, but has turned it down, without telling his wife, because he is ashamed of his Christian names. 'Sir Lemuel' or 'Sir Gengulphus', in knee breeches and with a sword between the legs walking backwards, would make him the laughing stock of the Palace, the press and his friends. And now, if he is to buy *Milady's Boudoir*, Mrs Trotter insists that Anatole comes to her kitchen in Liverpool as part of the deal.

Aunt Dahlia yells for Jeeves, who fixes everything. He spots that Mrs Trotter's pearls are false – not the ones her husband gave her. He provides a cosh for Aunt Dahlia to fell Spode/Sidcup, an expert, just as he is about to spot that *her* pearls are false, too. Enter Daphne Dolores Morehad, best-selling writer and very beautiful. Stilton falls for her. Florence briefly is re-engaged to Bertie, but then changes to Percy Gorringe, side-whiskered poet who has dramatised her novel *Spindrift* and writes successful thrillers under another name. Jeeves cures L. G. Trotter's dyspepsia with one of his miracle mixtures, and Trotter buys the *Boudoir* and refuses to consider taking Anatole – all that nasty continental cooking. Bertie calls for soap and a razor and forfeits the lip-fungus.

All very fresh and fizzy.

FRENCH LEAVE 1956

The Wodehouses had lived in France, on and off, for about six years. This is the most French of the novels. It is set mostly in the holiday resort of Roville. Jeff, the hero, is Jefferson Comte d'Escrignon, now a writer. He had been in the Resistance. His mother had been American. He has fallen in love at first sight with American Terry Trent, but he won't court her because he isn't rich and he thinks she is. (Actually she and her sister are pretending to be a rich girl and her maid.) Jeff's father, Marquis de Maufringneuse and a lot more, has had two American wives. He is a sort of feckless Uncle Fred/Ukridge/Mr Micawber combined with Jill (the Reckless)'s Uncle Chris and Lord Hoddesdon. He sponges cheerfully on his son, Jeff. He is called 'Old Nick' and his best friend is a prince, an old reprobate with three breach of promise cases against him.

This novel is distinctly related to an idea Guy Bolton sold to Hollywood, of three attractive sisters (in this case, Terry, Josephine and Kate, who are running a hens-and-bees farm on Long Island) setting out to blow a small legacy and find husbands and happiness.

If Wodehouse is trying to say something in this novel (and he stoutly denied that he ever had a message), it is that the fringes of the French nobility are just as lunatic as the English ditto; and perhaps not only the fringes.

SOMETHING FISHY 1957

Pre-October 1929, New York. A bunch of American millionaires amuse themselves making a secret tontine: $50,000 each into a kitty that will provide about a million dollars for whichever is the last of their sons to get married. Summer 1955, Valley Fields, London SE. Keggs, once butler to, among others, the multiest of those millionaires, is now living in one of the houses he owns in Mulberry Grove with, as lodgers, Lord Uffenham, another of his previous employers, and Lord Uffenham's niece, pretty Jane Benedick (? sister of Anne in *Money in the Bank*). Jane's dowry, is, Lord Uffenham hopes, to come from the profitable sale of his pictures at his ancestral Shipley Hall. The hall is now rented to Roscoe, unpleasant, grossly rich son of the above (late) multiest. Jane is, at first, engaged to a sculptor with marcelled hair. Anyone who has read more than half a dozen Wodehouse novels knows that the engagement of a pretty girl called Jane to a chap with marcelled hair called Stanhope Twine, and who addresses her uncle as 'Ah, Uffenham', will soon be broken up by a fresh young buzzer called Sam, Jeff or, in this case, Bill (Hollister). It proves that grossly rich Roscoe and rather poor Bill are the only survivors in the race for the tontine loot.

Roscoe had bullied Jane as a girl. He is very mean. He is afraid of dogs and prepared to feed drugged meat to a harmless bulldog. He had been sacked from school for usury. Remember Battling Billson? Remember the barmaid Flossie whom he married? Well, Flossie is Keggs's sister. And the Billson daughter, Emma, is the beautiful actress 'Elaine Dawn'. And Roscoe had proposed marriage to 'Elaine Dawn', with letters to prove it. It is the work of a moment for hired sleuth Percy Pilbeam (that two-timing rat again!) to steal them back for Roscoe. But Emma Billson's parents have a word with welshing Roscoe and

an immediate wedding has been arranged. Two, in fact. Emma gets rich Roscoe. *Nouveau riche* Bill gets Jane.

We wonder whether the Billsons invited Ukridge to their daughter's wedding.

COCKTAIL TIME 1958

Opposite the Drones Club is the Demosthenes Club. A brazil nut from the Drones window from a catapult in the hands of Lord Ickenham bashes the topper of pompous barrister Sir Raymond Bastable, Lady Ickenham's half-brother. Sir Raymond blames it on the young, and furiously writes a novel fearlessly attacking that generation of vipers. But, not wanting his name on its spine, he gives it to his sister Phoebe's scrounger son Cosmo to claim authorship. It becomes a *succes de scandale, Cocktail Time*.

It's a pity about 'Beefy' Bastable. He used to be a very proper young gentleman: had eaten seven vanilla ices on the trot at school, followed by only three days in the San; he was an Oxford rugger blue; he was often thrown out of the Empire. Now he's a stuffed shirt: he bullies his sister and proposes to stand for Parliament for Bottleton East. Just the man for Lord Ickenham to get to work on.

'Beefy's' butler, Peasemarch, ex-ship's steward (*The Luck of the Bodkins*) is a friend of, and ex-Home Guards warrior with, Lord Ickenham. Lord Ickenham's godson, Johnny Pearce, writer of suspense thrillers, has rented a country house to 'Beefy'. Barbara Crowe, once engaged to 'Beefy', works at the literary agency that handles *Cocktail Time*. So, as end

products of Lord Ickenham's spreading of sweetness and light, a nicer, more spiritual 'Beefy' will marry Barbara, Peasemarch will marry Phoebe, Johnny will marry his Belinda and Johnny's limpet-like ex-nannie will be taken off his back and marry a policeman.

Three elderly romances, one younger. We meet, briefly, Sir Roderick Glossop again, a second (or is it third?) Bishop of Stortford (he preaches against *Cocktail Time* in the pulpit of the church of St Jude the Resilient), crooks Oily and Sweetie Carlisle again, and an eminent literary agent, Barbara's boss, who knits socks to keep himself from smoking. Also the policeman, Cyril McMurdo, who wins £500 in a football pool, which delays Nanny Bruce's acceptance of his courtship. And we learn that Lord Ickenham's nephew, long-suffering Pongo, is safely married now to Sally Painter.

Wodehouse is seventy-seven and his vintage years are nowhere near ended.

A FEW QUICK ONES 1959

Ten stories: four of them from the Drones Club, all with happy endings, three of them of tight-wad Oofy Prosser losing money and (pimply) face, one of Bingo and his boss Purkiss lying like mad to preserve their marital honour; another of Bingo putting little Algernon Aubrey Little up for the Drones in gratitude to him for saving his father's marital honour; two Mulliners, two Oldest Members, one Ukridge and one Bertie/Jeeves (originally, long ago, a Reggie Pepper story). In publishing dates this is the final Ukridge, and Ukridge, last seen, is in the soup.

In 'Oofy, Freddie and the Beef Trust', told by a Dronesman, the dialogue of everybody – greasy cockney Jas Waterbury, Oofy, two plug-ugly professional wrestlers and Freddie Widgeon – converges into a single slush-parody style, e.g. 'purged in the holocaust of a mighty love'. Perhaps the golden heart of Wodehouse's linguistic humour is slush-parody. In their weaker and most wonderful moments all his best fat-heads seem to show that they've been to too many silly silent films and absorbed their captions complete.

JEEVES IN THE OFFING 1960

In Jeeves's *Times* Bertie sees the announcement of his engagement to Bobbie Wickham. Panic! But this is Bobbie's way of softening up her mother to accept her engagement to Bertie's friend 'Kipper' Herring. And, of course, Bobbie had forgotten to warn either Bertie or Kipper that she was going to do this. Staying at Brinkley is Aubrey Upjohn, quondam HM of Bertie's and Kipper's prep school, of the filthy food of which Kipper tells horror stories. Kipper, on the staff of the *Thursday Review*, scathingly and anonymously reviews a book about prep schools by this Upjohn. And dear Bobbie, reading the final proof, sees that he has left out the splendid stuff about the Malvert House food, and puts it in, again without asking or warning Kipper. So Upjohn will see the *Thursday*, and know who wrote the piece.

With Upjohn at Brinkley is his step-daughter Phyllis, rich (inherited from her late mother), 'a well-stacked young featherweight' who is Aunt Dahlia's goddaughter. There is a rich young American pursuing her and reading poetry to her. He is believed to be the much-marrying playboy, 'Broadway Willie', and Sir Roderick comes down to 'observe' him, and becomes a butler for the purpose. Kipper will marry Bobbie, after a quarrel which drove both of them in pique to get engaged to others (Phyllis and Bertie, for the record).

Jeeves is away shrimping at Herne Bay for most of the novel and Bertie has to drive there and fetch him to solve all the problems, which he does, finally, by putting the blame on the young master and labelling him as a loony and kleptomaniac – not the first or last time for this drastic way out in a last chapter. The plots creak a bit. Some of the writing is 'short'. Many of the images, quotations and verbal handsprings are recognisably old. New and surprising is that Jeeves has taken Bertie to the Louvre to see the *Mona Lisa*. Now, at last, they get that quotation from Walter Pater right – it's 'ends' of the world that come on that head, not 'sorrows' as so often before.

ICE IN THE BEDROOM 1961

Here we must say goodbye to Freddie Widgeon.[1] He's off to Kenya with Sally (*née* Foster) whose tip-tilted nose twitches like a rabbit's, with a £3,000 loan from old Mr Cornelius of Valley Fields, and the blessing of Sally's boss, best-seller Leila Yorke, who has found a long-lost husband, too.

But let's start at the start. Freddie, who has a lowly job in the solicitors' office of Shoesmiths (four of them), shares Peacehaven in Valley Fields with a policeman who was a college friend. Sally and Leila normally live in Sussex where 'Leila Yorke' turns out very successful 'predigested pap' (her own phrase) novels. Irked by the critics who refer to her stuff in much the same phrases, she decides to show them she can write a Hardy/Gissing type of novel too, 'grey as a stevedore's vest', if she can only find somewhere grey to live for a while for atmosphere. Bottleton East? No, says Freddie, they live for pleasure alone in Bottleton East. Come to grey, grey Valley Fields – the house next to mine is vacant etc., etc. So Leila and Sally come to Castlewood, which, as it happens, Soapy and Dolly Molloy had rented previously and where they had stashed some nice diamonds that Dolly had lifted off Mrs Oofy Prosser. (Wait a minute. Aren't we back to *Ice in the Bedroom*? – Well, yes, but you should have forgotten that in the last thirty-six years.)

---

[1] He appears in 'Bingo Bans the Bomb' in *Plum Pie* (1966): but that's the Widgeon of old, bachelor and butterfly.

Soapy has been selling his dud 'Silver River' oil stock regardless of age or sex – to Leila, to Lord Blicester (Freddie's uncle), to Oofy Prosser (twice) and to Freddie. Lord Blicester as a young man, Rodney Widgeon, has been engaged to Leila, but she had broken it off because he got so fat. Oofy Prosser has the majority of the shares of Popgood and Grooly, the publishers of Leila's books. And so it goes, round and round. And it's just as well that Leila brought her shotgun to Valley Fields with her. *Bang, bang*, and Chimp Twist regrets he has taken up burglary again.

Wodehouse wrote that he thought *Sam the Sudden* was 'darned good'. So is *Ice in the Bedroom*. And Leila Yorke is a great addition to Wodehouse's beloved female best-sellers. She has been making £15,000 a year for the last fifteen years, has saved most of it and has sold her last novel to Hollywood for $300,000. And she is very funny about it all. The Aunt Dahlia of the book world.

N.B. Popgood and Groolly (with two ll's) were the publishers waiting to be offered the never-ending *Typical Developments* book in *Happy Thoughts*, by F. C. Burnand, serialised in *Punch* in 1866 and onwards.

SERVICE WITH A SMILE 1962

Lord Emsworth is sorely tried. He has got Wellbeloved back as pig-man, but Connie has got him, as secretary, Lavender Briggs, who irritates him. The horrible Duke of Dunstable has invited himself to stay at the castle again. And Connie has allowed the Church Lads Brigade to camp in the castle grounds, squealing, throwing crusty rolls at his top-hat, making him jump into the lake fully dressed to save a boy, who turns out to be a log of wood. And Connie has brought Myra Schoonmaker, daughter of an American millionaire, down to the castle as, left in her care in London, Myra has fallen in love, and tried to elope, with a penniless curate, Rev. 'Bill' Bailey. Connie invites the Duke's nephew, Archie Gilpin, down to keep Myra company and help her to forget her curate.

At the opening of Parliament Lord Emsworth meets Lord Ickenham, who says he will come and sort things out, bringing with him a young friend, Cuthbert Meriwether, from Brazil (*alias* of the Rev. Bill Bailey, Myra's beloved).

Keep an eye on Lavender Briggs. She needs £500 to start her own secretarial bureau; and blackmail comes easy to her to that end. Keep an eye on the horrible Duke. He's out to steal the Empress and sell her to Lord Tilbury, who has long coveted her for his farm in Bucks. The plots thicken so fast now that at one stage Lord Emsworth, whose grandson has secretly photographed him secretly cutting the guy-ropes of the Church Lads' tent, and who is now held to ransom for his crime, is prepared to buy his own thrice-medalled pig back from the Duke, his guest, for £3,000. Wellbeloved is sacked and re-reinstated. Myra's widower father will marry widow Constance Keeble. Bill Bailey will marry Myra. Lavender

Briggs has got her £500. Archie Gilpin, who needs £1,000 to buy into his cousin Ricky's onion soup bar, gets that and rejoices.

All thanks to Lord Ickenham's virtuoso counter-plotting. He has spread sweetness and light all around except to the horrible Duke.

STIFF UPPER LIP, JEEVES 1963

Bertie has bought himself a jaunty little Tyrolean hat, and Jeeves dislikes it. Gussie still hasn't married Madeline, so Bertie is still in danger of having to do it himself. The Rev. 'Stinker' Pinker begs Bertie to get Madeline to invite him down to Totleigh as there is something his fiancée Stiffy Byng wants Bertie to do. (*They*'re not married yet, either. Sir Watkyn hasn't come across with that vicarage for Stinker which would enable them to marry.) And Gussie, on his way to Totleigh, speaks to Bertie of Madeline in a way no fiancé should. 'Madeline makes me sick!' he says and buzzes off.

So Bertie, silly ass, decides to go to Totleigh and try to heal the Gussie/Madeline rift; plus Alpine hat, plus Jeeves. Madeline has put Gussie on a meatless diet and he is being fed steak and kidney pie at midnight by the sympathetic young cook – a temp: in fact Emerald, kid sister of that Pauline Stoker, now Lady Chufnell, who had led Bertie such a dance in *Thank You, Jeeves*. A guest at Totleigh is Roderick Spode, now Lord Sidcup, always keen to break Gussie's neck if he thinks he's not treating his beloved Madeline right. When Spode sees Gussie kissing the cook, he feels that the neck-breaking cannot wait. First to Gussie's rescue is Stinker (who has boxed heavyweight for Oxford. One day someone must count the number of Wodehouse characters, mostly heroes, who have boxed for their universities. I'm sure I could find twenty-five without a small-tooth comb.). He knocks Spode out with a sweet corkscrew left. Then Emerald does it again, with a kitchen basin. Gussie elopes with Emerald. Madeline says she is going to marry Bertie. Spode says, 'Oh no you're not. You're going to marry me!'

There has been a sub-plot. What Stiffy had wanted Bertie to come to Totleigh for was to steal a black amber statuette that Sir Watkyn had acquired by apparently dirty-dog methods from Major Brabazon Plank, that explosive explorer who had operated in *Uncle Dynamite*. Jeeves, pretending to be Chief Inspector Witherspoon of the Yard, rescues Bertie from Plank's threatened knob-kerrie. And he rescues Bertie from imprisonment, by Sir Watkyn, JP, by agreeing to become Sir Watkyn's valet ('*psst* ... only temporarily, sir'). But Bertie must forfeit that hat. Sir Watkyn's butler is glad to have it to add dash to his courtship of a widow in the village.

It's marvellous the way Wodehouse can get the same actors into new imbroglios using the same scenery; and the way innocent Bertie has only to see a noose to stick his fat head into it. It is comforting to know that, in the tea-tent at the school treat at Totleigh, Sir Watkyn received a well-aimed hard-boiled egg on the cheek-bone from an anonymous donor.

FROZEN ASSETS 1964

Two years ago English journalist Jerry Shoesmith had met American journalist Kay Christopher on the *Mauretania* (the *Mauretania* was in fact taken out of service in 1935. Oh, well.). And now they meet again in a Paris police station – a very good scene this, for openers: Wodehouse was obviously remembering how he and his wife had been pushed around by the Paris police in 1944. Kay is engaged to a stuffed-shirt Englishman at the Paris Embassy. Her brother Biff had saved the life of Lord Tilbury's brother and will inherit a million pounds on condition he is not arrested before the age of thirty. Only a week to go, but the urge to drink is strong and, when drunk, he finds the urge to sock cops strong. And, working for Lord Tilbury, who thinks *he* should have his brother's million pounds, is Percy Pilbeam, who tries to get Biff drunk and seeking cops to sock. Lord Tilbury's secretary is Gwendoline Gibbs and he is in love with her and will marry her. Lord Tilbury's niece, who is his hostess in the Wimbledon Common mansion, Linda Rome, will marry Biff. They had been engaged years before. Jerry will marry Kay.

There is a sequence of debaggings in Valley Fields. Henry Blake-Somerset (he's the mother-dominated stuffed-shirt Embassy chap) had twice been debagged by rowdies at Oxford. Now he is debagged by the debagged Pilbeam, and Lord Tilbury and Biff Christopher make up the chain, each clothing himself in the bags of the next comer. Surprisingly funny as told here, but hasn't Lord Tilbury been debagged, in Valley Fields, before? Yes, in *Ice in the Bedroom*.

We find in this book a whole new list of authors from whom Wodehouse quotes: Shelley, Du Maurier, Robert Service, Alexander Woollcott, Theodore Dreiser, Horace (in Latin), Shakespeare (*Henry IV*), Malory, Burke, Defoe, Raymond Chandler and Mickey Spillane.

GALAHAD AT BLANDINGS 1965

In which Lord Emsworth finds Dame Daphne Winkworth being shoved at him as a prospective second Countess; in which Dame Daphne's horrible son Huxley is determined to release the Empress for cross-country exercise; in which the Empress gets pie-eyed on whisky and bites Huxley's finger; in which Dame Daphne hears Lord Emsworth calling the vet to ask if biting Huxley can have done the Empress any harm; in which Gally introduces a pseudo-Augustus Whipple to the castle and the real one wants to visit too; in which beefy Monica Simmons, the Empress's current guardian, is wooed and won by little Wilfred Allsop; in which Tipton Plimsoll and Veronica Wedge head for the registrar's office.

Lady Hermione Wedge is in the hostess's chair now that Connie has become Lady Constance Schoonmaker, married in New York. Tipton still hasn't married Veronica and

when Lord Emsworth mistakenly announces that Tipton has lost all his money, Veronica's parents find he has lost all his charm as a prospective son-in-law.

At this late stage Wodehouse ravels as tangled a plot as ever, but he unravels it with a rather unseemly rush. Gally has to 'tell the tale' (i.e. lie) briskly in all directions to get the right endings.

PLUM PIE 1966

Nine stories here. In the first, 'Jeeves and the Greasy Bird', Bertie, engaged again to Honoria Glossop, tries to get out of it by compromising himself with Trixie, actress niece of greasy Jas Waterbury. Jeeves and Aunt Dahlia perjure themselves to get Bertie out of that mess, and he and Jeeves are now off to Florida, where Jeeves hopes to catch tarpon. We must suppose that Honoria will now marry Blair Eggleston and be off her father's hands so as to let him marry Myrtle, Lady Chuffnell (as he seems to have done already, six years ago, in *Jeeves in the Offing*. You can't win trying to equate publishing dates with Wodehouse's calendar.). In 'Sleepy Time' hypnotism produces strange golf scores. 'Sticky Wicket at Blandings' isn't about cricket, but about Freddie Treepwood giving away his wife's beloved Alsatian dog to an attractive neighbouring girl. 'Ukridge Starts a Bank Account' finds Ukridge (so does his aunt) selling Aunt Julia's antique furniture. Corky as usual pays for the lunch. There are two Bingo Little stories. In one he gets arrested for sitting in Trafalgar Square at a Ban-the-Bomb rally with a beautiful redhead who he had last met in a water-barrel. Her father, Lord Ippleton, is a good buzzer. 'George and Alfred' is a Mulliner story about twin brothers and Jacob Schnellenhamer and his yacht at Monte Carlo. Only so-so. 'Life with Freddie' is about the dog-biscuit salesman supreme again. And its length and course suggest that it might have been planned to go to a full novel. Ditto 'Stylish Stouts', which ends with a surprising clang. There is a fine drunk scene in 'Stylish Scouts' and the first paragraph of 'Sleepy Time' is a gem even among what might be a slim anthology of Wodehouse's best opening paragraphs.

COMPANY FOR HENRY 1967

Wodehouse is eighty-six now and this is a tired book, especially at the finish. My first edition hardback has several glaring misprints in the last chapter. There is a highly suspect poesy-paragraph in it which might have come in, or from, something fairly gooey he'd have written before the First World War. And I strongly suspect that about ten pages have actually dropped off at the end. *Did* Stickney buy Henry Paradene's awful old mansion? Surely some nice, competent girl would have come and taken nice, incompetent Algy Martin in hand. What about that flock of extra staff, hired for Ashby Hall in the early chapters in case Stickney came to stay? Did the broker's man marry Mrs Simmons the cook, or run away from her hymn-singing?

Henry Paradene could sell Ashby Hall if anybody would buy it. But he isn't allowed, by the entail, to sell a rare French eighteenth-century paperweight, an heirloom, which Mr Stickney covets. Henry's pretty niece is engaged to interior decorator, silky moustached Lionel Green (what, him again?), and when Bill Hardy (who looks like a plug-ugly gangster until he smiles, and who wants to chuck his job and write thrillers in a country cottage somewhere) comes along, you know he'll get Jane in the end, if the end hasn't dropped off. He rescues a cat up an elm in Valley Fields (we're back to *Ice in the Bedroom* yet again) and he gets into Ashby Hall by impersonating the Duff and Trotter bailiff.

There are some good items, verbal 'nifties' and incidentals. 'Bill' Hardy's real name is Thomas. As he can't use Thomas Hardy on the spines of his books, he calls himself Adela Bristow, hoping this might sound, to a bookseller, like 'Agatha Christie' and make him stock up with a lot. Otherwise it's deckchairs on the lawn, swims in the lake, gazing at a girl's bedroom window in the moonlight, going up to London to hire an instant valet, going for a walk 'to think' and going to a bedroom to search it. Even though Lionel Green is a stinker and breaks his engagement to Jane (she is delighted, but no gentleman breaks an engagement), it is good news that he may marry the daughter of an American millionaire client of his shop, Tarvin and Green.

DO BUTLERS BURGLE BANKS? 1968

This novel feels as though it may have started out as a light comedy play script, with all characters on stage for the finale of the last act. A privately owned Worcestershire bank, insolvent through bad management, is now inherited by Mike Bond, Cambridge boxing blue, once third in the Grand National etc. The pretty nurse-companion of Mike's aunt, who lives with him and has broken her leg, is daughter of an impecunious country squire and she is in love with Mike. The butler says his father is ill and a temp takes his job. This is Horace Appleby, head of the Appleby Gang, late of Chicago, now active in England, robbing country houses. Appleby, who lives in Valley Fields, sharing house with Ferdy the

THE OTHER SHORT STORIES

The Man Upstairs (1914), The Man with Two Left Feet (1917), The Clicking of Cuthbert (1922), The Heart of a Goof (1926), Meet Mr Mulliner (1927), Mr Mulliner Speaking (1929), Mulliner Nights (1933), Mulliner Omnibus (1935), Blandings Castle (1935), Young Men in Spats (1936), Lord Emsworth and Others (1937), Eggs, Beans and Crumpets (1940), Nothing Serious (1950), A Few Quick Ones (1959), Plum Pie (1966).

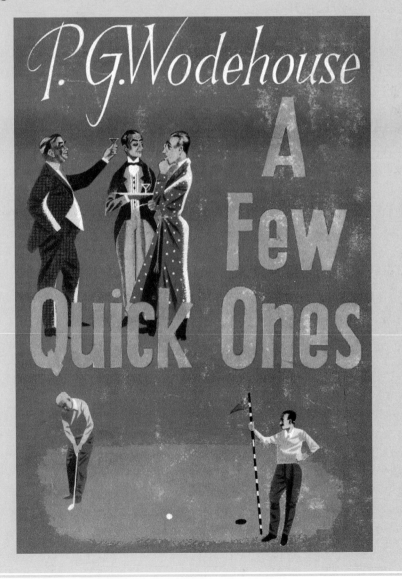

Fly (porch-climber) as his bedmaker/cook, likes to get into country houses first as a butler and then plan the burglary in comfort. Appleby was one of the Duplessis mob on the Riviera. He plans to marry Ada Cootes, Mike Bond's secretary, and retire to the south of France to a house where he has done a burglary job. This time he has bribed the Mallow Hall butler to say his father is ill and leave the post vacant.

Appleby's safe-opening expert, Llewellyn ('Basher') Evans, colossal in size, soft in heart, gets 'religion' at a revivalist meeting (Ukridge's Battling Billson did the same thing) and opts out of the burglary at a critical moment. Charlie Yost, gunman from Chicago, is angry because Appleby has docked his wages for carrying a gun against orders.

Mike's bank is saved when its debts are paid by investments in it by three rich ex-burglars.

Happy endings for all.

A PELICAN AT BLANDINGS 1969

In *Uncle Fred in the Springtime* (1939) Lord Emsworth, weighed down in a sea of troubles (the Duke of Dunstable being the worst), had enlisted Lord Ickenham's help in taking arms against them. Now, with remarried Connie back for the summer and the disgusting Duke once more self-invited, Lord Emsworth summons his brother Galahad to his aid. Galahad is more and more doubling his part with Lord Ickenham these days: spreading sweetness and light; mornings in the hammock; the great sponge in the bath (Lord Ickenham's was 'Joyeuse', Gally's is not named); blackmail; telling the tale; godsons; unsundering young hearts; ringing in impostors.

The Duke has brought his pretty niece Linda with him and of course John Halliday, her ex-fiancé (there had been a flaming 'take back your ring' row), is one of Gally's godsons. And sundered hearts make Gally sick, so he'll have to bring Linda and John together again. For instance, why, when the call comes, shouldn't John come to the castle as Sir Roderick Glossop's junior partner, to keep an eye on the suspected pottiness of Lord Emsworth? Meanwhile there's this American heiress (is she an heiress?) Vanessa Polk that Lady Constance met on the boat. And Wilbur Trout, much-married American playboy. And the painting (is it a forgery?) of the reclining nude that the Duke has bought, brought with him and hung in the gallery. It's up to Gally to find answers to all these problems. He does.

You learn in this book that the oak staircase at the castle is slippery. And if you're trying to work out what rooms were on which floor of the castle, and how to get on to the roof over the semi-detached west wing, this is required reading. It leaves even architects as baffled as ever. Remember, Wodehouse, after years of living in America, could make 'first floor' mean the ground floor. And so on up. Or not.

Wodehouse was eighty-eight when this book was published. The writing is now thin and tediously stretched in places. The ribs of the plot often stare out gauntly with too little flesh on them. Just for a laugh poor Lord Emsworth falls face down into the Empress's sty in the small hours in dressing gown and pyjamas. Many of Gally's old Pelican stories are repeated, often *verbatim*, as though from notebooks. But there are some lovely plums in the duff still.

THE GIRL IN BLUE 1970

Crispin Scrope, middle-aged bachelor, has inherited vast, decrepit Mellingham Hall (not the same one as in *Pearls, Girls and Monty Bodkin*). He runs it as a guest house and he hasn't enough money to pay the repair bills. His butler is really a broker's man. His younger brother Willoughby is a prosperous London solicitor, from whom Crispin has to borrow. Willoughby passes on to Crispin some rich Americans as double-paying guests: Homer Pyle, corporation lawyer and (slightly) a poet: Barney Clayborne, Homer's sister, widow, a sort of Aunt Dahlia and, actually or seemingly, a shoplifter/kleptomaniac.

Willoughby is trustee for young Jerry West, but refuses him his money if he intends to marry gold-digging and imperious Vera Upshaw, daughter of Dame Flora Faye, actress. Jerry, on jury-duty, falls in love with Jane Hunnicutt, air-hostess, also on jury-duty. She hears from Willoughby Crispin that she is inheriting one or two million dollars from someone she was kind to in a plane. So Jerry can't now ask her to marry him – he has scruples about seeming to be a fortune-hunter.

Willoughby has just bought a Gainsborough miniature. It disappears from his office and the fingers of suspicion point to Barney. Several people, for rewards, search her bedroom at the hall for the picture. Vera Upshaw, thinking that Homer Pyle is going to propose to her (she is a writer), ditches Jerry. Then she hears that Jerry has got his money and she tries to switch back. But Jane's legacy doesn't materialise, so Jerry can marry Jane. And rich Barney will marry Crispin Scrope and take over the management of Mellingham Hall. Willoughby warns Homer against Vera Upshaw and Vera remains single and discomfited while all the others rejoice in happy endings. (The Gainsborough turns up, and it wasn't Barney who took it.)

Plotting and narrative are rather lacklustre. But there's some excellent dialogue, very crisp for an eighty-nine-year-old. And there is a good situation moment when the broker's man/butler blackmails his master, Crispin, JP, into agreeing to push the local cop into a stream while he is dabbling his hot feet after the day's duty. In fact Crispin funks it, but Barney does it for him.

One idea for making Barney disclose the Gainsborough, if she had it, was to sound the fire alarm – the principle being that, in a fire, everybody grabs the things most dear to him/her to escape with. Not new, but funny here.

MUCH OBLIGED, JEEVES 1971

This is the one in which we learn Jeeves's Christian name, in which Bertie is Jeeves's guest at the Junior Ganymede Club, in which Bertie is unwillingly, briefly and almost simultaneously re-engaged to Madeline Bassett and Florence Craye, in which Spode, 7th Earl of Sidcup, gets hit in the eye with a potato in an electioneering fracas and is thus cured of his idea of renouncing his title and standing for Parliament.

We're back at Brinkley, and the house is full of guests for the Market Snodsbury by-election, Bertie's, and Aunt Dahlia's, friend Ginger Winship is standing as Conservative candidate and has asked orator Spode to speak on his platforms. Spode's fiancée, Madeline Bassett, comes too. Winship is engaged now to Florence Craye and she comes, a very bossy fiancée as usual. Ginger falls in love with his new secretary and will do anything to get Florence to break their engagement. A final guest at Brinkley is financier L. P. Runkle, who became rich on something that Tuppy Glossop's late father, a research chemist, had invented. But Runkle had not rewarded the inventor and Aunt Dahlia is determined, by Anatole's cooking, theft or blackmail, to get Runkle to give the long-owed money to Tuppy so that he can marry Angela.

A newcomer to Market Snodsbury is Bingley, once Brinkley, Bertie's valet in a period (*Thank You, Jeeves*) when Jeeves had left him. Now, thanks to a deceased grocer uncle, he is a man with a house, property and a butler; though still a country member of the Junior Ganymede. He was once also Ginger Winship's 'man', and Runkle's. And he has 'borrowed' the Junior Ganymede Book of Revelations, containing facts about Ginger which, if published, would turn the strait-laced electors of Market Snodsbury against him.

Just what Ginger would now hope, since it would turn Florence against him too. But Jeeves, with a knock-out drop, steals the book back from Bingley. The book contains stuff about Runkle also. Ginger, on Jeeves's advice, makes a speech advising the electors to vote for his opponent. Florence's self-willed re-engagement to Bertie after that lasts for a single page and she is still unattached, a proud and bossy beauty, when we hear of her, here, for the last time.

When the Book of Revelations goes back to the Junior Ganymede, it will not contain the seventeen pages Jeeves had contributed over the years about Bertie.

A tired book, full of misprints and misprisions – e.g. Bertie says that Arnold Abney, M.A. was the HM of his prep school (of course he meant the Rev. Aubrey Upjohn, HM of Malvern House, Bramley-on-Sea), Jeeves misquotes Lucretius and Brinkley has changed his name arbitrarily and without explanation. Wodehouse is writing very short now.

PEARLS, GIRLS AND MONTY BODKIN 1972

Rich Monty (Montrose) Bodkin must put in another year's employment with Ivor Llewellyn, the Hollywood tycoon, if hockey international Gertrude Butterwick's father is to allow him to marry her. Now he is Llewellyn's secretary, and pint-sized Sandy Miller, who had been Monty's secretary in Hollywood, is now Mrs (Grayce) Llewellyn's secretary, and the Llewellyns have taken Mellingham Hall in Sussex, furnished, for a season. Sandy has long been in love with Monty, but has let concealment, like a worm i' th' bud etc., as she knows he's engaged to that beefy English girl. Grayce has a valuable ($50,000) pearl necklace, and you know what that means – a detective to watch it (Chimp Twist, of course) and that nice couple they met in Cannes, the Molloys, Soapy and Dolly, soon to be watching Chimp and their own opportunity. And, wouldn't you know (Ivor Llewellyn does, because he did the switch – poor chap, he has a joint bank account with Grayce, so how else can he get spending money for gambling? See Sigsbee Waddington in *The Small Bachelor* 1927), the pearls are fake. Besides which Grayce has put Llewellyn on a diet, and Chimp is disguised as his valet with orders to report if he eats or drinks anything he shouldn't. Grayce makes Chimp shave off his moustache for the part.

The old problems: a) a tycoon shackled by a joint bank account with his wife and b) an English gentleman (Monty) wanting to get out of his engagement with a girl. Monty, you see, is now in love with Sandy. When he saw her pull a dustbin full of bottles down over a policeman's head in a raid on a nightclub, he knew that there was the girl he must marry. It all ends happily, with Grayce divorcing Ivor Llewellyn, Monty and Sandy teamed up and Gertrude to marry the dustbin-crowned cop, who is an Old Etonion and also a hockey international. And Chimp, Dolly and Soapy are stuck with a lot of dud pearls.

There is an affinity between this story and *Money in the Bank* (1946).

BACHELORS ANONYMOUS 1973

Her former employer, Laetitia Carberry, of the Anti-Tobacco League, has left to journalist Sally Fitch a Park Lane flat, and £25,000 if she doesn't smoke for two years. And a detective, Daphne Dolby, must share the flat and keep an eye on her and report.

In Hollywood a number of businessmen form 'Bachelors Anonymous', to save friends, clients and themselves from matrimony. The prime mover is Ephraim Trout, lawyer who has handled Ivor Llewellyn's five divorces. Trout always carries Mickey Finns as a last resort to save a soul. He is determined to save Llewellyn from a sixth marriage. When Llewellyn goes to London, Trout arranges for a firm of solicitors there to provide a man to dog his footsteps and save him, especially from Vera Dalrymple, who has just wrecked the chances of Joe Pickering's first play, in which she took the lead. Joe meets Sally Fitch and falls in love with her when she comes to interview him. Sally had once been engaged to Sir Jaklyn Warner, 7th Bart. and a no-good sponger. Hearing about Sally's legacy, Sir Jaklyn courts Sally again, and, in pique because she thinks Joe has stood her up on a dinner date, she accepts him. Sally smokes and loses her £25,000.

Ivor Llewellyn buys Joe's play for $250,000 for a movie. Joe will marry Sally. Daphne Dolby, the detective, drags Sir Jaklyn to the altar, or registry office, and will probably make something of him. Ephraim Trout is bitten by a dog in Valley Fields and the dog's owner, a widow and ex-nurse, bandages him up and feeds him tea and home-made scones and strawberry jam, and Trout will marry her. Happy bachelor Ivor Llewellyn, having escaped Vera Dalrymple, will join Bachelors Anonymous enthusiastically when he gets back to Hollywood.

A most benign, autumnal novel: formulaic but much simpler in plot than Wodehouse in his long summer would have thought fair to his cash customers.

AUNTS AREN'T GENTLEMEN 1974

Plots now run so much in grooves that the fun is almost one hundred per cent linguistic. Bertie and Co. get into fun situations – he is tied up and gagged, horsewhipped, made to fall in a middenish puddle and later a swimming pool. But it's the narrative grammar and syntax murdered by Bertie that is the main strand of humour. When it's fresh and new, it's good. But there is quite a lot of old, cold stuff, too. Sad, but, dash it, Wodehouse is rising ninety-three.

Bertie, with spots on his chest, is told by a doctor to go to the country and live a quiet, fresh-air life. He goes, with Jeeves, to Maiden Eggesford, to a cottage on the estate of a Colonel Briscoe, brother of the Vicar. Aunt Dahlia is staying at the Colonel's house. Jeeves has an aunt in Maiden Eggesford, too. Colonel Briscoe has a racehorse, Simla, which is hotly rivalled by his neighbour Colonel Cook's Potato Chip for an important local race. Potato Chip pines in his stable if his friend the cat isn't there. Aunt Dahlia and all the

Briscoes, including the Vicar's daughter Angelica (remember her from the fizzing short story 'Tried in the Furnace'?) have their shirts on Simla and Aunt Dahlia thinks to safeguard their investments by stealing the cat from Potato Chip so that he'll pine and lose the race. Of course she expects Bertie to house the hijacked cat until after the race.

The young love interest is Orlo Porter, an Oxford Union Communist, who yearns to marry Vanessa Cook, whose father, Colonel Cook, above, is Orlo's sole trustee and who won't unbelt Orlo's money to let him marry his daughter. Vanessa (to whom Bertie had proposed marriage some time previously) quarrels with Orlo because he hasn't the guts to go and thump the table with her fierce horse-whipping father. At one stage she says, 'Right, Bertie, I will marry you.' This would be for Bertie worse even than Florence Craye. Vanessa is dominant and disapproving and proposes that Bertie shall, when they are married, give up smoking, his silly laugh and the Drones.

Simla wins the race on a technicality. Orlo and Vanessa elope. Colonel Cook and his friend (Bertie's enemy in the last book) Major Plank are made to look silly. Why Plank, and Jeeves's aunt for that matter, are there at all is a mystery. Aunt Dahlia wins a lot of money and Bertie and Jeeves escape to the quiet life in New York, far from aunts.

SUNSET AT BLANDINGS 1977

Wodehouse (at long last Sir Pelham Wodehouse) died before he had finished this novel. It was in the form of a rough typescript (he had typed it himself as usual) of the bare-bones narrative and dialogue of the first sixteen chapters of a planned twenty-two. Its story keeps to the Blandings formula: a pretty niece brought to the castle to separate her, and cool her off, from an 'impossible' (i.e. poor) suitor in London; suitor infiltrated under an assumed name by Gally, as artist come to paint the Empress for the portrait gallery; Lord Emsworth innocently blowing the gaff to an angry sister. But there is a lot of good fresh stuff, even in this first-draft *precis*. Two new sisters (that gives Lord Emsworth ten in all) appear, one formidable as usual, the other, uniquely, nice. The formidable one is separated from a 'weak' husband. The Chancellor of the Exchequer, Sir James Piper, wants to propose to the nice one, but cannot do so with his Scotland Yard bodyguard always hovering. It goes practically without saying that Jimmy Piper had been a Pelican and a bit of a lad when young and indigent. But now he too needs Gally's help.

The sixteen chapters at this stage run to scarcely 30,000 words. At that rate the whole novel would have worked out at about 40,000. A finished Wodehouse novel is minimum 60,000. Which shows – and it shows when you read it – that the sixteen chapters would all have been considerably fleshed out. When he was young Wodehouse wrote long and, in the last stages of a novel, enjoyed cutting and simplifying. In his old age he wrote short and enjoyed, but less, the fleshing-out process.

NUGGETSGolf

W odehouse played golf when young, by the light of nature. A big man and strong, he somewhat resembled the 'First Grave-Digger' gentleman of the Wrecking Crew in the story 'Chester Forgets Himself'. The First Grave-Digger, you will remember,

> ...differed from his colleagues – 'The Man with the Hoe, Old Father Time and Consul, the Almost Human – in that, while they were content to peck cautiously at the ball, he never spared himself in his efforts to do it a violent injury.

But golf was a splendid subject for his typewriter, and he could have set his green-fees and club subscriptions down against income tax for the wealth they – or the game – brought him. Unlike cricket, it was played and enjoyed in America too. Its ardours, endurances, agonies and exultations produced stories that could be sold on both sides of the Atlantic.

On the short fourteenth he got one of those lucky twos which, as James Braid once said to J. H. Taylor, seem like a dome of many-coloured glass to stain the white radiance of eternity.

William's sister was one of those small rose-leaf girls with big blue eyes to whom good men instinctively want to give a stroke a hole and on whom bad men automatically prey.

'After all golf is only a game,' said Millicent.
Women say these things without thinking. It does not mean that there
is any kink in their character. They simply don't realise what they are saying.

I attribute the insane arrogance of the later Roman emperors almost entirely to the fact that, never having played golf, they never knew that strange, chastening humility which is engendered by a topped chip-shot. If Cleopatra had been outed in the first round of the Ladies' Singles, we should have heard a lot less of her proud imperiousness.

'I have never put a club into the hand of a beginner without something of the feeling of a sculptor who surveys a mass of shapeless clay. I experience the emotions of a creator. Here, I say to myself, is a semi-sentient being into whose soulless carcase I am breathing life. A moment before, he was, though technically living, a mere clod. A moment hence he will be a golfer.'

Reggie was a troubled spirit these days. He was in love, and he had developed
a bad slice with his mid-iron. He was practically a soul in torment.

Agnes Flack was the undisputed female champion of the club. She had the shoulders of an all-in wrestler, the breezy self-confidence of a sergeant-major and a voice like a toastmaster's. I have often seen the Wrecking Crew, that quartette of spavined septuagenarian golfers whose pride it was that they never let anyone through, scatter like leaves in an autumn gale at the sound of her stentorian 'Fore!'.

There is nothing sadder in this life than the spectacle of a husband
and wife with practically identical handicaps drifting apart.

The Wrecking Crew were just leaving the eighteenth tee, moving up the fairway
with their caddies like one of those great race-migrations of the Middle Ages.

The least thing upsets him on the links. He misses short putts
because of the uproar of the butterflies in the adjoining meadows.

FICTIONAL AUTHORS AND THEIR BOOKS FOUND IN WODEHOUSE

Sir Buckstone Abbott: *My Sporting Memories*

Rosie M. Banks: *A Kiss At Twilight, All for Love, A Red, Red Summer Rose, By Honour Bound, Mervyn Keene, Clubman, Only A Factory Girl, The Courtship Of Lord Strathmorlick, The Woman Who Braved All, Mapcap Myrtle.*

Sir Raymond Bastable: *Cocktail Time* (Cosmo Wisdom named as author).

Mrs Cordelia Blair Blakeney: *Hearts Aflame, Grey Mildew, Sewers Of The Soul, The Stench Of Life.*

Stultitia Bodwin: *Offal.*

Lavender Botts: *How To Talk To The Flowers, Many Of My Best Friends Are Mosquitoes, My Chums The Pixies.*

James Braid: *On Taking Turf, On Casual Water.*

Adela Bristow: *Deadly Earnest.*

Lady Carnaby: *Memories Of Eighty Interesting Years.*

Ann Chester: *The Lonely Heart.*

James Corcoran: ghosted *The Memoirs* of Sir Rupert Lakenheath.

Clarissa Cork: *A Woman In The Wilds.*

Lady Florence Craye: *Spindrift.*

Adela Cream: *Blackness At Night.*

Blair Eggleston: *Offal, Worm I' The Root.*

Professor Farmer: *Sleepy Time.*

Dora Faye: *Theatre Memories* (ghosted by Reginald Tresilian).

Clifford Gandle: *Watchman, What Of The Night?* (sold 43 copies).

Jeremy Garnet: *The Manoeuvres Of Arthur, The Outsider, The Brown-Haired Girl* (projected).

John Gooch: *Madeline Monk, Murderess, The Mystery Of The Severed Ear, Saved From The Scaffold.*

Percy Gorringe (pseudonym 'Rex West'): *Blood Will Tell, Inspector Biffen Views The Body, Murder In Mauve, The Case Of The Poisoned Doughnut, The Mystery Of The Pink Crayfish.*

Mrs Horace Hignett: *The Spreading Light, What Of The Morrow?*

Marcia Huddleston: *Percy's Promise* (Popgood & Grooly 1868 3 vols).

Colin Jeffson: ghosted *Life On The Links* for Sandy Mc Hoots.

The Rev. Aubrey Jerningham: *Is There A Hell?*

Sandy Mc Hoots: *Life On The Links* (ghosted by Colin Jeffson).

Emily Ann Mackintosh: *Roses Red And Roses White.*

Ralston McTodd: *Songs of Squalor.*

Ashe Marson (pseudonym 'Gridley Quayle): *The Adventures Of The Secret Six.*

'George Masterman': see Lady Wickham.

Gwendolyn Moon: *Autumn Leaves, 'Twas In An English June.*

Jane Emmeline Moss: *Her Honour At Stake.*

Francis Pashley-Drake: *My Life With Rod And Gun.*

Louella Peabody: *My Friends The Newts.*

Evengeline Pembury: *Parted Ways, Rue For Remembrance.*

Nesta Ford Pett: *A Society Thug, At Dead Of Night.*

Leila Pinckney: *Heather O' The Hills, Rupert's Legacy, Scent O' The Blossom, The Love Which Prevails.*

Bishop Pontifex: *Collected Sermons* (1839).

Lora Delane Porter: *Principles Of Selection, The Dawn Of Better Things, What Of Tomorrow?*

Charlton Prout: *Grey Myrtles.*

'Gridley Quayle': see Ashe Marson.

James Rodman: *The Secret Nine.*

Paul Sartine: *The History Of The Cat In Ancient Egypt.*

Muriel Singer: *The Children's Book Of American Birds.*

Horatio Slingsby: *Strychnine In The Soup.*

Rodney Spelvin: *The Purple Fan.*

Benedictus de Spinoza: *The Works Of*, authoritatively annotated.

Reginald Sprockett: *Prose Ramblings Of A Rhymester.*

Clare Throckmorton Stooge: *A Strong Man's Kiss.*

J. H. Taylor: *On The Push Shot.*

Reginald Tresilian: ghosted *Theatre Memories* for Dame Dora Faye.

Julia Ukridge: *The Heart of Adelaide.*

Vera Upshaw: *Daffodil Days, Morning's At Seven.*

Jerry Vail: *A Quick Bier For Barney.*

Lady Wensleydale: *Sixty Years Near The Knuckle In Mayfair.*

'Rex West': see Percy Gorringe.

Augustus Whiffle or Whipple: *On The Care Of The Pig* or *The Care Of The Pig.*

Lady Wickham (pseudonym 'George Masterman'): *Blood Will Tell, Agatha's Vow, A Strong Man's Love, A Man For 'A' That, Meadowsweet, Fetters Of Fate.*

'Uncle Willoughby' (Bertie's uncle at Easeby): *Recollections Of A Long Life.*

Cosmo Wisdom: named as author of *Cocktail Time*, written by Sir Raymond Bastable.

P. G. Wodehouse: *On The Niblick.*

Alexander Worple: *American Birds, More American Birds.*

Leila Yorke: *Cupid, The Archer, For True Love Only, Heather O' The Hills, Sweet Jennie Dean.*

Some Book Titles Given Without Their Author's Names:

*The Lads of St Ethelberta's, The Personality That Wins, Gingery Stories, The Spinning Wheel,
With Rod And Gun In Little Known Borneo, Types of Ethical Theory.*

In Lord Emsworth's Library:
Gardens As A Fine Art
Pigs At A Glance
British Pigs
Diseases In Pigs
Pigs And How To Make Them Pay

Various Mystery Stories:
Blood On The Bannisters
Excuse My Gat! Gore By The Gallon
Guess Who!
The Casterbridge Horror
Murder At Mistleigh Manor
Murder at Bilbury Manor
The Man With The Missing Toe
Murder at Murslow Grange
The Murglow Manor Mystery
The Poisoned Pen
Severed Throats
Three Dead on Tuesday

THE FRENCH FOR WODEHOUSE

I mentioned earlier, when discussing the Knut-language which gave something of their conversational style to Psmith and that early Bertie Wooster, that Wodehouse's Lord Tidmouth, in the play *Good Morning Bill*, produced six separate slang variations for 'Goodbye'. They ranged, in the course of the play, from 'Teuf-teuf' to 'Tinkerty-tonk'. Wodehouse's books have been translated into hosts of modern languages. But how? What foreign language do you know? Well, do you in that language, know six separate ways, comparable with 'Teuf-teuf' and 'Tinkerty-tonk', in which a blah young English peer with butter-coloured hair and a receding chin could say 'Goodbye'? And that's only the beginning of the difficulties. The mish-mash of elusive allusion of Wodehouse's buzzers and burblers, the hotch-potch of slangs, the quotations, direct or veiled, the wild imagery...

French is the only language in which I might begin to judge a Wodehouse translation. The last time I was in France, I bought *Jeeves, au secours* (Amiot-Dumont, Paris). '*Ce livre paru en langue anglaise sous le titre*: JOY IN THE MORNING.' The translators are Denyse and Benoit de Fonscolombe.

Joy in the Morning is my favourite Bertie/Jeeves novel. *Bref*, as the French say, and in Bertie's own words, it is 'the super-sticky affair of Nobby Hopwood, Stilton Cheesewright, Florence Craye, my Uncle Percy, J. Chichester Clam, Edwin the Boy Scout and old Boko Fittleworth ... or, as my biographers will probably call it, the Steeple Bumpleigh Horror'. (...*cet embrouillamini ou ... pour prendre la définition qu'adopteront probablement mes biographes ... l'horrible drame de Steeple Bumpleigh auquel furent mêlés Nobby Hopwood, Stilton Cheesewright, Florence Craye, mon oncle Percy, J. Chichester Calm* [sic], *Edwin le Boy Scout et ce vieux Boko Fittleworth*).

I knew that my depth-analysis of the translation wouldn't be easy, as soon as I discovered that two of Bertie's ways of saying 'Goodbye' ('toodle-oo' and 'pip-pip' – neither of which was used by Lord Tidmouth) became in French *bye-bye*. And 'Shropshire' becomes *Skropshire*. This word only appears in the book once, so the French rendering may be a misprint. But I must take it as it comes ... e.g. *chez Droves* for 'at the Drones' and variously *Catsmeat Ploter-Pirbright*, *Potter Pirbright-tête-de-mou* and *Potter Pirbright dit Tête de mou* for 'Catsmeat Potter-Pirbright'. (*Mou* is the French for butcher's lights.) And Lord Worplesdon becomes an armaments, not a shipping magnate.

Anyway, let's take slang and imagery. You might like to paste the following in your Michelin Guide as vocabulary for your next travels in France:

A bucko mate of a tramp steamer .... *un bosco de caboteur*

A nice bit of box-fruit, what! .... *une belle mélasse*

That will bring home the bacon .... *ça rabibochera tout*

A joke salt-shaker .... *une salière surprise*

Rollicking .... *désopilant*

To render unfit for human consumption .... *mettre à mal*

To tear limb from limb .... *déchiqueter*

To give the little snurge six of the best .... *flanquer au maudit galopin une volée*
   with a bludgeon   *de martinet*

To mince yourself to hash .... *se faire hacher la viande*

Some rout or revel .... *quelques parties ou quelques bamboches*

Stinko .... *parti*

My dear old soul (Jeeves) .... *mon petit vieux*

The beasel (Florence Craye) .... *la pécore*

A girl liberally endowed with oomph .... *une fille amplement pourvue de chien*
   (Nobby Hopwood)

To pull someone's leg .... *monter un bateau à quelqu'un*

Cookoo (mad) .... *toqué*

A flop .... *un loupé*

Oofy .... *pourvu de galette*

Rannygazoo .... *la corrida*

A bloke .... *un zèbre*

Acts of kindness .... *des B.A. (bonnes actions)*
   (as enjoined to Boy Scouts, daily)

Nobby and Boko have hitched up, have they? ...... *ça biche Nobby et Boko?*

Everything is gas and gaiters .... *ça gaze à bloc*

To write stinkers (letters) .... *écrire des engueulots*

A blunt instrument .... *un instrument massif*

Loony to the eyebrows .... *complètement dingo*

To go to the mat and start chewing .... *être en bisbille et commencer à se dire*
   pieces out of each other   *des 'vacheries'*

A sterling chap .... *un crac*

To dot him one .... *lui en coller un dans la figure*

A bottle from the oldest bin .... *une bouteille de derrière les fagots*

A bearded bozo (King Edward the Confessor) .... *un bonze barbu*

A wet blanket .... *un vrai parapluie*

To snitch .... *souffler*

To thrash that pie-faced young wart-hog .... *rosser, à deux doigts d'en crever, cette face*
    Fittleworth within an inch of his life   *de tarte, cette jeune verrue de Fittleworth*

His eyes popped out of his head and waved .... *ses yeux étaient hors de la tête et erraient*
    about on their stalks   *de-ci, de-là au bout de leur tige, le nerf*
    optique sans doute

He moved, he stirred, he seemed to feel the .... *Il remuait, s'agitait comme si la vie dans*
    rush of life along his keel   *sa puissance toujours jeune, lui*
    chatouillait la colonne vertébrale

He realises that dirty work is afoot at the .... *Il se rend compte qu'une vilaine besogne*
    crossroads and that something swift is   *est en train de s'accomplir et qu'une*
    being slipped across him   *peau de banane va lui être*
    incessamment lachée dans les pattes

To zoom off immediately .... *faire un départ à l'anglaise sur le champ*
    (for fear of Aunt Agatha)

The bean (head) .... *le chef*

The napper (head) .... *la cafetière*

The onion (head) .... *la caboche*

The old bounder .... *le vieux rustre*

You bloodstained (Bertie) .... *espèce d'ignoble individu*

You horrible young boll-weevil (Edwin) .... *espèce d'horrible graine de charançon*

You fat-headed young faulty reasoner (Edwin) ..... *espèce de nigaud de raisonneur à l'envers*

You outstanding louse (Bertie) .... *espèce de vermine*

You degraded little copper's nark (Edwin) .... *infecte petit rabatteur de police*

You blasted object (Bertie) .... *espèce de détritus*

To hammer the stuffing out of someone .... *étriper quelqu'un*

To spot oompus boompus .... *mettre le doigt sur les manigances*

He loved like a thousand of bricks .... *il était amoureux comme pas un*

Love's young dream had stubbed its toe .... *le rêve de jeunesse et d'amour avaid*
    les ailes coupées

I shall probably play on the old crumb .... *je jouerai probablement sur les fibres de*
    (Lord Worplesdon) as on a stringed   *cette vieille noix comme sur un*
    instrument   *instrument à cordes*

We Woosters can read between the lines .... *nous, Wooster, savons lire entre les lignes*

The menace was null and void .... *la menace était nulle et non avenue*

He ground a tooth or two .... *il grinça des dents*

Her ladyship (Aunt Agatha) .... *Madame la Baronne*

Butler .... *maître d'hôtel*

Butler .... *valet de chambre*

NUGGETS Smells

Wodehouse gives us some memorable musty interiors. They are vivid and polite in his fiction, even with his pig-men who niffed noticeably. They are vivid and less polite in one or two passages in his broadcast talks from Berlin after his internment. He had had the duty of cleaning some Belgian Army latrines on his way to Tost in Upper Silesia. The dormitory at Tost (which had been a lunatic asylum), designed for thirty beds, was now occupied by sixty-six, many of the incumbents British fellow-internees who had married French wives and were now converted to the French rule – bedroom, railway carriage and lavatory windows to be kept tightly shut against the danger of fresh air.

The lamp-and-mop room at the station was a dark and sinister
apartment, smelling strongly of oil and porters.

Like all antique shops it was dingy outside and smelly within.
I don't know why it is, but the proprietors of these establishments
always seem to be cooking some sort of stew in the back room.

A well-defined scent of grease, damp towels and old cabbages
told her that the room through which she was creeping was the kitchen.

(At the election meeting) I sat among the elect on the platform at the Associated
Mechanics Hall, and there came up to me a mixed scent of dust, clothes, orange
peel, chalk, wood, plaster, pomade and Associated Mechanics ... the whole forming
a mixture which, I began to see, was likely to prove too rich for me.

A Frenchwoman of the sturdy lower middle class considers that to inhale
air in which a spoon will not stand upright is to court pneumonia.

(Lord Ickenham coaches his nephew Pongo
in yet another instant impersonation.)
'You are the local vet, my boy, come to minister to my parrot.
I should like to find you by the cage, staring at the bird in a scientific
manner. Tap your teeth from time to time with a pencil and try
to smell of iodoform. It will help to add conviction.'

(From the Berlin broadcasts)
The cell smell (or stink) is a great feature of all French prisons.
Ours in Number 44 at Loos was one of those strapping, broad-shouldered,
up-and-coming stenches which stand with both feet on the ground and
look the world in the eye. When the first German officer to enter
our little sanctum rocked back on his heels and staggered out,
we took it almost as a personal compliment.

HOW DO I LOOK? (SOUND ETC)
Wodehouse's Similes

A melancholy-looking man, he had the appearance of one who has searched for the leak in life's gas-pipe with a lighted candle.

'You look like Helen of Troy after a good facial.'

'Gussie was looking so like a halibut that if he hadn't been wearing horn-rimmed spectacles, a thing halibuts seldom do, I might have supposed myself to be gazing on something a.w.o.l. from a fishmonger's slab.'

He now retreated to the wall and seemed, as far as I could gather, to be trying to go through it. Foiled in this endeavour, he stood looking as if he had been stuffed by a good taxidermist.

He was uttering odd, strangled noises like a man with
no roof to his mouth trying to recite 'Gunga Din'.

Stilton Cheesewright is a man with a pink face and a head that
looks as if it has been blown up with a bicycle pump.

A sharp thrill permeated his frame and he sat up in his chair as if a new,
firm backbone had been inserted in place of the couple of feet of
spaghetti he had been getting along with up till now.

A full-throated baying, a cross between a bloodhound on
the trail and a Scotsman celebrating New Year's Eve.

The eyes glaring, the moustache bristling and the *tout ensemble* presenting a strong
resemblance to a short-tempered tiger of the jungle which has just seen its peasant shin up a tree.

He looked haggard and care-worn, like a Borgia who has suddenly remembered that he
has forgotten to put cyanide in the consommé, and the dinner gong due any minute.

Bingo laughed in an unpleasant, hacking manner as if he were missing on one tonsil.

His eye, once so kindly, could have been grafted on to the
head of a man-eating shark and no questions asked.

A large, red-haired man in a sweater and corduroy trousers who looked
as if he might be in some way connected with the jellied eel industry.

He shot up like a young Hindu fakir with a sensitive skin
making acquaintance with his first bed of spikes.

'Lady Constance looks on me as a sort of cross between
a leper and a nosegay of deadly nightshade.'

He resembled a frog that had been looking on the dark side since it was a slip of a tadpole.

He was a man who was musing on the coming Social Revolution.
He said nothing, merely looking at me as if he were measuring me for my lamp-post.

As for Gussie Fink-Nottle, many an experienced undertaker would have
been deceived by his appearance and started embalming him on sight.

Her face now was pale and drawn, like that of a hockey centre-forward at a girls' school
who, in addition to getting a fruity one on the shin, has just been penalised for 'sticks'.

She looked like something that might have occurred
in Ibsen in one of his less frivolous moments.

Wilfred Allsop was sitting up, his face pale, his eyes glassy, his hair disordered.
He looked like the poet Shelley after a big night out with Lord Byron.

His resemblance to a corpse that had been in the water several days was still pronounced,
but it had become a cheerier corpse, one that had begun to look on the bright side.

The general's eye was piercing him through and through, and every moment he felt more
like a sheep that has had the misfortune to encounter a potted meat manufacturer.

In moments of excitement she had that extraordinary
habit of squeaking like a basketful of puppies.

Lady Constance started irritably, like the Statue of Liberty stung
by a mosquito which had wandered over from the Jersey marshes.

Mrs McCorkadale was what I would call a grim woman. She had a beaky nose, tight thin lips,
and her eye could have been used for splitting logs in the teak forests of Borneo.

Her face was shining like the seat of a bus-driver's trousers.

Abbott, Jane 173
Abbott, Sir Buckstone 173, 210
Abercrombie, George 173
Abney, Arnold 96, 205
Adair 96, 142
Adventures of Sally, The (1922)
 30, 154, **155**, 185
Agatha, Aunt (Mrs Spenser
 Gregdon/Lady Worplesdon)
 57, 64, 70, 73, 75, 76, 88,
 90, 94, 104, 109-10, 111,
 123, 127, 135, 147-8, 149,
 164, 179, 182, 217
'Ahead of Schedule' (story) 146
Alcester, Gertrude 35, 38
Alderman Blenkinsop, Mrs 189
Aldridge, John 70-2
Allsop, Wilfred 108, 198, 222
'Amazing Hat Mystery, The'
 (story) 101, 171
Ambose, Wiffen 46-7
Anatole (chef) 75-6, 96-7, 98,
 110, 124, 158, 170, 174,
 189, 204
Annie, Aunt 90
'Anselm Gets His Chance'
 (story) 176
Anstey, F. 16-17
Anstruther, Mr 47, 97
Appleby, Horace 200-2
'Archibald's Benefit' (story) 146
Archie 153
Arnold, Matthew 180
'Artistic Career of Corky, The'
 (story) 149
Asquith, Cynthia 83-4
'Aunt Agatha Takes the Count'
 (story) 102
'Aunt and the Sluggard, The'
 (story) 149

Aunts Aren't Gentlemen (1974)
 57, 69, 106, 123, 172, 206-7
'Awful Gladness of the Mater,
 The' (story) 163

Bachelors Anonymous (1973)
 30, 113-14, 206
Bagshott, Boko 131
Bagshott, Sam 126, 131
Bailey, Rev. 'Bill' 195-7
Banks, Cuthbert 153
Banks, Rosie M. 59, 90, 112,
 116, 156, 176, 210
Bannister, Ann 172
Bannister, Bill 167
Bannister, Ruth 150
Barmy in Wonderland (1952)
 30, 185
Barrie, Sir James Matthew 83-4
Barrymore, John 143
Basham, Plug 131, 133
Bassett, Madeline 60, 63, 77,
 97-8, 106, 108-9, 120, 127,
 170, 174, 182, 197, 204
Bassett, Sir Watkyn 76, 88, 90,
 97-8, 102, 174
Bastable, Sir Raymond 101,
 192-3, 210
Bates, Braid Vardon 160
Bates, Stiffy 131, 132
Bates, William 160
Baxter, Rupert 10, 19, 41,
 98-9, 100, 106, 157, 163,
 168, 173, 175
Bayliss, Myrtle 29, 30
Beach, Sebastian 39, 41, 43-4,
 45, 79, 99-100, 122, 125,
 133, 164, 168, 173, 185-7
Beamish, J. Hamilton 162
Bean, Elsie 181

Bellamy-Johnstone, Jack 131
Belloc, Hilaire 39, 64, 67, 93
Belpher, Lord 39
Bender, Blinky 131
Benedick, Anne 128, 177
Benedick, Jane 190, 192
Benger, Puffy 131
Bennett, Wilhelmina 154
Bennison, Jeff 45
Berlin Talks 2-4
'Bertie Changes His Mind'
 (story) 158
Bevan, George 12, 100, 149-50
Bevan, Joe 140-1
Bickersdyke, Mr 143
Biddle, Conky 184
Biffen, Fruity 131
Biffen, Mrs 93
Biffy 158
Big Money (1931) 30, 105,
 136, 164-6, **165**
Biggar, Captain 188
Bill the Conqueror (1924) 30,
 123, 158
Billson, Battling 25, 32, 157,
 190-2
Billson, Emma (Elaine Dawn)
 190-2
Billson, Flossie *see* Keggs,
 Flossie
Bingham, Rev. Rupert 35, 38,
 118
Bingham-Reeves, Alistair 93
Bingley/Brinkley 101, 169,
 204-5
'Birth of a Salesman' (story)
 184
Biskerton, Lord ('Biscuit') 164,
 166
Bittlesham, Lady 93

Bittlesham, Lord 112

Blake-Somerset, Henry 126, 198

Blakeney, Mrs Cordelia Blair 210

Blandings Castle (1935) 37, 108, 113, 115, 119, 121, 170-1

Blandings saga 2, 4, 10, 12, 19, 37-45

   see also specific characters/ novels

Blicester, Lord (Rodney Widgeon) 195

Blissac, Vicomte de ('Veek') 167

Blore, Eric 81, 171

Blossom, Lottie 100, 171

Blunt, Lady Julia 142, 143

Blunt, Sir Thomas 142

Bodkin, Monty 19, 100, 102, 168, 171, 205

Bodmin, Jno. 101

Bodwin, Stultitia 210

Boffin, Joe 101

Bognor, Bishop of 132

Bolton, Guy 3-4, 107, 187, 190

Bond, Mike 200-2

Bosham, Lord 39, 42, 121, 175

Bostock, Hermione 52, 181

Bostock, Sir Aylmer 181

Bott, Gladstone 160

Botts, Lavender 210

Bowles the butler 28, 32, 79, 157

Bowles, Sam 131

Bowman, Bill 131, 132

Boyd, Elizabeth 147

Bracken, Lady Beatrice 167

Braid, James 209, 210

Brancaster, Lord 89

Braythwayt, Daphne 156

Brewster, Daniel 153

Brewster, Lucille 153

Bridgnorth, Lord 89

Briggs, Lavender 195-7

Brimble, Hermoine/Heloise 185

Bring On the Girls (1954) 84

Brinkley/Bingley 101, 169, 204-5

Brinkmeyer, Beulah 172

Brinkmeyer, T. P. 172

Briscoe, Angelica 171-2, 207

Briscoe, Colonel 206-7

British Broadcasting Corporation (BBC) 3, 182

Brock, H. M. 27

Brown, Sue 42, 43-4, 94, 99, 102, 119, 132, 163, 168

Bruce, Nanny 193

Brusiloff, Vladimir 153

Bryant, Nelly 153

Buchan, John 83

Bulpitt, Sam 173

Burgess, Mary 156

Burnand, F. C. 195

Burns, Peter 144

Burns, Robert 17

Burper, Lord 132

Busby, Mortimer 173

'Butter-and-Egg Man, The' (Kaufman play) 185

'Buttercup Day' (story) 33

Butterwick, Gertrude 100, 171, 205

Byng, Lady Caroline 39

Byng, Reggie 39

Byng, Stephanie ('Stiffy') 7, 35, 72, 76, 91, 94, 102, 146, 174, 175, 197

Callender, Sally 131

Captain, The (magazine) 26, 139, 146

Carberry, Laetitia 206

Cardinal, Mike 180-1

Carlisle, Gertrude 'Sweetie' 103, 193

Carlisle, Gordon 'Oily' 103, 167, 193

Carmody, Hugo 19, 119, 162, 163

Carmody, Lester 162-3

Carnaby, Lady 210

Carroll, John 162, 163

Carry On, Jeeves (1925) **56**, 57, 77, 96, 106, 110, 112, 149, 158

Chaffinch the butler 172

Charteris ('the Alderman') 11, 138, 139

Chavender, Beatrice 176, 177

Cheesewright, D'Arcy 'Stilton' 72, 88, 104, 106, 179, 189, 215, 221

Chester, Ann 148-9, 210

'Chester Forgets Himself' (story) 208

Chesterton, G. K. 83

Christopher, Biff 198

Christopher, Kay 198

Chuffnell, Little Seabury 46, 110

Chuffnell, Lord (Chuffy) 62, 87, 90, 110, 168-9

Chuffnell, Lady Myrtle 110, 169, 198

Chugwater, Clarence 141

Chums (magazine) 21, 69

Clam, J. Chichester 127, 179, 215

Claude (Bertie's cousin) 110, 156

Clayborne, Barney 203

Clicking of Cuthbert, The (1922) 118, 153

Clowes 11, 139

Cloyster, James Orlebar 104, 141

'Clustering Round Young Bingo' (story) 96, 123, 158

Cobbold, Adela 180

Cobbold, Ellery 180

Cobbold, Stanwood 180, 181

Cobbold, Teresa 180-1

Cocktail Time (1958) **48**, 49, 51, 103, 171, 192-3

Code of the Woosters, The (1938)
57, **71**, 76, 97, 98, 102, 109,
111, 120, 146, 174-5

Coker, Judson 158

Coming of Bill, The (1920) 30,
46, **136**, 150, **151**

'Company for Gertrude' (story)
170

Company for Henry (1967) 30,
200

Connor, William 'Cassandra'
3, 182

Conway, Berry 164-6

Cook, Vanessa 77, 207

Cooley, Joey 172

Cooper, Alfred Duff 3, 182

Coote, Looney 28

Cootes, Ada 202

Cootes, Eddie 157

Cootes, Edward 102

Corcoran, James (Corky) 17,
26, 27-8, 29, 30, 31, 32-3,
92, 104-5, 157, 184, 199,
210

Cork, Adela Shannon 184

Cork, Clarissa 210

Cork, Mrs 94, 177

Cork, Smedley 184, 185

Cornelius, Charles 105

Cornelius, Mr 105, 194

Cornwallis, Frederick Altamont,
fifth Earl of Ickenham 13, 14,
15, 41, 42, 44, 49-53, 66,
82, 88, 110, 171, 175, 180,
181, 192-3, 195-7, 202, 219

Craye, Edwin 46, 69-70, 73,
106, 127, 158, 179, 189,
215, 217

Craye, Lady Florence 72, 75,
76-7, 88, 104, 106, 116, 127,
158, 179, 204, 205, 207,
210, 215, 216

Craye, Percy (Earl of
Worplesdon) *see* Worplesdon,
Lord

Cream, Adela 211

'Creatures of Impulse' (story)
82

'Crime Wave at Blandings, The'
(story) 82, 98-9, 125, 172,
173

Crocker, Billy 148

Crocker, Jimmy 148-9

Crocker, Mrs 148

Crowe, Barbara 192, 193

Cullingworth, James 26

'Custody of the Pumpkin, The'
(story) 119, 121, 170

Cyril, Uncle 90

Dadd, Philip 139

Daily Mirror (newspaper) 3

Daily Telegraph (newspaper)
182

Dalrymple, Vera 206

Damsel in Distress, A (1919)
12, 30, 37, 39, 100, 149-50,
185

Davenport, Horace 175

Davenport, Joe 184-5

Davies, Marion 185

Dawlish, Bill 147

Dawn, Elaine *see* Billson, Emma

Derrick, Phyllis 140

Dingle, Steve 150

Do Butlers Burgle Banks?
(1968) 30, 200-2

Dobbs, Constable 90, 182

Dobson, Constable 169

Doctor Sally (1932) 13, 167

Dolby, Daphne 206

Don Quixote 59

Donaldson, Aggie *see*
Emsworth, Aggie

Donaldson, Penny 187

Doyle, Arthur Conan 11, 16,
26, 58-9, 84

Duff, J. B. 176-7

Dunstable, Alaric, Duke of 41,
42, 45, 55, 99, 106-7, 132,
175, 195, 197, 202

Eggleston, Blair 94, 110, 116,
167, 199, 211

Eggs, Beans and Crumpets
(1940) 25, 101, 104, 112,
115, 176

Elizabeth, Queen Mother 1

Emerson, George 146

Emsworth, Lord 9, 10, 19, 20,
37-45, 53, 98-100, 102, 106,
107, 108, 118-19, 121, 125,
126, 127, 130, 132, 146,
149, 157, 163, 168, 170,
173, 175, 180, 184, 185-7,
195, 198-9, 202-3, 207, 214

Enter Psmith (1935) 9-10

Escrignon, Jefferson Comte d'
189-90

Eustace (Bertie's cousin) 110,
156

'Extricating Old Percy' (story)
127

'Extricating Young Gussie'
(story) 57, 73, 74, 84, 147,
149

Fairbanks, Douglas, Sr. 143

Farmer, Professor 211

Farnie, Reginald 138-9

Farrar, Dean 13

Faye, Dora 211

Fenwick, Claire 147

Ferdy the Fly 200-2

Few Quick Ones, A (1959) 25,
57, 105, 112, 115, 118, 193,
201

Finch, George 160-2

Finglass, 'Finky' 105

Fink-Nottle, Augustus 'Gussie'
22, 60, 63, 74, 76, 88, 98,
108-9, 111, 120, 170, 174,
182, 197, 220, 222

Fish, Miles 132

Fish, Ronnie 7, 42-4, 94, 102,
132, 149, 162, 163, 168

Fishbein, Isidore 113

Fisher, Bradbury 160

Fitch, Sally 206

Fitch-Fitch, Freddie 176

Fittleworth, Boko 93, 106, 111, 127, 179, 215, 216, 217

'Fixing It For Freddie' (story) 57

Flack, Agnes 115, 163, 209

Fleming, Peter 53

Flores, Carmen 184

Foljambe, Reggie 93

Fonscolombe, Benoit de 215

Fonscolombe, Denyse de 215

Ford, Elmer 144

Ford, Ogden 109, 144, 148

Foster, Jerry 154

Foster, Sally (later Widgeon) 105, 194

Fotheringay-Phipps, Cyril 'Barmy' 171, 185

Franklyn, Packy 167

Fred, Uncle *see* Cornwallis, Frederick Altamont, fifth Earl of Ickenham

French Leave (1956) 30, 189-90

Frisby, Paterson 164

Frohmann, Charles 141

Frozen Assets (1964) 30, 113, 120, 123, 126, 198

Full Moon (1947) 37, 41, 108, 123, 179-80

Galahad at Blandings (1965) 37, 108, 123, 126, 127, 131, 198-9

Gandle, Clifford 211

Garland, Lady Dora 180

Garland, Prudence 180

Garnet, Jeremy 27, 28, 58, 140, 211

Garroway (policeman) 162

Gedge, Mr 167

Gedge, Mrs 103, 167

Gentleman of Leisure, A (1910) 30, 142-3

'George and Alfred' (story) 199

Gessler, Hermann 139

Gethryn, Alan 138-9

Gibbs, Gwendolyn 123, 198

Gilbert, W. S. 59

Gilpin, Archie 195, 197

Gilpin, Ricky 175, 197

Girl in Blue, The (1970) 30, 203

Girl on the Boat, The (1922) 30, 94, 154

Globe (newspaper) 2

Glossop, Honoria 75, 77, 88, 94, 95, 109-10, 156, 158, 199

Glossop, Oswald 46

Glossop, Sir Roderick 60, 62, 70, 83, 88, 109-10, 169, 175, 193, 194, 202

Glossop, Tuppy 17, 63, 64, 109-10, 124, 125, 164, 170, 204

Glutz, Jacob 113

Glutz, Sigismund (Sam) 113

'Go-Getter, The' (story) 170

Gold Bat, The (1904) 21, 139

Gooch, John 211

'Good Angel, The' (story) 82, 146

Good Morning, Bill (play) 14, 167, 213

Goodwin, Margaret 141

Gorringe, Percy 106, 189, 211

Graham, Tony 138

Green, Lionel 177, 200

Gregson, Thos 46, 47, 64, 69, 76, 110, 111, 182

Haddock, Esmond 182

Haggard, Rider 13

Halliday, Eve 19, 157

Halliday, Johnny 132, 202

Halliday, Stiffy 107, 132

Hancock, Tony 25-6

Hardy, Bill 200

Havershot, Reggie 58, 67, 172

Hay, Ian 13

Hayward, John 69

Head of Kays, The (1905) 21, 140, 142

Hearst, William Randolph 185

Heart of a Goof, The (1926) 118, 160

Heavy Weather (1933) 37, 100, 102, 108, 119, 123, 168

Heloise, Princess von und zu Dwornitzchek 107, 173

Hemmingway, Aline 102, 121

Henderson, Dolly 42, 102, 122, 130, 132, 163

Henley, William Ernest 65

Herbert, A. P. 20

Herring, 'Kipper' 70, 77, 94, 193-4

Hicks, Seymour 9

Hignett, Eustace 94, 154

Hignett, Mrs Adeline Horace 154, 211

Hoddesdon, Lord 166

Hogg, James 126

Holbeton, Lord 176, 177

Hollister, Bill 190, 192

Holmes, Sherlock 11, 16, 58-9

Homer 37-8

Hong Kong and Shanghai Bank 2

Hopwood, Nobby (Zenobia) 7, 76, 111, 127, 179, 215, 216

Hot Water (1932) 30, 103, 167

Houghton, John W. 139

Howard, Jane 94, 154

'How's That, Umpire?' (story) 184

Huddleston, Marcia 211

Hunnicutt, Jane 203

Hunstanton, Lord 162

Ice in the Bedroom (1961) 30, 103, 105, 119, 123, 194-5

Ickenham, Lady 49, 50, 51, 52, 181, 192

Ickenham, Lord *see* Cornwallis, Frederick Altamont, fifth Earl of Ickenham

If I Were You (1931) 30, 166

'In Alcala' (story) 114, 146

Indiscretions of Archie (1921) 30, 153

Ingall, Isaac 78

Intimitable Jeeves, The (1923) 57, 109-10, 112, 156

Ippleton, Lord 199

Jabberjee, Hurry Bungsho 16-17

Jackson, Bob 142

Jackson, Joe 143

Jackson, Mike 10, 11, 14, 19, 26, 28, 39, 96, 111-12, 142, 143, 146, 147, 156-7

Jackson, Phyllis 39, 112, 156-7

Jane 173

Jane 200

Jardine, Hank 150

Jarvis, Bat 144, 146, 147

Jeeves, Reginald 17, 19, 58-9, 61, 64, 67, 69, 70-2, 73-4, 76, 77, 79, 81-93, 96, 97, 98, 101, 102, 109, 112, 120, 124, 127, 146, 147, 148, 149, 158, 164, 168-9, 170, 174, 175, 179, 182, 187-9, 193-4, 197, 199, 204, 205, 206-7, 213, 216

'Jeeves and the Chump Cyril' (story) 149

Jeeves and the Feudal Spirit (1954) 57, 70, 97, 104, 106, 110, 120, 189

'Jeeves and the Greasy Bird' (story) 110, 199

'Jeeves and the Hard-Boiled Egg' (story) 149

'Jeeves Makes an Omelette' (story) 57, 149

Jeeves in the Offing (1960) 57, 70, 77, 83, 193-4, 199

'Jeeves and the Old School Chum' (story) 112

Jeeves Omnibus, The (1931) 57, 77

'Jeeves Takes Charge' (story) 106, 127, 158

'Jeeves and the Unbidden Guest' (story) 149

Jeffson, Colin 211

Jellaby, Myrtle 35

Jellicoe 14

Jenkins, Herbert 40

Jerningham, Rev. Aubrey 211

Jevons, Mr 82, 98-9

Jill the Reckless (1921) 19, 29, 30, 125, 126, **136**, 150-3, **152**, 154, 185

Johnson, Dr Ben 16-17

Jones, Evan 157

Joy in the Morning (1947) 57, 75, 104, 106, 111, 127, 179, 215

Julia, Lady 168

Kaufman, George 185

Kay, Mr 140

Kayite 140

Keats, John 18

Keeble, Joe 112, 121, 157

Keeble, Lady Constance *see* Threepwood, Lady Constance

Keggs, Flossie (later Billson) 157, 190-2

Keggs, S. E. 39, 190

Kegley-Bassington, Muriel 68

Kemp, Ginger 154

Kennedy (prefect) 140

Kern, Jerome 1, 100

Kipling, Rudyard 87-8

'Kissing Time' (song) 4

'Knightly Quest of Mervyn, The' (story) 168

Lakenheath, Lady 157

Laughing Gas (1936) 30, 58, 67, 172

Lawlor, Boko 31, 32-3

Leave it to Psmith (1923) **8**, 9, 10, 12, 14, 18-19, 37, 39, 49, 98, 102, 112, 121, 143, 156-7

Lehman, Fanny 185

Lehman, Joe 185

'Life with Freddie' (story) 199

Linda (niece of the Duke of Dunstable) 106, 202

Lister, Bill 180

Little, Algernon Aubrey 46, 112, 184, 193

Little, Bingo 17, 46, 69, 74, 75, 86, 88, 91, 93, 95, 96, 112, 156, 158, 164, 176, 184, 193, 199, 221

Little Nugget, The (1913) 21, 30, 96, 109, **136**, 144, **145**

Little, Rosie 94, 95, 96, 112, 158

Littlewood, Daphne 127

Llewellyn, Evans 202

Llewellyn, Grayce 113, 205

Llewellyn, Ivor 100, 113-14, 171, 184, 205, 206

Lloyd, Marie 77

'Lord Emsworth Acts for the Best' (story) 170

'Lord Emsworth and the Girl Friend' (story) 170

Lord Emsworth and the Others (1937) 25, 37, 99, 104, 112, 115, 172-3

Lorimer (school boy) 139

Lorimer, Mabel 139

Louder and Funnier (1932) 66, 128

Love Amongst the Chickens (1906/1921) **24**, 25, 26-8, 32, 58, 140, 141, 157

'Love That Purifies, The' (story) 97

Luck of the Bodkins, The (1935) 30, 100, 113, 171

Luck Stone, The (1908) 21

Mabel 91

Mabel of Onslow Square 29-30

Mc Hoots, Sandy 211

McAllister the gardener 39, 41, 43

McCorkadale, Mrs 222

McEachern, John 142

McEachern, Molly 142-3

Mackail, Denis 84

Mackintosh, Emily Ann 211

McMurdo, Cyril 193

McMurdo, Sidney 163

Macpherson the gardener 39

McTodd, Ralston 211

Mainwaring, Peggy 93

'Making of Mac's', The' (story) 148

Man with Two Left Feet, The (1917) 57, 73, 115, 147-8, 149

Man Upstairs, The (1914) 82, 114, 146

Mannering, Eggy 22, 172

Mannering-Phipps (Bertie Wooster) 73, 74, 147-8

Mannering-Phipps, Gussie 147-8

Mariner, Jill 125, 150-3

Marlowe, Peggy 185

Marlowe, Sam 154

Marriott 11

Marsh, Lady Maud 100, 149-50

Marshmoreton, Lord 7, 39, 100, 149

Marson, Ashe 12, 39, 43, 146, 211

Mason, Wally 29, 153

Masterman, George 211

Mating Season, The (1949) 57, 68, 82, 90, 98, 109, 111, 127, 182, **183**

Maude, John 143-4

Maufringneuse, Marquis de 190

Maxwell, Rutherford 114

Meadowes the butler 83, 90

Meet Mr Mulliner (1927) 115, 162

Meriwether, Cuthbert 195

Mike (1909) 9, 11, 14, 21, 26, 111, 142

Mike and Psmith (1953) 9, 14, 21

Mike at Wrykyn (1953) 21

Miller, Jeff 52, 128, 129, 177

Miller, Sandy 100, 205

Mills and Boon 144

Milne, A. A. 182, 184

Mitchell, Abe 153

'Mixer, The' (story) 148

Molloy, Dolly 103, 104, 105, 160, 162-3, 177, 194, 205

Molloy, Thos G. ('Soapy') 103, 104, 105, 160, 162-3, 177, 194-5, 205

Money in the Bank (1946) 11, 30, 52, 94, 103, 128-9, **136**, 177-9, **178**, 205

Money for Nothing (1928) 30, 103, 162-3

Moon, Ann 164

Moon, Gwendolyn 211

Moon, Sebastian 70

Moore, Dinty 185

Moore, George 43

Morehead, Daphne Dolores 104, 189

Mosley, Sir Oswald 120, 175

Moss, Jane Emmeline 212

Motty, Lord Pershore 17

Mountford, Rollo 156-7

Mr Mulliner Speaking (1929) 115, 163

'Mr Potter Takes a Rest' (story) 171

Much Obliged, Jeeves (1971) 57, 96, 97, 98, 100, 110, 111, 120, 125, 169, 204

Mullett 162

Mulliner, Anselm 176

Mulliner, Rev. Anselm 35

Mulliner, Archie 83, 171

Mulliner, Augustine 162, 167

Mulliner, George 162

Mulliner, John San Francisco Earthquake 22

Mulliner, Mr 22, 69, 113, 114-15, 162, 163, 171, 172, 193, 199

Mulliner, Montrose 115

Mulliner Nights (1933) 115, 167-8

Mulliner Omnibus, The 115

Mulliner, Sacheverell 168

Mulliner, Wilfred 162

Mulliner, Uncle William 22

Murray, Gilbert 37

Muspratt, Beefy 132

My Man Jeeves (1919) 57, 73, 77, 149, 158

Nicholas, Fillmore 154

Nicholas, Sally 154

'No Wedding Bells for Him' (story) 27

Not George Washington (1907) 104, 141

Nothing Serious (1950) 25, 37, 104-5, 112, 118, 184

Oakley, Jane 143, 144

Oakshott, Bill 52, 79, 82, 181, 184

Old Reliable, The (1951) 30, 113, 184-5

Old Stinker 46

Oldest Member 118, 160, 172, 184, 193

'One Touch of Nature' (story) 148

'Oofy, Freddie and the Beef Trust' (story) 193

Opal, Jane 167

Opal, Senator 167

'Ordeal of Osbert Mulliner, The' (story) 22

Orwell, George 32, 142

Over Seventy (1957) 14, 26, 66

Oxford Book of Quotations 5

Index

Packard, Jane 160

Painter, Sally 49, 51, 181, 193

Paradene, Henry 200

Parker the butler 79

Parkinson-Willoughby, Esmerelda 131

Parsloe-Devine, Raymond 116

Parsloe-Parsloe, Sir Gregory 6, 7, 40, 44, 99, 107, 108, 110, 118, 122, 123, 132-3, 163, 168, 170, 185-7

Parsloe-Parsloe, Lady (Maudie Stubbs) 99, 118, 164, 187

Parsloe-Parsloe, Tubby 118, 187

Pashley-Drake, Francis 212

'Passing of Ambrose, The' (story) 46-7, 163

Peabody, Louella 212

Peake, Adrian 107, 173

Pearce, Johnny 192, 193

Pearls, Girls and Monty Bodkin (1972) 30, 100, 103, 113, 114, 205

Peasemarch, Albert Eustace 52, 171, 192, 193

Peavey, Aileen 102, 157

Peggy 114

Pelican at Blandings, A (1969) 37, 41, 45, 106, 108, 123, 202-3

Pembury, Evengeline 212

Pendlebury, Gwladys 77, 164

Pepper, Reggie 57, 73, 74, 115, 149

Performing Flea 2, 16, 49, 69, 115

Pershore, Motty 22

Peters, Aline 43, 146

Peters, J. Preston 12, 43, 146

Pett, Nesta Ford 148, 212

Pett, Peter 148

Phipps the butler 184, 185

Piccadilly Jim (1918) 19, 30, 109, 148-9

Pickering, Joe 206

'Pig-Hoo-o-o-o-ey!' (story) 119, 170

Pigs Have Wings (1952) 37, 40, 108, 119, 123, 131, **136**, 185-7, **186**

Pilbeam, Percy 22, 100, 102, 119-20, 123, 160, 163, 168, 190, 198

Pinckney, Leila 116, 212

Pinker, Rev. Harold 'Stinker' 35, 72, 94, 102, 120, 174, 197

Piper, Sir James 207

Pirbright, Catsmeat 22, 68, 182, 215

Pirbright, Corky 7, 68, 77, 182

Pirbright (pigman) 107-8

Pitt, Jimmy 142, 143

Plank, Major Brabazon 181, 197, 207

Plimsoll, Tipton 22, 94, 180, 198-9

Plum Pie (1966) 25, 37, 57, 105, 110, 112, 113, 115, 123, 199

Plumpton, Uncle 184

Polk, Vanessa 202

Ponderby, Legs 133

Pontifex, Bishop 212

Porter, Lora Delane 150, 212

Porter, Orlo 207

Pothunters, The (1902) 11, 21, 138, 139

Pott, Edwin 108

Pott, Mustard 175

Pott, Polly 51, 175

Potter, Mervyn 22, 185

Potter, policeman 181

Potts, Eustace 133

Potts, Freddie 133

Pound, Percy 132

Powell, Baden 141

Prefect's Uncle, A (1903) 21, 138-9

Price, Cuthbert 108

Price, Mabel 27-8, 29-30, 157

Prince and Betty, The (1912) 30, 143-4

Pringle (school boy) 139

Prosser, Oofy 6, 25, 46, 193, 194-5

Prout, Charlton 116, 212

Psmith 5, 8-20, 49, 96, 111-12, 121, 142, 143, 146-7, 156-7, 215

Psmith in the City (1910) 9, 10, 112, 143

Psmith Journalist (1915) 9, 10, 11, 12, 14, 16, 18, 19, 112, 144, 146-7

Public School Magazine, The 139

Pulbrook, Eustacia 182

Pulbrook, Sir Eustace 182

Punch (magazine) 1, 13, 16, 66, 83, 139, 195

Punter, Mrs 180, 181

Purkiss 176, 193

Pyke, Roderick 123, 158

Pyke, Sir George *see* Tilbury, Lord

Pyle, Homer 203

Quick Service (1940) 30, 176-7

Ramsbotham, Sir Peter 1

Ranelagh, Lord Frederick 89-90

Reed, Talbot Baines 18

Richards, Frank 18

Right Ho, Jeeves (1934) 17, 57, 60, **80**, 98, 109, 124, 170

Ring for Jeeves (1953) 57, 73-4, 81, 88, 90, 187-8

Robb, Augustus 180-1, 184

Robinson, Robert 2

Rodman, James 212

'Rodney Has a Relapse' (story) 184

Roegate, Lord 173

Rollo 146

'Romance is an Ugly Policeman, The' (story) 148

Rome, Linda 198

Ronald, Master 99

Rooke, Freddie 29, 125, 153

Roscoe 190-2

Rowbotham, Charlotte Corday 156

Rowcester, Lord 74, 90, 187, 188

'Rummy Affair of Old Biffy, The' (story) 158

Runkle, L. P. 97, 110, 204

Sackville-West, Victoria 43

Sally 176-7

Salt, Gloria 118, 187

Sam the Sudden (1925) 105, 119, 123, 158-60, **159**, 195

Sartine, Paul 212

Schnellenhamer, Jacob 113, 115, 199

Schoonmaker, Lady Constance *see* Threepwood, Lady Constance

Schoonmaker, Myra 49, 163, 195

Scobell, Benjamin 143-4

Scott, Walter 105

Scrope, Crispin 203

Scrope, Willoughby 203

Seaman, Owen 66

Selby, Chris 150, 153

Seppings, Butler 97

Service With A Smile (1962) 37, 44, 49, 53, 106, 108, 123, **136**, 171, 195-7, **196**

'Shadow Passes, The' (story) 112

Shakespeare, William 17, 62, 63, 64, 65, 66, 69, 114, 117, 171, 184

Shannon, 'Bill' 184, 185

Shannon, Kay 184-5

Shaw, T.E. 36-7

Sheen 140-1

Sheridan, Felicia 158

Shoesmith, Jerry 120, 198

Shortlands, Lord 180

Shotter, Sam 28, 105, 158-60

Silver, Betty 143-4

Silver, Jimmy 11, 140

Silversmith, Charlie 68, 82, 90, 182

Silversmith, Queenie 90

Simmons, Monica 108, 185-7, 198

Singer, Muriel 212

Sipperley, Oliver 164

Slattery, 'Soup' 167

'Sleepy Time' (story) 199

Slingsby, Horatio 212

Small Batchelor, The (1927) 30, **136**, 160-2, **161**

Smith, Rupert 144

Smith, Sally 167

Snettisham, Lady Jane 76, 97

'Soapy Sid' 90, 102

Something Fishy (1957) 30, 120, **136**, 190-2, **191**

Something Fresh (1915) 12, 37, 39, 40, 43, 45, 59, 90, 98, 99, 121, 146, 154

'Something Squishy' (story) 163

'Something to Worry About' (story) 146

'Sonny Boy' (story) 112

Spelvin, Rodney 117, 212

Spencer, Sanders 126

'Spennie', Earl of Dreever 142

Spenser Gregdon, Mrs *see* Agatha, Aunt

Spenser/Spenser-Gregson/ Spenser Gregson 75, 111

Spink the butler 180, 181

Spinoza, Benedictus de 212

Spode, Roderick (later Lord Sidcup) 2, 6, 73, 88, 98, 109, 120, 174, 189, 197, 204

Spottsworth, Rosie 188

Spring Fever (1948) 30, 180-1, 184

Sprockett, Reginald 212

Steptoe, Mabel 176, 177

Stickney, Mr 200

'Sticky Wicket at Blandings' (story) 199

Stiff Upper Lip, Jeeves (1963) 57, **85**, 90, 98, 102, 106, 109, 120, 181, 197

Stoker, Dwight 46, 169

Stoker, Eileen 180, 181

Stoker, Emerald 120, 197

Stoker, J. Washburn 169

Stoker, Pauline 62, 77, 87, 110, 169, 197

Stoker, Pop 17, 62, 77, 88, 90

Stooge, Clare Throckmorton 212

Strand Magazine, The 16, 82

Struggles, Buffy 133

Stubbs, Maudie *see* Parsloe, Lady

'Stylish Scouts' (story) 199

'Success Story' (story) 184

Summer Lightening (1929) 5, 37, 99, 102, 108, 119, 121, 123, 162, 168, 170

Summer Moonshine (1938) 30, 107, 173

Sunset at Blandings (1977) 37, 44-5, 94, 108, 123, 125, 126, 127, 207

Swoop, The (1909) 141-2

Swordfish the butler 83, 110

Tales of St Austin's (1903) 21, 139

Taylor, J. H. 209, 212

Tennyson, Ambrose 113, 117, 171

Tennyson, Lord 83, 113, 117, 154

Tennyson, Reggie 171

Thank You, Jeeves (1934) 57, 62, 83, 92, 101, 110, 168-9, 170, 197, 204

Thistleton, Digby (Lord Bridgnorth) 89

Thomson, Allen 138

Waterbury, Jas 193, 199

Watkyn, Sir 197

Watson, Dr 58-9

Watson, Jane 93

Waugh, Auberon 5

Waugh, Evelyn 3, 4, 5, 45, 120, 142

Weatherby, Joss 176-7

Webster, Montague 154

Wedge, Hermione 179-80, 198

Wedge, Veronica 42, 94, 179-80, 198-9

Welch, Fanny 162

Wellbeloved, George Cyril 40, 107, 118, 119, 170, 185, 195

Wensleydale, Lady 213

West, Bill 158

West, Jerry 203

Westbrook, Herbert 104, 141

Wetherby, Lady Pauline 147

Whiffle/Whipple, Augustus 126, 198, 213

White the butler 144

White Feather, The (1907) 21, 26, 140-1

Whittaker, Prudence 173

Wickham, Bobbie 7, 12-13, 70, 76, 77, 83, 94, 95, 115, 163, 164, 171, 193-4

Wickham, Lady 115, 116, 163, 213

Wickhammersley, Cynthia 35, 77, 156

Widgeon, Freddie 69, 105, 154, 171, 173, 184, 193, 194-5

Widgeon, Rodney (Lord Blicester) 195

William Tell Told Again (1904) 139

Willie, Broadway 194

Willoughby, Uncle 158, 213

Wilson 146

Winch, Gladys 154

Windsor 146-7

Winfield, Bill 46, 150

Winfield, Kirk 46, 150

Winfield, Ruth 46

Winkworth, Dame Daphne 127, 182, 198

Winkworth, Gertrude 182

Winkworth, Huxley 107, 127, 198

Winship, Ginger 106, 204-5

Wisdom, Cosmo 192, 213

Wisdom, Mrs 164

Wisdom, Phoebe 52, 192, 193

Wodehouse, Lady Ethel 1, 3, 128, 129, 157

Wodehouse, Leonora 1

Wodehouse, Sir Pelham Grenville 1-2

  on alcohol 22-3

  on animals 128-9

  Berlin Broadcasts 2-4

  Bertie Wooster 57-77

  Blandings 37-45

  books 136-207

  on children 46-7

  on the Church 34-5

  death 1

  fictional authors and books in 116-17, 210-14

  French translations 215-17

  on Gally's associates 130-3

  on golf 208-9

  insults 54-5

  Jeeves 81-93

  knighthood 1, 3

  on manservants 78-9

  58 memorable characters 96-127

  nationality 1

  Psmith 8-19

  RAF bombing incident on Le Touquet 3-4

  residences 2-3

  similes 220-2

  on smells 218-19

  TV interview 2

  Ukridge 24-33

  Uncle Fred 49-53

  on women 94-5

Wooster, Bertie 2, 4, 5, 13, 15, 16, 17, 28, 37, 46, 57-77, 81, 86-9, 90, 91-3, 96-7, 98, 101, 102, 104, 106, 108, 109-10, 111, 112, 115, 120, 122, 123, 125, 127, 146, 147-8, 149, 156, 158, 164, 168-9, 170, 171, 174, 175, 179, 182, 187, 189, 193-4, 197, 199, 204-5, 206-7, 215, 217

  see also Mannering-Phipps (Bertie Wooster)

World of Jeeves, The (1967) 126

World of Psmith (1974) 9, 20

Worple, Alexander 213

Worplesdon, Lady *see* Agatha, Aunt

Worplesdon, Lord 22, 75, 89, 94, 104, 106, 111, 127, 158, 179, 215, 217

Wyvern, Colonel 162

Wyvern, Jill 188

Wyvern, Pat 162, 163

Yates, Dornford 18-19, 43

Yaxley, Lady 164

Yaxley, Lord 7, 74

Yorke, Leila 116, 117, 194-5, 213

Yost, Charlie 202

Young Men in Spats (1936) 49, 101, 115, 171-2

Zizzbaum, Ben 113

'Those in Peril on the Tee' (story) 163

Threepwood, Aggie (*née* Donaldson) 41, 121

Threepwood, (Keeble/Schoonmaker) Lady Constance 12, 39, 41, 42, 45, 94, 98, 99, 102, 106, 107, 112, 118, 122, 125, 127, 143, 156-7, 173, 175, 187, 195, 198, 202, 221, 222

Threepwood, Diane 44-5, 94, 125

Threepwood, Florence 45

Threepwood, Freddie 10, 14, 17, 19, 38, 39, 41, 42, 43, 45, 49, 99, 121, 146, 157, 180, 184, 199

Threepwood, Galahad ('Gally') 5, 15, 40, 41, 42, 43, 44, 45, 51, 102, 107, 118, 119, 121-3, 126, 130-3, 163, 168, 175, 180, 185-7, 198, 199, 202, 203, 207

Threepwood, George 173

Threepwood, Georgina 94

Threepwood, Hermoine 94, 125

Threepwood, Julia 94, 102, 132

Threepwood, Millicent 119, 163

Threepwood, Robert 41

Thurston, Frank 83-4

Tidmouth, Lord 13, 215

Tilbury, Lord 6, 100, 119, 120, 123, 131, 133, 158, 160, 168, 195, 198

Times Literary Supplement, The 57

Times, The 25-6, 77, 81

Tipton, Chet 133

Todd, May 131

Todd, Montague 89

Todhunter, Hash 160

Topham, Lord 184

Topping, Desborough 180

Townend, Bill 2, 16, 26, 115, 171

Travers, Angela 73, 75, 76, 99, 110, 123, 124, 125, 170, 204

Travers, Aunt Dahlia 6, 58, 63-4, 66, 67, 70, 75, 76, 88, 89, 96-7, 98, 101, 110, 112, 120, 123-5, 135, 158, 170, 174, 189, 194, 199, 204, 206-7

Travers, Bonzo 46, 75, 123, 124

Travers, Uncle Tom 75-6, 96, 97, 98, 123-4, 170, 174

Treacher, Arthur 81

Trent, Terry 190

Tresilan, Reginald 213

'Tried in the Furnace' (story) 171-2

Trixie 199

Trotter, L. G. 124, 189

Trotter, Mrs 97, 189

'Trouble at Tudsleigh' (story) 154

Trout, Ephraim 206

Trout, Wilbur 202

Trumper, Eustace 94

Tupper, George 28, 29, 31, 32, 157

Twemlow, Mrs 43

Twine, Stanhope 190

Twist, Alexander 'Chimp' 103-4, 105, 119, 160, 162-3, 177, 195, 205

Twistleton, Gladys 133

Twistleton-Twistleton, Pongo 49, 50, 51, 52, 110, 171, 175, 181, 193, 219

Twistleton-Twistleton, Valerie 50, 175

Uffenham, Lord 52, 177, 190

Ukridge (1924) 25, 27, 32-3, 104, 157

Ukridge, Aunt Julia 25, 28, 31, 32, 82, 157, 199, 213

Ukridge, Millie 25, 26, 27, 29-31, 140, 157

Ukridge, Stanley 17, 24-33, 55, 69, 82, 88, 140, 141, 157, 172, 176, 184, 192, 193, 199

'Ukridge Starts a Bank Account' (story) 199

Uncle Dynamite (1948) 49, 50, 51, 171, 181, 197

'Uncle Fred Flits By' (story) 49, 171

Uncle Fred in the Springtime (1939) 37, 42, 49, 51, 99, 106, 108, 121, 171, 175, 202

Underhill, Sir Derek 29, 125-6, 150-3

Underwood, Lady 150

Underwood, Vicky 45

Uneasy Money (1917) 30, 147

Upjohn, Phyllis 194

Upjohn, Rev. Aubrey 70, 193-4, 205

Upshaw, Vera 203, 213

Vail, Jerry 19, 131, 187, 213

Valentine, Joan 12, 43, 146

Valentine, Kitchie 164

Vanity Fair (magazine) 141

Vanringham, Franklin 107

Vanringham, Joe 173

Vanringham, Tubby 173

Venner, Sir Alfred 138

Very Good, Jeeves (1930) 57, 97, 110, 112, 164

Vokes, Siffy 133

Vosper the butler 79, 160

Vosper, Lord Orlo 187

Voules, Sergeant 169

Waddington, Molly 160-2

Waddington, Sigsbee 22, 160-2, 205

Wallace, Edgar 141

Warblington, Lady Ann 39

Warner, Sir Jaklyn, 7th Bart. 206